*Other people's
diaries*

Also by Kathy Webb
(writing as Kris Webb and Kathy Wilson)

Sacking the Stork
Inheriting Jack

Happy Reading! Kathy Webb

Other people's diaries

KATHY WEBB

MACMILLAN
Macmillan Australia

First published 2008 in Macmillan by Pan Macmillan Australia Pty Limited
1 Market Street, Sydney

National Library of Australia
Cataloguing-in-Publication data:

Webb, Kathy.
Other people's diaries.

ISBN 978 1 4050 38508 (pbk.)

1. Diaries – Fiction. I. Title.

A823.4

Typeset in 12.5/14pt Bembo by Post Pre-press Group
Printed in Australia by McPherson's Printing Group

Papers used by Pan Macmillan Australia Pty Ltd are natural, recyclable products
made from wood grown in sustainable forests. The manufacturing processes
conform to the environmental regulations of the country of origin.

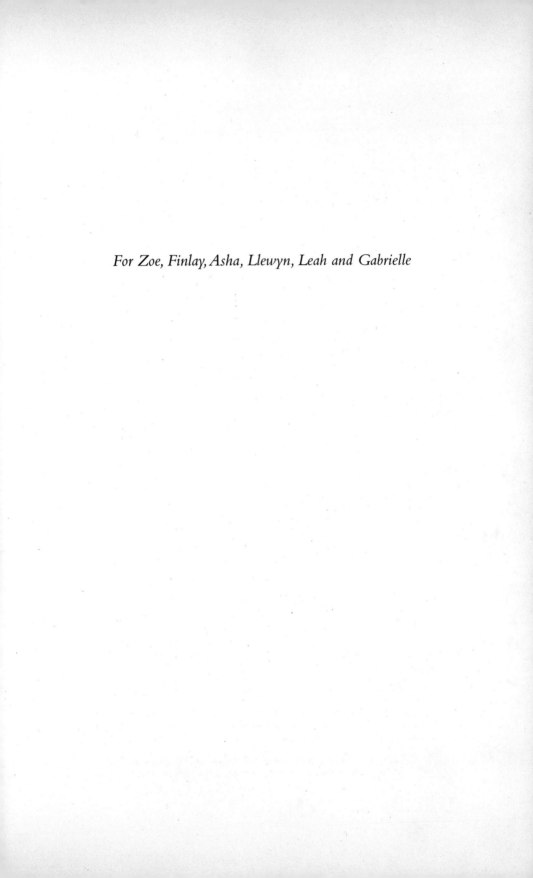

For Zoe, Finlay, Asha, Llewyn, Leah and Gabrielle

Sometimes when I consider what tremendous consequences come from little things . . . I am tempted to think there are no little things
Bruce Barton

Prologue

The website didn't look like anything special.

Designed in shades of purple and green, it resembled a hundred similar sites.

Looking for scented candles to burn in your bathroom? Click here.
Like to find out how to grow healthy herbs? Click here.
Need a natural medicine to help you sleep better? Click here.

If a website could be fragrant, this one would have smelt like a combination of sandalwood and lemon floor cleaner.

If you didn't know better, you'd stop there, close the site and forget you'd ever looked at it.

Unless, that is, you clicked on the small button halfway down the page. The button with the words *The Red Folder Project.*

Nothing changed with the design of the page.

But the references to homemade soaps and natural essences were replaced by something much more interesting.

A group of people have embarked on an experiment.

They are strangers, but each has the secret fear they aren't living the best life they can. They are too busy, not busy enough. Have lost love, are losing love, have never known it . . .

They agree to make some changes. Nothing shocking, nothing dramatic. Just little steps toward making their lives happier.

These are their diaries . . .

Alice

Alice looked at the shoes again and wondered if she was brave enough. They hadn't seemed quite so red in the shop . . . Or so high . . .

She looked at her watch: five past seven. There was no time for second thoughts. Resolutely, she slipped on the shoes, straightened up and took one last look in the mirror.

Amazingly, the woman who stared back at her didn't look as though she was so nervous she could throw up at any moment. Her brown hair sat, for once, in stylish waves on her shoulders. Her dark eyes were dramatically outlined, just a hint of apprehension showing in their depths.

The recently purchased fashion magazines had known what they were talking about. The patterned wrap dress, for which she'd paid way too much, did all the right things in the right places. She ran her hands over her hips, which appeared smaller than usual, and looked approvingly at the illusion of a flat stomach. Thanks to the new underwear she'd bought on impulse, her breasts looked almost voluptuous, rather than just very large.

Alice wondered briefly if her bra could become a tax deduction if she actually got this crazy idea off the ground.

She walked over to the closet and drew a large leather-bound jewellery box from the back of a shelf. The inner felt was emerald green and glowed through the tangle of necklaces and earrings.

Alice picked through the winding strands, her fingers catching on a cascade of silver chains with diamantes dotted throughout. She pulled it out, dislodging the other pieces that came with it.

It was probably worth the least of anything her grandmother had owned and it was years since she'd worn it. The silver clashed with Alice's gold wedding and engagement rings so she slipped them off.

Alice reached behind her neck and fastened the clasp of the necklace.

This was it.

Alice picked up her bag and strode out of the bedroom.

Rebecca

Claire was the only reason I went that first night. She was desperate to meet Alice Day, but wouldn't go on her own. Guilt is something that factors largely in my life — guilt that Bianca is like she is because she doesn't know her father, or because I spent so little time with her when she was young. Guilt that I never sit down and do jigsaws with Sam, guilt that it's nine days since I initiated sex with Jeremy . . . Guilt about secrets I've never told. I figured at least going along for one glass of champagne would mean I wouldn't have to feel guilty about not helping Claire.

'I think that legal action might be a bit of an overreaction.' Jeremy's voice was low and calm.

'But they're blackballing me,' Rebecca thundered. 'I am being blackballed by a bunch of nannies.' She paced the length of the kitchen and back again, her tailored trouser legs whipping against each other.

'You're right. It's outrageous. But just slow down for a moment.'

'Slow down?' Rebecca retorted in amazement. 'How the hell can I slow down when the whole Brisbane nanny network has been instructed not to take my calls?'

'All I'm saying is that sometimes your immediate reaction

in these situations is a little extreme. Remember when that girl called Bianca a loser on her first day of high school?'

'Yeah, okay.' Rebecca looked slightly shamefaced. 'Sneaking laxative into her drink bottle would have been a little over the top.'

'Laxative? You were talking about arsenic when you first found out.'

'Come on Jeremy, that was a joke, obviously.'

Rebecca pushed her hands into her long hair, dark red strands spilling over her fingers and onto her face. 'If I'd known this would happen I'd have put up with that prima donna's problems a bit longer. Seriously though, what is going wrong with the service industry in this country? Lorraine earned more than I did after working for ten years, yet she still refused to extend herself beyond popping food in Sam's mouth and taking him on play dates.'

Jeremy slipped off his suit jacket and draped it over the moulded back of a chrome and white chair. He leaned on the chair and looked at his wife. She was tall anyway, but wearing high heels and burning with anger, she was a formidable sight. He spoke calmly.

'What did the nanny agency say?'

'Apparently people who don't respect their nannies are not sought-after employers. Can you believe it? They acted like I'd chained her in the attic overnight! I simply told her she needed to start helping out with a few things like the washing and keeping the kitchen clean.'

'And you were kind and understanding when she said no?'

Rebecca picked at the polish on her long nails. 'Perhaps not as much as I could have been.'

Jeremy said nothing.

'All right, I told her she was a selfish little cow who had to discover some get-up-and-go if she was going to make anything of her life.'

The silence stretched. Jeremy loosened his tie and waited, knowing from experience that there was more to come.

'And that I was glad she was going anyway because I couldn't have my child growing up around someone who didn't know the difference between the words "bought" and "brought".'

'Mmmm.'

'Yeah, okay. Not my most diplomatic moment. It's just this whole scene. It's like a modern caste system. Cleaners, nannies, tradespeople loftily perched above mothers, who finish all the bits no one else wants. My suggestion, that Lorraine might actually give the kitchen floor a quick mop when it's disgusting, was greeted as though I'd asked her to scrub the toilet with her toothbrush. The other night I was hanging out our bedroom window cleaning the outside of the glass because the cleaner only does the insides. What the hell is going on here?'

Jeremy opened the stainless-steel fridge door and pulled out a bottle of wine. In an automatic response, Rebecca pulled two large wine glasses from the cupboard behind her head and clattered them onto the island bench. Jeremy winced, but decided now was not the time to mention their price. A wine glass aimed at his ear was a distinct possibility.

Wordlessly he poured a large glass and handed it to Rebecca. She took a gulp and slumped onto a chair.

'Bec, you've got to learn to think before you act. You're right, Lorraine's a prissy little piece of work. But she was good with Sam and a hell of a lot better than no nanny.'

'I know,' Rebecca said in a low voice, adrenalin rush spent. 'I just got so sick of biting my tongue, running around at midnight doing all the things she could have done but didn't. But I was sure there'd be someone else who would be better. Talk about a sellers' market . . .' Rebecca looked at her wine glass, vaguely registering it was almost empty despite the fact that she had no memory of picking it up. An early sign of alcoholism, she thought with resignation.

'What the hell will I do now?'

'How about I give Mum and Dad a call and see if they'd come down next week? That'll give us a bit of time to sort something out.'

Rebecca grimaced. 'And give them another chance to see how I can't look after their grandson's wellbeing.'

Jeremy said nothing, his mouth a thin line.

This was heading down a well-worn path and Rebecca held up her hands. 'I know. I'm sorry. Your parents are great with Sam. Just not so great with Bianca or me.'

'And your other options would be?'

'All right. You're right, obviously. Mum is working – so it's got to be your parents.' She hesitated. 'Could you just not mention I had a fight with Lorraine? Please?'

'Okay, so I tell them what exactly?'

Rebecca paused, pursing her lips. 'She eloped to Brazil? Or suddenly developed a deadly allergy to playdough?'

Jeremy shook his head, smiling. 'I'll come up with something. Forget about it for now, I'll call them in the morning. Have another glass of wine.' He refilled her glass.

Rebecca looked at her watch. 'God,' she grimaced. 'How on earth did I let Claire convince me to go to this thing tonight? I'd rather clean windows than sit around chatting to an author who hasn't published anything in a decade. At least I'd achieve something.'

The front door slammed and Rebecca tensed, her head turning in the direction of the doorway. Bianca stormed into the room in a flurry of black.

Claire

I can still remember the first time I read Her Life, My Life. *It was a week before Peter's graduation ceremony and I borrowed it from the library for the commute to the dental surgery where I worked. Back then, we lived a forty-five minute bus ride from the middle of Hobart. Without something to read, I'd spend the whole journey thinking about teeth, which always made the day seem so much longer.*

The book was one of those that seemed to absorb you as soon as you opened the cover. It was so deliciously old-fashioned and made me want to be a magnificent matriarch just like Alice Day's grandmother. Maybe nine children in this day and age would be a shade too many, but I knew I'd have at least four.

So when Peter came home after his first day as a qualified physio, I met him naked at the door with a glass of champagne and the news. Effective immediately, I was no longer a dental nurse but a stay-at-home-mother-in-waiting. Obviously I tempted fate.

'No, another couple won't make any difference. Just check that they eat seafood, will you? . . . Yes, I know seafood is expensive, but it's a risotto so I didn't have to buy much.'

Claire listened for a moment, rolling her eyes in irritation.

She looked critically at the pyramid of lemons on the kitchen table, repositioning the two on top.

'Well, I've already bought it, so it's too late. I just need to be sure no one is allergic – or that they just don't like it. You'll have to call them back. Please, I don't have any more time to talk about it – I still have pastry to make for the lemon tart and then the ice cream to get into the ice-cream maker. I have to be gone just after seven, so there will be instructions for the entrees on the table. I'll be home in time for the main course.'

She paused again, listening.

'We've had this discussion already, Peter. I'll be gone for an hour and a half. It's really important to me. Okay, bye. Oh, Peter . . . make sure you use the good plates. I'll leave them out on the bench and set the table.'

Claire pressed the off button on the cordless phone and placed it carefully back on the base. Was it terrible to skip out on her own dinner party? She and Peter had moved back to Brisbane four months earlier. They'd planned this dinner party over a month ago in an attempt to get to know some people. Now Peter had invited two more people. What would they all think of her?

Claire picked the telephone up again. This was ridiculous. She should just forget about the drinks. She didn't even know why it felt so important that she go. Sure she'd loved Alice Day's book, but she'd loved lots of other books too. It was just that it sounded fun – and exciting.

The clouds that had blanketed the sky all morning released the sun for a moment. The small windows only let a fraction of the sunlight into the living room and Claire looked around disapprovingly. That whole wall had to go – a huge bank of concertina doors opening onto a large deck was what it needed.

With the sun, though, came a surge of optimism. It would be fine. She'd have everything set up for Peter and would be back in plenty of time to manage the main course.

Claire pulled her long brown hair off her neck, twisting it into a loose knot and securing it with a few pins.

Glancing at the glossy recipe book in the stainless steel holder, she took a perfectly ironed apron out of a drawer, dropped it over her head and set about making pastry.

Megan

It was all kind of weird. The entry form had said that a number of lucky people would win an evening with Alice Day. That was weird because although she used to be really well known, I hadn't heard of Alice Day in years. It was also weird that the drinks were in a bar just down the road from where I live. Even weirder was the fact that I received an invite, given that I never win anything. Ever. Even when I cheat.

Still it did solve my most pressing dilemma, which was what to get my mother for her seventieth birthday which was looming like a train smash. I figured that during the course of the 'evening' I could convince Alice Day to sign a copy of Her Life, My Life *for Mum.*

In all honesty I can't remember whether or not Mum liked Her Life, My Life. *I do remember her reading it, though – I guess when it was all the rage. At one time it seemed like just about everyone owned a copy of it.*

It was certainly better than my other idea which was a day spa voucher. I had suggested it to my sister, who delighted in telling me that Mum hates having her head and feet touched.

Dear Mum

Megan cursed as her pen smudged. She wiped the ink blob onto one of the many pieces of paper that littered her kitchen table. Her dark hair was short, but in need of a cut, and she pushed her fringe irritably out of her eyes, leaving a smear of ink across her forehead.

Megan flicked the card back to look at the front, suddenly doubting the wisdom of her choice. Out of the sepia photo stared maybe twenty women, clearly sixties housewives complete with scarves and aprons. They were each armed with a cleaning implement, some a broom, some a mop, some wicked-looking dusters. They looked as though they were at a battleline, bracing for a fight. The writing at the bottom said: *Maybe housework never killed anybody, but why take the chance?*

It had seemed funny to Megan in the shop but maybe it was completely inappropriate. After all, her mum had been a sixties housewife and to Megan's knowledge had never fought against anything.

She searched the table for a cleanish piece of paper. Maybe a heartfelt letter would do the job better than a card anyway.

Dear Mum, she wrote. *Thank you.*

There, that wasn't so hard.

Thank you for being there when I needed you.

Except, she added silently, for all the times my sisters treated me like crap and you were too busy to notice.

Megan scribbled angrily over the page.

She pushed herself away from the table and moved to her real desk in the study, where her sleek computer sat, looking incongruous on top of an old formica-topped table.

At some stage the house's small verandah had been enclosed and this narrow room was where she worked. The positive side of the room's transformation was that it was light and airy. The downside was that the window sat at eye level, right in front of the footpath. It was quite disconcerting when a passer-by looked straight in at her. Usually, though, she felt like an invisible voyeur, watching the busy goings-on in the street outside.

Now, without conscious thought, she clicked on the internet icon on her screen.

Her eyes caught the exercise books, perched on the edge of the desk. In an attempt to hide them from view, she grabbed a towel from the floor and threw it – too hard – over the stack. The books tumbled onto the lino floor, taking a glass of water with them.

'Damn it!' Megan yelled. 'Bloody students with their stupid bloody homework, which I only set to make pushy bloody parents happy!'

She sat and watched the liquid seep into the thin pages, picturing it being sucked up over the fine red and blue lines. Those HB pencil marks, put there under sufferance.

Maybe she'd like teaching without the parents? Each morning she braced herself for the inevitable welcoming committee at the classroom door. Someone always had an issue. The problems varied, but the parents unfailingly believed their children to be faultless. Perhaps the parents' defensiveness wore off a little as the school years wore on, but in Year 3 it was still holding strong.

She reflected for a moment. Nope – removing the parents wouldn't be enough. They'd have to remove the children too for her to enjoy her job.

There were a few kids she genuinely liked. But since the day they were born, most had been led to believe their views were brilliant and deserving of full attention. Maybe it worked in a home where a mother or a father could listen to little Johnny's every utterance. But in a classroom with twenty-five other equally self-centred children, it was a nightmare.

Megan's mother had always wanted Megan to be a teacher. Her older brother Ben was a doctor, one of her sisters was a lawyer and the other had been born to be a wife and mother. But Megan's mother had insisted teaching was the career for her youngest child.

Megan had drifted through high school, never really knowing what she wanted. So without much thought, she'd taken the line of least resistance and applied to do teaching at university. Four years later she had found herself in front of a horde of eight year olds wondering what the hell she'd done.

Her mother . . .

Megan glanced at the clock at the bottom of her screen: *18:45*. She had to make a decision. She could stay here and finish her marking and have nothing but a bunch of flowers to give her mother at her birthday lunch next weekend. Or she could go out to these drinks, get a book autographed for her mother and face school tomorrow with no marking done.

One glance at the exercise books and the decision was made. The kids would have to live without their marks for another day. Megan picked up the brown paper bag which contained a copy of *Her Life, My Life* and stuffed it in her knapsack.

In a rare moment of forward planning, Megan had dropped into a bookshop several weeks ago, looking for a present for her mother. Nothing had seemed right, but she had picked up the latest issue of *Byte*, a computer magazine she bought each month.

As Megan was paying, the shopkeeper had taken a form off a stack next to the cash register and slipped it into Megan's magazine. Another customer had asked the shopkeeper a question and she'd turned away for a moment, Megan's change still in her hand.

Megan had picked up one of the forms, wondering what it was about. Seeing Alice Day's name, an idea had struck her and she'd grabbed a handful of the forms and pushed them inside her bag. Later that day she'd filled out all ten entry forms and posted them, in the vague hope that if she met Alice Day she could get her to sign a book for her mother.

Now, Megan walked past the galley kitchen and out to the bathroom, which opened off the back landing. Fifteen minutes in the tub would improve her mood, and she turned the taps on to full.

It was the bathroom that had convinced her to rent this place. The rest of it was distinctly tired. The floor was covered in two versions of seventies patterned lino, triangular-shaped tears showing where previous tenants' furniture had sat. The walls were desperately in need of paint, and the bedroom windows were hung with drooping venetian blinds, their cords irretrievably tangled.

But the bathroom was divine. Dark red walls framed a deep, glowing white bath and the floor was covered in heavy slate tiles. It was as though the house owners had decided they could bear anything if the bathroom was beautiful.

As the bath filled, Megan wandered back into the living room. She pulled off her T-shirt and dropped it on the floor. A lack of flatmates was an expensive luxury, but one she thought she deserved after ten years of sharing houses and apartments.

After a brief glance across at the study, Megan left the exercise books sitting in their pool of water and headed back to her bath.

They were a problem for tomorrow.

Lillian

Apparently Buddhists regularly contemplate their own death — in a good way. Not in a ghoulish way. In a way that makes them appreciate today.

Clearly I am not a Buddhist. I am contemplating my own death, but not in a good way. In a there-is-an-envelope-in-my-purse-that-has-a-referral-for-an-MRI-scan kind of way.

The entry form to win an evening with Alice Day was inside a book a friend gave me for my birthday.

I don't even know why I filled it out and posted it back. Maybe it was because Her Life, My Life still stuck in my memory. I read it when the children were teenagers. It was at the same time my daughter Kyla decided she needed a tattoo. Predictably, I was horrified and we had several heated discussions about it, with much door slamming and many unkind words.

The day after I finished Her Life, My Life I drove Kyla to a tattoo parlour. Suddenly something as minor as a tattoo didn't seem important enough to cause damage to our relationship.

The funny thing was, she backed out while we were waiting.

Still, when the letter saying that I was invited to drinks with Alice Day arrived, I threw it on the pile of junk mail next to the door. I had no intention of going. What would I have in common with a bunch of strangers and a well-known author?

I'd deliberately not mentioned it to Kyla when she called on *the weekend, knowing she'd tell me I should go and meet some different people. That's the thing about my children, they believe nothing is too hard or daunting and that life is there for the taking. How I produced offspring with such a well of confidence I will never know. I wish I had some of it now. It might make it possible to contemplate my own death in a good way.*

The church wasn't as big as she remembered. Or as daunting. Probably, she reflected, because when she was last here she'd been twelve years old.

Keeping her head bowed she looked around. Except for a five year old boy and his mother several pews away, she was at least twenty years younger than the average age of the room.

Lillian wasn't sure exactly why she was here. She'd been driving past the church on the way home from the neurologist's rooms. The doors were open, a few cars scattered around the carpark. She could think of no reason why there'd be a service on Friday evening, but something made her pull into the driveway.

Lillian had grown up in a little workers' cottage less than a kilometre away.

Although they weren't religious, her mother had insisted the family attend the local church when it counted. So every Christmas and Easter, Lillian and her four brothers had been cleaned up and marched down the road.

Just about everything in the area had changed, but not the little church on the corner.

The couple in front were at least eighty-five and whenever they stood up to sing, Lillian was terrified the woman would fall over. Each time, the man took his wife's elbow and she leaned on him heavily, slowly coming to her feet. Her burgundy hat, bag and gloves matched perfectly. These were high-fashion items, but from another era.

Despite the elderly lady's frailty, her voice soared out above the rest, as if defying the march of time.

Lillian hadn't been too bothered by her sixtieth birthday the year before, assuming that she would be fit and strong for years to come. And deep down, she still believed that. Regardless of the long examination involving hammers, pins and tuning forks, followed by the neurologist's diagnosis of 'possible' multiple sclerosis.

Over a year earlier, Lillian had been struck by bouts of dizziness. These had stopped within a few days, though, and the doctor hadn't been too concerned. But recently the dizziness had returned. This time the episodes had also affected her coordination and the sight in one eye and made it almost impossible to walk in a straight line. Lillian's doctor had referred her straight to the neurologist.

She still needed a battery of tests to exclude other diseases – some relatively minor, some even worse than multiple sclerosis. The MRI scan would give more information, apparently, but would not be conclusive. The symptoms had disappeared again by the time she saw the neurologist, and he had told her they might recur tomorrow or never again. He'd also explained that if it was multiple sclerosis, the disease's symptoms could be mild and slowly progressing. Or, as he'd calmly finished, very serious and quickly advancing.

The small amount Lillian knew about multiple sclerosis was that it typically affected women between twenty and forty. Somehow it seemed like a bad joke, having a young persons' disease when you were no longer young. But it happened, apparently.

She knew she should be devastated. But all she felt was numb, as if her emotions had been suspended.

Lillian glanced at her watch. Despite the fact her children had been overseas for years – Kyla in Paris, Daniel in New York – she still found it difficult to figure out the time differences. Was it the middle of the night there? The time calculation was nothing more than a reflex though; she knew she wouldn't tell them yet.

The service finished. Lillian followed the old couple slowly down the aisle, wondering if they, like her, were thinking how different things were when they first made that walk as husband and wife.

She caught herself, angry at how maudlin she was being.

Another empty weekend looming in front of her didn't help. A glance at the calendar before leaving home had confirmed that she had no social engagements for the next week. So there was little else to think about other than the impending MRI scan.

The gravel crunched under Lillian's feet as she walked slowly to the car.

With one hand on the car door, she paused and looked down at the gold watch her mother had left her. The fine hands showed fifteen minutes after seven.

She didn't have the invitation, but remembered the details clearly. *7:30pm – Bocca Bar – for Champagne and Conversation.* Without consciously looking for it, she had spotted the bar the week before.

Dated beige trousers, white linen shirt and flat brown shoes were almost certainly inappropriate for evening drinks. But right now that seemed totally irrelevant. With sudden decision, Lillian got in, put the car into gear and drove out of the carpark.

Kerry

The last time I wrote a diary, I was in sixth grade. My teacher, Mr Bradley, made us keep a journal of our Easter holidays. My father had been out of work at the time and, with four boys to feed, things were pretty tight. He'd built us a hutch out of old packing cases, though, and on Easter Sunday we came out to find not chocolate eggs but a real live white rabbit waiting for us.

To this day, it is the best present I have ever received.

I remember the diary though, because I spelt rabbit with only one b the whole way through. Mr Bradley (who in hindsight may well have been more than a bit crazy even for a boys' school that prided itself on old school values) counted all the mistakes and made me come out to the front of the class. Ten cuts I got that day.

Haven't kept a diary since.

Kerry had been warned by friends that post-divorce dating was a special kind of hell.

Conjuring up Old Testament images, they told stories of desperate women with talon-like fingernails who would be determined to make Kerry commit to eternal love from the first date. He'd refused to believe it, liking the idea of meeting women who'd already been around the block a time or two and were happy just to have a good time.

The stories had been half right. Some of the women were horrendous; over made-up, over blow-dried, they drank their wine with one eye on the rest of the bar. The others, though, were normal. In a way the normal ones were the worst. As far as he could make out most of them were lonely and genuinely looking for someone to share their lives.

Although he and Sandra had been divorced for almost two years, it still felt as though he was cheating whenever he was out with someone else. Pretty soon he had started avoiding the whole scene, preferring a few beers in front of the footy with a mate.

Kerry had found the entry form for the evening with Alice Day in a copy of *The Da Vinci Code*. He had never been much of a reader before Sandra left. But now he found thrillers and mysteries helped fill the empty evenings. Figuring there must be something to a book read by just about everyone in the western world, he'd bought *The Da Vinci Code* from *Words*, his local bookshop. The entry form had dropped onto his chest that night and had made an excellent bookmark for a few days. Catching sight of it as he threw the doona cover over the wrinkled bed one morning, he'd impulsively tossed it onto a pile of mail. Without thinking too hard, he'd scrawled his name and number across it and dropped it in the box with the rest of the letters.

Kerry hadn't given it another thought until the invitation had arrived in the mail. Nursing a beer in the Paddo Tavern that evening, he'd mentioned it to his mate.

'Yeah I remember that *Her Life, My Life* book,' Brian said. 'My mother, my sister and my girlfriend all bawled for hours after they read it. I started it, but couldn't see the point. No plot – no action. Some of it was set in the war, but not enough to count. As far as I could make out it was just chick stuff.'

They moved on to another topic and Kerry assumed the conversation was over, but Brian came back to it later.

'You know, mate, I've been thinking. That book thing might be worth checking out. I'd bet my last dollar there'll be a bunch of women there and not too many men – it could be a good place to meet someone.'

Assuming Brian was just giving him a hard time, Kerry shrugged. Brian ignored the gesture and pressed on.

'It's not natural, mate,' he said. 'How long since you've done the deed? A year? More?'

'What's it got to do with you?'

Brian held up his hands. 'All I'm saying, mate, is that you're in a drought and it ain't healthy.'

Kerry had tried hard to forget the conversation, but Brian's words had haunted him all week.

The idea of 'Champagne and Conversation' had depressed him. But by Friday evening another night at home watching reruns of *Law and Order* seemed unbearable.

Kerry rummaged under the bed and found a red checked shirt that Sandra had once bought in an attempt to smarten him up. She'd always liked it when he'd worn it.

As he set up the rickety ironing board, he wondered if they'd have beer.

The Red Folder Project

Alice felt as though she had been painted into place. Like one of those stylised cafe scenes, she was seated on a high stool next to a round table, back ramrod straight. Unfortunately her posture was a matter of necessity, not choice.

The stool was fixed to the floor, way too far from the table. She could either put her elbows on the table and lean forward, cyclist style, or sit bolt upright. Neither option was working for her.

She wouldn't have felt quite so self-conscious if she hadn't been overdressed. The same magazines that had recommended the wrap dress had counselled that it was far better to be over- than under-dressed. The authors had obviously not visited a bar recently.

The top part of the bar was a narrow rectangle, a long bench stretching along one wall. On warm nights such as this one, the bank of ceiling-high windows was pushed back, opening the bench to the footpath. From Alice's position in the far corner, there was a line of denim-clad legs stretching along its length. Not a skirt or dress in sight.

Off to Alice's right was a sunken area containing more seating. She'd clearly given too much detail to the manager while in the first flush of enthusiasm for her idea. There was an embarrassingly large sign on one of the tables, which bore her name in red letters.

Although it was past seven-thirty, the table was empty. She almost hoped no one would show up. Alice knew she should sit down at the table, but couldn't bring herself to do it.

Sitting here for much longer wasn't an option though. She tried crossing her legs at the calves, to see if that felt any less awkward. It didn't and the heel of one foot slipped out of her shoe. The shoe see-sawed on her big toe before plunging to the floor.

Suddenly all her enthusiasm vanished, leaving her feeling merely tired. Tired and rather silly. She had tried so hard to do this well, but it hadn't come off. What on earth had she been thinking? She was a mother of three children pretending to be something she wasn't. The days when she'd had queues of people lining up for her autograph felt not only as though they'd been in another lifetime, but like they'd happened to another person.

Slipping off the stool she bent down to retrieve her shoe, making no attempt to do so gracefully. Jamming it savagely onto her foot, she stood up.

'Alice? I thought it was you. You look just like your pictures.'

The petite woman at her shoulder was beaming at her in a way Alice remembered from the old days. Alice's first thought was that the other woman embodied the kind of effortless style which had always eluded her. She wore a simple black dress with a long string of expensive-looking beads looped around her neck. Her hair fell thick and straight over her shoulders, her eyes just a slightly darker shade of brown. The ballet slippers on her feet had a discreet bow at the toes and her handbag probably cost more than all of Alice's outfit put together.

'I am so thrilled to meet you – I loved your book. My name is Claire Menzies.'

A large group moved into the bar, pushing the two women together. Alice forced a smile, feeling trapped and hoping it wasn't apparent. This was all a huge mistake and she didn't want to be here any more.

'Hello. I'm so pleased you could make it.'

Unbelievably the woman's name was gone from her mind. How on earth could she have forgotten it in the space of two seconds? She had promised herself she would repeat everyone's name as soon as she heard it, in an attempt to make it stick in her brain. She mentally ran through the names of people who had replied. Claire, that was it.

'I just arrived myself,' she added.

The lie tripped easily and unnecessarily off her tongue and she felt the heat rush to her face. Alice had a sudden fear that Claire would see the half-drunk glass of wine on the table behind her. But Claire was turning to a tall red-haired woman standing beside her.

'This is my friend Rebecca Jackson.'

Rebecca was much taller than Claire and dressed for the office in a tailored trouser suit. Resisting the temptation to look, Alice would have put money on the fact that Rebecca was wearing the three-inch heels that her magazines had named the 'perfect marriage of power and princess' for businesswomen this season. The insecure part of Alice was quite pleased to note some mascara had smudged onto the other woman's eyelid.

'Nice to meet you, Rebecca.'

She'd remembered to repeat the name. What had seemed like a good tactic last night made her sound in real life like a used-car salesman.

Rebecca Jackson was one of the names on the list, but how did these two women know each other? Part of Alice's concept was that everyone involved would be strangers.

'You two know each other?' Her words came out more aggressively than intended and she flushed again.

Rebecca either didn't notice or didn't care.

'Claire and I went to school together,' she said, almost as if having to explain herself bored her. 'We hadn't seen each other for years, but were having lunch together at a bookshop cafe and Claire bought some cookbooks that had your entry forms inside. She entered for both of us.'

Alice flicked a glance at Claire. Rebecca was clearly here under sufferance, but Claire seemed oblivious.

Alice ducked her head, stomach clenching. What in God's name did she think she was doing, bringing these glamorous women here to talk about fixing their lives?

She concentrated on the mascara smudge on Rebecca's eyelid and took a breath. But before she could say anything, Rebecca gestured at the sign on the table behind them.

'I assume that's for us?'

'Yes . . . good idea. Ah – why don't you follow me?' Alice stammered.

She led the way down two steps and toward the table. There was a long padded bench on one side and chairs around the rest of it. Alice took the seat at the head of the table, having thought about this while she was waiting. The other two women looked at her questioningly.

'There's no seating plan. Sit wherever you like.'

Alice waved vaguely at the table and Claire slid into the middle of the bench. Rebecca chose a chair. One of the closest to the door, Alice noticed.

Claire and Rebecca waited expectantly. Alice looked back blankly, unable to think what was planned next.

Drinks – that was it.

'Would you like a glass of champagne?' she asked.

'Absolutely,' Claire answered and there was an answering nod from Rebecca.

Alice caught the eye of a waiter.

'Would you mind opening the champagne?' She gestured at the ice bucket in the centre of the table, in which a bottle of Moët was angled.

The waiter removed the foil and wire and eased the cork silently from the bottle.

Alice smoothed her dress over her lap, pushing down hard on her thighs with the heel of her hand.

There was another long silence as the waiter filled their glasses. Alice suddenly remembered the script she'd prepared so diligently. If nothing else, she'd planned this part meticulously. Stomach still churning, she pictured the words she'd laboured over. She'd printed them on her archaic printer and practised in front of the mirror.

This was it.

It was time to start. Even if there were only two people here, who would both decide she was a loser within seconds. It was unfortunate she'd booked such a big space – the empty chairs gave away her high expectations. But there was nothing she could do about that now.

As rehearsed, she looked at her watch, despite knowing full well it was seven-forty.

'Let me begin by saying thank you for coming and please – enjoy your champagne. It's a little strange I know. An invitation to drinks with someone who wrote a book over a decade ago. But if you'll bear with me, I'd like to tell you a little about myself and then we'll get to the reason I invited you here.'

Her words sounded unnatural, as if she was still addressing the mirror. She tried to slow down and relax.

'It seems like a lifetime ago that I wrote *Her Life, My Life*. Since it was published I have had three children and my world has been taken over by the practical things that keep a family going.'

As she spoke, two more women walked toward the table.

Alice stood up.

'Hello. I'm Alice Day,' she smiled, holding out her hand to the older of the two women.

'I'm Lillian Grant,' the woman introduced herself. Lillian's grey hair was short and feathered softly around her face. She held her handbag against her hip, the strap stretched tight. Her lipstick had obviously just been applied, the muted pink precisely covering her lips, the lines at the corners of her mouth accentuated rather than disguised by a dusting of face powder.

'And I'm Megan Jones.'

Megan was younger than everyone else – somewhere in her late twenties, Alice guessed. A tiny jewel glittered from a piercing on her nose. She wore tight jeans and sneakers with what looked like an old-fashioned cowboy shirt.

Alice's eyes were drawn to someone standing behind Megan, near the door. It was a man of about forty, with curly hair reaching his shoulders and a goatee. Definitely not one of her invitees, but he was still looking their way. Alice smiled automatically and was surprised to see him walk toward the table.

He held his hand out to Alice. 'Ah, I'm Kerry Jenkins,' he

ventured. 'I feel like I've got something mixed up here. Is there a blokes' table over the back?' He peered over at the clearly empty tables further along.

Despite her tension, Alice laughed. 'No, just us. Have a seat.' She gestured to a chair next to Rebecca.

So much for an all-women group – she'd automatically assumed someone named Kerry was a woman. Not much she could do about it now, though. It was blindingly obvious this was going to be a disaster. If only she hadn't come up with this bloody stupid idea in the first place. She wanted to be at home sorting the washing so much that it almost hurt.

Miraculously the waiter reappeared. Alice nodded in response to his silent request and he filled the extra glasses. She made a mental note to leave him a big tip.

Alice had received thirty entry forms. That was too many, even allowing for the ten forms which Megan had sent. In the end she'd chosen the ten people with Paddington addresses, fig-uring it would make any gatherings easier. She'd had no idea how many would come.

Everyone was looking at her expectantly.

Follow your script, she reminded herself.

She'd just say her bit, they'd all think she was odd and then she would disappear as soon as possible. She'd pay the bill, feel like an idiot, but pretend it had never happened. It wasn't a big deal.

At least she hadn't told Andrew. That was one less humiliation she'd have to face.

Figuring if she started again it would be clear she was follow-ing a script, she decided to just keep going.

'As I was saying . . . I don't think I am the first woman to discover that domestic life and writing aren't always wonderful bedfellows. My second book was what's known in the trade as a stinker and I figured that maybe one good book was all I had in me.'

She'd thought long and hard about whether or not to men-tion the second book and decided it would be dishonest not to.

'But recently I had an idea that follows on from *Her Life, My Life* and try as I might I can't make it go away.'

She smiled. This was the bit when they were all supposed to smile back sympathetically.

They didn't.

She wished she could somehow make them all drink faster. This would sound much better if they weren't sober. For want of any better options, she took a large sip herself.

This wasn't working. Mentally she drew a thick red line through the next few paragraphs and skipped right to the end of her speech.

She looked at the ring of faces, their expressions ranging from interest through to clear suspicion.

'Before I wrote *Her Life, My Life* I was studying at university. In one of my subjects the lecturer told us that the biggest challenge facing society would be how to use all of the spare time that modern technology was going to deliver. Big chunks of time were going to open up to the whole population. He said we'd be living in the Age of Leisure.'

She paused for a moment.

'I often recall that lecture, because he was absolutely and totally wrong. For all the promises of efficient technology, we somehow have less time than ever. Everybody I know is juggling a thousand things, running from one thing to another without enough sleep.'

Alice caught herself. That hadn't been part of the script.

'I travelled overseas to promote *Her Life, My Life*. The thing I still remember about my trip to France is that everyone stops for lunch. It doesn't matter how busy their day is, lunch is non-negotiable. They have a cooked meal, cheese and at least one glass of wine.

'I tried to explain to a Frenchman that in Australia we usually just have sandwiches and often eat at our desks. He just looked at me and said, "But why?"

'I started carrying on about getting things done and he kept just looking at me, with no understanding of what I was trying to say.'

With relief, Alice noticed a slight softening of the expressions in front of her.

'I've been thinking about this a lot lately. It sounds strange, but do you know anyone who is really happy? Not someone who's just got a good marriage, or nice kids, or a well-paid job. Someone who is exactly where they want to be, who gets up every morning looking forward to what the day will bring.

'When my children were small, I used to think I'd be happy when they were older. I remember thinking, if only they were toilet trained . . . If only they could clean their own teeth . . . And then I used to think it would all come together when they were in school. Well my youngest started school this year and still I find myself thinking – if only . . .

'People seemed to love my book because it was about the simple stuff that was the essence of my grandmother's life. And the question readers asked time after time was how she managed nine children. I could never really answer that. To her it wasn't a matter of managing the children or my grandfather, they just were her life. She wasn't trying to do a million other things or wanting to be somewhere else. I know that's not the answer for any of us. But maybe there's something we can take away from it all.'

Alice took a gulp of champagne. Finally the alcohol was doing its job. She could almost feel it seeping into her bloodstream and relaxing her muscles. She took another sip for good luck.

'I have a theory,' she proclaimed, her smile taking the serious-ness out of her words. 'I think we need to try to make things a little simpler, find some more time for things like a long lunch. Maybe even to cook it ourselves . . . I think the balance in our lives is wrong. We're the slaves of what we're doing – we need to change that so we do things that make us happy.'

Rebecca was looking cynical and Alice's brief feeling of suc-cess faded.

'I'm not talking about dramatic changes. You have jobs, com-mitments . . . But maybe, by doing a few small things, you can make life more worthwhile or happier. Perhaps even figure out some parts of it that you could do without.'

Enough said, she decided. Either she was totally off course or they got what she was talking about.

'I'd love to see if what I'm thinking has any value and write about it. I'd like to see if there are some values my grandmother held that could help make us happier in today's world. I don't know anything about any of you. Maybe I've got it totally wrong and everything is perfect in your lives. If so, that's great. But maybe things aren't as good as they could be. If they're not, then maybe what I'm saying makes a bit of sense. So – here's my idea . . .'

This was it, she thought. Make-or-break time.

'What I'd like is for you to join me in a kind of experiment. What I want to do is to see if, by reclaiming some simple things in our daily lives, we can find more happiness, more fulfilment.

'I thought about doing this myself and writing about it. But while I'm great at picking what's wrong with other people's lives, I'm not so good with my own. So I spoke to my boss at the bookshop where I work. She liked the idea and we put the entry forms in all the books we sold over a couple of weeks.'

Alice paused, searching the faces in front of her for a clue as to how this was all being received. Claire looked captivated, Rebecca seriously unamused, the rest fell somewhere in between.

'What I want to do is see what happens to a group of people who actually try to change things . . . All of you – if you're willing. If you could each tell me a bit about your lives, I'll send you an email every week or so. The email will ask you to do something differently. Nothing dramatic, nothing weird. Just little things that you can't see for yourself when you're so stuck in the middle of everything. Some of the tasks may be related specifically to your life, some may not be.'

Alice was speaking freely now, moving away from her carefully prepared words.

'And so I know what's going on, you post a diary entry on my website. The entry can be one sentence or five pages, just write what you feel like. Even a diary entry before you receive your first task would be great – maybe talking about what you thought this whole invitation was about. There's a password, so no one other than the people here can look at the site. It would also be good, I think, to get together each month or so for a drink, just to talk face to face.'

She was getting a couple of suspicious looks.

'Look, to be honest, I'm not really sure how this will work. I don't have any complicated analysis or tests to apply to outcomes. I just want to read your stories and see if my ideas make a difference. You might decide it's a waste of time. If you don't like it just stop. But if it does work I'd like to write about it. It goes without saying that I would change your names in any book and make sure you weren't identifiable at all – I give you my word on that.'

Alice took a deep breath. She was into the home straight.

She pulled out a pile of folders bound in soft red leather from the large paper carry bag and placed them on the table. They'd been expensive, but as soon as she'd seen them, she'd known they were right.

'That's it. If it doesn't work for you, that's fine. But if it does, then have a look in these folders, fill out the questionnaire and send it back to me. We can go from there. I thought,' she added hesitantly, 'that perhaps we could call it the Red Folder Project.'

Picking up her glass she drained the remainder of the champagne.

'I'm going to leave you to it. There's plenty of champagne for you all – on me. Thank you for coming and I hope to hear from some of you soon.'

Alice walked away as confidently as she could. About to sweep out the door, she felt a hand on her elbow.

'Alice?'

'Look, this is weird I know, but would you mind signing this for my mum? It's her birthday on the weekend and she's a huge fan of yours.'

Alice looked at the copy of *Her Life, My Life* in Megan's hands. At least that explained why Megan was here – and why she'd sent so many entry forms.

'What's your mum's name?' Alice asked.

'Ah – it's Patricia, she's turning seventy,' answered Megan, holding out a pen.

Alice wrote on the title page with a flourish, slipping easily back into the habit of years ago.

'Thanks,' Megan said. 'You've saved my life.'
'Well that was easy,' Alice laughed.
And with that she left.

Kerry

Kerry threw his keys onto the table. They skidded along the wooden surface, halting against a pile of dirty washing. He swore quietly, out of habit. But remembering that Annie wasn't there he swore again – loudly this time. Just for the hell of it.

Feeling marginally better, he looked back at the wrinkled heap of clothing. A single person's washing was depressing. His mother had drilled into him that clothes had to be sorted and each colour group washed separately. Putting a pair of jeans in with his father's white shirts had been a serious crime in their household, second only to running the machine without a full load.

It hadn't taken him long to get over that once Sandra left. Black trousers were washed with white T-shirts and fluffy bath towels. But he couldn't put on one of his mottled loads without thinking about the tiny growsuits and lacy bras that used to tangle with his jeans.

That was the trouble with divorce – the little things like the washing.

There were the obvious issues – like feeling you'd lost the person you were meant to spend the rest of your life with. But those you could deal with and keep locked away in separate compartments. It was the little things that were the bastards.

Just when you were sailing along, having a nice day like normal people, something small would jump out and smack you between the eyes.

Take yesterday, for example. He had been in the supermarket, deliberating between penne and fettuccine, when he'd remembered a *Play School* episode featuring pasta necklaces, which he and Annie had watched together the week before. He'd reached for the large packet of penne, but the words *Family Pack* had jumped out at him. With a sudden surge of anger, he'd thrown two small packets into the trolley instead.

Sandra had worked at a hairdressing salon down the road from the garage where Kerry had done his apprenticeship. Each day he and some mates would walk to the corner shop for a burger or a sandwich. Kerry wasn't the first to comment on the pretty brunette hairdresser who always had a smile for them. After work one day, he parked his motorbike in front of the salon and went inside. Half an hour later he had the shortest haircut of his life and a date.

His hair hadn't had a chance to grow much longer during the time they were together. After Sandra had left, Kerry let it grow, in what he knew was a childish form of rebellion. Now the curls fell loosely around his face, much like Annie's. It was the resemblance to Annie that made him keep it long. Somehow seeing strangers smile at the two of them together made him feel more closely bound to her.

Kerry dropped the red folder onto the table beside the keys.

The second he'd spotted the group of women circled around a bottle of champagne, he'd known he'd made a terrible mistake. He had been about to turn around and leave when the woman at the head of the table had looked straight at him. She certainly wasn't beautiful, but there was something real about her. And she had been nervous. From where he was standing, Kerry had seen her foot jiggling under the table, as if that was the only bit of her she couldn't quite keep under control.

Brian's words had rung in his ears. 'It ain't healthy, mate.' Somehow he'd found himself at the table, registering the surprise in her eyes when he introduced himself.

It was such a chick thing – all that feel-good stuff about happiness and small moments.

He wasn't the only person who'd felt out of place. The tall redhead had looked at her watch about five times and left before the last bottle of champagne was even opened. Her friend, though, had looked completely star struck.

Of course the woman who had looked at Kerry as he'd been about to walk back out of the bar was Alice Day. She wasn't what he'd expected – not that he'd given it much thought. If he had, he would have pictured her as an ageing hippie, maybe in a caftan, most definitely not wearing a bra.

But she wasn't like that at all. He'd have guessed that she was pushing forty. She had on a fancy dress and high heels – and no wedding ring, he noticed later. She wasn't the type of woman he would normally be attracted to, but there was something about her, a warmth, that he really liked.

Kerry picked up a glass from the sink and filled it from the tap. He leaned his back on the counter and took a mouthful of water. The house looked much as it had when Sandra had lived there. They'd been talking about moving somewhere bigger when Annie was born, but when things had started going bad the idea had been forgotten.

Previous owners had knocked out the hallway of the small workers' cottage. Now two bedrooms opened straight off the kitchen/living area. The bedroom at the back of the house was still Annie's, although a bed covered with a pink gingham doona cover had replaced the cot a couple of years earlier. As a second-birthday surprise, he'd spent a whole weekend painting fluffy clouds on one wall, and on her third had added pink fairies and birds everywhere. It was by no means a work of beauty, but Annie loved it.

Kerry had thought about selling after Sandra had moved out. Annie always seemed so happy there though, he could never quite bring himself to do it. He didn't really want to live anywhere else anyway.

Besides, if he moved, he'd have to deal with ten years of accumulated crap in the storeroom downstairs.

Kerry clicked the television on and flicked through the channels, knowing it was a waste of time. Even SBS, usually good for some naked euro flesh at this time of night, had let him down. It seemed to be some dark foreign thing about two women but there was far too much talking for his liking.

He turned it off again, restless, and picked up the red folder which he'd only glanced at in the bar. It was pretty fancy – red leather with cream stitching around the outside. Annie would like it, he thought idly.

There were two sheets of cream paper inside with four or five typed headings on each page and a blank space underneath. At the top of the first one was written:

The only time I ever remember my grandmother getting angry was when I was about ten and I told her I was bored.

'Alice,' she said, 'if you can't figure out a way to entertain yourself with all the things you have here, then you don't deserve to be happy.'

I've thought about what she said a lot lately and have decided that advice doesn't just apply to a little girl. I think we can all be a lot happier than we are, but that maybe we have to work a little to make that happen.

Humour me here. To start with, go and put on a song you like. Then find yourself a drink you enjoy, sit down and have a look at this.

Kerry almost looked over his shoulder to see if anyone was watching. This was like something out of a reality TV show. Pretty soon Brian would walk in with a six-pack laughing about what an idiot Kerry was.

Hell, if Brian even knew he was reading this stuff, he wouldn't be worrying about Kerry's drought. He'd be thinking that he batted for the other side.

But the champagne was still creating a warm fuzz in his blood. He walked over to the CD player and flicked through the discs splayed across the top.

A Janis Joplin CD caught his eye and he slipped that into the machine. He waited for her throaty voice to begin and adjusted the volume at the dial.

A drink . . . Normally a beer would be his beverage of choice, but after champagne, somehow that didn't seem appropriate. Instead, he pulled a bottle of port down from on top of the kitchen cabinet. A quick search of the cupboard found no port glasses. He poured a good measure into a mug instead.

Back at the table, Kerry pulled the red folder back toward him. Instead of the expected questions about marital status, job, hobbies, etc, the first heading was *What are some of the things that make you feel good (alcohol and drugs excluded – sorry)?*

Kerry smiled. At least she had a sense of humour. He picked up a pen.

Rebecca

Rebecca closed Sam's bedroom door and trudged down the hallway. Every part of her was weary, from her gritty eyes to her aching soles.

She paused in the doorway to her and Jeremy's bedroom.

Once again the tidying fairy hadn't appeared.

All the children's stories proclaimed that you had to really believe in something to see it. Rebecca believed, with every fibre of her body, in a good spirit that would restore her house to order when she wasn't there. But the doona cover was still crumpled at the foot of the bed. The sheets which should have been changed a week ago were still dirty and lying in uneven hillocks across the mattress.

Rebecca had met Jeremy through a friend who worked with him at a stockbroking firm. She had been actively avoiding romance since her last boyfriend had disappeared after a run-in with her daughter Bianca. Rebecca had walked into the kitchen one Sunday morning to hear a then ten year old Bianca commenting that the best thing about having Charlie sleep over was wondering which revolting shade of pastel his polo shirt would be the next morning. Things had declined rapidly after that.

Jeremy had been living in Hong Kong before he and Rebecca met. Friends had muttered dire predictions. Apparently any unattached man in Hong Kong was single for a very good reason, which might or might not be immediately obvious. Unable to commit, used to a smorgasbord of women, preferring the company of mates to a demanding partner.

If Jeremy's reason existed, Rebecca was yet to find it. He was unremarkable looking. As you might expect a spy to be. Average height, average build, brown eyes and hair . . . Nothing about him that would particularly stick in your mind. Except if you got him into bed that was . . .

Several days after they'd met, Jeremy had called Rebecca at work and they'd met for a drink. The next week, dinner, and the week after that, dinner and a movie . . . Rebecca had tried to prepare him for Bianca and the two had met briefly on a couple of occasions. She had put it off as long as possible, but after several months he spent the night at home with her.

Jeremy had showered and dressed before her on the Saturday morning. Watching him walk out toward the kitchen, Rebecca had felt rather like a Roman sending a Christian out to a pack of ravenous lions.

Rebecca had taken her time getting ready, preparing herself for the worst. But she'd found both Jeremy and Bianca sitting at the kitchen table, each calmly reading part of the Saturday paper. Neither of them had ever disclosed what had occurred that morning, but Jeremy's calm and easy relationship with Bianca had continued.

If the joking complaints of Rebecca's friends' husbands were halfway correct, regular marital sex was a pretty rare commodity. Admittedly she and Jeremy had only been together for five years, but their time behind the tight-fitting bedroom door was something special and fundamental to their marriage. That had continued through her pregnancy and Sam's baby days.

Rebecca's eye caught on the paperback angled across the bedside table. Reading had been one of her pleasures once. But her old favourites – writers like Vikram Seth and Ian McEwan – had been unable to withstand the exhausted ten-minute read Rebecca would throw at them each night before she could no longer keep her eyes open. Now it was back to airport thrillers – where it didn't matter if you read something twice, or missed a couple of chapters.

Just for a moment, she pictured kicking off her shoes and lying down on the unmade bed. She would pick up the book, read for half an hour and then fall asleep with it sitting on her chest. But that would mean ignoring dinner for Jeremy and Bianca and the two hours of work she needed to have done before she sat down at her desk tomorrow.

Did everyone's idea of nirvana sink so low, she wondered.

She unbuttoned her blouse slowly, dropping it in the wash basket. The skirt went into the dry-cleaning pile and Rebecca pulled on a pair of threadbare jeans and a deep musk T-shirt.

With one last look at the novel, whose plot she couldn't even bring to mind, she left the room and headed back to the kitchen.

Despite the fact that Rebecca knew exactly what was, or more to the point, what wasn't, in the fridge, she opened it. Perhaps the tidying fairies had left a slowly stewed casserole instead of making the beds today.

No . . . the only thing that vaguely resembled the makings of a meal was a slab of mince which should have been eaten days ago.

Jeremy's parents couldn't come until the following day and so Sam had spent the day with one of Rebecca's friends. As kind as her friend had been about looking after Sam, Rebecca had felt guilty and had rushed to pick him up soon after five o'clock. Sam hadn't wanted to come home and had thrown a tantrum when Rebecca tried to strap him into his car seat. Unable to face stopping at the supermarket with a screaming child, Rebecca had driven straight home.

Rebecca's hand hovered over the mince for a moment. Who had ever heard of people getting food poisoning from bad mince? Prawns maybe, or chicken. But not good old hormone-crammed mince. It would probably last another month or so without any problems.

Botulism aside, nothing great was ever created out of mince. Maybe in Delia Smith or Jamie Oliver's worlds. But in her world it meant spaghetti bolognese or tacos. Neither of which she had ever particularly liked.

But tacos would require some kind of salad accompaniment, which ruled that out. Spaghetti it was. Again . . . And for Bianca, who at sixteen had already been a vegetarian for two years, bolognese sauce without the mince. Wearily Rebecca pulled the necessary cans from the pantry and started dinner.

Claire

It's kind of sad to be writing two entries before I even receive my first email.

'Too much time on her hands . . . She needs a job; no children, you know . . .'

I actually found myself lying about what I did the other day. Someone asked me how I passed my time. For some bizarre reason I heard myself saying airily that I do charity work. Which is a lie. It sounded good though.

I didn't set out to be a cliché. If ten years ago I'd had to describe what I'd be doing now, I would have said I'd be run off my feet with a house full of children. Flipping pikelets for afternoon tea and buying those huge packets of cereal which would take Peter and me a year to eat by ourselves. But here I am, still waiting for that houseful of children . . .

I've just re-read what I wrote and almost deleted it. But I didn't. At least everyone else will look incredibly balanced compared to me.

Claire spread the A3 plans out in front of her. The table, which had come from their last house, was all stainless steel and glass and looked ludicrous against the old hardwood deck. But that was all about to change. The architect's design was great.

The kitchen and the deck would disappear, to be replaced by a glass pavilion which would hover over the backyard.

The security door gave off a metallic clunk. Claire scraped her chair backwards, taking brief pleasure from not having to worry about damaging the floorboards. 'Hi,' she called out.

Peter walked down the hallway and gave her a half-hearted smile. Reaching the deck, he slumped into a chair beside her. Claire had realised several months ago that Peter no longer kissed her hello or goodbye. She couldn't put her finger on exactly when he had stopped, but the lack of that perfunctory kiss cut her every morning and every afternoon.

'Ah, the plans,' Peter said, looking at the pages on the table.

'They're fantastic,' Claire enthused. She pushed the papers in front of him. 'Have a look – this area out here will be amazing.'

Peter glanced at them briefly. 'Uh huh. And has he given you any ideas on how much it will all cost?'

'Not really, but I think it might be a bit more than we originally planned.'

'Jesus, Claire!' Peter jerked his head to the side, not looking at her.

After a moment he turned back to her. 'Money does not grow on trees, you know. If the renovation costs are higher, we have to push our mortgage out further. You don't seem to have noticed, but my income is only just covering the mortgage repayments as it is. And if interest rates go up again, we're going to be in serious trouble – even without a bloody renovation.'

The words were delivered with a cold, closely reined fury. There was no trace of familiarity on his face and Claire felt the sharp pang of isolation again. She'd been stupid to show Peter the plans now. He was still barely talking to her after last Friday night.

Claire had been taken aback when Alice had left the bar straight after telling them her idea. But gradually the awkward silence had loosened and conversation had flowed. Claire had quickly felt drunk, the sense of doing something for herself like a double shot of vodka. Rebecca had left early, but Claire had decided to have just half a glass more.

She remembered quite clearly thinking she really should get going – she couldn't miss her own dinner party. And then the guy – was it Kerry? – had picked up yet another champagne bottle and silently offered it to her, eyebrows raised in question. She'd hesitated, then nodded.

After that, she'd pretended not to hear her mobile ringing or see the screen flashing, *Home.*

By the time she left the bar, she knew she was in serious trouble. Unable to find a taxi she had driven home to save time.

The key had refused to fit into the front door and she had been on her third attempt when Peter had wrenched it open.

'Where have you been? I've been worried sick.'

Claire's first thought had been that he didn't look worried – just furious. She'd felt like a fifteen year old who'd stayed out past curfew. She had barely managed to suppress a giggle. 'Um, out.' Even she could hear the laughter in her voice and she bit the inside of her cheek, feeling even more like a delinquent teenager.

She'd pushed clumsily past Peter and strode into the entertaining area. 'Where is everyone?'

From where she'd stood, she could see that the kitchen was a disaster. Judging by the trail of debris, Peter had attempted to make the risotto and it hadn't gone well. So not well, in fact, that it seemed he'd decided on a Plan B. Greasy cardboard pizza boxes were strewn all over the suede caramel couches. Any other time Claire would have been horrified, but she had calmly pushed one of the boxes onto the floor and sat down.

Peter had suddenly looked genuinely concerned. He'd sat down on the opposite sofa. 'They went home half an hour ago. Are you all right?'

'I'm great.'

'Claire, where were you?'

'I told you. I was having drinks with Alice Day.'

Peter hadn't even glanced at his watch. 'It's almost ten-thirty. You said you'd be home two hours ago.'

Guilt had snuck past the alcohol and Claire had started to feel bad. She'd felt the bubble of happiness leaking out of her. 'For

God's sake, Peter. This is not a national disaster. I was having a good time, I got carried away.'

'Yeah well, while you were getting carried away, I was left looking like an idiot. I had to order pizza.'

It was pretty obvious she'd done the wrong thing. She'd known she'd feel desperately bad later, but right then she hadn't.

'Okay, I'm sorry. I'll call them all tomorrow and say . . .' her imagination had failed her, '. . . something.'

Peter had sworn under his breath. 'Right, "something" will really help.'

'I really am sorry, Peter.'

'Not as sorry as I am. How much did you spend?'

'Spend? Nothing. I told you it was free.'

'With you, nothing is free.'

And then they'd gone down the same old path.

Finally Peter had stormed off to sleep in the spare room. Claire had opened the most expensive bottle of wine she could find and sat down to fill in the questionnaire.

Claire looked at Peter now, cursing herself for not putting the plans away for a more opportune time. She'd been so excited about them she'd not thought of the possibility that Peter might not be enthusiastic.

'But we talked about this and agreed it was what we wanted. Maybe it won't cost more anyway,' she managed weakly.

Peter leaned his elbows on the table, hands across his eyes. After a moment he looked up at her. 'Yes I agreed, because house renovation is the only thing in this world besides having a baby that seems to interest you. But it's a goddamn expensive hobby.'

His last words dropped into silence.

The money complaint was a well-used one, Claire's spending habits having always been a source of irritation to Peter. But in all these years of her not working she'd believed the time she spent renovating and decorating their houses had been worthwhile.

Claire willed him silently to stop, but Peter had obviously been stewing over this for a while and now the words tumbled out, unstoppable.

'It was bearable in Tasmania. Everything was cheap and the market was rocketing anyway. But it's different now. This place cost twice the one in Hobart and we still haven't started on your fancy architect's plans.'

He pushed the plans fiercely and they skidded off the table and onto the floor.

Claire felt the hurt swell inside her. She'd actually believed this was something she was contributing to their finances. She hadn't had a job, but she'd worked hard at their renovations. Managing the renovation work and then doing the interior decorating had been her responsibility. She truly believed that she had done it well and that it was her input that had made their properties in Hobart sell so quickly.

Claire looked down at the buckled plans and back at Peter. 'So you want to stay here, like this?' She gestured vaguely at the house.

'You know, I don't actually care,' Peter said. 'It's perfectly fine. People have lived in it in this state for years – it doesn't have to be all modern and beautiful just to impress our friends. If we had any friends, that is.'

'Perhaps we should have stayed in Hobart,' Claire said glibly.

Peter looked at her levelly. 'You know, perhaps we should have.'

Claire looked back at him in surprise. The move to Brisbane had been Peter's idea.

Claire had adjusted to living away from Brisbane years ago. Her father had been dead for a long time and her mother had recently moved to country New South Wales with her new husband. Claire had no brothers and sisters and her friends had dropped off steadily during her years away. Coming back here was almost like starting in a totally new city.

But she'd done it because Peter had been so enthusiastic about a physiotherapy practice up here which had a partnership for sale. There was another reason too, one that neither of them had voiced. The hope that maybe a new start would give their marriage fresh life.

Peter sat back in the chair, his chino-covered legs spread wide. 'It's really hard being the new boy at the practice. Roger started it himself years ago and figures he's the boss even though it's a three-way partnership. I'm starting to figure out why there was a partnership for sale.'

He took a breath.

'And the business I was supposed to take over from the old partner just isn't there. A lot of patients have followed him, but somehow Roger seems to feel that's my failing.'

For the first time Claire could remember, Peter looked vulnerable. She stretched out her hand and put it over his. 'It'll get better. It's always hard in a new job at first.'

Peter left his hand under hers for only a second.

He stood up. 'I've got to go. Cricket training tonight.'

Claire nodded. She knew that. Peter had started coaching a local cricket team two evenings a week. The team was made up of a group of fifteen year old boys from local schools and Peter loved it. Claire also knew that he didn't really need to leave for another half an hour.

She moved toward the bench and picked up the plastic container which held the sandwich she'd made earlier. She handed it to Peter and he took it with a nod of thanks. He looked as if he was going to say something more, but then shrugged and walked into the house.

Claire watched him leave. Slowly she bent down and picked up the plans, trying to smooth out the creases. Then she stopped. Slowly and carefully she picked up the top sheet and crumpled it tightly into her palms. She deposited the misshapen ball on the table beside her and started on the next sheet. When she had a pile of them, she gathered the balls into her arms and walked into the kitchen. One by one she dropped them into the stainless-steel tidy bin – an Alessi she'd kept from their last kitchen. After a moment she picked up the bin and traced Peter's steps down the hallway. She reached the big green rubbish bin which stood next to the front steps, opened it and threw the tidy bin in.

It clanged satisfactorily in the evening air and she stood there quietly listening. Then she turned around and walked back up the steps and into the house.

Alice

Alice pushed open the front door and looked at the usual scene of devastation. With the children in the house, the mess looked vaguely purposeful. As if maybe someone was about to claim the library books spread across the hallway. Or pick up the cardboard rocket on the sofa to take to school.

The state of the house was less important than the maelstrom of activity which existed between seven and eight-thirty each morning. But without footsteps clattering up the staircase, or someone dropping a dirty cereal bowl on the counter, it changed. Now the mess was dominating. The washing needed hanging on the line, the kitchen was a disaster and various items of clothing spread from one end of the house to the other needed to be put away.

Alice dropped her keys on the shelf next to the front door. There was a tangled heap of shoes, hats and items discarded from school bags that morning. She bent and sorted the shoes, slotting them into place. Hats went next and she collected a handful of school notices and artwork.

Slowly she walked down the hall and leaned on the side of the refrigerator, surveying the kitchen.

Growing up, if she'd ever thought about tidiness, she'd have been pretty clear that it was a simple concept. It either existed or it didn't. Now she could write a thesis on how wrong that was.

The state of her house veered between under control and total devastation. The place could be untidy but easily fixable – the stray items all having somewhere to go, the beds makeable. Then sometimes everything looked all right but was only a hair's breadth from chaos. There would be items stacked on tables or shoved in drawers, which could erupt as soon as there were more bodies in the house again. It was like a sinking ship – the second she stopped bailing it all went horribly wrong.

The water was lapping at the deck this morning.

Alice hadn't realised how much the expectation and planning for the night in the bar had buoyed her over the last couple of weeks. Now all she had to show for it was an outfit she'd never wear again and a bill for expensive champagne. She'd hoped that if it was a failure she'd be able to move on, happy that she'd given it her best shot. Instead she was left with a sense that something should have been done differently.

Irritably, Alice kicked off her shoes. Last week she'd broken her rule of never buying a pair of shoes that weren't perfectly comfortable in the shop. She couldn't even blame the saleswoman – it was her job to tell stupid women like Alice that rigid leather would stretch.

The floorboards were cool underfoot and Alice walked slowly to the sink, stacked with the remnants of school lunch preparation. She turned on the tap, staring out the window as the sink filled. The water ran over her hands, relaxing her. She left her hands in the water, looking out the window.

The sky was the blue no photo or painting ever seemed able to replicate exactly. It didn't seem to begin or end anywhere and she suddenly pictured herself floating up and disappearing. A cereal-encrusted bowl wedged in a cloud would be the only remaining evidence of her existence.

It had been a difficult year. Alice's youngest child, Alex, had started school in January and for the first time she was home by herself between nine and three each day. After twelve years of only brief moments to herself, it was very strange. At first it had been wonderful. She'd spent hours sitting in cafes reading the paper and drinking too much coffee. She'd sorted all the children's old clothes, which had been stuffed into high cup-boards in her bedroom for the last few years. And she'd even finished Alex's baby book.

But soon the hours had started to stretch. The things she'd ached to have time for were no longer appealing. And she was sick to death of people asking what she was doing now the chil-dren were at school. At least they didn't ask if she was writing. Those enquiries had dried up years ago.

Alice had been browsing in *Words*, her favourite bookstore, when she'd seen a notice about a position as a salesperson. She had no experience in retail, having worked in pubs and restau-rants when they lived in London, and then with Andrew setting up the business.

Bridget, the bookstore owner, had waved away her concerns with jewelled fingers. 'You're a writer and you love books. That's good enough for me. The rest you can learn.'

So Alice worked in the shop two days a week between nine-thirty and two-thirty. Strangely, it was the people not the books that interested her most about the job. Most of the customers were women and many stopped for a coffee in the small cafe. The cash register Alice worked from was close by and she eaves-dropped shamelessly.

The thing that struck her about most of the women was that they were unhappy. They laughed and joked with friends, but there was always an underlying sense of discontent. Too tired, too busy, ungrateful children, absent husband, having a job, not hav-ing a job . . .

At first it made Alice feel vaguely better. At least other mar-riages weren't perfect and other women brought up their families by themselves while their husbands worked long hours and trav-elled. But after a while it just depressed her. These were all people with enough money to buy a book and a coffee whenever they felt like it. They weren't on the poverty line. Somehow, though, they couldn't manage to find happiness.

Alice knew that she was the same as those other women, but she couldn't seem to kick free of the fog dulling the edges of her life. Lately, though, she had felt an urge to write. The only problem had been having no idea what to write about. Until the concert six weeks ago.

The smoke-filled darts of light had fallen from the ceiling, encircling the slight figure on the stage. He had looked up at the sharply shelving rows of seats, rubbed a hand over his shaved head and smiled slightly. Pick gripped between his thumb and fingers, he plucked two notes from his guitar. The silence was broken by a hum of pleasure as the audience recognised the introduction to one of the singer's best known songs.

Alice let the music wash over her, savouring the long-forgotten feeling of being immersed in music. Her life in London had been a tour of band venues. From Hammersmith Odeon to little joints in dingy suburbs, the live-music scene had been an important part of her life. And after their move to Brisbane, she and Andrew had been regulars at small dark clubs in the Valley. Then the children had been born and practicalities had prevailed. Too late, too smoky, too loud . . . She'd never consciously decided to stop going, it had just happened. And her music collection had stayed fixed firmly somewhere in the late 1990s. She'd heard everything she owned too many times to be bothered to even turn the CD player on these days.

This however, was something she couldn't let pass. A four-night concert with a hundred different songs from Paul Kelly. She'd loved the singer ever since the first day she'd arrived in Australia. The taxi driver at the airport, a lanky young man who looked barely old enough to drive, had taken one look at Alice's enormous pile of luggage and figured she wasn't your everyday backpacker.

'If you're planning on staying here,' he'd said, 'you'll need to know about this guy.' With a flourish, he had pushed a tape into the old cassette deck and the strains of 'From St Kilda to Kings Cross' came floating out.

Alice had booked tickets as soon as she'd heard about the four-night concert and had scored front-row seats for every night. The last two hours were a glorious melange of songs she loved and some she'd never heard but delighted in.

Alice watched the singer strum the chords which he must have strummed a thousand times and watched his face form the expressions it must have formed a thousand times. And then she saw the sheer joy on his face as his fingers danced around the guitar and the sweet sound wrapped itself around the auditorium.

Alice realised suddenly that there was nothing in her life which gave her that intense personal joy. The children were different. She loved them fiercely, but taking pleasure in them was different from what the man on the stage was experiencing. Something for him alone – a skipping of fingers across guitar strings which clearly made his heart dance.

Surely that's what made everything else worthwhile. The hours wheeling a recalcitrant trolley around a supermarket, the mind-numbing routine of school drop-offs and pick-ups. They all made sense if there were moments of joy dotted through the hours.

So what were her moments? What made her happy? And what about those women she overheard in the bookshop cafe, what was it that kept them going between the tedious episodes of everyday life?

Alice had always believed that immersing oneself in children was a cop-out. Surely that defeated the purpose if every life cancelled out the next by folding in on itself. So apart from the children, what did she have? A job in a bookshop which, if she was brutally honest, was no better than something to fill empty days. The faded love of her husband who either no longer knew her well enough to realise how much these concerts meant to her or, even worse, knew and didn't care.

She looked at the empty seat beside her and back up at the stage.

The surge of modern life didn't have room for those little pockets of joy. Alice's last twelve years had been spent swamped in the minutiae of family life. All of the things she'd loved, like music, had fallen away.

Something her grandmother had said not long before she died came into Alice's mind. 'You know what I don't understand about your world? It's why things are always so complicated.

People focus on doing everything quicker and more efficiently and then run around just finding more to do.'

At the time Alice had been young and full of energy and had figured there wasn't much to be done about it anyway – it was just the way things were. And surely being able to do more could only be a good thing.

Now she was pretty sure it wasn't.

She pictured the lean-to outside her grandmother's tiny house that had been known by everyone in the family as 'the patio'. Although it hadn't been much bigger than an average bathroom, it had been the place where her grandmother had 'taken' tea twice a day.

For as long as Alice could remember, no matter what she was doing, her grandmother would stop at ten o'clock and half past three to sit amongst the flowers and drink tea out of her fine bone china. There had been no view to speak of, unless you counted the neighbour's dog's kennel. Yet Alice couldn't remember ever having been in a more wonderful place.

Maybe that was the answer to everyone's problems – they should pass a law requiring everyone to stop for tea twice a day. And make tiny pink cupcakes with sprinkles compulsory.

Except it didn't work like that. Tea was her grandmother's thing. Just because it had given her pleasure didn't mean it would help anyone else. Even with cupcakes and sprinkles.

There was something in it though, she was sure. Little things. Every day. Maybe in their desperate rush to get to all the big things, everyone had lost track of the little things that made it worth the effort.

She suddenly wondered what it would be like to watch a group of people try to find their 'little things'. The things that made them happy every day. Maybe she should write to Channel Ten and pitch the idea. They were clearly struggling for material. Just last night she'd seen an ad for a new reality show with a host claiming to be a supernanny for dogs.

She warmed to her idea. They could call the show *Cupcakes or Candlesticks*. Or better still, *Your Favourite Things*. She could see it now. Someone like Julie Andrews could host it. They'd follow a group of people who each day had to make one small change and then live with it until it became a habit.

Kind of like *Big Brother* but without the sex and nudity. Actually, nothing like *Big Brother*.

Actually, it would make a terrible TV show.

But maybe a wonderful book.

Alice became aware that the singer was halfway through a song she hadn't even heard him start. She brought her eyes back from the middle distance, a faint feeling of excitement coursing through her blood.

Standing at the sink, her hands still soaking in the water, Alice grabbed on to that thread of excitement she'd felt at the concert and started to wash the dishes.

Rebecca

E ven as Rebecca threw herself off the edge of the ferry and felt the downward pull of water, she knew the dream wouldn't last.

The water disappeared and her world solidified on white sheets. She tried desperately to picture herself back in the water. There was no doubt in her mind that drowning was preferable to being awake. But the dream slipped from her grasp.

It was early.

There was no sign of daylight, but something in the stillness told Rebecca that dawn wasn't too far off.

Superstitiously she always avoided looking at the clock radio when she first woke. As if somehow not seeing the digital evidence would send the hours spinning backwards and give her more precious sleep.

She rolled onto her stomach, forcing herself to think of something calming. But thoughts of her confrontation with Jeremy last night squirrelled their way past the image of an open white beach. Her shoulders tensed and she felt a queasiness in her stomach.

Rebecca opened her eyes in a squint: *05:10.* As always, she tallied the number of hours she'd been asleep. It was never enough. She reached for the earplug on the bedside table and screwed it into her ear. There was no way she could face this day yet.

She turned onto her back, searching for a way to slip back into the thoughtless abyss of sleep. Beside her Jeremy stirred.

'Are you all right?' he muttered.

Rebecca never knew how he expected her to answer that question. She was awake after only five hours of interrupted sleep and knew she wouldn't be able to sleep again. Did that count as all right?

Sarcasm wasn't going to help anything though, and she bit back her immediate response. Soft snores from the other side of the bed solved her dilemma. She flipped onto her other side in annoyance, grinding the earplug deeper. Why couldn't she sleep like that? Jeremy had just as much going on as she did, but he could shelve his problems for as many peaceful hours of sleep as were available and take them up again when he woke.

This was always the hardest time, wondering how she could possibly survive the endless stretch of hours until she was next able to put her head on the pillow. She knew it would be better once she was in the shower. Better even once her feet were on the floor. But for now, gritty eyes screwed tight, the day looked insurmountable.

Rebecca knew from past experience that she wasn't going to go back to sleep. Her mind jumped from one worry to another, staying with each one just long enough to set her heart beating, but not long enough to come up with a solution. Inevitably, though, it returned to today and who was going to look after Sam.

Jeremy and Rebecca had reached an icy stalemate last night, both claiming that the next day's work was critical. Jeremy's last comment, delivered as she lay fuming beside him in the darkness, was that as she had chased his parents off after only one day, she should stay home to look after Sam.

Jeremy's parents had arrived on Tuesday morning, an hour later than arranged, making Bianca late for school and Rebecca late for work. They'd fussed over Sam, taken him out for a sugar-laden lunch (grandparents' privilege, they'd said) and only put him down for his sleep at 3 pm. Sam hadn't been awake long when Rebecca arrived home at five-thirty to find everyone waiting expectantly for her to cook dinner. But as they'd forgotten to buy the things Rebecca had asked for, she'd had to go back out to the shops first. Sam had been starving, then had refused to go to bed and dinner had been a tense and stilted affair.

Rebecca had kept telling herself just to get through it. That Jeremy's parents were helping and she should be grateful. But then Jeremy's mother had asked whether Rebecca perhaps thought that Sam's speech development was suffering from Rebecca being at work so much.

Rebecca had looked at Jeremy. She'd registered his pleading look and had known she should turn the other cheek. But she simply couldn't.

'If you think he has speech problems, Marilyn, perhaps his father should be spending more time with him. Have you thought of that possibility?' Rebecca had tried to soften the words with a smile, but it hadn't worked.

'That's not how things work, Rebecca,' Marilyn had retorted.

'Maybe not in your generation, Marilyn, but in mine we run our lives differently.'

'Do you really, Rebecca?' Derek had asked. 'Then you won't need us any longer. We've got things to do at home which frankly we'd rather do than be here. I think it's better for everyone if Sam comes and stays with us sometimes.'

They'd had their bags packed when Rebecca came downstairs the next morning and left before breakfast.

So Rebecca had called in sick yesterday. And it seemed to be the only option for today. No nanny, no friends she could bring herself to impose upon again. But just the thought of telling work she wasn't coming in today – again – made her head ache.

Her boss had recently moved into the position from Sydney and had made no secret of the fact that he thought working mothers were taking jobs from people who would really earn them. He seemed to make a point of scheduling meetings at the end of the day, clearly not caring if they ran over time. At least two afternoons a week Rebecca was forced to sit, stewing, as he pontificated on whatever topic took his fancy. Finally at six o'clock she'd blurt out that she had to leave, facing a barrage of stony faces as she walked out the door. There'd be a stressful drive out of the city through the snarls of traffic and then she'd be met at the door by an irate nanny reminding Rebecca that her 'contract of employment' had her clocked off by 6 pm. Invariably on those nights the house would be in chaos. Sam would be in tears and Bianca on the warpath as Rebecca hadn't been home in time to drive her to her band's jam session.

Now, Rebecca stared blindly into the darkness. Bianca was definitely getting worse. Their relationship had been wonderful until almost two years ago. Then, soon after Bianca turned fifteen everything had changed. She'd been transformed from a happy, loving girl who teachers adored, to one filled with anger at the world in general and Rebecca in particular.

Nothing Rebecca tried helped. A month ago she had signed them up for a series of Thursday-night lectures about why vegetarianism was going to save the world. She'd thought that maybe it was something they could learn together. But Bianca had refused to go along even once.

Her thoughts spun around again. She just couldn't miss work today. The recruitment agency she worked for had one client bigger than the next ten put together. The client wanted to fill a very senior position and she had finally pinned down the top candidate. He had a high-profile job elsewhere and his interest in this position was highly confidential. Rebecca had arranged several hours of meetings between the candidate and the client's senior management and rescheduling because of a personal problem was inconceivable. This was her biggest placement in a year. She simply couldn't mess it up.

Jeremy hadn't seen it that way. 'What if you were sick? Or the candidate was? You can do the same thing tomorrow or the day after. My clients are expecting me to do their trades as soon as the stock market opens tomorrow. Leaving it a day is simply not an option.'

She turned her head slowly to look at Jeremy again. His arm was flung back, his lightly tanned and still slender chest bare. Regular cycling had helped him avoid the middle-aged spread which had caught so many of their friends and he looked ten years younger than forty-five.

An idea entered Rebecca's mind. She rejected it immediately. She simply couldn't do it.

She lay there for a moment, picturing the phone calls she'd have to make to reschedule the meetings, the transparent lies she'd have to tell.

The idea itched at the back of her mind, offering a way out. Maybe it wasn't impossible.

Slowly, she inched her body across the bed. The cotton sheets rasped under her pyjamas, the sound magnified in the quiet room. Several times she stopped, heart pounding, certain she'd woken Jeremy. Finally Rebecca dropped her legs onto the floor and stood up, slowly removing her weight from the bed. She held her breath, but Jeremy's only response was to roll slightly away.

Walking gingerly on the balls of her feet, she eased the wardrobe open and pulled out the first outfit she saw. Then, on hands and knees, she rummaged amongst her shoes until she found two that matched. Finally, she pulled out her underwear drawer gingerly, throwing lingerie and stockings over her shoulder.

Slowly she walked toward the door, acutely conscious of the sucking sound of her feet lifting off the polished floorboards. One step at a time, she inched down the steps, keeping to the outside of the treads to stop them squeaking.

She stood indecisively at the kitchen door, taking in the mess in the kitchen. As usual, she'd been too exhausted the night before to do anything more than scrape the plates and run the dishwasher. The saucepan sat inside the greasy frypan, congealed sauce dripping down its side. The stainless-steel bench was covered with crumbs and a few wilted pieces of rocket.

Somehow she hadn't expected to get this far, had thought that Jeremy would wake and the decision would be taken out of her hands. The consequences of this would be horrendous, she knew that. But she could face them tonight, once she'd nailed this placement.

Her eyes found her keys she'd tossed on the counter the previous night. Slowly she walked across and weighed them in her hand.

Could she really do this?

It wasn't as though she was abandoning anyone. She was

leaving Bianca and Sam with Jeremy. Sam was his responsibility as much as hers. And Bianca hadn't let anyone look after her for years.

Decision made, she stepped into her skirt and pulled the suit jacket over her pyjamas. She'd shower at work. She always kept make-up and toiletries there for when she went to the gym. The gym that had averaged two hundred dollars a visit this year, given her level of attendance.

Rebecca pulled the magnetised shopping list off the fridge. She drew out the pencil. *I'm sorry, but I just had to go to work,* she scrawled.

She hesitated. Her usual sign-off, *I love you,* seemed wildly inappropriate, but its omission seemed even worse. *Love, Rebecca,* she finished finally.

Her handbag was next to the front door and she slung it over her shoulder. Without looking around, she opened the door. With a soft click, she closed it carefully behind her.

Lillian

Lillian took a deep breath, pulling air down into her lungs. It was cool, but warm whispers promised a hot day. Spring had lasted for only a heartbeat and already the long summer was underway.

She walked faster, relishing the feeling of her muscles stretching, her stride covering the ground easily. Her first thought each morning was whether or not the dizziness and loss of balance were back. Each time she swung her feet to the ground without the feeling that the world was tipping around her, she felt a rush of relief.

Around Lillian the city still slept. A morning walk had been her ritual for years. It had begun when Kyla and Daniel were small. She would bundle them out of the door early with three bananas stuffed in a plastic bag. They'd walk down the street to the creek, its bank shrouded in scrub.

In the early days she'd sing to them. She'd sing different things – children's songs and her own favourites. But it was always the morning song they asked for, the song she made up as she went along and was different each day. She'd delight them with references to themselves, and her memories of those mornings were of laughter and her arms wrapped around both of them.

As with so many other things, though, the children had grown out of it without her quite noticing when it happened. One day she had realised they hadn't sung the morning song for a week and that most of the time she sat by herself while they climbed the trees and chased each other madly. And then the children had started sleeping in, not wanting to leave their beds.

So Lillian had started going alone. She'd been walking these streets for years, yet she never tired of it. She never went the same way, never saw the same thing. Except for Ross of course. Regardless of which way she walked she always saw him.

As if her thoughts had conjured him up, his tiny van appeared around the corner. He had to have spotted her in plenty of time. The street was long and straight and there wasn't another soul about. But Ross only began to slow down twenty metres from her, the piercing whine of his brakes hanging in the morning air.

Ross reminded her of a six year old boy, testing his nerve and his BMX to see how long he could make a skidmark. Far from worrying about the people sleeping in the nearby houses, he seemed to delight in as much early-morning noise as possible. Lillian smiled and stepped off the road.

'Lillian!' he called out of the window. 'How are you this beautiful morning?'

'I'm fine, Ross,' Lillian smiled. 'And you?'

'Great,' he replied and Lillian marvelled at his unfailing enthusiasm.

Ross rested his elbow on the window frame. 'It's a dark day for Liverpool,' he said, shaking his head.

'I'll say,' Lillian agreed.

Ross delivered the local area's newspapers and Lillian had noticed him going about his rounds more than a year before they'd first spoken. Then one morning, Lillian had turned into a street to find Ross standing beside his van staring at a flat tyre.

She'd kept walking, expecting to exchange a brief nod and perhaps a small comment of commiseration. Instead, he'd looked at her and asked cheerfully if she'd like a cup of tea. 'Reckon the lazy buggers can walk to the shops to get their paper this morning,' he'd said, grinning.

Before she could make her excuses, he'd pulled out a steaming thermos and matching mugs and poured her a cup of hot, sweet tea.

He had leaned against the bonnet, looking down the quiet morning street. Lillian had stood awkwardly to one side and they had drunk in silence for a few moments.

'Did you watch the football last night?' Ross had asked.

She'd noticed the score when she'd been flicking channels looking for something to watch. Her son, Daniel, was a huge soccer fan and Lillian had thought that he would have been happy with Australia's performance against a higher ranked team.

'A draw,' she'd said without thinking.

Ross had looked at her, silently impressed.

From then on he'd assumed Lillian to be a soccer fan. She hadn't bothered to set the record straight, figuring that they'd just wave at each other from a distance whenever they crossed paths.

But Ross kept pulling over for a chat whenever he saw her. Before too long it seemed impossible to tell him she really didn't like soccer. It was just easier to smile and nod whenever he raised the topic. Apart from soccer, Ross loved to read. Autobiographies were his passion and he and Lillian often swapped books and opinions.

Now, almost a year later, he looked at her earnestly. 'I hope Benitez knows what he's doing,' he said. 'He went and picked Harry Kewell again, didn't he.' Ross shook his head mournfully. 'That damn boy spends too much time hanging out with his wife's soapy friends to actually get fit.'

'Mmm,' Lillian murmured.

'She's a looker, I'll give him that. She's an actress from some English soap or other. Was it *Brookside*?' He looked at Lillian enquiringly.

She shrugged, her expertise on soap operas no greater than her expertise on football.

'Anyway. We won the Champions League – maybe this year we'll crack the big one.'

Lillian smiled encouragingly, despite having no idea what the 'big one' was. As she did every morning she vowed to ask Daniel to tell her something about English football.

'Beaut morning, isn't it?' Ross asked, looking over Lillian's shoulder at the curve of sky, its blue still soft and powdery at this hour.

'Just lovely,' Lillian relaxed now she was back on comfortable territory. 'It's going to be a hot summer though.'

'Yep, you're right. Just as well I've got my airconditioning.' Ross stuck his arm through the open window with a grin.

Lillian laughed. 'Not going to replace the van this year?' she asked, already knowing the answer.

'Absolutely not,' Ross proclaimed. 'I'd only bang it up.

'Heard from the kids?' he asked.

Lillian shook her head. 'Not for a week or so. How about you?'

'Melanie was round with her lot yesterday. God they make a lot of noise. Bloody glad when they were gone actually.' His words were light-hearted. Ross loved his grandchildren and hated his ex-wife with equal passion. She had left him long ago for his business partner at the time.

For a friendship which existed only in short bursts on the side of the road in the dawn hours, they knew a lot about each other.

'So you're okay then?' Ross looked closely at Lillian.

His words caused a sudden wave of panic in her. 'No,' she wanted to scream. 'I'm not okay. I have no idea how to handle this.'

But she smiled shakily instead. 'I'm fine thanks, Ross. No problems at all,' she lied, glancing away.

Ross looked at his watch and sighed. 'I'd love to talk some more, but I've got to go.' He gestured at the stacks of newspapers in the back of the van. 'I'm a bit behind this morning. See you tomorrow.'

With that he was gone, leaving behind the smell of burned rubber.

Megan

M egan couldn't believe how many different ways there were to encourage a team.

Her three nieces had been bitten hard by the cheerleading bug and she had just endured forty-five minutes of bum wiggling and invisible pompom waving. The most frightening move had involved them doing a handstand while simultaneously winking. Still, it was better than what was waiting for her inside.

Growing up the youngest of four, she was used to criticism, but these family get-togethers tested even her armour. It didn't help that Ben, her brother and ally against all things family, was living overseas.

At least her mum had seemed genuinely happy with the auto-graphed copy of Alice Day's book. Even though it had paled into insignificance beside the gift of a return flight to the Maldives from Jennifer, Megan's eldest sister.

Jennifer had spent the first twenty minutes after she'd arrived telling Megan how there were no good teachers any more because their training was so inadequate. To hear her tell it, her kids were being educated by brainless robots, all of whom coincidently had it in for her children. Jennifer's husband was busy telling his obligatory racist jokes, every one of which he prefaced with, 'I'm not a racist but this one is really funny . . .' To make matters worse, Megan had foolishly opted to drive, which meant she couldn't numb the pain with vast amounts of alcohol. Consequently, she had been delighted when she'd been invited to be an audience for the family cheer squad.

'I got booty, I got class.

Betcha, betcha love my . . . .'

'Do you think they get extra curriculum points for this?'

Megan barely suppressed a laugh as her other sister Jane, who was only two years older than her, crawled onto the ancient trampoline.

'Probably . . .'

The three girls in front of her were trembling on the brink of teenagerdom and they were so beautiful it almost hurt to look at them. All blonde hair and long legs. And yet, despite the suggestion behind the words and movements, Megan was sure they had no idea of the power they were about to wield.

For a moment, the two sisters watched the show in silence.

It was Jane who spoke next. 'Remember how Dad would clout us if we used the word "stuffed"?'

This time Megan did laugh.

'And "bum"? I don't think kids even use those words now. Too boring.'

'I used to be convinced Dad didn't actually know any really bad words,' Megan said. 'And that was why he fixated on words like "stuffed".'

'Yeah, I know. I always had my doubts, though. I saw him swear once when he was mowing and a stone spun up and hit him on the shin. I was too far away to hear what he said, but it didn't look polite.' Jane smiled at the memory.

'We should ask Mum if he ever worked out we used to drink the booze in the liquor cabinet and replace it with water,' said Megan.

'Course he did,' Jane answered. 'There was never anything much in them to start with. Didn't you ever wonder why we didn't get drunk?'

'Really? Why didn't he ever say anything?'

Jane shrugged. 'Dunno, guess he figured it was keeping us busy.'

There was another silence, this time broken by Megan. 'Mum's not looking much better. I've barely seen her smile all day.'

'What can you expect? Dad's been dead less than six months. She's hardly going to be out dancing on tables.'

'I know . . . I just hate to see her so . . . beaten.'

Jane shrugged. 'You try being married forty-eight years and then have your partner die.'

Megan exhaled quickly. 'Well at least that's not something I need to worry about any time soon.'

'Why, what's happened to that engineer you met a little while ago?'

'Nothing's happened to him. It's just that he's already married.' Megan said the words without thinking and instantly wished she could call them back.

'What?' Jane spun around, giving up any pretence of watching the cheerleaders.

Megan tried to play it down. 'It's no big deal.'

'No big deal! Megan, are you insane? If Mum finds out, she'll kill you.'

'Jane, we're not ten any more. I'm a grown-up, you know.'

'Well, not a very good one obviously. Who the hell sleeps with someone else's husband?'

'Would you keep your voice down?' Megan looked around, but the cheerleaders were practising handstands against the fence.

'Jane, I swear if you tell anyone I'll never speak to you again.'

Jane looked at her silently for a second. 'Think about it, Megan. What is in it for you with this guy? It's not like you have years to waste on a married loser. You need to do something about your life. Everyone was talking about it before you arrived.'

'They were *what*?' Megan's words were icy and Jane started back-pedalling.

'Well, not really talking about you. Just commenting really . . .' Jane met Megan's cold stare and gave up trying to pretend. 'On how you have no direction . . . no kids.'

'Neither do you!' Megan couldn't believe her family had been discussing her.

'Sure I have no kids – yet. But Stewart and I are going to start trying next year.'

'Well whoopie for you!' Megan was stung. 'I have direction. Plenty of direction. For your information, I'm a founding member of a group that is working toward changing lives.'

Jane looked doubtful.

'It's all about the little things,' Megan added, trying to remember Alice's exact words. 'About trying to make things better by putting small pleasures back into life . . .' She trailed off, hoping Jane didn't ask for more information.

'Right.' Jane looked doubtful. 'That doesn't sound like you.'

Megan ignored her. 'It's run by Mum's favourite writer actually – Alice Day.'

'Goooooooo Reading!!'

Megan wasn't sure if her nieces were finished or just perfecting a move but she was delighted by the distraction. She stood up on the trampoline and wolf whistled.

'Great work, girls,' she said as she slid off the side of the trampoline and headed toward the house. She needed a stiff drink, even if it meant she had to walk home.

Alice

'Hello?' Alice spoke into the phone, a bundle of dirty sheets under one arm.

'Hi – it's me.'

Alice felt a jolt of happiness. Andrew must have thought about what happened this morning and realised he'd been unfair. Maybe he was ringing to apologise.

'Just a quick call,' his voice was brisk, businesslike. 'I wanted to tell you that I'm probably not going to Jakarta this week.'

Right. Clearly no apology.

Alice gave him a moment to say more, knowing now he wouldn't.

'Okay then,' she said finally. 'Thanks for letting me know. I'll see you tonight.'

Alice replaced the phone on the handset and looked around her. Of course he hadn't apologised. Andrew never apologised.

She looked down at the urine-soaked sheets she had stripped from Alex's bed and released her grip. They flopped onto the polished floorboards and she stared at them for a moment.

This morning's fight seemed to have blown up out of nowhere.

Ellen had woken up grumpy and had proceeded to irritate Andrew and her brothers in quick succession.

Andrew had chosen to take his favourite position in times

of family crisis. Keeping his toes safely out of humdrum family issues, he pronounced a dour judgement on the children's and Alice's behaviour.

By the time Andrew had left for work, he and Alice had been silently fuming at each other, Alice for his total inability to provide any form of assistance, Andrew for the unacceptable way in which he believed his wife and children were acting.

It wasn't so much the arguments any more as the silences. Their disagreements went down well-worn paths. They'd look at each other and know what the other was thinking and what they were about to say. Then they'd look away, Alice to the sink full of dishes, Andrew to the pile of papers he was stuffing into his briefcase. Even without words, the air vibrated with their silent vitriol.

Alice had always assumed a long-term relationship would have its issues blown away by early fights. But she had been totally wrong. She knew couples who had been married for fifty years and were still bickering over the same things as when they first met. It was the same with her and Andrew. Child rearing had added a whole extra dimension to the arguments, but they were essentially over the same issues.

Two of Alice's grandmother's mantras were that the sun should never set on an argument and that husband and wife should never sleep in separate beds. During the many nights that Alice and Andrew seethed with spoken or silent words, Alice's only solace was the bed in the spare room. The clean white space around her allowed her the sleep which Andrew's proximity chased away.

She wondered sometimes if it was the truncated fights that were the problem. Maybe a full-throttle screaming match would blast the cobwebs from their relationship and let in a fresh breeze of change. But somehow it never seemed the right time to really thrash something out. Inevitably the children were around, they were both too tired, or it seemed churlish to ruin what otherwise was a rare moment of peace. So things continued as they were.

Alice walked through to the study. Sitting on the desk were three large envelopes, their tops ragged where she'd opened them earlier.

For some reason Alice had put their post-office box address

on the red folders. She realised that was rather ridiculous, given that if anything she was the one acting suspiciously.

It was not normal behaviour to gather a group of perfect strangers, promising to fix their lives for them.

'Physician heal thyself . . .' The words jumped into Alice's head. There was no point in dwelling on the fact that she couldn't even sort her own life out. That's what this whole idea was about – figuring out what was important and getting rid of the crap. She was trying. That had to be enough for now.

Andrew's company sold natural health remedies and he spent a lot of time at the factories in Asia which produced them. In the eighties anything other than vitamin C was considered the province of hippies. The early nineties had seen natural medicines become mainstream, but the new millennium had brought a boom, which had exceeded even Andrew's expectations.

Andrew liked to tell people he was the world's worst plumber. He'd left Australia the day after he finished his apprenticeship and ended up working in a bar in London. While there he'd picked up both Alice and his idea for a business. Two years later he had returned to Brisbane, with Alice following him. They'd started a small company, both of them trailing around the suburbs trying to convince health food stores and chemists to stock their products. One of the smaller chemist chains began buying from them and they bought a fax machine in celebration. Six months later they started their own brand, sticking on the labels and packaging them up themselves.

Alice had returned to England when her grandmother was ill, living with her for the three months before her death. She'd begun writing her book as soon as she returned. Andrew had hired staff and the business soon bore no resemblance to the one born from a business plan drafted over two bottles of red wine. Now there was an office, a warehouse near the airport and twenty employees. But they rarely discussed the business these days and Alice's involvement was limited to organising the annual Christmas party.

The thing about having three children and a business was that you didn't have to discuss much at all.

For the last twelve years the children had absorbed most of Alice's energy. When they were very young Andrew had rarely been home before they went to bed. She'd clean the kitchen and then summon the energy to cook a second meal for the two of them. They'd talk about their day. Alice would try to dredge some nugget of interest from a day like any other, while Andrew said very little, clearly craving silence after hours of dealing with customers and suppliers.

Weekends were usually better. Andrew adored Ellen and would kick balls with the boys for hours. The evenings would mean a quiet meal and a bottle of wine, or occasionally a night with friends.

Alice had spent a long time trying to figure out when the special connection between them had disappeared. The sense that Andrew was the person who knew her better than anyone and cared the most.

They were a good partnership – the division of responsibility was clear, each normally respectful of the other's role. Their mutual love for the children bound them together and they laughed or worried together about whatever was going on with them. But they no longer knew what the other was feeling. Alice would often recognise signs of Andrew's hidden irritation or anger, but she no longer cared enough to try to fix what was wrong. Andrew would ask after Alice's day, but not listen to her reply.

A month earlier Alice had mentioned to Andrew that she had thought about writing again. He'd been reading the sports section of the weekend newspaper.

'That's good, sweetheart,' he'd murmured, not even looking at her.

Alice had left the room, shut herself in the bathroom and cried. Then she'd splashed water on her face, walked back into the kitchen and scribbled a first draft of the Red Folder questionnaire.

The night at the bar had been during one of Andrew's business trips. Alice had always intended to tell him what she was doing, but the time had never been right before he'd left. She wasn't sure whether it was his opposition or indifference which would have hurt the most. Now it seemed too late to tell him.

Alice twisted her hair loosely onto her head and looped it in place with an elastic band.

She'd become so used to Andrew's frequent travelling that she now found it far more relaxing being alone. When he was home, she felt like she had to make an effort. She couldn't skip dinner, or eat scrambled eggs on toast every night for a week.

Alice had left it until this morning, over a week since the night in the bar, to check the post-office box. She'd prepared herself to receive nothing. But amongst the white envelopes with cellophane windows had been three bulky envelopes addressed by hand.

Claire, Kerry and Rebecca.

Alice was astonished at the frankness of their answers. At least she assumed they were being frank . . . Maybe they were just taking her for a ride, planning on having a good laugh at her emails.

Somehow though, she didn't think so. Under the heading *Worries and Fears*, Claire had listed ten items. A lot of her fears were pretty common, such as public speaking and sharks, but some were much more intimate, such as her fear of her husband leaving her for someone more interesting.

But it was Rebecca and Kerry who had surprised her the most.

Rebecca had sat in the bar the entire time Alice had been talking, looking seriously scary and contemptuous of the whole idea. Alice had been sure she'd never hear from her again.

Even Rebecca's scrawled handwriting gave the impression she had a million other things she needed to be doing.

What could she possibly offer this woman?

And yet Alice had been surprised by some of Rebecca's answers. Under the heading *What do you see as your greatest success?*, she'd written, 'Still having a great sex life despite the chaos that is my world'. Under *Greatest Failures* was, 'Raising my sixteen year old daughter'. Asked to name a weakness she'd supplied, 'Having lost the ability to relax'.

Sure they were throwaway lines, written without much

thought, but still, there was an honesty there she hadn't expected.

Alice had been astounded when she'd seen Kerry's name scrawled on the back of one of the envelopes. Apart from being male, he was vibrant and outgoing, seemingly having no need for what she was suggesting.

After reading his questionnaire, though, she wasn't so surprised. Kerry had been divorced for two years and yet references to his ex-wife and daughter were dotted throughout what he'd written.

Alice looked at the pile of books beside her. Pulled at random from the spirituality and self-help sections of the local library, they weren't providing the inspiration she had hoped for. She opened a pocket-sized one with a teal cover entitled *Road Map to Happiness*.

'Smile at a stranger,' it exhorted. 'Pretend today is the last day of your life.'

She dropped the book on the sofa. If she emailed that to anyone, this project would be over before it had started and there wouldn't even be one diary entry.

After Alice had decided that she would ask the members of the group to write their diaries online, she'd remembered oldtimes.com. The website had been her idea. Online sales, based more on the appeal of old-fashioned remedies than alternative medicines. It had been her last foray into the business just before Alex was born.

It hadn't worked.

Mainly because she had lost focus amongst the chaos of three small children. Andrew had never really been interested and it had been quietly forgotten about. Without much hope Alice had pulled up the site, expecting the domain registration to have been dropped years ago. But it was still there and thankfully she'd used her own name as the password to access the site administration. Even she couldn't forget that.

After dropping the kids at school one morning, she'd sat down with some internet books from the library. Her plan had been to redesign the site, to create something inspirational for the group.

Five hours later she'd still been sitting there. After almost destroying the entire site, she'd abandoned any attempt to do something major. Finally she'd figured out a way to amend the text which appeared on a password-secured page. If she gave the password to everyone, they should be able to post their diary entries there. It was the best she could do.

Now Alice stood up and walked across to the bookshelf, pulling out a copy of *Her Life, My Life*. She stopped, looking at the green vinyl tape case beside it.

During Edith's final illness, Alice had convinced her to make some tapes recording her memories. Alice had listened to them while she had been writing *Her Life, My Life* but had then put them away once she'd finished the manuscript. She hadn't listened to them in years.

It was extraordinary how quickly technology changed. They didn't even have a tape player in the house any more. Stumped momentarily, Alice remembered an old walkman of Ellen's she'd noticed discarded in a toy box.

It had no batteries so she pulled a newish set out of a remote-control car lying in the corner.

Alice chose a tape at random, its spool halfway wound through. Finally, she sat back at her desk, the familiar voice filling her ears.

'*I didn't really meet your grandfather at the pictures you know – that was just a story we made up for the family.*' Even on the old tape recording Alice could hear the smile in her grandmother's voice.

'*He stole my bike.*'

There was a silence as the spools went around.

'*My father owned a billiards hall near Victoria Station – back before they had pool tables in hotels. I had been working there for a couple of months and then one day your grandfather came in. I used to tell him I'd been watching him but I hadn't – I just told him that to make him feel good.*'

There was another silence and then she added more softly, '*Good thing to do with men, you know. Make 'em feel good – even if you have to make it up. They don't usually know the difference.*'

Her voice resumed its storyteller's tone as she continued.

'He'd just come into town and had been hustling pool all day – made a bit, so he said. But he'd got a few beers in him and got overconfident. First I knew about it was when someone tried to break a cue over his head. He bolted out the back door, grabbed my bike and took off.'

There was a slight chuckle.

'He brought it back that night as I was closing up. Asked me to take a walk with him.'

With tears in her eyes, Alice stopped the tape.

Who'd have thought a little walk would lead to a lifetime of love and nine kids?

It wouldn't work now. From what she read, dates were big business these days. Anything less than a dozen roses and a fancy restaurant, and a guy looks cheap. The funny thing was that the people were still the same whether the first date was a stroll through a quiet city or an extravaganza.

Alice looked back at the flickering cursor on her computer screen.

'All right,' she murmured finally. 'Let's get this started.'

Kerry

Kerry peered out the front window. A package was sticking out of the postbox. He pulled on a pair of faded work shorts, zipping up the fly as he walked out the door.

The lid to the postbox squeaked as he lifted it, and a large flake of white paint drifted onto the grass verge which was badly in need of cutting. But Kerry's attention was on the parcel.

It occurred to him that to a casual observer it could easily look like he had a porn addiction.

Every couple of weeks he received magazine-shaped parcels in suspiciously innocent-looking brown paper wrapping. He glanced at the return address and almost laughed. Hell, this one was even from Canberra, the porn capital of Australia.

He headed back inside and glanced at the fridge. It was almost three o'clock. Well and truly time for a beer.

He twisted off the top and took a large satisfying mouthful before pulling the package toward him. Picking up a pair of scissors, he cut through the wrapping and pulled out its contents.

A much younger Mick Jagger sneered out at him from under the now famous *Rolling Stone* banner. The seller had been right. This was a pristine copy.

Kerry had first gone onto eBay a year earlier, searching for fairy-themed mosquito nets for Annie. He'd stumbled onto someone selling a *Rolling Stone* magazine from 1968. Out of curiosity, he'd made a bid and been surprised when he'd won it for less than five bucks.

It had arrived, much more battered than had been described but still a solid reminder of a past he'd been too young to know. He'd stayed up late, devouring the news from what seemed like a far simpler time. Janis Joplin, Jim Morrison, Jimi Hendrix. They were all there looking young and immortal, with no sign of the tragedy to come.

By the time Kerry had finished the magazine, he'd decided to try to collect every edition sold in the sixties – the decade he was sure contained the most musical talent.

Now he had more than a hundred. And his collection had spread to early editions of other music magazines like *Hit Parader* and *Downbeat*. As addictions went, he figured his was pretty harmless.

Kerry put the magazine beside the computer. He'd made a bid on a copy that had come out shortly after Woodstock. He'd just check how it was going.

No movement – he was still the highest bidder. The icon for new email flashed and he moved his mouse to look at it.

Alice Day. He grabbed another beer from the fridge and downed half of it, considering what to do.

In the cold light of day, this Red Folder Project was kind of ridiculous. As if cute little email instructions were going to change his life, or anyone else's.

Mentally Kerry listed his problems. Failed marriage – check; job he hated – check; eBay obsession – double check.

It was simple to get out of this group thing. An email to Alice Day would do it. Just something short, saying that he didn't think it was for him.

He knew he wouldn't.

He drank too much. Each day, he promised himself he'd give up or at least cut down, but each day he came up with another reason to justify the first beer. After that the pull of the second one was harder to resist and before he knew it, half a carton was gone.

He was still living in the house he'd shared with his ex-wife because he was still in love with her and couldn't bear to break the final link. He knew that too.

Something had to change and he had no idea where to start.

At least small things couldn't make things worse.

Besides, Alice Day was kind of sexy in her own way. Who knew? Maybe she might be the one to break his drought.

Smiling a little at that thought, Kerry double-clicked on the message.

Claire

Claire stared at the red blood, vivid against the white silk of her underwear.

It was right on time as always, just like clockwork. Which made it ridiculous to feel so disappointed.

Slowly Claire pulled clean underwear out of her handbag. There were two women waiting for the toilet, but she couldn't seem to go any faster.

It was almost fifteen years since that day a naked Claire had declared herself a mother-in-waiting. Nevertheless, she still nursed a sliver of hope each month. It was tucked at the back of her mind, but grew a little each day. Not even a conscious thought, it was just something that was always there. Occasionally she'd allow herself to take the hope out and turn it over, picturing herself with a round belly or with a baby. Then, precisely twenty-eight days after the last time, that hope would shatter. All she'd have to think about then was another month of temperature taking. That and trying to convince Peter that she genuinely wanted to have sex. That it was a mere coincidence that her desire coincided with ovulation.

As usual she felt no urge to cry. She figured she'd used up her allocation of tears many years ago – long before the fourth failed IVF attempt.

Claire had known this was a bad idea and she hadn't even ordered a drink yet.

Another bad idea, just like the one to move back to Brisbane.

After high school, the university in Hobart had been the only place where Peter had been accepted to study physiotherapy. To the horror of both sets of parents, Claire had moved to Hobart with him and they'd married three years later. After graduation, Peter had joined a small practice and he'd worked there until they had moved back to Brisbane four months ago.

Peter was finding it difficult working in a much bigger city where he had no local contacts and Claire often caught him staring into space with a worried frown.

Someone knocked on the toilet door. Claire straightened her skirt and stepped out of the cubicle, ignoring the baleful stares of the women waiting.

She could walk out of the bar and forget all about this task Alice had set for her. It would be simple to email Alice tomorrow and make up some story about what she had done. Or better still, tell her she'd reconsidered and didn't want to be involved with this crazy experiment. But Claire knew she wouldn't. Peter wouldn't be home until later and the thought of another evening by herself was even less appealing than being here.

She tousled her hair and ran a lipstick over her already vivid red lips. Then, with a deep breath, she pushed open the swing door and re-entered the wine bar.

Maybe she'd picked the wrong kind of place for this experiment.

Waiting for the first of Alice's emails to come, Claire had tried to imagine what it might say. Despite Alice insisting that she had no magic formulas, Claire had been convinced the project would help her.

Once she'd calculated that Alice would have received her questionnaire, Claire had checked her emails hourly. But when the message had finally arrived that morning, she stared at it in bemusement.

Go to a bar alone and sit at a bar stool. Order any kind of drink you like as long as it has a maraschino cherry in it. Stay there until you have written down at least three things that you know you are good at.

Claire knew the dumb task was her own fault. It was all because she'd been drunk when she'd filled in the questionnaire.

Claire had chosen the same bar as the week before. She had only been to one or two since they'd moved back to Brisbane. Anyway, it seemed kind of fitting.

This was her second attempt. She'd walked into the bar ten minutes ago, acutely aware of the fact that everyone else was in couples or groups. Alice's instructions had been precise and Claire had walked toward the stools next to the bar. But she had caught sight of the toilet doors further on and, with a sudden loss of nerve, had kept walking.

Claire looked longingly toward where they'd sat last week. She could tuck herself into one of the corner tables and not be at all conspicuous. But the email had been quite specific. After only a slight hesitation she slid onto a spare stool in front of the bar.

The bartender flipped a drink coaster in front of her. 'Evening,' he smiled briefly. 'What can I get for you? The wine list? Or would you rather wait for your friend?'

'Ah, there's no friend. I mean I have friends, but not tonight . . .'

The bartender was regarding her silently. Claire cursed her tendency to ramble when she was nervous. What was it about her that forced her to fill any available silence with words?

'I'm alone,' she finished abruptly. 'And I want a cocktail. Please,' she added as an afterthought.

'Yes m'am,' he smiled, and she relaxed a little.

The bartender opened a leather-covered list and turned it toward the back. 'These are our cocktails. I'll give you a second.'

'Ummm, one question?' she called after him as he headed to serve a sleek-haired girl at the other end of the bar.

He turned back toward her.

'Do any of these have cherries?' she asked.

'Cherries,' he repeated flatly.

'Mmmm, you know the red sweet ones.'

'You know, I don't think we do cherries.'

'Okay,' she conceded. Presumably the garnish wasn't critical to the whole process.

Suddenly she changed her mind. If she was going to do this, she'd do it properly.

'Ah, do you think maybe you could check? It's kind of important.'

He looked at her for a moment. 'No problem. Just give me a sec.'

He served the girl a glass of wine and then walked back into the kitchen.

'On my cherry mission,' he murmured as he passed her.

Looking for something to do, Claire flicked through the menu. The thought of a glass of white wine appealed greatly. She didn't even like cocktails.

The man reappeared, bearing a saucer with several red spheres in the centre.

'You're in luck.' He brandished the plate proudly.

'Now, what kind of cocktail do you want with your cherry?'

'Um, any will be fine. Can you just choose for me?'

He started to say something and then stopped. 'No problem.'

Claire watched a succession of bottles upended over the cocktail shaker. This was a bad move – she had planned to drive home after her one drink. Peter had said he'd be back by about nine. She hadn't made a conscious decision to keep Alice's group a secret, but that night had become a topic they both steered around and she knew he'd think it was ridiculous to be involved. So somehow she just hadn't mentioned it.

A huge frothy glass was deposited on the coaster in front of her. Claire regarded the orange- and yellow-layered concoction topped with not one but three cherries and laughed.

'That is fantastic. Just what I needed. Thank you.'

The bartender gave a small bow and left her with her drink.

Claire pulled a small notebook and pen out of her handbag. The bag was awkward on her lap and so she dropped it onto the floor.

Right. Drink – notebook – bar stool. She perched awkwardly on the stool, back straight, feeling incredibly conspicuous.

How the hell were you supposed to sit at a bar anyway? If she sat with her back to the room, she could see absolutely nothing. But if she turned the other way, she'd look like some kind of loser, waiting desperately for someone to talk to her.

As a compromise, she turned slightly to her right, drink at her left elbow and notebook balanced in her lap. She crossed her boot-clad legs. This pencil skirt and high boots always made her feel good, but she didn't normally sit balanced on bar stools. Right now, the gap between skirt and boots felt metres long. She longed suddenly for a pair of trousers.

The bar was busy and the air was full of that certain murmur of conversation produced by alcohol. An occasional laugh spiked the noise levels. Gradually Claire felt less of an object of interest. New people arrived, some left and no one much seemed to be paying attention to her.

A blue and yellow straw poked out the top of her drink and Claire sipped on it tentatively. Her experience of cocktails was that they didn't taste as though they had any alcohol in them. This one tasted like lemon-flavoured rocket fuel. That's what you got when you asked a bartender to choose for you. She didn't want to think about what it would cost.

Three things she was good at. Surely that couldn't be so hard. She'd do this, have a few more sips and then go. She certainly wasn't going to finish the lethal concoction in front of her.

The pen was heavy in her hand, a Mont Blanc she'd bought for Peter last Christmas. He had never used it, claiming it had been too expensive and that he was scared of losing it. She rolled it in her palm, watching the reflection of the lights above the bar in its silver surface.

Three things she was good at . . .

Once she'd been a good dental nurse. But that was too long ago to count. She could produce successful dinner parties without spending too much money – but simply following recipes couldn't be a skill.

Claire took another long sip, this time enjoying the feel of the alcohol seeping through her body.

So, she wasn't pregnant. Again . . .

In a way it was easier now that her friends' children were at school. The years when they were nursing babies and trundling toddlers on trikes had been the hardest. At first she'd spent time with them, feeling like she was learning. But over time, the possibility that Claire would never have a baby had grown. She had felt angry at friends who complained about sleepless nights or crying children. Sometimes she just couldn't keep smiling over the pain in her chest when she looked at a friend's baby. So she'd started to keep her distance.

It was around the same time that she'd discovered the satisfaction that renovating could bring. First the little workers' cottage outside Hobart, and then the one on Battery Point overlooking Salamanca. Both had been in an awful condition when they bought them. Claire had worked with architects and builders to turn them into appealing properties which sold within days of being on the market. Claiming any great skill was dishonest though. She was just the middleman who provided the cash to the architect and the builder.

The cocktail suddenly wasn't looking so undrinkable any more. It was half gone and Claire drew on the straw again. The toothpick-speared cherries bobbed in the remainder of the drink. Picking one up, she slid the cherry off with her teeth.

Claire looked around the bar, drink in hand. Her eyes rested on a woman sitting at a nearby table. She had on a black round-necked shirt. Automatically Claire registered how much better the woman would look in something open necked in a lighter colour. She could pick what would suit either herself or a friend within five seconds in a shop. Hardly a skill though.

She ran her pen around the spiral wire at the top of the page. This was not going well. Desperate, she drew on the straw again, jumping as an embarrassing slurp signalled the end of the drink.

If she had another one of those, she wouldn't be able to find the car, let alone drive home. This was ridiculous. Claire scribbled one word on the page and signalled for the bill.

Rebecca

I crossed a line last week. And I'm not sure if I can go back.

We didn't have anyone to look after our three year old son, and Jeremy and I couldn't agree on who would stay home. I had a really important day lined up with someone I was trying to recruit. So I snuck out before Jeremy woke.

Are you shocked? I think I am.

To make things even worse (if that's possible) Jeremy won't even talk about it. Just fixes me with this look of cold fury whenever I try to raise the subject.

I ended up having to grovel to our last nanny to have her come back to look after Sam. She now knows that she has me over a barrel and does even less than before.

Oh yes, and the person I was trying to recruit called me the next day to say he'd decided he was happy where he was.

I agreed to join this group for Claire, but was thinking I'd probably find a way to get out of it. My life needs major surgery, not gentle tinkering. But what the hell, I'll give it a go.

Rebecca slid onto her office chair, depositing her styrofoam coffee cup on the corner of the desk. The velcro of her laptop bag protested as she ripped it open. She plugged the computer in and logged in quickly.

The emails dropped onto the screen and she sat there for a moment wondering how there could be so many more since she'd last checked them at midnight. About to pick up her coffee, she spotted an email from Alice Day.

Her hand hovered above the mouse.

What on earth was she doing? She had an in-tray that was overflowing, a sixteen year old daughter who wouldn't talk to her, a nanny with a major attitude and a husband who might never smile at her again. The last thing she needed was some freak show of a self-improvement group telling her that it was the little things that mattered most.

She had to admit, though, there had been something interesting about the other night. The people there weren't the losers she'd expected. Somehow she'd imagined sad, downtrodden individuals who just wanted to talk about themselves. But they were all surprisingly normal and not old either. There had even been a bloke who was seriously good-looking.

Still, by anyone's definition, the speech that Alice woman had made was weird. The whole time she was speaking, Rebecca kept thinking of a time-share sales pitch she'd been conned into once. She'd practically had to knee the salesman in the groin to escape.

She had started planning her excuses while Alice was still talking. She was too busy; she already volunteered on several boards. Hell, if she had to, she'd say it was just too weird.

Then Alice had just gone. Leaving them with six bottles of champagne already paid for (Rebecca had checked with the waiter).

Suddenly, the five of them were left all alone with nothing in common except a very strange experience and some champagne. It was all a bit disconcerting.

Typically, the only guy there had taken charge and asked the waiter for another bottle. Rebecca would have left, but the likelihood of another run-in with Bianca wasn't very appealing either.

With nothing else to do, the five of them had flicked through the fancy red folders, laughing nervously about the strange idea.

Blessedly, a jazz duet had started up near them, removing the ability to talk at anything less than a shout.

The older lady had been the first to leave, going around the table shaking each person's hand as if they'd just left a business meeting.

Rebecca had been next. She'd driven and was probably already pushing her luck with two glasses on an empty stomach. Claire pushed the folder under Rebecca's arm as she left.

'Come on, Rebecca, let's do it,' she'd yelled over the band. 'What have we got to lose?'

Just as she'd expected, Claire had called her the next day. 'Well, it's definite now, I need someone to fix my life.'

'Really? Why?'

Rebecca had only been half listening while she seasoned a piece of beef she was cooking for lunch.

'Well . . . I managed to miss my own dinner party.'

Rebecca laughed despite herself. 'But it was only eight-fifteen when I left. What happened?'

'Well, the champagne tasted good and I don't get out much any more . . .' Her voice trailed off and Rebecca stayed silent.

'Actually that's not really true. It was like I just couldn't do it any more. Couldn't smile while I put the perfectly presented food on the table . . . Couldn't pretend that everything was good between Peter and I, when we barely talk. It was a stupid way to deal with it, I know. But I think maybe I was exhausted from being sensible and doing what I was supposed to do.'

Rebecca was silent for a moment. They'd only seen each other twice since school, but Claire had slipped back into the friendship as if the past seventeen years hadn't happened.

'What time did you get home?' Rebecca asked.

Claire groaned. 'I'm not sure and I can hardly ask Peter – he hasn't spoken to me all day.'

'He wasn't too pleased?'

'Not so much, no . . . But it's okay, because it's only the whole bunch of people Peter had targeted as our Brisbane friends that I offended.'

'Mmmm . . .'

'Rebecca. I can't do this by myself. I really need you to do it too.'

'Oh, come on. What the hell will it achieve? Let's just go buy that *Chicken Soup for the Soul* or whatever it is and be done with it.'

Claire was silent for a moment. 'Something has to change. I cannot go on like this.'

Her words were low and flat.

'Claire, there are other things to do. A counsellor maybe – or even a job?'

Rebecca regretted the words as soon as they were out of her mouth, but Claire didn't seem offended.

'I know. I should have gone back to work years ago. But there was always another possibility just around the corner. Another shot at IVF maybe, or a different fertility drug that might change everything. And all the doctors said that the less stressed I was the more likely it was that I'd conceive. I feel as though I've lost years in this endless longing for the next month. But it's time finally to stop and do something positive. This feels right. It really does. Please do it with me. Please . . . ?'

'I'm sorry, I just can't. I have more than enough in my life to worry about at the moment. I really don't need another thing.'

'But that's just the point, don't you see? It isn't another "thing", it's you.'

Rebecca rolled her eyes. 'Yeah, I heard what she said too. I just don't buy it. Let's face it. This Alice Day person is just a failed writer trying desperately to make some more money. That's fine, but I don't need to be part of the process.'

'Rebecca . . .' Claire's voice was openly pleading now. 'I can't have a baby. My marriage is on the rocks and I know no one in Brisbane any more. I really, really need your help.'

Rebecca was silent. It was as dangerous to maintain her friendship with Claire as it had been all those years ago. But the despair in Claire's voice made it impossible for her to refuse.

Mentally she added the group to her to-do list.

'Okay,' she sighed. 'Count me in.'

Even so, Rebecca had put off filling out the questionnaire.

Until last Thursday.

When she'd arrived home after her early morning departure, Jeremy had simply picked up his keys and walked out, not even meeting her eyes. He hadn't been home by the time Sam was asleep and Rebecca had sat at the kitchen bench, jumping every time she thought she heard a car. Finally she'd picked up the red folder and a pen and scrawled out some words in an attempt to take her mind off the inevitable confrontation.

And now she'd received her first email. Well it wasn't like Alice Day could make things any worse . . .

She clicked on the email entitled simply *From Alice*.

Rebecca,

My guess is that you're reading this at your computer with a foam coffee cup at your elbow. Here is today's task. Throw the coffee in the bin, go back downstairs, order a proper cup at the nearest cafe and sit there and drink it. Oh, and don't take those files you're thinking about. No pen or paper, no newspaper. Just sit there and look around.

Rebecca deleted the email and picked up her cup. It was seven-thirty already and she had a million things to do before her first appointment.

She paused, the plastic lid resting on her lip.

'Okay Alice,' she muttered reluctantly. 'I'll try it today. But you're going to have to do better than this next time.'

Alice

A lice turned into the long hallway, almost tripping over the sneakers strewn across the floor. She shifted the roll of dirty washing to her left hand and picked the shoes up with her right. The washing went into the machine, the shoes were dropped next to the back door. The pile of hand-washing sat on the laundry shelf, untouched since she had put it there a month earlier.

Alex's feet sped across the floor upstairs. Alice heard John thump after him and tensed. It was all so predictable. If she belted upstairs as fast as she could, she'd probably be just in time to head off the confrontation. But suddenly she couldn't be bothered.

Several seconds elapsed before she heard Alex's screech followed by a silence. His ability to suck in his breath mid-scream still surprised Alice. Often she'd think Alex had stopped, just as he let out his breath again in a burst of outrage.

John pounded down the stairs in a futile effort to disassociate himself from the carnage.

'It wasn't my fault, Mum. Really.'

He had yet to learn about protesting too much.

Alice ignored him and walked into the kitchen. She leaned her back against the sink. The bench was covered with the remains of breakfast and the lunches she'd made for everyone this morning. It was three months since she had started work at the bookshop, but she was still physically incapable of getting them all out the door on time and leaving a clean kitchen behind as well.

At least Alex had stopped crying. That meant that John's infraction hadn't been too bad. Or else he had fallen into a coma . . .

Maybe Andrew was right. They should renovate this place. Open up the kitchen to the living room and put some more bench space in here. Perhaps that would stop it constantly looking so like a pigsty. Or perhaps it would just make for a larger pigsty.

Alice looked at the clock. Three forty-five. Late afternoon was the low point of her day. The last traces of the morning's caffeine lost the battle with the tiredness that always lurked behind her eyes. John came home from school exhausted but still hyped from staking his place amongst his peers. Alex, desperate for his time, received only offhand attention from his brother. Or else John tried to continue his playground games, which usually ended in tears. Ellen just retreated to her bedroom, refusing to associate with either of her brothers.

In the first years Ellen and John were at school, afternoon tea had been a ritual. Alice had baked cakes or biscuits, feeling delightfully domesticated as they'd all sat around the kitchen table drinking Milo and talking about their days. But at some point that had stopped. The appeal of iPods and PlayStations outweighed Alice's company and the children now helped themselves to food when they felt like it.

Even the prospect of a glass of wine once the children were in bed was too remote to help.

As it often did these days, the lyrics to Marianne Faithfull's 'Ballad of Lucy Jordan' skimmed through her mind.

It was Dr Hook's less elegant version that had jammed in her memory, but still, the words were no less poignant.

Without even thinking about it she hummed the tune under her breath. She'd grown up hearing the song, but had never understood the lyrics until one day several years ago.

Alex was still a baby and she had been forcing John's squirming foot into a small sandshoe while yelling the school library books' last known location to Ellen.

Trying to ignore Alex's hungry wail, she'd suddenly understood the desperation of the woman in the song. The woman whose children were at school and husband at work, who had suddenly realised that her youth and her dreams had disappeared. An image of a woman much like herself abandoning it all and wandering naked through the suburban streets had burned behind Alice's eyes. Suddenly it hadn't seemed so ridiculous. In fact it had seemed like a bloody good idea.

Alice's handbag was where she had dumped it on the kitchen floor, the day's mail spilling out the top. She had seen the heavy cream envelope as soon as she'd opened the post-office box, but had thrown it into her bag with the rest of the mail. It had sat there temptingly while she picked up the children.

Abruptly Alice decided she could simply not be bothered traipsing upstairs to check on Alex. Instead she filled the kettle and plugged it in. Mind drifting, she warmed the heavy teapot and measured in a spoonful of leaves.

Alice rubbed her bare ring finger, not used to the absence of her wedding ring. When she'd gone to put it back on after the night in the bar, she'd realised how tight it had become. It had always been a little small, but with the weight she'd put on recently her finger bulged uncomfortably either side of the gold band. She'd left it with a jeweller to be resized.

Tea made, Alice tucked the mail under her arm and carried the teapot and her favourite cup to the soft bench seat running along the windows. It was a habit she'd acquired during the heyday of her book. Each mail would bring lovely notes and letters from readers and she'd sit down with a pot of tea and read them. It had amazed her that hundreds of thousands of people had read the words she'd typed on her computer.

Slowly, the flow of letters had ebbed and then stopped entirely. Now the mail comprised glossy brochures, bills and the occasional party invitation for one of the children. But still Alice would open each day's mail religiously, cup of tea at her elbow.

The inside of the envelope was lightly patterned with flowers. Alice knew it was from Lillian even before she read the questionnaire.

Quickly she skimmed the pages, her eyes abruptly catching on the final paragraph, which looked like it was added almost as an afterthought. Lillian didn't have a computer and had also included a diary entry to be posted on the website. Alice read through it, her heart sinking.

With an effort, Alice forced her eyes back to the rest of the questionnaire. Lillian had been widowed several years ago and lost her mother last year – she had a son living in New York and a daughter living in Paris. Scanning further down the page, Alice read that Lillian never felt she got her clothes right and suspected that maybe she'd missed the great adventure of her life.

Alice stared out over the railing. What on earth did she think she was doing? She was acting like an irresponsible charlatan dabbling in things she knew nothing about. These were people's lives she was playing around with.

She looked back at the last paragraph.

And their deaths . . .

Lillian had some kind of terrible illness. That wasn't something she was going to fix with some pithy words of wisdom.

Alice took another sip of her tea. The liquid warmed her throat, the scent of the blend of spices calming. This was an illicit pleasure – a brand of herbal tea produced by one of Andrew's competitors. He'd be horrified if he knew she bought it and kept it stashed at the back of the pantry.

The walkman containing her grandmother's tape was sitting at the other end of the bench seat. Pulling it toward her, she slipped the headphones over her ears and pressed play.

'I would have liked a fancier wedding but we couldn't afford it. We'd planned it to be wonderful – we were going to have everyone talking about it. I was going to have nylons and a dress made by a professional dressmaker.

'Your grandfather had sent his war wage home to his mother – four years' worth he sent. We talked about it a lot in our letters. That money was going to set us up. Pay for our wedding and then buy us a little house.

'Except that by the time he got home, there was no money. Your grandfather's brother had convinced their mother to give it all to him. He told her he was going to invest it.'

There was a pause.

'*Except that he spent it instead. The whole lot.*'

The silence crackled on the tape again for so long, it seemed as though she had finished the story. Finally she spoke again.

'*I'd like to say I was graceful about it but I wasn't – I behaved dreadfully.*

'*I cried because we couldn't afford a reception at the Gresham Hotel in the city like my sister. I told your grandfather I hated that my mother had to make my dress. I even told him I was thinking of calling the whole thing off.*

'*He never said a word.*

'*Until finally I asked him why he wasn't angry. Didn't he care what kind of wedding we had?*

'*He took a long pull on his cigarette and said, "I want a wedding that makes you my wife."*

'*I never complained about money again. Not once.*'

Alice picked up Lillian's form again. There was nothing she could do about her illness. But that wasn't what this was about. Small things, she reminded herself.

Megan

Well at least being part of this group means that for once I'm the youngest.

I'm starting to become a little paranoid about the age of everyone around me. All right, at thirty I'm not exactly over the hill. But when you find yourself doing the same things as people ten years younger than you, you've got to stop and take a good hard look at yourself.

Unfortunately, though, my new boyfriend is also someone else's husband. So doing grown-up public things with him is not an option. That means I can either go to sedate dinner parties and Sunday barbecues with married friends and their babies, or to bars and gigs with other, much younger friends who still have an idea about what constitutes a good time.

Taking a sip of her Diet Coke, Megan opened her email. Two messages from her brother who now lived in Dubai. One from a friend in Sydney.

And one from Alice Day.

God, that was quick.

The questionnaire had sat on her kitchen bench for over a week. The idea of a whole bunch of women (and a guy who was clearly just hoping to get lucky) trying to fix their lives didn't really work for her. She had no issues with anyone else doing it – each to their own and all that. She just didn't want to be part of it.

Still, since she'd stupidly told Jane that Greg was married, her entire family had been on her back about it. Jane had of course told Jennifer, and her mother had known about it before Megan had finished her first drink.

The way they had all performed, you'd think she was the only one in the world who had ever shagged a married man. Megan's argument that as she wasn't married, she wasn't doing anything wrong, had just inflamed the situation. Telling them that it was nothing serious had been a mistake as well – Jennifer lectured Megan that she shouldn't be putting someone else's marriage in jeopardy for a whim.

Her mother had fallen on this thing with Alice Day as though it had the potential to save Megan from eternal damnation and had insisted on calling every day to find out how it was going. The first couple of days Megan had lied and said she had filled in the forms and was waiting to hear back. But it was clear her mother wasn't going to give up.

So the night before last she'd sat down to fill in the questionnaire, a glass of wine in her hand, her favourite singer, Bill Callahan, playing on the stereo. She'd surprised herself with how honest she was with her answers – maybe it was the wine, but she just couldn't be bothered making up lies.

Under the heading *What would you like to be doing in five years?* Megan had written that she would like to be a computer programmer for a gaming company, working from home and having nothing whatsoever to do with children.

She'd even written about Greg and admitted that he was married, although she'd made it quite clear that she didn't consider it to be the soul-damning crime everyone else seemed to believe it was.

Megan had also told Alice that the way she was running the diary entries on her website was the technological equivalent of using a horse and cart instead of a car and she couldn't stand not to fix it.

Now, Megan clicked on Alice's email.

Hi Megan. I'm really pleased you've decided to do this.

Thank you for your offer to upgrade the website. As you can tell, the technology revolution has largely passed me by and my kids tell me frequently I am a dinosaur. The administrator password is currently Alice (yes, I know, not very clever). Please feel free to bring us into the twenty-first century.

Now, to your task. I have to admit, I found your first email task one of the most difficult to come up. I'm not sure why, maybe because you live such a different life.

That was obviously the closest that Miss Perfect Alice could come to acknowledging her having sex with a married man, Megan thought sourly.

It sounds to me that you are frustrated with life because you've done things others wanted you to do – like teaching. Perhaps a good place to start is to think of something you truly want to do today – for you, not anyone else.

I am trying hard not to sound like that line of greeting cards which features birds flying into sunsets and asks you to follow your dreams. But today, I want you to do one thing just because you want to.

Megan looked at the computer screen. After a moment she closed her email program so that the screensaver came up. It was a picture of Greg she'd taken on her mobile phone a few days ago. His dark eyes looked at her, his smile enigmatic.

What Megan had said about not being serious about Greg wasn't true. Megan liked him a lot. He was the head of some department in a mining company, used to making things happen. He was smart and confident and seemed to listen to what she said. Almost perfect actually – except for the wife and two children.

Even so, her family's reaction had made her re-think their relationship. It seemed inevitable that it was all going to end badly and she should just finish it now. Suddenly though, she changed her mind.

Okay Alice, she thought. Something just for myself and no one else . . . Well, then, I choose to keep seeing Greg.

Megan pulled up Greg's number on her phone.

Need a drink. R U free?

Within seconds the answer came back.

Yep – normal place 30 mins.

Megan hit the shutdown key on her computer.

Her immortal soul would just have to wait a little longer for redemption.

Lillian

Kyla called on Sunday and I told her about the drinks and Alice's idea. She surprised me by being strongly against the concept, thinking it all sounded very weird. Which I guess it is. But I found myself trying to explain how I'd thought the same things that Alice had been talking about, but had never actually put any of it into words.

After the MRI scan I needed something to think about that didn't involve long scientific words or 'likely scenarios'. So I filled in the form and sent it back. I also sent Alice my first diary entry about why I decided to go to the drinks in the first place. I must admit it felt quite nice to do something of which my daughter disapproved. Perhaps I'll try a tattoo next . . .

The note from Alice had come in the mail – a small piece of bright pink notepaper in a matching envelope.

Dear Lillian

Your task is to go and buy yourself a piece of jewellery. Nothing expensive, but it must include beads and at least two different colours. And you need to wear it!

Lillian had been taken aback, almost irritated. What on earth was that supposed to achieve? Disappointed, she screwed the note up and dumped it in the bin. She didn't know what she had been hoping for, but shopping for accessories wasn't it.

She couldn't believe she'd wasted the effort of filling in the form.

Annoyed at herself, she found her big hat and gardening gloves and headed outside. After two days of rain, the garden had finally started to show some life. Lillian spent the morning pulling out weeds and cutting back unruly branches. Finished by lunchtime, she washed her hands and headed upstairs. Pulling off her hat, she tried to push her sweaty hair from her forehead.

She had nothing else planned for the remainder of the day. The pile of reading material the doctor had given her sat on the dining room table.

With sudden decision she strode into the bathroom. Thirty minutes later she was ready, hair washed and dried and make-up on. She had never understood the ability of her children to walk out the door in whatever they happened to be wearing without so much as running a brush through their hair. She'd been brought up to believe that you dressed up when you went out, and old habits died hard.

Lillian settled herself at a cafe table as a well-dressed couple in their early forties stood up to leave a neighbouring table. The man dragged a beautifully clad baby from where she had been crawling around the table legs. As he lowered her into the stroller, the baby arched her body and launched into a full-throated yell. Rattled, the man fumbled with the straps and the baby rolled sideways off the pram and toward the floor. The woman caught the child with one hand, dumping her into the pram.

'Grab the stuff, Adam, I'll wait further down,' she instructed the child's father over her shoulder.

The man looked over at Lillian, who made a commiserating face at him. He smiled thinly. From under the table, he collected a macerated piece of toast, soft toy and an expensive-looking pair of sunglasses.

'Makes me wonder why we do this to ourselves,' he muttered to Lillian.

'Don't worry, they do grow up,' she replied. 'Before you know it, you'll be pulling her out of bars.'

'Roll on the day,' he ground out. 'Drug addictions will be just fine if she sleeps in occasionally.' He smiled to soften his words, but it came out more like a grimace.

Lillian watched him stride down the street, blissfully unaware of the patch of mush covering his designer right buttock.

Raising children today wasn't easy. Parenting seemed to be incredibly self-conscious, people thinking and double thinking actions or decisions which in her day had been automatic. How to discipline your children, what opportunities to offer them . . . Thirty years ago the answer to the first had been smacking and to the second had been playing in the backyard. Now it seemed that neither of those scenarios existed.

She guessed that Kyla would be the same if she ever had a child, treating motherhood like a career. Lillian didn't envy her the task – sometimes having fewer options was a good thing.

Grandchildren . . . She'd thought that when they came they would bring more purpose to her life. Her mother had come to live with her soon after David's death. There'd always been someone to look after until last year. But now, perhaps she wouldn't be around when Kyla or Daniel had children. Or if she were, maybe she wouldn't be able to take them for walks, or even hold them . . .

The waitress interrupted her thoughts and Lillian placed her order.

She pushed thoughts of illness to the back of her mind and concentrated on enjoying the outing. There was absolutely no reason not to do this more often, but somehow she didn't. She'd never even had a coffee alone until about five years ago. A night out for dinner had been something done with the children at the local Chinese once in a blue moon.

But here she could sit back and watch the world go by. That at least was one benefit of being invisible.

Lillian sometimes felt like a modern version of a ghost. People could hear her if she spoke to them, feel her if she touched them. But otherwise she was completely invisible. Too old to draw a second glance, too young to need helping in the door or up the bus steps . . . It seemed that the presence of a sixty year old woman simply didn't register on the consciousness of most people. She understood now why people became eccentric. It was simply a way to maintain a place in a world that had forgotten them.

Lillian wondered briefly if that was why Alice had sent her off to buy a striking necklace. To make her noticeable. It was unlikely though that Alice understood. Alice was under forty, a successful author and had young children. It was probably just that she couldn't think of anything else to suggest to a boring old woman with a disease that could well be going to destroy her life.

Suddenly Lillian didn't care why she was here. It was a beautiful day and the food the waitress had delivered was excellent. She was about to wander through the shops with a purpose, rather than her usual aimless anxiety. There'd been enough bad buys over the years to put her off shopping altogether. Nothing terribly dramatic, just items that looked good in the shop but either looked ridiculous at home or went with nothing she owned.

Lillian finished her meal and paid the bill.

Thirty minutes later she was standing in a boutique, fingering a long string of pearl-coloured beads. It was beautiful, but only one colour and so didn't fit Alice's criteria.

'Lillian?'

She turned to see one of the women who'd been at Alice's drinks evening.

'Lillian? It is you. I'm sorry, you probably don't remember me, but we met the other night. I'm Claire.'

Lillian smiled and quickly took her hands off the beads. She felt as though she'd been caught doing something wrong.

'Hello.'

She did remember Claire, although she wasn't sure she would have spoken to her if she had seen her first. After all, they hadn't exactly met under normal circumstances.

'Doing a bit of retail therapy?' Claire held up the smart-looking paper bag she was carrying. 'They have a great sale on at Spark. I had to use incredible willpower not to buy more.'

Lillian shook her head. 'For me, retail is anything but thera-peutic. If I could just wear my pyjamas everywhere I'd be a much happier woman.'

Claire looked as though she wasn't sure whether Lillian was joking or not. 'You really don't like shopping?'

'Hate it. Mostly because I always seem to get it wrong.'

Lillian hesitated. This whole project of Alice's was ridiculous. She felt stupid admitting that she was actually in the shop fol-lowing Alice's instructions. But then Claire was part of it, wasn't she?

'Alice told me to buy some beads,' she confessed. 'Coloured ones. But I have no idea which ones to buy.' She gestured at the rack in front of her.

Claire looked at them briefly. 'None of them,' she said. 'To get away with beads like that, you need to be a six foot supermodel or a teenage girl. They'd make anyone else look frumpy.' She looked sideways at Lillian and hesitated before adding, 'No offence.'

Lillian tried hard not to take any. At least she hadn't actually bought them. Frumpy – just the image she was looking for.

'But,' Claire was saying, 'they have some wonderful necklaces on sale at Spark. I was just looking at them but knew my husband would go ballistic if I spent more money. Come on, I'll show you.'

'No, really, I should be going. It's not as though I need any-thing, I was just browsing . . .'

'Please, I'd love to show you. Besides, they're half price.'

As if that settled the matter Claire headed out of the store, leaving Lillian no choice but to follow.

Rebecca

Bianca looks almost normal when she goes to school. Apparently the headmistress walks up and down amongst the girls during assembly, checking that their uniforms comply with the rules.

She's been teaching a long time has Miss Shepard, and rumour has it that she once expelled a girl for wearing eyeliner. No warning – just gone.

Personally, I don't believe it. If it is true, it happened a long time ago before students' rights became more important than their education.

But it's a good rumour.

Each morning I drop Bianca off at the school, a pimple-prone teenager with a stuffed backpack. Each afternoon she emerges from her bedroom, eyes ringed with kohl, and dressed in black drainpipe jeans, a shirt with cuffs dripping over her fingers and at least one item which includes a skull. Apparently emo wear is about developing a look of your own. If yesterday's green fingerless lace gloves are anything to go by, though, I'd say a bit of conformity wouldn't go astray.

See, there I go again . . .

Apparently I have no idea whatsoever about where she is at. Actually she's right about that.

For a long time I tried really hard to stay with what was happening in Bianca's world. I read her magazines and forced *myself to listen to emo rock on the way to work, despite the fact that the emo band label is apparently an 'artificial and consumerist label with no value'.*

But somewhere between the Wiggles and Panic at the Disco, I lost her. I can't seem to catch her again. She treats my attempts to understand where she's coming from with a very adult type of pitying disdain. And then sometimes I can see the sixteen year old girl who is desperately hurt that her mother has not a clue what she is about.

She alternates between breaking my heart and arousing in me a fury no one else can produce.

'It's not like I remember them or anything. Couldn't you just take along a picture?'

'Bee . . . please.' Rebecca knew she should be chastising Bianca for the way she was speaking, not pleading with her. But she had neither the time nor the energy. She'd had to threaten Bianca with missing tomorrow's band practice just to get her in the car. Rebecca couldn't think of a threat big enough to make her pretend to be pleasant.

She continued, desperate to make everything right. 'Claire hasn't seen you since you were a baby – and she's cooking you a special meal.'

Bianca rolled her eyes. 'Yeah great. No dead animals. What a huge favour that is.'

Her tone was even more rude than normal. Rebecca threw a despairing look at Jeremy but he was concentrating on driving in the heavy rain and said nothing.

She wondered, not for the first time, whether it would have been different if Jeremy had been Bianca's father. Maybe as a united force they could have stood firm against her assaults on happy family life, instead of allowing her moods to wash over them all.

Jeremy had married Rebecca knowing that a then eleven year old Bianca was part of the package. If anything he had a better relationship now with Bianca than did Rebecca. He was infinitely patient and would correct Bianca in a stern but calm voice which she appeared to actually heed. But when things got too heavy he always deferred to Rebecca. Tired of the sound of her own shrieking voice, Rebecca yearned for Jeremy to lose it – just once.

'I should have stuck to my guns and said no,' she said heavily to no one in particular. 'Or we could have gone out to dinner in a restaurant, left the kids at home . . .' Rebecca received no response from anyone and her voice trailed off.

She had tried to refuse the invitation, but Claire had kept coming up with different options until it was virtually impossible to do so without being blatantly rude. Claire had insisted that her house was great for kids – completely unrenovated and tough as nails, she'd said.

'We'll see about that,' Rebecca thought grimly.

Rebecca sighed and returned her attention to the map on her lap, trying to figure out when they should turn off the major road they were on. They must be getting close. She peered at the jumble of streets, trying to match a name to something she could see. Before she could manage it, Jeremy pulled the car over. They'd long ago agreed she couldn't navigate to save herself and she handed him the street directory wordlessly.

He looked at it for a moment. 'Nearly there.'

Jeremy closed the heavy book and handed it back to Rebecca, ensuring his hand was nowhere near hers. Since the morning over a week ago when she sneaked out of the house at dawn, Jeremy had spoken to her only when absolutely necessary.

Two syllables constituted a long conversation.

As soon as Rebecca had arrived at work on that morning, she'd known she'd made a terrible mistake. She'd gone through the motions of coordinating the interviews, but had been unable to concentrate, a feeling of panic twisting in her stomach.

Jeremy had only tried to call her mobile once, not even leaving a message.

Eventually, though, she'd had to go home.

As Jeremy waited for a break in the traffic, Rebecca looked at the side of his face, searching for some sign that he had forgiven her. There was none, his face set in the mask she was starting to think might be permanent.

It had never been like this before. They had fights, but those were always solved quickly, often in bed. But now Jeremy turned his back toward Rebecca every night, falling asleep quickly and leaving Rebecca to her swirling thoughts.

What she'd done had been stupid – guaranteed to fail and to hurt everyone. Rebecca wondered how she could have ever thought it might be a good idea. It was a plan that only a sleep-deprived mind could have thought viable and then only in the pre-dawn hours. But Jeremy had rebuffed each of Rebecca's attempts to apologise.

Jeremy accelerated quickly and swung across the oncoming lane, into the next side street.

The rain had brought down the evening early and Rebecca frowned as she tried to make out the house numbers. This bit she could do.

'Eighty-seven – there it is.'

The numbers were large and stuck onto an immense faded green retaining wall which blocked all view of the house from the street.

Jeremy pulled up next to the wall.

She tried one last time. 'Okay guys. Please behave. Bianca. I promise, we'll have dinner and then go straightaway.'

Bianca just snorted in response.

'Yes, Sam, what is it?'

Rebecca turned around to look at him, his incessant drone of 'Mum ... Mum ... Mum ...' having finally broken through her focus on Bianca.

'Need to go potty.'

Sam was in the process of being toilet trained, but it was still pretty hit and miss. Anticipating this exact situation, Rebecca had slipped on a nappy when she dressed him this evening.

'Sweetheart, can you hold on for just for a minute?'

Sam sucked his thumb and shook his head.

'Okay, don't worry. Just do a wee into your nappy – this once won't hurt.'

Instantly a dark stain bloomed across the front of his khaki trousers.

'What the . . .'

'Oh yeah – Sam asked me to take it off before we left home, so I did.' Bianca's voice couldn't have been less concerned.

'Oh for God's sake!'

Rebecca flung her door open and stepped out into the downpour. Before she'd even made it to the boot to get the umbrella she was drenched. Without looking, she knew that her pale green shirt was sticking to her dingy grey bra which should have been thrown in the bin months ago.

The rusted blobs on the umbrella stem jammed its action. Cursing, she jerked it hard, pinching her finger in the process. Ridiculously her eyes filled with tears. She stood for a moment in the downpour, took a deep breath and finally pushed the umbrella into position.

Rebecca opened Sam's door, trying to force a smile. 'Don't worry, darling. No harm done.'

There was no way she could take Sam inside like this.

Balancing the umbrella, Rebecca unbuckled the car seat and quickly pulled him out. She tried not to grimace as he wrapped his wet little legs around her waist.

Taking shelter under the large tree which spread its branches over the footpath, she quickly stripped off his trousers and replaced them with some ancient shorts she'd found on the floor of the car.

Bianca stood next to Jeremy under an umbrella. Their ease with one another cut at Rebecca like it always did.

The gated entrance through the high wall was vaguely castle-like in a shabby kind of way. Rebecca pushed it open and climbed three steps to the path which led to the house's front stairs.

Finally they were all assembled, dripping wet, on the top step. Rebecca rang the bell.

The first thing Rebecca noticed when Claire opened the door was her white, perfectly ironed shirt. Rebecca knew the shirt would make her look like a waitress, but on Claire it looked great. Must be the jewellery, she thought, or the shoes. Either way, it worked.

Claire leaned forward and kissed Rebecca on the cheek. Rebecca caught a faint whiff of perfume which reminded her that she hadn't even managed deodorant.

'Jeremy,' Claire put out her hand, smiling. 'So lovely to meet you.'

She seemed so genuine, Rebecca thought. And so together. She didn't even mention the state of them all.

Jeremy returned the smile as he shook hands.

'Sorry we're late,' he said. 'My fault, I'm afraid – a work thing.'

Rebecca looked at him gratefully, but he avoided her eyes.

'No problem at all. Peter's only just home himself. Bianca – I've heard a lot about you.'

Bianca looked at the outstretched hand and for one terrible moment Rebecca thought she was going to ignore it. But slowly she reached forward and took it briefly.

Rebecca looked at Bianca through Claire's eyes. Dyed black hair, black lips, red eye shadow, black nail polish. Short black lace skirt belted over footless tights with a heavy studded belt. Her red and black basketball shoes clashed fiercely with her tight-fitting pink top.

Claire bent down and took Sam's hand. 'Hi Sam.'

Unused to such attention, Sam smiled shyly from underneath his fringe. She absolutely must get his hair cut this week, Rebecca thought again.

Claire stood up. 'So, follow me . . . please excuse the house. It is definitely a renovator's dream . . .'

Rebecca noticed Claire throw an awkward look at Peter.

'Looks pretty good to me,' Jeremy said lightly. 'You should have seen our place before we knocked it down and started again. Rain like this would have brought the roof in.'

Rebecca saw a couple of bedrooms off to the side, a lounge area to the right. And then they were through the kitchen and dining room and out onto an enormous old covered deck.

Peter turned from the table where he'd been opening a bottle of red wine.

Claire made the introductions. 'Peter, this is Jeremy. And Bianca and Sam.'

As Peter and Jeremy shook hands, Rebecca looked at Peter. He was almost a head taller than Jeremy and still good-looking. If anything he looked better than he had at school. At school he had been one of the sporty ones – lanky and lean. He'd filled out in the intervening years, and while he still looked fit, it was the fitness earned at a gym.

Peter and Claire looked every inch the successful physiotherapist and his wife. His chinos and loose button-up shirt had clearly not been cheap. And, as usual, Claire looked divine. Not over the top or ostentatious, just that perfectly groomed point that Rebecca reached perhaps half-a-dozen times a year when all the stars aligned and she had more than five minutes to dress.

Sam wandered off toward the steps which led off the deck. Bianca followed him, Sam being the only person in the family she cared for unequivocally.

'Rebecca!' Expecting a polite peck on the cheek, Rebecca was surprised when Peter put his arms around her. 'It's been a long time.'

She tried to relax into his embrace, but was too conscious of the fact that she was wet and almost certainly smelt of urine. Peter clearly felt her unease and released her after a brief moment.

Rebecca took a step backwards. 'It must be strange being back in Brisbane after all this time.'

Peter thought about her question for a moment. 'I guess so. I feel a bit like we left as kids and came back grown-ups. The last car I had in Brisbane was that old tan Toyota – I used to be able to see the bitumen through the rust holes. My new car is definitely a step or two up from that.'

'I remember that car,' said Rebecca without thinking, and instantly regretted it.

There was a tiny silence before Peter spoke again.

'We need a drink,' he announced. 'Claire thought we should celebrate seeing each other again with champagne. But there's also beer, or wine if you'd rather.'

'Champagne would be great, thanks,' Jeremy answered.

'Me too,' Rebecca added.

Claire turned to Rebecca. 'I wonder if Bianca might like a small glass as well? It's just such a treat to see her again.'

Rebecca forced a smile. She had no problems with Bianca drinking alcohol. However, she did have a problem with Bianca pouring the champagne onto the floor in protest at middle-class excess and, knowing her daughter, that was a distinct possibility.

'Well, maybe a small glass . . .' She fixed the back of Bianca's head with a stare, willing her to behave.

'Excellent.' Claire set the glasses on the table. Peter opened a bottle of champagne and started to pour. Claire handed out the glasses, taking one over to Bianca, who in a rare moment of good humour actually managed a half-smile.

Claire returned to the others and raised her glass. 'So here's cheers. To old friends.'

They each raised their glasses. 'To old friends,' they replied, Rebecca forcing a cheerful smile.

Claire turned back to Rebecca. 'It only seems like ten minutes ago that we heard you were pregnant with Bianca.'

Rebecca nodded stiffly. She didn't like the way the conversation was going. As far as she was concerned that was all a very long time ago and she had no need to revisit it.

Out of the corner of her eye, Rebecca saw Bianca stand up a little straighter. It occurred to Rebecca that she hadn't told Bianca how she knew Peter and Claire.

Rebecca was relieved when Jeremy spoke.

'How long has it been since you saw each other?'

'Before we had lunch a few weeks ago, the last time I saw Rebecca was the year after school. Bianca was only tiny.'

'So you knew my father.'

They were the first words Bianca had spoken. That, though, wasn't the reason they were shocking. It was the aggression behind them. It wasn't a question, just a furious statement of fact.

Claire flicked a nervous look at Rebecca. Her voice was hesitant. 'Yeeees . . .'

'So you know how I could find him?'

'Um . . . no. I . . .' Claire was clearly completely unprepared for this.

Rebecca tried to rescue the situation. 'Bianca, this isn't the time or the place for this. We'll talk about it later.'

Bianca turned on her. 'Every time I try to talk to you about my father I get the same crap. He was an exchange student at your high school. You found out you were pregnant after he left Australia and never told him about me. You said we'd talk about trying to find him when I turned fifteen – and sixteen . . . Fuck later. I want to know now.'

Alice

Alice could remember clearly when she'd realised she was getting old.

She'd known that she didn't look like those nubile babes on the beach with their stomachs as flat as their surfboards. But that was okay. She could still run a brush through her hair, pencil on a smudge of eyeliner and feel okay about how she looked.

She'd had a rather average haircut, nothing too awful, just a bit short, with too many layers that made her think of an ageing eighties rock chick. Each time she glanced in a mirror she was slightly taken aback by how average she looked. It wasn't that she looked terrible, just ordinary. The type of person you'd walk past on the street without noticing. But she figured it would be better once the haircut settled down.

A week passed and she still looked ordinary, even on a couple of evenings when she'd gone to a bit of effort. Not even her favourite deep red T-shirt helped. The colour just accentuated the veins in her eyes and the blotches on her cheeks.

She started looking closer at the mirror and noticed the lines, not just at the corners of her eyes, but under them too. Her chin wasn't as firm as she remembered, and there were a couple of those flat moles at her hairline. A sign of age, a GP had depressingly told her when she had had them checked out. And her eyes looked flat. She looked at the children just to check she hadn't imagined things. No, their eyes definitely sparkled – where the hell had her sparkle gone?

Andrew looked older too, but damn it, age looked good on a man. There were lines under his eyes and his hair was thinning. But somehow he was looking more like Sean Connery to her Barbara Cartland.

Alice pulled five plates from the dishwasher, carelessly clattering them onto the kitchen table. Her days of reading until the early hours were long gone. Still, though, the seduction of another world pulled her in at the end of a day of mundane chores and it had been way too late last night by the time she'd forced herself to close her book.

Andrew had pulled her toward him then, curling his body around hers. Alice had tensed, the tantalising lure of sleep pulled away. She'd forced herself to relax.

His hand moved over her stomach and she wondered whether he immediately compared it to the way it had been when they met. Before three children and too many full-fat coffees. She had forced herself not to think about it and concentrated on the sensations his hand was creating. They fell into their long-established pattern, giving each other pleasure in the way they had so many times before.

Lying curled in Andrew's arms afterward Alice had felt closer to him than she had in months. She opened her mouth to say something, anything, she didn't know what. But Andrew had muttered 'Night,' and rolled over onto his side.

Alice had lain sleepless for an hour afterwards, listening to Andrew's deep breathing. Then, soon after she had fallen asleep, she was wrenched back to consciousness by a persistent, 'Mummy, Mummy . . . Mummy?'

Looking up she had seen Alex, knowing immediately that he'd wet the bed again. She had pulled a nightgown over her head and followed him down the dark hall, changing sheets and pyjamas in a semi-trance. An hour later John had woken crying, terrified again of the nightmares she blamed squarely on the latest Harry Potter film.

Alice had no idea what time she'd closed her eyes again but it had seemed only moments before the alarm shrieked beside her.

The table set for breakfast, she moved on to the school lunches. Six slices of bread sat neatly on the breadboard awaiting a fabulous filling. Alice didn't feel up to fabulous this morning, though – Vegemite and cheese was as good as it was going to get.

Knife in the Vegemite jar, she paused, glancing at the chrome clock on the wall. Its black hands showed that she was ahead of schedule. Suddenly the lure of a world outside her morning's domesticity appealed. Her computer was in a spare bedroom off the kitchen and she switched it on, the screen glowing in the early morning light. She settled into the chair, and checked her emails. The usual raft of penis enlargement and share trading spam mail sat there in black type. She deleted them one at a time, marvelling at the fact that someone must actually answer them. About to delete the last one, she saw her name in the preview box on the right of the screen.

She clicked on the email.

Dear Alice

Just wanted to drop you a line and tell you your first email was inspired. I had a great chat to an old mate on Thursday. Turns out he will be up in Brisbane in a couple of months – he's going to crash with me for a couple of days.

The email had come from Kerry.

Alice had the feeling Kerry was lonely, despite the front he put on. Not lonely for someone to go out for a beer with, he clearly had lots of those sorts of friends. It was more as though he needed someone he had a history with. He'd been with his ex-wife since they were both twenty. When a marriage like that broke up, she figured there was a lot of history lost with it.

So Alice's first instruction to Kerry had been to call a friend he hadn't spoken to in at least five years. She was outrageously delighted it had gone well. Conscious she was no longer ahead of her morning schedule but falling further behind every moment, she quickly scrolled down the page.

> *You may also be pleased to know I haven't made a bid on eBay for coming up to thirty-six hours. Maybe I should come up with a twelve-step plan for eBay junkies?*

Alice laughed out loud. Under areas he'd like to change, Kerry had admitted to spending hours online adding to his collection of 1960s *Rolling Stone* magazines.

> *Better go — I can feel eBay's tentacles reaching out . . .*
> *Talk soon,*
> *Kerry*

Alice hit the reply button.

> *Delighted to hear of your successes!!! There is life after eBay. I became compulsive about finding the perfect Polly Pocket set for my daughter a few years ago and spent hours searching online for it. I think I was cured when I found it at Target at half the price.*
> *I don't want to sound like a school ma'am but you need to write on the site or this thing won't work.*
> *Alice*

She quickly pressed send and logged onto her website. Excellent. There were more diary entries.

Hearing loud thumps from upstairs, she quickly closed the site down. She'd look at the diaries after the kids were at school.

Her computer pinged signalling a new message. She clicked on her inbox.

> *A school ma'am . . . Hmmm. I like the sound of that.*

Alice stared at the screen.

Was he flirting with her?

She hesitated for a moment, then typed a reply.

Shouldn't you be getting ready for work or something?

The reply came back quickly.

Or something. Got the day off. Any suggestions for me today, oh oracle?

Alice smiled.

Nope, today you are on your own. Just enjoy it.

'Alice, are you here?'
    Andrew's voice echoed in the room. Guiltily Alice pressed the send button and hurried back to the kitchen.

Claire

Well, I went. It actually wasn't as bad as I thought, drinking cocktails by myself. Rather depressing outcome though. I sat there for an hour and the only skill I could think of was shopping for clothes. How incredibly shallow and useless to be unable to come up with anything better than that.

The house was perfectly tidy and dinner ready to cook. Claire hated looking idle when Peter came home and always tried to be in the middle of some activity.

She knew he thought she should be looking for a job. Peter's new practice was bringing in far less than they'd been banking on when they'd bought the house. Just making the minimum payments on the mortgage each month was becoming increasingly stressful.

It had become so bad, she'd started hiding her purchases from Peter, lying if he asked if something she was wearing was new.

He was right about a job, she knew that. It was just that after all this time, she had no idea where to start and even less of an idea what she was capable of doing.

Claire sat down at the computer to check her emails. She wasn't looking for another email from Alice. The last one had been a total waste of time anyway. This group was obviously yet another of her short-lived enthusiasms with no long-lasting outcomes.

Just like the florist course. Or the meditation retreat. Thank God she hadn't told Peter about it when she was in the full flush of her enthusiasm.

Still, when she saw the email from Alice Day she couldn't help clicking on it anyway.

Dear Claire

I did promise little and there is no arguing that's what this one is.

Tonight, cook a meal for you and Peter but a little different to your normal standard. In your questionnaire, you said you felt one of the pressures in your day came from coming up with new menu ideas each night.

So tonight I have for you a challenge. What would happen if you made a meal that took you less than five minutes? Your parameters are that it must cost less than $5.00 in total and involve at least one can. Personally I recommend baked beans on toast but you can choose.

Don't go to the shop — just use whatever you have. Remember, it doesn't have to be glamorous. In fact, it doesn't even have to be good.

Claire looked over to where the rib eye fillet was sitting on the counter. It had cost a fortune, but she'd bought it on impulse, sick of worrying how much everything cost.

She was planning on serving it with the jus she'd made and frozen into small portions several weeks ago — the flavour of it was amazing. Mash and broccolini as side dishes would complete the meal.

Where did Alice get these ideas from? What good would it possibly achieve to have a lousy meal tonight? She almost laughed as she thought of Peter's reaction to baked beans on toast.

She was still staring at the email when the front door opened. Closing the computer down, she walked toward the doorway.

'Hi,' she said as Peter walked in the door.

'Hi,' he replied, dropping his shoulder bag beside the couch.

'Good day?' she asked.

'Yeah, not too bad. I've been with the Demons this afternoon.'

'How are they looking for the season?'

Claire couldn't care less whether Peter's cricket team won or lost. She figured, though, that she should at least make an effort to get past the fight over the house plans.

'So, so,' Peter replied. 'They're a rough bunch and this is their first season together. You never know, though.'

'Do you feel like a glass of wine?' Claire asked hopefully.

Years ago a drink together when Peter came home from work had been a lovely part of the day for both of them.

'No thanks,' Peter replied casually. 'Think I might have a shower. Do I have time before dinner?'

'Sure,' Claire replied, trying hard not to show the hurt his words had caused.

It was as though they had both just run out of love. Maybe it was because they'd married too early. They'd had their tenth anniversary before most of their friends had even married and they had missed those exciting twenty-something adventures in different relationships.

Or perhaps it was their inability to have a baby.

Maybe the years of timed and highly organised sex and the endless failures had killed the spark they'd once had.

Peter said that he had accepted they wouldn't have a child, but Claire never had. She had no idea how to make the endless ache for a baby go away. It was with her every day. Every mother and child she saw on the street, every happy family on television, sent a stab of pain into her chest. She'd been hard to live with at times – she knew that. It was like a part of her was missing, though, like she couldn't function properly without having the chance to become a mother.

Perhaps she should have pushed Peter harder years ago about the idea of adopting a child from overseas. He'd never been enthusiastic and Claire had let the idea slide, always hoping that she would fall pregnant. Now, though, they couldn't even agree over what to watch on television, let alone something like adoption.

Claire had kept trying to breathe some life back into what had once been very good. She tried to be bright and cheerful, the lovely social wife. But now suddenly she was tired.

Peter disappeared into the bathroom and Claire walked back into the kitchen. She pulled a saucepan out from under the bench, filled it with water and set it on the stove. Reaching for the peeler, she picked up one of the potatoes neatly positioned next to the cutting board.

She pushed too hard on the peeler and it skidded off the potato, cutting into the side of her thumb. Tears leapt to her eyes and she fought hard to stop the sob that filled her throat.

Claire looked down at the cutting board for a moment, then picked up the potatoes and put them away. The steak and the jus went back into the fridge.

She opened the pantry and looked at the cans neatly set out there. As she'd thought, there wasn't a tin of baked beans to be seen. There were several of artichoke hearts and chickpeas, but nothing she could see that would make an easy meal. Pushing aside a tin of salmon, she spotted a lone can of spaghetti right at the back.

She pulled it out, ripped open the pull-top lid and tipped the contents into a small pan.

By the time Peter wandered into the kitchen dressed in shorts and an old T-shirt, she was finished.

Claire handed him the large white plate, half smiling. Alice hadn't said anything about presenting it well so she'd served the spaghetti on toasted sourdough and garnished it with cherry tomatoes, chives and grated Parmigiano.

It didn't look too bad really, considering.

Peter didn't notice the smile, or if he did, he didn't acknowledge it.

'Thanks,' he murmured, barely glancing at the plate. 'Looks good.'

And then, as he did every evening, he walked over and sat down in front of the huge plasma screen and flicked on the seven o'clock news.

Lillian

This is the fourth time I've started this diary entry. The other three attempts are lying in screwed-up balls on the kitchen table and before I started this one I made myself a rule. I'm going to write what first comes to my mind without editing it. So my apologies if I split my infinitives or say something inappropriate.

Can it be, Alice, that your simple plan isn't so simple after all? Have you managed to weave a tangled web of organisation in which you had Claire stalking me in order to pounce and take me shopping?

I actually don't think so, but in any event don't really care. As well as a fabulous beaded necklace (in three colours actually), I am now the owner of four new items of clothing. After years of hating everything in my closet I've found myself going into the bedroom just to look at them. When I put them on I know how superheros feel in costume . . . The only problem with owning clothes that will 'take me everywhere', however, is that I don't currently have 'everywheres'. Actually, I don't even have 'any-wheres' – unless I count doctors' surgeries.

(Sorry about those last words, awfully self-pitying sounding I know. But rules are rules.)

Lillian

Next-door's dog heralded the postman's arrival without fail. Normally Lillian paid no attention, only vaguely registering the demented yapping.

But since she'd posted her third diary entry to Alice, she had found herself listening for the intermittent buzz of the postman's motorbike. On Wednesday his orange jacket and white helmet continued inexorably past, shoulders hunched against the rain. Yesterday he stopped in front of her house, but delivered only a bank statement and a phone bill.

This morning the dog started its desperate barking as she was sweeping the kitchen floor.

Her feeling of anticipation was ridiculous, she knew. It was a serious reflection on how little she had to fill her days. But she propped the broom next to the fridge and walked out to the back verandah.

David had enclosed the verandah in the seventies. She couldn't remember why exactly. Possibly because that's what everyone else in the street was doing. Or possibly because he was in a lull between research projects. David had been a scientist involved in medical research right up until he had died. Most of the time home handyman jobs had been totally ignored, but every now and then he'd focus on a certain job. For a while, whatever task it was would take on the importance of stem-cell research.

Lillian would have loved to strip out the glass windows and have somewhere cool to sit in the evenings. But somehow it seemed like too much trouble.

With a faint screech of brakes, the postman stopped abruptly in front of the low red brick wall, which had always been totally ineffectual at containing either children or dogs. Lillian watched him reach into his saddlebag and caught a flash of colour before he pushed something into the galvanised-iron slot in the bricks.

She walked down the splintering steps and onto the concrete path where wet weeds elbowed their way through the cracks. David's mother had always been quick to busily rectify the deficiencies in Lillian's homemaking. Weeding had been one of her mother-in-law's specialties. It had not been uncommon for her to pause on her way up the path, drop her beige vinyl handbag and spend ten minutes ripping out offending plants. Lillian's small act of rebellion had been to silently cultivate the green upstarts and she'd grown to like their gutsy stamina and blowsy flowers. Even now, decades after her mother-in-law's death, she could only bring herself to uproot them when they threatened to take over the place.

The curtains across the road twitched and she waved at Mr Adams. As he had every day for the last thirty-five years, he ignored her. Which was just as well, Lillian decided. An answering wave at this point could only herald some cataclysmic change in the world.

Years ago Mr Adams had had something to watch. While not exactly edge-of-the-seat action and intrigue, there'd been a lot going on when the children were growing up. They and their friends had trailed in and out, dropping school bags and dragsters at the front gate. David had loved a chat and there was often a beer or two drunk on the front steps with a mate who happened to be passing.

There'd been a time when they'd had street parties. As far as Lillian could remember, no one had ever actually planned them. They had just sort of happened. Chairs would be pulled out onto the street, bottles of wine opened. Someone would produce a packet of chips, someone else a French-onion dip from the fridge. As it grew dark the women in the street would feed whichever children happened to be still there.

Now, though, the whole street seemed to have pulled back into self-contained bubbles. The last few years had brought another influx of young families, but they all seemed to keep to themselves. The street was deathly quiet even on weekends, everyone imprisoned in their own little space, watching television or manipulating joysticks.

So maybe her trip to the letterbox was the highlight of Mr Adams's day. Lillian smiled slightly, remembering the family competition to see who could make him wave back. The prize of two weeks free of washing-up was still unclaimed.

There was a red envelope in the box and she pulled it out, ignoring the others.

Lillian perched on the fence. *From Alice* was scrawled across the triangle on the back of the envelope.

She clumsily pushed her forefinger through the paper. As she did so, an image of her mother using her silver letter opener to cleanly slice open each letter came to mind. The familiar pang of loss throbbed in her chest. Her mother had been old and weary and happy to die. But Lillian still expected to see her seated at the kitchen table first thing in the morning, halfway through *The Courier Mail* crossword.

She thumbed open the sheet of paper inside.

Dear Lillian

I'm delighted that your shopping trip was successful. My intention was for you to buy something different which made you feel good. It sounds like you've achieved that and more. And by the way, that was just extraordinary good luck that you came across Claire. The organisation required to make that happen is way beyond me.

I've just re-read your diary entry. Yes, rules are rules . . . And I'm about to break all of mine here.

I told you that I wouldn't ask you to do anything major, that they'd all be small changes. But then your having a serious illness has got to be against some kind of rules too, hasn't it?? I came up with, and discarded, about ten ideas for your next task. But they all seemed a bit of a waste of time, to be honest. So here it is . . .

You have money from your mother and you need an adventure. Go overseas. Kyla in Paris, Daniel in New York. Pretty good options . . . You choose. But I think you should go.

Alice

Lillian stared at the paper. Her feeling of anticipation had vanished, replaced by disappointment and a strong sense of irritation.

'Join the queue,' she muttered.

Kyla had been lobbying for years to have her mother visit her in Paris.

'C'mon Mum – live a little,' she'd say.

Lillian had lost track of the number of times she'd tried to make Kyla understand that it just wasn't that simple.

Alice's generation seemed incapable of appreciating how different their life was from Lillian's. For Alice, or for Kyla or Daniel, travelling to the other side of the world by themselves was purely a mechanical exercise. The only issues for them were whether they had sufficient money and time.

But Lillian had lived her whole life in Brisbane. She'd been a good mother, a reasonable wife and had read enough to have an understanding of how much went on outside the boundaries of her small life. But she could count on one hand the number of times she'd been on an aeroplane, and the only time she'd left the country was for a brief trip to New Zealand.

When David was alive, they'd always done things together. Except for the occasional shopping lunch in the city with a female friend, all their social occasions involved each other. Confidences with friends were things shared while making salads for the BBQ, not over a glass of wine in a bar. It was just the way things were.

Sometimes she wondered guiltily how much of her grief at David's death had been genuine sorrow and how much had been terror for herself left alone.

Time had passed. She'd learned to write out a cheque, mow the lawn and take out the rubbish on Tuesday nights. The loneliness hadn't disappeared though.

And despite Kyla's urgings, she hadn't gone out to do things by herself.

Asking friends to go to the movies or dinner with her always seemed like a favour, dragging them away from their family. And then her mother had needed her first hip replacement operation and had moved in with her afterwards. She wasn't well enough to be left alone so Lillian had settled into a gentle and very uneventful life.

There were days when the only person she spoke to was Ross. And she didn't understand half of their conversations. This morning's football update had been that Liverpool's coach was having some fight with the club's American owners. Ross had shaken his head. 'Don't they understand football clubs need money?' he'd asked her. 'You know that, I know that, why the hell don't they?'

If she couldn't manage to socialise in Brisbane, how on earth would she manage on the other side of the world?

The last thing she wanted was to be a pathetic old woman who sat inside all day in a foreign city, waiting for her child to come home and take her out. But the thought of even getting to somewhere like Paris or New York by herself terrified her, let alone finding her way around once she got there. She didn't speak a word of French and what she knew of New York made it sound dangerous and violent.

Really, what would it achieve anyway? She'd spend the small nest egg her mother had left and come home to exactly the same place as when she'd left.

The breeze waved through the branches of the jacaranda tree on the footpath and Lillian watched the purple blossoms rain down onto the concrete. Suddenly she had a vision of herself looking at the same trees in bloom next year, and the year after. With nothing else having changed, except perhaps her health. The days between then and now stretched endlessly, punctuated only by rare visits from the children or occasional drearily predictable social occasions. It all seemed unbearable.

Lillian had read only one of the latest genre of books about middle-aged women finding themselves. She'd picked up the book in *Words*, surprised to find it was about a woman of her generation, a group who seemed only to exist in popular culture as cranky mothers-in-law or eccentric but wise old women.

But halfway through she'd put it down, more bored than offended. Yes, she had a life yet to lead and, yes, she had all kinds of options. But walking away from everything she'd spent her life working for and believing to 'find herself' seemed rather stupid and distinctly self-absorbed. She'd wondered where women who did this would find themselves in five years without the family they'd discarded on the way.

Perhaps, though, it didn't have to be that way. For a moment she pictured herself in a Parisian cafe. For there'd be no competition between Paris and New York. America appealed not at all, but France . . . well, that was different.

Intensely intelligent students on the Left Bank, an open barge drifting down the Seine, smoke-filled cafes patronised by brooding dark-haired men called Pierre . . . It had always seemed like a magical place to Lillian, even before Kyla brought back stories of dimly lit restaurants off cobbled streets and brilliant green parks filled with metal chairs for sun worshippers.

The thought of doing something totally and utterly different was intoxicating. Lillian gave it free rein, pretending for a moment that it was possible. Then, though, she pictured an eternity crammed on an aeroplane next to a complete stranger, the huge cost, days spent alone in a big city, strange trains and buses . . .

Lillian slowly crumpled the paper in her hand, then walked back down the path, feeling years older than when she'd left the house.

Megan

I had no idea that Greg was married when we first started seeing each other. In fact, I wasn't even sure he was male.

Sounds kind of weird, I know, but we met in a virtual world. A whole alternative world where you can do anything or be anything you want.

You just logon, pick yourself a name, conjure up how you want to look and off you go.

I, of course, was a willowy dark-haired temptress. Think Wonder Woman in edgy clothes.

The very first person I chatted with turned out to be Greg. Except he didn't call himself that. His character was a huge musclebound guy called Knowledge Seeker.

So we started talking.

It was 5 am in Los Angeles which was where most of the players come from. So it probably wasn't that much of a coincidence that he turned out to be Australian as well.

We both seemed to have the same routine and kept finding ourselves online together around about midnight. So we became friends. We started visiting the online nightclubs together and listening to bands, each sitting comfortably in our own living rooms.

It was six months before we discovered we both lived in Brisbane (he never asked and I figured to do so must be uncool).

It was another two before we talked about meeting up in real life and another three before we actually did.

The funny thing was . . .

Megan deleted the words she'd just typed. Why on earth would she put that out there for the group to see?
She was supposed to report on the effect of Alice's last task. Okay Alice, she thought. Here you go.

My task was to do something for myself, something which wasn't for anyone else. So instead of breaking up with Greg, which was what I'd figured pretty well everyone and his dog was telling me to do, I met up with him again. One thing led to another as they do and – well, I actually think I'll keep seeing him.

Megan hesitated for a moment then pressed Enter so that the words were added to Alice's website. She made a mental note to do that work on the website. It was so bad at the moment, she was embarrassed to be associated with it.

Walking into her bedroom, Megan grabbed her running clothes from their customary place on the floor. Despite her defiant words in the diary entry, she'd had an uneasy feeling since she'd met up with Greg. Perhaps a long run would shift it.

She'd told Greg about the Red Folder Project and he'd laughed with her at the predicament her family had put her in, all because they believed her moral compass was faulty.

He had shifted position, leaning more comfortably against the headboard of her bed. Megan had tried not to stare at his bare chest. Presumably, Greg's wife didn't get a thrill in her stomach just looking at him. It wasn't that he had a perfect body – far from it. He was nearing forty-five with a lifetime of good living behind him. But she'd never got accustomed to having a man in her bed and there was something compelling about him.

'That's exactly why you're so hot,' he had said, running a finger along her shoulder and over one breast. 'I love a woman with suspect morals.'

Megan had smiled her most vampish smile. 'Tell me more,' she'd whispered, pulling his mouth toward hers.

Now, Megan pulled on her sneakers. Although she never would have admitted it to anyone, Greg's barb about her morals was bugging her.

On their first real-world date Greg had seemed anxious, constantly glancing at his mobile as if he expected an important call. She'd ignored it, trying to convince herself it was just nerves, and by his third gin and tonic he'd begun to relax.

Megan had been in the middle of telling Greg why she hated teaching when he'd interrupted her mid-sentence. 'I'm married,' he had blurted out.

There had been a long echoing silence and then, with the bravado of too much alcohol, Megan had thrown back the last of her drink.

'I'm not,' she had replied, heading off to the bar for another round.

When she returned, she'd merely picked up the conversation from where he'd interrupted. The last thing she wanted to hear was how his wife didn't understand him. They'd moved bars again, done tequila shots and finally ended up back at Megan's place. By the time Megan had woken late the next morning, convinced this was the hangover that was going to kill her, Greg had gone. Not only had he not left a note, there was no evidence at all that he had ever been there.

Feeling let down and miserable, Megan had stepped into the bathroom, turned the shower on hard and let the hot water pour over her head. Willing herself not to throw up, she'd stayed there until the hot water had run out. To hell with the drought.

Stepping out, she'd glanced in the mirror. Words had appeared there as if by magic.

Last night was amazing. G

She later found out Greg had written the words using an old candle he'd found in the lounge. The white wax had remained invisible until the mirror had fogged up with steam.

Over the following days, in between disconcerting flashes of the two of them naked in her enormous bath, she'd given the whole thing a lot of thought.

It wasn't her problem, she'd reasoned, if Greg and his wife didn't much like each other any more. If anyone should be feeling guilty about what was going on, it was Greg, not her.

If Greg wasn't doing the nasty with her, he'd be with someone else. It wasn't like she owed Greg's wife anything. She'd never held much with female solidarity anyway. Every woman for herself and all that.

By the time Greg called again, she'd made up her mind and had never once asked him why he'd come looking for her or what went on in his other life. He had once mentioned in passing that his wife, Deborah, was a freelance journalist, and even that small piece of information had been more than Megan wanted to know.

With Greg's words about her morals echoing in her ears, she closed the front door behind her and slipped the key into the letterbox. She took off slowly, easing into her pace.

It was a long way to the river from Megan's house, but it was the route she took most days. An old folks' home sat at the point where Megan joined the path along the river bank. The nurses would wheel some of the patients out onto the grass in the late afternoons and Megan had got into the habit of waving as she went past. Usually no one responded, but there was one old man who would occasionally wave back. Once he even called something out to Megan, but his words had been lost on the wind. For weeks afterwards Megan had wondered what he had said.

Megan increased her pace. She sucked in air to drive her legs faster, and the pressure in her chest pushed all thoughts from her mind.

Alice

The handwriting was small and precise – it reminded Alice of the little sentences of encouragement her children's teachers sometimes wrote in the margins of the children's homework books.

Dear Alice

I understand why you sent me that last instruction. But you also have to understand why it's not possible.

We come from different points of view, you and I. I grew up reading the Brontës and admiring the Impressionists. But I never had any expectation that I'd see the English moors or look at anything other than calendar prints of Monet's garden. I was to have a husband and a family – which I did.

You, like my children, learn of something in one moment and wonder in the next when you can see it for yourself. To be honest, I'm not sure which way is better. You have more opportunities, yes. But do more opportunities always deliver more happiness? I'm not so sure.

For you, doing something alone means that you are independent and unbound by another's desires. For me doing something alone means that everyone is looking at me and wondering why I have no husband or friend. So what to you is an adventure on the other side of the world is to me an expedition fraught with intimidating experiences and challenges.

Am I doing a good job of explaining this? I don't know. I'm figuring it out as I write. But my solution, if there is such a thing, lies closer to home. I'm sure about that.
    Yours sincerely
    Lillian

Alice looked down at the crumbs on her plate in disgust.

'That was awful. Why on earth did I eat it?'

'It looked good,' Lillian supplied, trying to be helpful.

'Yes – they always do. I seem to have this ridiculous compulsion to buy muffins. They always sound fabulous – raspberry and coconut, apple and cinnamon – but inevitably they are incredibly ordinary – no matter what they claim to have in them.'

She paused for a moment.

'Think about it, have you ever eaten a good muffin?'

Lillian's brow creased. 'Not that I can remember. They always seemed to be about twice the size any one person could possibly eat and leave an aftertaste like mothballs.'

Alice drained her last mouthful of coffee and set the glass down firmly on the table. The cafe was almost half full even though it was a weekday morning.

'All right, that is officially my last muffin ever. This is definitely the new me. Unless I see a double chocolate one – I'd have to make an exception for that.'

Her casual words were a cover. When she'd received Lillian's last letter she'd been incredibly disappointed. Without stopping to think, she'd posted a reply asking Lillian to call her so they could arrange to meet for a coffee. Lillian had sounded reluctant, but too polite to refuse.

Alice was dressed in a pair of wide-legged linen trousers and a pink cotton shirt she'd had for years and always made her feel good. Without a hairdresser's straightening iron, her hair decided where it kinked and where it sat flat. So today she'd abandoned the fight, pushing it back into a wide hair band.

The hairdresser, who had also done her make-up the other night, had waved a couple of brushes over her face, somehow putting the features back into the right proportions. Alice knew better than to attempt it herself, though, and this morning had merely applied a touch of mascara. She felt a little like Batman after the Joker had stripped off his mask. But this was real life and there was no point in pretending to be something she wasn't.

If Lillian had noticed the marked slide in Alice's personal grooming she didn't show it.

'Do you actually enjoy writing?' Lillian asked.

'I loved writing *Her Life, My Life*,' Alice answered slowly. 'My second book was written for all the wrong reasons and for everyone else. It was a struggle to write every word and it showed.'

She propped her elbows on the table and rested her chin on her fists. 'But my first book was different. The best thing was actually not the writing but the noticing. When I'm writing, or even just thinking about writing, the whole world looks more vivid. I look at people differently and see things I wouldn't normally notice. Nothing terribly revolutionary, just little glimpses or edges of things that make me think. Sometimes it's depressing, but sometimes I see some marvellous things that I might not normally notice.'

'Like what?' Lillian asked.

'Like that man,' Alice nodded at an elderly man off to one side of the cafe. 'He was here before us and was just finishing his coffee when we came in. He's been looking around and whenever anyone looks at him he just smiles a bit.'

Lillian smiled politely, obviously thinking both Alice and the man were distinctly strange.

'He's not creepy,' Alice said quickly. 'You can tell. He moved that table when a woman with a stroller was trying to get out. He's just happy to be around people and being a part of everything that's going on here.'

'He sounds a little sad,' Lillian replied.

'Maybe,' Alice conceded, 'but he doesn't look sad. Those people look sad.' She gestured discreetly at a couple waiting for their coffees at a table nearby. They both stared into middle distance, matching vacant looks on their faces.

'They're not even bored, at least that would be an emotion.

They've got nothing to say to each other, but they don't even notice because they're so used to it.'

Lillian turned back from the couple, about to say they looked pretty normal to her, but something in Alice's face stopped her. She twisted the teaspoon in her cup, absently stirring the caramel-coloured froth into the milk, and then looked up.

'It doesn't make me any better at making my own life work, but I've got twenty-twenty vision for everyone else's.' Alice paused. 'I'm sorry if I offended you, suggesting you go overseas.'

Lillian shook her head. 'I'm not offended. A little uncomfortable to have had to explain why I don't want to do it. But not offended.'

Alice nodded. 'I'm having serious second thoughts about starting this whole thing and your letter made me panic – I'll understand if you'd like to stop now.' After a slight pause, she continued. 'I'll instruct my staff to see you get a full refund,' she smiled. 'No questions asked.'

Lillian didn't return the smile. 'I think that is probably the best plan,' she nodded. 'I'm not sure I'm really a group person.'

Alice felt as if someone had poured cold water over her; she hadn't really expected Lillian to take her up on the offer. She'd only made it because she'd felt she should. Lillian was supposed to brush it aside as if it wasn't an option.

But she hadn't and Alice could tell this was the beginning of the end. She could feel her little group unravelling.

Megan was clearly not taking the group seriously. Her last entry about not breaking up with her married lover had seemed almost like a taunt. Alice had no idea why Megan had joined the group. She had thought about suggesting that Megan drop out, but decided against it. She had to take what this group brought up, regardless of whether or not she liked it.

Now Lillian didn't want to be involved. Alice's book was never going to be written. Never even get off the ground.

She cleared her throat. 'Okay then.'

Lillian looked uncomfortable.

'Well . . . thanks for the coffee.'

'No problem. It was probably not a great idea anyway.'

Lillian put her hand gently over Alice's where it rested on the table. 'Just because I'm not the right person for it doesn't mean your idea won't work. I think in a lot of ways you are right and that it is the little things that hold it all together. But I sometimes think all I have ever done my whole life is little things. Tea and scones, flowers always on the hall table . . .'

She opened her mouth to continue but Alice interrupted, words tumbling over themselves without thought. 'But don't you see – that's why we need you in the group. It's not about flowers or tea – that was just an example. It's about making changes that make you happy. It's about people who should be happy, being miserable. People whose husbands are strangers. People who used to be interesting but now are the ones who listen to everyone else's stories . . .

'People like me,' she finished weakly.

She paused and sat back in her chair, tipping her head back for a moment.

Lillian said nothing and Alice spoke again.

'I didn't suggest that you go overseas so that you could visit the Louvre or see the Statue of Liberty. I just thought maybe now was your time to spread your wings and see what you're capable of. And that's much harder to do when you're at home doing the same things you have for the last forty years.

'You might find Parisians rude or New York filthy and wish you were home. But maybe being somewhere different, with nothing to do but wander the streets and see fabulous things, might just help you find your adventure.'

Alice stopped herself and laughed self-consciously. She could tell by the look on Lillian's face the older woman hadn't changed her mind.

She held out her hand. 'It has been a pleasure meeting you and I wish you well.'

Lillian grasped it. 'The same to you, Alice,' she said quietly.

Kerry

Why don't you see if you can make a new tradition? Something small, but something that both you and Annie enjoy.

Last night's beers were taking turns with the vodkas, which had seemed like such a good idea at the time, to pound the back of Kerry's eyeballs. He took the opportunity of a red traffic light to allow his eyelids to droop closed, only opening them reluctantly at the sound of the horn behind.

Under other conditions he could imagine himself having been inspired by Alice's email. One of the things he'd confessed to Alice on his questionnaire was his sense of loss for the rituals he had enjoyed when they were a family.

Sunday morning walks with Annie to the bakery to buy sticky pastries for breakfast weren't the same when there was no one to bring them home to. And sneaking out together for an early morning walk was rendered pointless when there was no one left at home for a sleep-in.

But today, all he could think about was survival. He had planned to take Annie to a kids' session at the art gallery. Right now, though, that seemed the idea of a madman. Just the prospect of negotiating the carpark crammed with overzealous parents filled him with horror. Hours watching Annie make rubbings or other artistically worthy objects made torture seem a viable alternative.

Normally he enjoyed receiving Alice's emails. She was so different from Sandra. Older obviously and not as good-looking as Sandra. But there was something about her that made him want to make her laugh and to like him. And so he'd found himself flirting a little in emails. She hadn't objected and so he'd continued.

But right now writing a witty response to Alice seemed on a similar level of difficulty to developing a cure for cancer.

The only reason he'd seen the email was that he'd logged onto the internet to see whether the Wallabies had won their match in Scotland overnight. He'd had a sneaking feeling of déjà vu when he saw the scoreline, more likely caused by alcohol amnesia than some sixth sense. The possibility that he'd been out late enough to see the final score and drunk too much to remember something so critical made him feel immediately sicker.

He and Brian had just been going out for a quiet beer. But they'd run into an old mate of Kerry's who had been at lunch all afternoon. A drink together had turned into about a hundred and the last thing Kerry remembered was a nasty nightclub somewhere in the Valley. Vague recollections kept flashing through his mind like a hazily recollected movie.

'What you cannot remember did not happen.' Kerry repeated Brian's mantra under his breath, determined not to push his day even deeper into a ditch with an avalanche of embarrassing memories from the night before.

There, at least, was an advantage of not having Sandra around.

She'd drunk with the best of them in their early days together. But motherhood had drained her party-girl fire. She'd start well with a few quick drinks, but by eleven o'clock was generally sober as a judge and ready for bed. It wasn't what she said the next morning, as much as what she didn't say. When he surfaced at what he felt was a hellishly early hour she'd give him a long, amused look, followed by a 'So how do you feel this morning?'

In a throwback to teenage hangovers in his parents' house, he'd be forced to pretend to feel like a million dollars, on one memorable occasion even pushing Annie's stroller up and down Paddington's merciless hills in searing summer heat.

At least his appearance in front of Sandra today was a mere cameo. Nothing that a baseball hat and a pair of sunglasses shouldn't get him through.

He pulled up outside the shopfront, the old feeling of resentment coursing through him. This was what it had all been about.

For a while he'd found himself wishing there'd been another man. At least he'd have had something tangible to hate. Perhaps a couple of toe-to-toe confrontations, curses spat and punches thrown might have cauterised this feeling inside him. Having lost his wife and family to a beautician's parlour seemed like some kind of bad joke.

He'd thought Sandra was joking at first. Annie was a baby. His business selling plants at farmers' markets was growing, but slowly. The last thing that they needed was the risk of a second small business. That had seemed blatantly obvious to him.

But he'd been dismissive, apparently, patronising and failing to respect her needs and skills.

'You've got to grow up sometime, Kerry,' Sandra had said once. 'It's not enough to sit around complaining that things aren't how you want them. If you don't like the plant job then find a new one. If you'd rather live somewhere else, we can figure that out too. But drinking too much and covering everything up with jokes is not going to change anything.'

She'd paused and then looked straight at him. 'I'm not going to just sit around watching you be miserable.'

There'd been long talks, and then silence. They didn't even fight, reduced to sarcastic comments and blistering looks.

Sandra hated his drinking and Kerry had made a few half-hearted attempts at giving up over the years, but it had never stuck.

Kerry's vintage Aston Martin was another bone of contention. Kerry had spent many hours and an incalculable sum of money restoring the sports car. It rarely moved from under the house, using too much petrol to drive further than the corner shop. Sandra had never understood the pleasure Kerry found in working on the car and had always wanted him to sell it.

Kerry had thought that Sandra had come to terms with the fact that her business would have to wait. He'd even thought things were improving between them. Then one Tuesday night, right after walking in from a day potting more bromeliads than he'd hoped ever to see in a lifetime, she'd handed him a set of keys.

Maybe they could have worked it out if it hadn't been for the key tag. It was a cheap plastic one – the type you buy from a hardware store for fifty cents. The type that you can't prise open and write on without a sharp knife and a great deal of patience. In handwriting neater than Kerry had ever seen her produce, Sandra had written the words *Sandra's Salon*.

He'd stared at the tag. Those carefully curled letters excluded him more than any tirade of bitterness could have. They meant she had gone ahead and done it without him, without even talking to him. For the whole time they'd been together decisions had been made jointly. They were a partnership. But Sandra had chosen her own way. The partnership was finished.

Kerry had held the keys out, plastic tag curled tightly in his hand. Perhaps if he crushed it this would all go away, he had thought for a wild moment. But when Sandra held out her hand he'd dropped the keys softly into her palm.

And then he'd turned around and walked out.

Try as he might, Kerry couldn't help feeling he was a living cliché of a divorced dad. The only things missing were an American accent and a four-wheel drive. Every time Kerry picked Annie up, he vowed he'd relax and act normal. And every time he didn't. Somehow their days together always felt as though they had to be planned, in a way that had never been the case when he and Sandra were together. There was always a defined start and a finish which somehow left the in-between time as something which had to be filled rather than just lived. Usually by the end of the weekend they'd find the old grooves and slip into them gratefully. But then it would be another few days or a week until the next visit and, like landing on the biggest snake on the Snakes and Ladders board Annie had got for Christmas, they'd slide right back to the beginning again.

He'd find himself standing in places like an art gallery, places that should be listed in some kind of Rough Guide to Divorced Fathering, trying to identify the single dads. Packed lunches were a giveaway. The guys who were sitting out on the gallery steps while the children munched Vegemite sandwiches were definitely just giving the wife some down time. But put Kerry in the gallery's cafe and he was in more like-minded company. If a guy said no to the huge slab of cake poised temptingly under the glass counter, he was definitely not a single dad; but when the cake was whisked out by the cafe staff accompanied by an 'Of course, darling, whatever you want, this is a special day!', Kerry knew he wasn't alone.

His personal giveaway was hot chips. Sandra had always been health conscious and while they were married Kerry and Sandra had presented a united front to Annie. Porridge or Weet-Bix were the choices for breakfast while Kerry thought longingly about the Coco Pops he'd craved every day of his childhood and eaten every day of his adulthood despite widespread derision. They'd both agreed when Annie became old enough to figure out that Daddy was eating something different that it was probably time for him to grow up anyway.

Hot chips had obviously been on the unacceptable list. Even Kerry knew how bad they were for you. One day after he and Sandra had been divorced about three months, Kerry took Annie to the beachside at Manly. They walked past a cafe on the corner and the mouth-watering smell of chips freshly drowned in litres of old animal fat wafted out of the doors. About to walk past, Kerry stopped.

'Do you know what I really feel like, sweetheart?' he asked Annie. She shook her head, presumably not even recognising the smell.

'A big plate of hot chips with loads of tomato sauce!'

Annie's look just about broke his heart. A two year old looking at him like it was Christmas. He cursed the years of the sensible diet he and Sandra had laid on her. Who cared if a few transfats ran around her bloodstream? One of the immutable characteristics of children was that they loved bad food. And if that was a way to make his little girl happy, when he only saw her for fourteen waking hours per week, well so be it.

So Coco Pops were back on the menu at Kerry's house.

Kerry pulled the cap down a little lower and pushed the sunglasses up a little higher. With a deep breath he opened the car door and pulled himself upright using the door frame. Conscious of the fact that Sandra could be watching from inside, he didn't collapse over the car as every muscle urged him to. Instead he closed the door softly and walked toward the door, willing himself not to vomit in the gutter.

Sandra and Annie lived in a small house attached to Sandra's Salon. It was perfect as she'd tried to explain to Kerry on various occasions. A one-off opportunity she couldn't let slip away by indecision.

The entrance was off to one side of the salon and Kerry knocked on the door, closing his eyes briefly behind the glasses.

'Mummy, Daddy's here!' Kerry could hear Annie screech from outside, and smiled to himself.

Seconds later Sandra's steps echoed on the polished floorboards and she opened the door. 'Hello Kerry,' she smiled.

Please couldn't this get a little easier soon? Kerry sent up a prayer to any entity who would deign to intervene in his screwed-up existence.

His wife – correction, ex-wife – stood in front of him as gorgeous as the day he'd met her. At least if they couldn't get back together again, she could get really fat, couldn't she? He sent that wish up after the first one.

'Hi Sandra. You're looking good.'

He wasn't sure if the contraction of facial muscles he managed constituted a smile, but it was the best he could do under the circumstances.

They were saved the ongoing humiliation of small talk by a slight figure in a pink leotard and tutu. Annie ran past Sandra and into Kerry's arms. 'Daddy!' she yelled in glee.

'Hello sweetheart.' He hugged her tight for a moment and then held her at arm's length. 'Now how did you know that you needed to wear a tutu today?'

Kerry could feel Sandra glower at them. That was the other part of divorced dad syndrome. Nothing he could do was right with Sandra. If he didn't do interesting things with Annie he wasn't giving her priority in his life. But if he did, he was spoiling her and trying to make Sandra look bad given all the humdrum things she had to do with Annie.

'Is it a fairy party, Daddy?'

'Nooo, not as such,' Kerry answered, shuddering at the mere thought. 'We're . . .' Rule one of parenting was not to tell a child what you were planning until the last available moment. Just in case you needed to change your plans. Rule two of parenting was to pay particular attention to Rule one if you happened to be desperately hungover. '. . . going to the kids' section at the art gallery.'

He listened to his words and felt any possibility of lying on the sofa while Annie played with her Barbies shrivel and die.

Ah well, in for a penny, in for a pound.

'And I read in the paper last week that there's an exhibition by Degas in the gallery at the moment. Which you obviously knew,' he tousled her hair. 'Because Degas's claim to fame is painting ballerinas. So grab your bag and we'll get going.'

Annie laughed in delight and bounced down the hall.

'Have you started going to exhibitions?' Sandra asked with what sounded even to Kerry's suspicious ears to be genuine interest.

'Not really,' Kerry confessed. 'I just noticed the piece in the weekend paper and then someone mentioned it at the stall yesterday. I thought Annie would like it, given her ballet obsession.'

He didn't think it was necessary to admit that until yesterday he'd always thought Degas was pronounced as it was spelt.

'Are you feeling all right?' Sandra asked.

'Me?' Kerry feigned surprise. 'I'm great thanks, never better. Had a really early night and went for a run this morning.'

He managed to stop himself before his burbling became even more ridiculous.

'How about you? Are things okay?'

As he asked the question, he looked at Sandra properly for the first time.

'Yeah, things are fine,' she answered without much enthusiasm. 'Business is good and Annie's been really easy this week . . .' She trailed off.

Kerry looked at her again and had a shock of memory. This wasn't just a woman who tried to make his life difficult. She was the person he'd spent most of his adult life with, the one who'd held him all night when the dog he'd had since he was fifteen died, who'd looked at him with wonder over the tightly bound bundle of their newborn daughter.

'Kerry . . .' she started to say something, but stopped as Annie barged past her legs dragging a princess trolley bag behind her.

Annie grabbed Kerry's hand and pulled him toward the car. 'Let's go, Daddy. I want to see the ballet pictures.'

Kerry twisted back to face Sandra, pulling back hard enough on Annie's arm to keep himself in one spot. But Sandra waved him away.

'Have a good day, I'll see you tonight. Maybe they'll have a fried breakfast at the gallery cafe for that hangover of yours,' she added, closing the door before Kerry could answer.

Rebecca

To be frank, the fact that I am still part of this group is a grave indication of what a disaster area my life is. Two years ago I would have done the first task, made Claire happy and then found any excuse to stop. But now I find myself actually wanting to write this diary.

Claire invited us all to dinner, which was horrendous (sorry Claire). Bianca demanded to know how she could find her father, swore at me, then burst into tears and rushed from the room. I told her again all there is to know. I got pregnant at the end of school to my boyfriend Sven (yes, really), a Swedish exchange student. By the time I realised I was pregnant, he was back in Sweden. There was never anything serious between us and I didn't tell him I was having a baby. I haven't heard from him for the last seventeen years.

I've always thought that I would be enough for Bianca, but now I'm not so sure. Is it the not knowing her father that changed Bianca? Or is it just something else she is using to be angry at me?

I don't know.

Bianca and I were always a team. For a long time it was just us. I smugly watched friends' unhappy relationships with their teenage children, thinking how good things were for us. Bianca was a star student loved by her teachers, with heaps of lovely *friends. Then she discovered ninemsn, text messaging and the colour black. Now it feels like my friend has gone somewhere else and left in her place a surly teenager who heartily dislikes me.*

'Bee?'

There was no reply and Rebecca looked at her daughter in the rear-vision mirror.

Bianca's headphones were clamped down tightly over her ears.

At the next lights Rebecca turned in her seat and gestured for Bianca to take the headphones off. Bianca complied, rolling her eyes. Rebecca ignored the attitude. A plan had been forming in her mind since she'd woken that morning.

She'd been annoyed by Alice's last email which had told her that her next assignment was to spend some time with Bianca. All Alice's children were no doubt perfect, she'd thought – probably still wearing pastel-coloured OshKosh and leather sandals. Alice knew nothing about Bianca or how to deal with her.

But even while Rebecca had been angry, she'd known Alice was right. It wasn't exactly rocket science, but having been rebuffed so many times, Rebecca had given up trying to get close to her daughter. A tense stand-off was about as good as it got at the moment.

'Do you have anything big on at school this morning?'

'Whadda you mean big?'

'Well, anything you really can't miss. Like an exam?'

Bianca, looking suspicious, shook her head.

'Any chance you could cut school with me?'

Bianca, looking even more suspicious, said nothing.

'It was just that . . . I noticed an ad for a new vegetarian cafe in West End. I thought we could go there for breakfast.'

'You hate vegetarian food.'

'No I don't.'

'You do. I heard you tell Jeremy it always tastes like wheat-germ.'

It wasn't a question but a quiet fact.

'Well . . . Yes, you're right, I did say that.'

Bianca went to put her headphones back on.

'I could have a coffee,' Rebecca added quickly. 'They'd serve coffee with caffeine in it, right?'

Bianca shrugged. 'Yeah.'

'So are you up for it?'

Again Bianca shrugged, clamping the headphones back onto her head. Taking that as an assent, Rebecca indicated right at the next lights. She wasn't sure what she was going to tell them at work – she'd used car trouble last time the nanny was sick.

Half an hour later, Rebecca was wishing she had broken down on the side of the road.

Although she and Bianca were alone, she felt distinctly like a third wheel as Bianca hadn't stopped text messaging the whole time they were there.

So accomplished was she that she could do it with the mobile under the table with only an occasional glance.

Rebecca's attempts at conversation had been met with monosyllabic answers and finally they had lapsed into silence, punctuated only by the sound of the keys on Bianca's phone.

Bianca had declared herself not hungry and ordered a carrot juice.

The coffee was bad, just as Rebecca had known it would be. She felt like Pollyanna, throwing conversation topics at her daughter with a lilt in her voice and a false smile plastered on her face.

Finally she'd given up the pretence that everything was okay.

'Why are you so angry with me?'

She was sure it was the wrong approach. But Rebecca didn't care. It was the only thing she really wanted to know.

Bianca's fingers didn't even pause on the buttons. 'What? Other than the fact that your whole generation has totally screwed up everything?'

Rebecca didn't quite know how to respond to that. 'What do you mean?'

Bianca looked at Rebecca with utter disdain for her lack of understanding. She was suddenly reminded of when, seventeen years ago, her mother had raised the idea of an abortion. Rebecca remembered looking at her mother in an identical way. Strangely the memory gave her some comfort.

'Do you really think it's a coincidence that it hardly ever rains?'

Rebecca looked at her, trying to figure out where this was going. 'It's a drought, it happens every twenty years. Always has. Always will.'

'Not this time.' Bianca sounded as though she was talking to Sam. 'The world is dying and your generation has killed it. When you were my age the future looked fantastic – my future is nothing like that.'

'Well it's not like it was just me,' Rebecca began, knowing what a terrible argument that was.

'No – just everyone like you. You leave your kids with someone else while you work to buy a fancy house and wanky wine. If I don't want to be part of the hours you allocate to "quality time" with me, then I'm being difficult.'

Bianca was clearly bored with the subject and smiled down at her mobile.

God, she was probably telling her friends about the conversation she was having with her mother before they'd even finished it!

Enraged, Rebecca reached across the table and pulled the phone out of her daughter's hands.

'Now hang on a minute, young lady.'

Bianca rolled her eyes again and for just a moment Rebecca longed to slap her.

'You are hardly blameless. Where do you think your computer came from, and your mobile? You can't sit in judgement on my lifestyle when you're part of it.'

Bianca looked at her calmly with all the confidence of youth. 'It doesn't matter what I do, your generation has destroyed everything. And I'm an accessory just like everything else.' She looked at her watch and added, 'I really need to get back to school. Are you going to drive me or do you want me to get a bus?'

Lillian

Lillian stepped inside her door.

All she could smell was dirty flower water. The roses in the vase were well past their best, but she hadn't been able to find the energy to throw them out.

She still couldn't.

Out of habit, she flicked on the kettle as she walked into the kitchen and then realised she didn't want a cup of tea. She didn't want anything.

Today there had been more tests. Now she knew she didn't have a tumour, Lyme's disease or about three syndromes whose names had slipped off the neurologist's tongue but hadn't lodged in her memory. That was another symptom, apparently – short-term memory loss.

It was a strange thing, excluding illnesses. She was pretty sure that she should be happy that there was no sign of a tumour. But Lyme's disease or the others on today's list? It was hard to know how to react when she didn't know anything about each of these conditions. They were just a line of black ink on the specialist's file, but a possible life sentence for her. One of the lesser diseases was surely a better result than multiple sclerosis, which seemed to be the last man standing.

Without knowing whether to cheer or be disappointed as the results of each test came in, Lillian had arrived at a strange kind of ambivalence. No complicated migraine? Okay then, move on to Parkinson's, then to diabetes . . .

Restlessly she headed into the bedroom. She'd felt unsettled ever since she'd had coffee with Alice the week before. Even though she knew she'd done nothing wrong, she felt as though she'd let Alice down in some way, and that annoyed her. It wasn't her fault Alice was miserable, or that she'd got it wrong when she suggested the answer for Lillian was to go overseas.

She didn't want to. Why was that so hard for everyone to understand? And if she were totally honest, she was more than a bit scared. It was all right for these younger women who had been practically brought up travelling to tell her to 'just do it'.

Changing out of her fancy 'Claire trousers', she threw them onto the bed and put on a sagging pair of jeans and a cotton blouse. Perhaps an hour in the garden would help clear her head.

It was strange, she thought as she looked around. Her whole married life she'd yearned to have a feminine bedroom, but David had always objected. She'd imagined huge pink roses on the bedspread, maybe some light green as a contrast. Maybe even a white mosquito net above the bed.

And yet, in the three years since David had died, Lillian had changed not one thing. The quilted bedspread was beige and the walls featured prints she'd stopped looking at a decade ago.

A faint enthusiasm stirred and she remembered a scrapbook she'd started years ago. Back when the children were young and money had been tight. She'd torn out pictures of decorating ideas she'd liked, even collected fabric samples. No doubt it was all hopelessly out of date, but it would be interesting to look at. Like everything else that had no other home, it would be in the storeroom under the house.

Lillian walked down the stairs, her hand running along the polished banister. Beneath the house was a cement-floored room which had been the children's playroom. These days Lillian almost never came down here.

Pausing only briefly in the room, she walked through the other door and outside. Underneath the front of the house David had built a fibro-sheeted storeroom which had become a sort of organic collection of memories. Photos shared boxes with junk and objects she couldn't even identify – all without any obvious logic or order.

Lillian wrestled with the bolt and finally jiggled it out of the position it had sat in for at least a year. She pulled the door toward her and looked in at decades' worth of boxes stacked on precarious shelving.

The floor of the small space was crowded with random items. Lillian picked up a skateboard and an old fan heater and piled them to one side. She smiled faintly. David had despaired of her inability to keep everything in the type of order he saw as perfectly normal. She'd never been able to make him understand that when you had two small children demanding your attention, there just wasn't time to place things in a careful pile. The children had grown, of course, but the habit had stuck and Lillian's standard practice had been to open the storeroom door, throw something in and slam the door shut before it could fall out at her feet.

An old beer carton was crammed onto one of the middle shelves. Lillian pulled it out slightly and saw it was full of yellowing *Women's Weekly* cookbooks. She shoved it back in. A box full of curtains from Daniel's teenage bedroom, one stacked with Mills and Boons she'd once read voraciously. There was no way she was going to find what she was looking for.

There was a pile of boxes off to her right. Lillian flicked back the cardboard flaps of the nearest one and saw that it was full of Kyla's stuff. God knows why she'd kept it, or anything else in this storeroom. Old high school reports. An end of senior year T-shirt signed by a hundred forgotten school mates. A tattered purple plastic ring folder with biology assignments.

Across the front of the folder, the corners curled up and blackened, was a rectangular sticker. Lillian remembered Kyla receiving it when she'd gone in her first ever street march. It had been to commemorate International Women's Day and declared boldly in green and purple letters: *Girls Can Do Anything.*

She stared at the words. That was it.

Kyla and Alice had been brought up on that slogan. It hadn't always worked out for them, but at least they hadn't been afraid to try.

'Girls can do anything.' That's what she'd told Kyla when she was growing up. Thinking back, Lillian was sure she'd believed it, but only in relation to others, not herself.

Kyla still believed it. Probably Alice did too.

What was the point in sitting here, money in the bank, waiting for some disease or, in the best-case scenario, old age to claim her? What exactly did she have to lose? She couldn't think of a single thing.

Lillian replaced the folder, closed the ancient cardboard box and headed upstairs to find a phone.

She had a travel agent to call.

The Red Folder Group

It was both the same as last time and very different. They were in the same bar, full glasses of champagne in front of them. Four people looked at Alice expectantly, waiting for her to tell them what they were supposed to do.

It would have helped had Alice known herself. A monthly get-together had seemed like a good idea when she came up with the idea of the group. They could talk over what had happened, share experiences, begin to know each other more. Except that now it came down to it she didn't have a clue what that meant.

'Look, I don't want to make this formal,' she began. 'I'm really pleased that we've come this far and that you're here tonight. Lillian has decided this wasn't something she wanted to do. So it's just the four of you. What I'd like to do is get your thoughts on what's happened so far. It's still early days obviously – changes don't happen in a couple of weeks – but maybe someone has something they wanted to say?'

As soon as the question was out of her mouth she knew it would be greeted with nothing but silence. What did she expect? An Oprah-type outpouring of emotions from all of them?

'Maybe I should start,' Alice broke the silence.

'I've found it difficult to try to identify what is important to each of you. I hope that as we go along I'll be able to do that better. But the more information you can put in your diary entries, the more likely I am to figure that out.'

'Look, I don't mean to be rude, but don't you think it's all a bit wishy-washy?' Megan asked suddenly. She continued without waiting for an answer. 'I mean, nothing you've asked me to do is going to change my life – not even close.'

Rebecca snorted in derision and everyone looked at her.

She was obviously still wearing her work clothes, her pant suit cut in at the waist and a tight-fitting T-shirt underneath. Her expensive-looking string of beads tipped forward as she leaned toward Megan.

'Sorry. It's just that you sound exactly like my daughter.'

Rebecca took a deep breath, trying to calm herself, but the memory of her conversation with Bianca at the vegetarian cafe was too fresh in her mind.

'Please explain to me what it is about your generation. Life's not about sitting back and knocking what everyone else does. It's you Alice is talking about with your short diary entries. Everyone else is actually writing real stuff. You do these glib little entries like you're sending a text message. Blind Freddy would know that you haven't done what you say you have.'

Megan sat back in her chair. 'Had a bad day, have we?' she asked patronisingly.

Rebecca's eyes darkened. 'See, it is never your fault. Life for Generation Y is just such a struggle. You were born with these exploitative parents who raped the world and are forcing you to endure the benefits. So what do you do? You spend hours on your computers and mobile phones, but any suggestion that you should actually step into the real world and participate is the most outrageous thing you've ever heard.'

'Look, Rebecca, it doesn't take a psychiatrist to figure out that your problem is with your daughter, not me. I've got as much right to be in this group as you. Just because I don't write pages about my screwed-up home life doesn't mean I'm not participating.'

'Participating . . . Yeah right. Like sleeping with your married boyfriend for one of your tasks? Give me a break.'

'All right.' Claire's quiet voice cut across the table. 'If either of you don't want to be part of this group, feel free to leave. But if you spend your whole time looking for reasons why it won't work, then of course it won't. None of us knows if this is something worthwhile or a waste of time. Unless you're both perfectly happy, though, I'd suggest you think about giving it a try.'

Claire ran her hand up the outside of her glass, the condensation pooling on her fingers. 'And before either of you say that I'm only here because my life is a mess, I'll say it myself. I'm almost thirty-five, I have no children, no career and not much of a marriage. It seems that even my feeble attempts at house renovation are an expensive waste of time. To be honest, I don't really know where to begin to fix things. But what Alice is suggesting seems as good a start as any.'

The silence stretched for long seconds.

'Whew,' Kerry said. 'Here I was thinking I was just coming for some free grog and a bit of a chat!'

There was a smattering of uncomfortable laughter.

'Look, let's not get too worked up about it. This isn't exactly outrageous stuff, it probably won't change anything, but I for one don't have anything more exciting to do on a Tuesday night. So far Alice has hooked me up with an old friend, which is great. What can be bad about that?'

He smiled across at Alice.

'Okay, sorry. I overreacted.' Rebecca nodded vaguely at Megan, not quite meeting her eyes. She picked up her glass and took a large sip. Megan did not volunteer her own apology.

The mood of the group relaxed slightly but the tension between Rebecca and Megan was palpable. Claire, however, seemed oblivious to it and eventually Alice managed to relax.

The champagne disappeared quickly and the conversation became less forced. A lot of it had nothing to do with the tasks or their diary entries, so Alice just sat back trying to absorb the nature of each of them. It wasn't until Alice was about to order a third bottle of champagne that Rebecca said she had to go, with Megan and Claire following soon after.

Alice was very conscious of the fact that it was just her and Kerry left in the bar. Kerry's email about liking the sound of her being a school ma'am had taken Alice by surprise. Despite herself she still felt a rush of pleasure when she thought of it. It had been a long time since someone had flirted with her. It hadn't taken long for Alice to remember she hadn't been wearing her wedding ring the first night and that Kerry probably assumed she was single. 'Not a biggie,' as Ellen would have said. Alice could have corrected Kerry's mistake with a quick email.

But she hadn't. Somehow jumping on top of a nice email with a statement that she was married seemed ridiculous. She had just decided to just keep the emails on a friendly level and drop in something about Andrew when it was natural to do so.

So why did she feel like a giggly schoolgirl now that Kerry was sitting beside her?

'Do you think I could have picked people with stronger personalities than Rebecca and Megan?' Alice asked.

Kerry laughed and Alice felt a strange thrill of excitement. She sat back in the chair and pushed her hair back with both hands.

'Is this what you were hoping?' Kerry asked.

'To be honest, I don't really know. I go through times when I think that this is a ridiculous waste of everyone's time, made up by a middle-class woman who should just get her act together. But then other times I wonder if we haven't just lost the whole point of living. It's like that old question, do you work to live or live to work. It's like there is no end goal any more – just more stuff to do.'

'You know, my dad has a theory,' Kerry said. 'Actually,' he corrected himself, 'he has lots of theories. But one of them is known in our family as the Porch Theory.'

Alice laughed. 'Tell me more.'

'When he was growing up, everyone had front porches. Not huge wooden decks over the backyard, a little porch looking onto the street. All the men in the street were home by four-thirty and dinner was all over an hour after that. In the evenings, his parents would sit on the porch while the kids played outside. They'd talk and the kids would gradually wind down, slumping on the steps as the sun went down. Sometimes a neighbour would walk past and chat from the bottom of the steps or sit on the porch if they were invited up.'

Kerry paused.

'Dad said that was the best part of the day. There was no one racing off taking kids to tap classes or saxophone practice, no televisions for people to sit in front of. It was just the way it was. He reckons society got screwed up when porches got closed in.'

'It's so different now.' Alice reflected silently on her own afternoons alone with the children.

'Anyway, I think what you're trying to do is great.' Kerry hesitated. 'But I'm a bit confused. I thought all wise women had to be eighty with a big mole on their nose or a goitre or something?'

Alice laughed. 'I gather I'm supposed to take that as a compliment?'

'You most certainly are.'

Kerry held Alice's gaze until she looked away.

'Shall we have another drink?' he asked. 'My shout this time.'

Alice's pulse was racing, her throat dry. 'No, I should go,' she answered automatically, then stood up abruptly.

'Okay,' Kerry said easily. 'I should get moving anyway.'

He joined her beside the table and put his hand under her elbow to steer her around a group of people near the door. His touch was perfectly proper but the point of Alice's elbow burned with the contact.

They stood together outside the bar.

'Right, well my car's over there,' Alice gestured toward the other side of the street.

'I'm the other way,' Kerry answered. 'I guess I'll be hearing from you then.'

'Yes,' Alice smiled at him. 'You will.'

Megan

Your latest instruction was to take the time to do something I like but normally rush over.

So I took Merlin, my dog, for a walk. Not a run and not just a twenty-minute duty walk around the block. A long one, along the river. I enjoyed it.

On the way we went past an old folks' home I've seen a lot of times. So I stopped and went inside to ask if I could help out with reading or something sometime. Turns out I could and I spent the next hour reading to a nice old lady who told me I reminded her of her granddaughter.

'Bugger ... bugger ... bugger.'

Megan knew she sounded like Hugh Grant as she leapt out of her ancient Toyota Seca, not even bothering to lock it.

Abandoning the tidy box of marked homework she had finally caught up with over the weekend, she bolted toward the staffroom even though she knew it was too late.

It was ten days before the annual school fete – the biggest deal of the year and, thanks to a defective alarm clock, she was almost forty minutes late for the final planning session.

When Megan had first started teaching, the annual fete had been just around the corner. The ancient deputy principal had leaned across toward her during a staff meeting. 'The best advice I can give you about this school,' he'd whispered confidentially, 'is never be late to a fete planning session. And if you are going to be late, make sure it isn't to the last one.'

The law of the staffroom was that anyone not present to defend themselves was 'volunteered' for all the hideous jobs no one else wanted. Megan's current school was no different. Last year a teacher had run away with his neighbour's wife, leaving vacant his job to walk the ponies around the school oval all day. Megan had always suspected it was his allotted task and not his wife that had caused his flight.

In the past, Megan had rather enjoyed seeing absent teachers allocated nasty jobs. She'd seen tardy colleagues get lumbered with coordinating the sale of raffle tickets all day, or being suspended over a pool of water for the 'Dunk a Teacher' game.

But this time she was the late one and she knew there was a good chance she'd have to pay for it.

Gently Megan eased open the staffroom door. She froze as the hinge squealed and the entire school staff turned to look at her.

Her smile felt weak and she could only imagine how it looked. Blushing furiously, she raised her hand in greeting.

'Sorry I'm late,' she mumbled, sliding into a chair at the back of the room. She looked down at her lemon yellow Converse sneakers, which she'd ordered from the States. Not even their cheery colour could remove her feeling of dread.

'So to conclude this meeting . . .' the principal resumed with an amused look in Megan's direction, which made her nervous, 'we are grateful to you all for volunteering your time. Let's make this year's fete the best yet.'

Chairs scraped harshly against the floor as the other teachers left, throwing styrofoam cups in the bin on their way out.

Trying not to expect the worst, Megan stood up. She might as well find out how bad it was. On butcher's paper taped to the blackboard were tasks along with the names of volunteers. Her eyes slid downward.

Her gaze snagged on her name and she jerked her eyes to the left.

Clothes stall – Megan.

She let out her breath in relief. There was a God. Clothes stall – she could handle that. It was probably just a matter of coordinating volunteers to sell donated clothes.

Glancing around, Megan saw the principal.

'Megan.' There was something about the way the older lady spoke that always reminded Megan of the Queen. 'Adriana has been networking and found us a great last-minute opportunity for the fete. The committee decided that you'd be the best person to make it happen.'

Megan nodded cautiously. Adriana was the only teacher younger than her on the staff. Despite their shared youth, they had yet to find anything in common.

'I see that. The clothes stall sounds fine. Is there a volunteer roster to coordinate?'

Megan could have sworn she saw the ghost of a smile on the principal's face.

'Not exactly.'

'Oh . . .' Megan's sense of dread returned.

'Adriana met the owner of a chain of boutiques and convinced her to provide us with some clothes to run a fashion parade next weekend. It's late notice, but well worth the effort, I'm sure you'll agree.'

The principal paused. Not hearing the expected agreement from Megan, she continued anyway. 'It won't be too hard – you just need to recruit about eight staff members to model the clothes for you. Only seven really, if you count yourself.'

'Oh,' Megan said again. Suddenly raffle tickets were looking good. She wondered if the person being dunked in freezing cold water would mind swapping jobs.

'In your absence it was decided that your unique style could be just what the parade needs to give it a bit of colour.'

Megan looked at the older woman desperately. 'But . . . I don't . . . I mean – surely Adriana could . . .'

The principal smiled as she turned away. 'As I said before, we are very grateful to all our volunteers.'

★

There had to be a better way to earn a living.

Megan's mother hadn't mentioned anything about fashion parades when she was advocating teaching as a career. It should be printed as a warning at the bottom of the university application forms, like on cigarette packets: *WARNING: The Surgeon General warns that a degree in teaching may lead to humiliation in many unspecified forms.*

At this point it was looking as though the fashion parade was going to be a one-man show. Despite her best attempts at both begging and pleading, not one other teacher had agreed to be in it. They'd all thought the position she was in was riotously funny. Megan had avoided Adriana. A tirade of four-letter words would almost certainly breach the 'professional respect' the principal felt so strongly about.

In desperation, Megan had gone to see the principal and suggested the event be cancelled.

'Unless,' she'd joked weakly, 'you'd like to participate. I have a cocktail number that would suit you beautifully.'

The principal had looked distinctly unamused. She had also made it very clear that the fashion show was going ahead one way or the other.

It had to be karma, Megan thought, logging onto Alice's website for a little light relief. The universe was making her pay for using Alice's task as an excuse to see Greg again – or for lying about reading to the old lady.

Every time she logged onto Alice's dinky old website, Megan wondered what the hell she was doing.

Judging by the calls she was getting from her family, though, she was still the problem child of the month. Megan had the distinct impression they would do something dramatic, like roster a family member to be with her at all times, if she told them she had quit the group.

She scrolled down through the entries, stopping on Claire's last one.

Well, I went. It actually wasn't as bad as I thought, drinking cocktails by myself. Rather depressing outcome though. I sat there for an hour and the only skill I could think of was shopping for clothes. How incredibly shallow and useless to be unable to come up with anything better than that.

Slowly an idea began to form in Megan's mind.

Alice

Alice threw her bag down beside the door.

The children ran into the house and up the stairs, still full of energy despite the two hours of after-school activity they'd just finished. Alice had dropped Ellen at her music lesson, the boys to football training, then retraced her steps collecting Ellen and returning to the park to wait for football to finish. She was exhausted even if they weren't.

'Five minutes, okay,' she yelled at their departing backs. 'Unpack your bags and change and then come back downstairs, we're meeting Dad at five-thirty.'

Alice considered the possibility of a shower and a change of clothes and quickly discarded it. Instead she walked into the kitchen. The old walkman was sitting where she'd left it on the kitchen bench, partly submerged in general family debris.

She slipped the headphones on and again, her grandmother's voice filled her head.

'*I actually had ten children you know, not nine. My first baby was a girl called Anna. She had more hair than any of my other babies . . .*'

Alice heard her grandmother's voice trail off and there was a small silence before she resumed.

'*They didn't have those sticks that change colour in those days. You figured out you were pregnant when you started vomiting or putting on weight. If you were unlucky, you did both. And then you pretty much waited until you went into labour.'*

The tape ran, faint crackles the only sound for several seconds.

'I knew she was dead as soon as she came out. It was the silence. Hours and hours of pain and then just . . . silence.'

There was the sudden sound of the tape recording being stopped. Alice remembered the moment. Remembered how she had quickly pushed the stop button, shocked by her grandmother's grief, despite almost fifty years and nine other children.

The tape recorder clicked a few times.

Edith's voice resumed. She'd recovered her composure, the old pain had been submerged once again.

'The only person who knew what to do was your grandfather. He didn't tell me we'd have more children or that it would be all right. He just held me and let me cry – night after night.'

Alice flicked off the tape and stared out the window.

She was hearing something different in the tapes this time. Something she hadn't focused on when she'd written *Her Life, My Life*. It was the love between her grandparents – the deep, uncomplicated love that rode all challenges life threw at them and surpassed everything else. Last time, Alice had been distracted by her grandmother's journey, the children, the drudgery, her incredible spirit. Maybe because she'd never really known her grandfather, she hadn't focused on him. But now, every time Alice turned the tape recorder on, all she heard was a huge, pulsing love between the two of them which had carried them for decades.

After a moment, Alice looked down at her watch.

They were late and she stood up abruptly.

'All right you lot, where are you?' She walked back into the hallway, looking up the stairs. 'We'll be late, let's go.'

Alice accelerated quickly and turned across the oncoming lane of traffic. The narrow road she was turning into was partially blocked by another car. She braked and stopped quickly, but without any real danger.

Looking out her window, she saw the driver of the other car, a middle-aged woman, shaking her head disapprovingly.

Alice rested her arm on the open window and smiled sweetly, obviously waiting.

Reluctantly the older woman rolled down the window, clearly not having intended any interaction outside her protective bubble.

'Hello?' Alice said questioningly, trying, not entirely successfully, to keep the note of sarcasm out of her voice.

'You could see that this car was parked here, so I was in the middle of the road. Really, you should be more careful. And you with children in the car.'

The woman shook her head in a disappointed manner that made Alice's blood boil.

'Thank you for that. I'll be going now.'

Alice was proud of her self-restraint. Road rage with three impressionable children was not a good look. Her views about young children being exposed to appalling behaviour by sporting stars would be somewhat blighted by their mother screaming like a fishwife.

She drove slowly over the edge of the gutter and back onto the road. Despite herself she felt unsettled and unhappy.

'Why did the lady say that, Mummy?' Alex piped up.

'She was just a bit grumpy, sweetheart,' Alice answered. 'She thought that I had done the wrong thing.'

'Why did she say that about having kids in the back seat?' John asked.

'Well, you should really drive more carefully when you have children with you,' Alice answered.

'Why?' Ellen asked. 'Shouldn't you be just as careful if you're driving with grown-ups?'

'Well, yes, you should I guess,' Alice said, waiting for the traffic light to turn green.

'She thought you were a bad driver, didn't she, Mummy?' John asked.

Alice closed her eyes briefly, willing herself to be patient. Children had an unerring instinct to pick away at things you wanted to forget. She couldn't get a word out of them when she asked about what they'd done at school. But her traffic incident was worth hours of discussion.

'Oh not really, John,' she lied. 'Now, who can see Dad?' she asked in her best Mary Poppins voice, trying to change the subject.

The children craned their heads toward the office block.

Andrew had been surprised when she'd suggested an early dinner with the children. There was a time when they'd gone out together every Friday night. It had been a ritual they'd all enjoyed, but somehow it had fallen away.

Alice had been thinking about Rebecca and Bianca that afternoon. She'd suddenly been struck by how she should follow her own advice and do something enjoyable with her family. Enthused with the idea, she had called Andrew and arranged to meet this evening.

Now, sitting in the car with the boys thumping each other in the back seat and the memory of the woman's disapproving look, the happiness disappeared, leaving her feeling only weary.

'There he is, Mum!' Ellen yelled.

'Daddy!' the three screamed in unison. Alice laughed. Maybe this had been a good idea after all.

Andrew swung open the car door and dropped into the passenger seat. He kissed Alice on the cheek and turned to the back seat. Unusually he was wearing a suit and he wrenched at the knotted tie around his neck.

'Hello team,' he smiled. 'Nice to feel appreciated, I must say.'

Alice looked at him sharply, wondering if the comment was meant for her.

He turned back to the front and reached for his seatbelt and she decided she was being oversensitive.

Alice indicated and pulled into the traffic.

'I thought we'd go to Giuseppe's. Is that okay?'

'Sounds excellent,' he smiled.

'Daddy?' Alex piped up from the back seat.

'Yes, mate.'

'A lady told Mummy she was a bad driver.'

Alice cringed. Andrew's lack of regard for her driving had always been pretty clear. He had never bought her argument that the law of averages meant that given the number of times she was in supermarket carparks it was inevitable she'd scrape the occasional pole.

'No she didn't, Alex,' Ellen corrected him pedantically. 'She said she should have been more careful because she had all of us in the car.'

Andrew looked across at Alice. 'Did something happen?'

Alice cursed the woman and her children simultaneously. 'It was nothing. Some woman was stopped halfway across the road and tried to tell me it was my fault.'

'Right.' Andrew was clearly unconvinced.

The children settled into a level of bickering just below the level which would require intervention.

'How was your day?' Andrew asked.

'Fine thanks.' Alice had been at home all day and could never bring herself to talk about the chores which filled her time between dropping the children at school and picking them up.

The core problem with being a housewife, she'd decided long ago, was that no one job was distinct from another. To put a load of washing on she'd have to first scrub the T-shirts stained from yesterday's activities. To be able to stand at the sink to scrub the T-shirts, she'd have to put away the bike which Alex had parked in the laundry. To put away the bike, she'd have to pick up the items that were strewn across the living room which led onto the garage. Each one job led into an endless spiral of jobs which, if you were really lucky, culminated in a reasonably tidy house for about ten minutes after the children came home.

She'd tried once to explain it to Andrew, but he'd clearly not understood.

'Just leave it all,' he'd answered. 'It doesn't matter if the dishes don't get washed up straight after breakfast.'

Which was right. But what he didn't understand was that his theory only worked if someone else eventually sorted it out. Otherwise the next lot of dishes would be piled upon the first lot and then the next and the next. And the whole lot would sit there festering and making her feel tense whenever she passed the kitchen.

It was so clichéd, she even bored herself. Frustrated house-wife, sick to death of the endless list of menial jobs and the fact that no one ever appreciated any of her efforts to make the family happy.

Alice would trundle a trolley around the supermarket, piling in favourite cereals and muesli bars while fighting a recalcitrant wheel and wonder whether she should just stop. Let them see how the milk cartons didn't automatically refill and the fresh bread didn't miraculously arrive on the kitchen bench each morning.

She'd asked herself what it was she wanted and she wasn't even sure.

If Andrew was to come home and say, 'My God, the kitchen window looks fabulously clean,' she'd think he was having an affair. And nobody, not even a cheating husband, was ever going to notice that what had been a basket full of dirty washing that morning was stacked back in the children's closets before dinner.

The only answer was to accept it and get over it. Which she could when she felt she was part of the whole family unit – moving them all forward to a goal that was good for everyone. But lately she felt as though she was nothing more than a fondly regarded housekeeper.

'And how was your day?' she asked Andrew.

He sighed and loosened his tie even further. 'I met up with some guys from a new supermarket chain today. They're interested in stocking our Home and Well range. I'm just not convinced that they're going to be up to the competition with the big super-markets. If they are, though, it could be an amazing opportunity. It could be worth millions.'

Alice was unmoved. Millions . . . It would be great obviously, but she'd never wanted to be rich. They were now, she guessed, and she had no desire to have more money. Most of her book royalties had gone into the business. They'd started pouring in just when the business needed to expand and there'd been no thought of keeping them for herself. Just as the royalty cheques had started to dry up, Andrew's business had started to make a profit and they'd been very comfortable financially ever since.

She stopped at a set of lights and looked across at Andrew. His face was expressionless and remote. Alice tried to picture the Andrew she'd fallen in love with in England. He didn't actually look that different – more lines around his eyes and a closed look to his face. Was he happy? Probably not. She tried to think of something else to ask and couldn't.

Alice thought of Kerry. He wasn't happy, but he still had an enthusiasm for life. Not like this grey-faced man sitting beside her.

Kerry treated her as though she was some sort of sexy wise woman, capable of guiding others. *With Great Power Comes Great Responsibility*, he'd emailed her yesterday, quoting Spider-Man's motto. She'd written back telling him to check his source, that the quote was in fact Peter Parker, Spider-Man's alter ego. He'd been impressed by her knowledge and she had chosen not to tell him that she'd learned it during John's obsession with Spider-Man several years ago.

The betrayal of her thoughts shocked her and she braked too hard at an intersection.

'Sorry,' she murmured to no one in particular.

This was something they hadn't done for ages. A simple thing – just what she preached to everyone else. And she was going to enjoy a nice calm dinner with her family, with nothing else to distract them.

As if evidence of divine blessing for her thoughts, Alice spotted a park on the street opposite the restaurant. She pulled up beside the car in front.

Andrew blew through his lips. 'That's pretty tight, sure you can fit?'

She wasn't sure at all, but nodded decisively and put the big car into reverse. Pivoting neatly, she slid into the space and turned off the engine.

She concealed her surprise at having succeeded, bending down to pick up her bag, hair falling in a shield across her face. When she sat back up, Andrew hadn't moved. She looked across at him and saw him looking at her with a grin. Involuntarily she smiled back. She sometimes forgot how much he knew about her.

'You are absolutely delighted you managed to do that, aren't you?'

She smiled slightly and opened the car door.

'Maybe,' she threw over her shoulder. 'Come on, let's eat.'

Lillian

Lillian had never thought that a pair of shoes would be her touchstone. But as the wave of panic threatened once again to engulf her, she looked down at her feet.

She hadn't owned a pair of high-heeled boots in her life, let alone brown suede ones. And yet, matched with her new beige slacks (tan trousers, she reminded herself) they felt right. It wasn't as though they were stilettos. The heel was only slight but it was enough to make her stand up straighter as she walked. They were the kind of shoes that someone flying to Paris by herself would wear.

The boarding call for her flight finally echoed through the departure hall. Lillian stood up and moved toward the silver chute leading to the immense aeroplane. Too late she realised that everyone else had done the same and she was standing halfway down a line that stretched back toward the duty-free shop. A handful of obviously seasoned travellers still sat, clearly waiting for the final call.

She pushed her handbag self-consciously toward her back. It wasn't terribly old, but it looked tired beside her new outfit. Perhaps she'd pick up a new one in Paris, she thought, a bubble of excitement racing through her and then popping just as quickly.

Lillian had oscillated from excitement to panic and back again over the last few days. The travel agent and Kyla had both convinced Lillian to fly straight away, while there was a special on flights and before winter settled in France. So after checking with her doctor, Lillian was leaving less than a week after she'd decided to go.

She'd be away for almost three weeks. Since booking her flight, she'd often looked around the house, feeling a sense of intoxicating release to be escaping its sameness. At other times, though, she had yearned desperately to be facing her normal routine of endless, uneventful days rolling one into the other.

But those days seemed to have disappeared anyway. The last few weeks had been dominated by medical tests, with the MRI scan and the lack of any other diagnosis pointing toward multiple sclerosis. There wasn't much to be done now but wait and see whether the symptoms recurred.

So here she was. But she hadn't told Alice. Maybe because doing so would make it seem too real. Or maybe because she wanted to keep this as her own adventure, not part of the group project. She would send Alice a postcard from Paris.

A friend had offered to take Lillian to the airport, but she'd refused. This was something she wanted to do by herself, without the need to make conversation or pretend that she was not scared stupid.

But Ross wouldn't be put off. He had refused point blank to accept her argument that she could take a taxi and badgered her for days until she told him her flight details.

He'd been waiting outside forty-five minutes before she had to be at the airport and had chatted cheerfully as he slung her luggage in the back and settled her in the front seat. He had closed Lillian's door for her and she had wondered if he was actually older than she'd thought. His old-fashioned manners were those that she associated with older men.

She had buckled her seatbelt and looked over at Ross, who was smiling at her.

'It's okay, I drive much better when there's someone else in the car,' he'd said.

She'd smiled nervously, not really believing him until they'd been driving for fifteen minutes without a tyre screech or running a red light.

Lillian had passed most of the drive in silence, staring out the window, terrified at the thought of what she was about to do. Ross, too, had been uncharacteristically quiet. As they approached the airport he had cleared his throat.

'I'm really happy to come in with you, but I think maybe you'd like to just get dropped off?'

Lillian had smiled gratefully at him. She'd been wondering how to say that without being rude.

'Thanks, that'd be great,' she'd said.

They had pulled up with a small screech in the drop-off zone in front of the airport.

'Sorry,' Ross had winced. 'Forgot for a moment.'

He had walked around to open Lillian's door, then pulled her suitcase out of the back.

'Well, bye I guess,' Lillian had said awkwardly.

'Hang on,' Ross had said. 'I almost forgot something.'

He'd opened the back door and pulled out a paper bag with a book inside.

'It's about female explorers in the eighteenth century,' he had said, smiling. 'I figured it was appropriate.'

Lillian smiled back at him, an ache in her throat. She had thought about hugging him, but a car waiting to pull into their spot tooted.

'All right, keep your shirt on,' Ross had muttered.

'Well, I'll see you in a few weeks.' Lillian had raised her hand in farewell.

'Yeah. Have a great trip, Lillian. See you soon.'

She had turned away, pulling the suitcase behind her.

'Lillian!'

Ross had been standing next to the car, ignoring the increasing agitation of the driver of the car double parked beside him.

'Forgot to tell you, I put a copy of Liverpool's match schedule inside the book. Just in case you want to pop across the Channel to London for a night!'

'Great, Ross, thanks,' Lillian had laughed.

Now, standing in the queue, Lillian rubbed her thumb rhythmically over her passport, the textured cover rough against her skin. She'd finally found it in the back of a drawer, where it had lain for years.

So here she was.

The man in front of her accepted a stack of passports back from the flight attendant and jammed them into his shirt pocket.

'Madam? Your passport and boarding card please.'

Lillian's attention snapped back to the stunning girl at the gate. Her uniform was patterned in coloured flowers against a royal blue background, the low neckline showing off beautiful collarbones and an elegant neck. The straight skirt fell to just above her ankles.

'I'm sorry,' she apologised, flustered. She felt old and pallid next to the girl's serene beauty.

The attendant handed Lillian's travel documents back to her. 'Have a wonderful holiday, madam,' she said.

Lillian looked down at her boots. Suede – and with a heel.

It was enough.

Kerry

Sometimes the very act of dreading something removes its sting.

I'd even go so far as to venture that it is better to visit the art gallery with a hangover than without. With a hangover your expectations are low – survival until bedtime is your only goal. Last Sunday there was nowhere else in the world (other than bed – clearly not an option) that I wanted to be. So the fact that Annie loved the paintings of the dancers made me happy too. And standing in one spot and staring, the only life skills left to me at that point, were by some extraordinary coincidence exactly what was required. Admittedly I did receive a few strange looks from people who noticed that my eyes were closed for most of the time. But I just smiled sagely and hoped they'd think I was contemplating deeply what I had seen. Perhaps the gallery's new slogan could be 'Drunk one Day, Brisbane Art Gallery the next . . .' Then again, maybe not . . .

Kerry pulled off his cap and wiped his forehead, flicking the sweat onto the ground. The sun was almost directly overhead and it was stiflingly hot, even in the shade.

He stopped for a moment and looked around.

This was by far the most glamorous of the markets he worked at. The people swarming the pathways between the stalls weren't here for a bargain. They were looking for boutique produce and price was an afterthought. Which was just as well because nothing was cheap.

Kerry charged almost double for his plants here. It was fair, he figured. New Farm residents with their Gucci sunglasses and Swedish-designed pull-along trolleys could bear a bit of a mark-up. With its renovated warehouse buildings housing thousands of glamorous apartments, the suburb was full of people with a high disposable income. Kerry was very happy to help in the disposal process.

He pulled another box of mother-in-law's tongue toward him. His own mother had refused to grow it for months, declaring it to be a toxic weed. Kerry had eventually convinced her that a few of the tall green blades stuck in a decent-looking pot sold itself. From Kerry's point of view, it had the additional benefits of being almost impossible to kill and having a name even he couldn't forget.

Hefting the box, Kerry struggled around the truck, dropping it on the ground beside the stand.

The teenage boy behind the counter looked over.

'Ah great. The lady over here wants three of them – biggest you've got.'

Kerry smiled broadly, pulling out three of the pots. 'Lovely choice, madam. These are a personal favourite of mine.'

Sometimes Kerry amazed even himself with his outrageous lies. They were harmless enough, but he felt vaguely uneasy about how easily they slipped off his tongue.

The stand was on the fringe of the market. This was the best place, Kerry had decided. People were ready to go when they reached him and happy to tuck a pot under their arm. His sales were almost double what they'd been when he'd been in the middle of the market, too many people promising to return on their way to the car but not managing it. Of course those figures were also before he'd come up with the idea of making a bit of a performance of it all.

It had started because he was bored with answering questions on plants which he couldn't care less about. Kerry's dad had been an auctioneer for a number of years. Kerry remembered standing in blistering hot sun in the ordinary backyards of ordinary houses all over Brisbane. It had been anything but glamorous but he'd loved the auctioneer's patter, absurdly proud of his father for motivating expressionless crowds to part with money.

'Well, I don't know what's so funny,' Kerry's voice, addressing no one in particular, was louder than the general hubbub. 'This rosebush is a family heirloom – each leaf carefully polished by my mother every day of my childhood. It broke my heart to dig it out of her garden to sell today. But I told her – you've got to do what you've got to do.'

'Mate, why are you looking at me like that?' He spoke to a smiling man in front of him. 'It's God's truth, I promise.'

'Okay, if that's not your thing, maybe the bougainvillea is for you – it was grafted in Los Angeles for a Hollywood superstar in honour of his latest wife. Sadly he fell on hard times and is selling off his best assets. The fleet of cars, the plants, the wife . . .'

As always tended to happen, people stopped in front of the stall. They smiled over at Kerry.

'You, madam,' Kerry gestured at a lady toward the back. 'I can tell by the look in your eye that you are desperately in need of something lovely and green for your kitchen table. Perhaps a . . .' Kerry paused for a beat, glancing at the prompt cards he'd stapled to the inside of the stall. 'Spathaphyllum,' he finished, raising his eyebrows.

The woman smiled slightly, shook her head and walked away.

Kerry grinned. It always took a little while – he saw it as a bit of a challenge now. Selling plants to people who never intended to buy one. He saw it as his small contribution to fighting global warming – and of course his own takings.

He searched the crowd, looking for a likely person to target. Someone who'd get into the fun and who other people would copy.

His eyes rested on a familiar face. Even behind large sunglasses and a hat, he recognised Alice. His rush of pleasure at seeing her surprised him.

She was aware of his gaze and gave a small wave.

Kerry wondered what she was doing here. New Farm was a fair drive from Paddington, too far to go for a nice piece of cheese. He wondered briefly if she could have come here to see him.

He looked back at Alice, aware that the silence was already a beat too long. She was dressed more casually than he'd seen her before, in faded jeans and a white T-shirt. Strangely she looked younger than when she was all dressed up.

He looked away. 'All right – what can I do to convince you to buy something? How about a little bonsai for that outdoor table? My Japanese suppliers got carried away this month and sent me a hundred all from the garden where the Karate Kid learned how to fight. Normally I charge a hundred dollars for these babies – they take years to grow and train in the right direction. But for you people today, just fifty. The offer's only on the table,' he looked at his watch, 'until eleven forty-five – five minutes away.'

'Okay,' a man at the front pulled out his wallet. 'I'll take a couple.'

'Me too,' a lady off to the far side said.

Kerry looked at Alice, tilting his head to indicate the side of the van.

Out of the corner of his eye, he saw her pushing through the crowd. After serving two people, he slipped out of the stall.

Alice was standing awkwardly beside the van, hat in hand and fingers pushing her sweat-flattened hair off her head.

'I wasn't expecting to see my beautiful guru here today.'

Kerry's words were low.

Alice laughed self-consciously.

'I needed some things and I was in the neighbourhood,' she waved a basket vaguely.

There was a silence.

'I'd like one of your bougainvilleas,' Alice said suddenly, a fraction too loud. 'Do you have any thornless ones?'

Kerry shook his head. 'Sorry, I don't do thornless. Seems like a good idea, I know, but they just aren't as good as the real thing. You just have to plant them somewhere the thorns won't drive you crazy. Where are you planning on putting it?'

'I need something to cover the wall of a carport.'

'Won't do.' Kerry looked serious. 'The thorns could puncture your tyres.'

He lowered his head, mouth to her ear. 'Buggers of things really,' he whispered. 'Wouldn't own one for quids.'

Alice stepped back quickly. 'Oh well, never mind. I should be getting along really anyway,' she said nervously.

Kerry suddenly wanted her to stay. 'Well, wait on a minute . . . I don't offer this to just everyone . . .' Kerry broke off as a boy stepped around the side of the van and stood beside Alice.

'Ah, I see you aren't travelling alone. Very wise. Can you vouch for this man?'

'This is John, my son.'

'Nice to meet you, John.' Kerry held out his hand, hiding his surprise.

He pulled out a stool and gestured for Alice to sit on it. He opened the door to the cabin and, keeping up the performance of secrecy, draped an old towel over something inside.

Alice laughed again.

He stood in front of her, hand poised on the towel.

There was a sudden silence.

'Ta dah.'

'It's jasmine,' Alice said.

Kerry was outraged. 'Jasmine? Jasmine? I present you with a plant that heralds the coming of spring with scent and mystery and all you say is, "It's jasmine."'

He turned to John. 'Just like a woman,' he said conspiratorially.

John shrugged. 'Women,' he said. 'Can't live with 'em . . .'

And the three of them burst out laughing.

Alice recovered first and reached for her purse. 'How much do I owe you?'

Kerry waved her away. 'I drank a lot of champagne that first night. The jasmine is on the house.'

Alice looked at John.

Sensing her discomfort, Kerry pointed John toward a large box off to one side. 'Have a look in there – I picked up a stack of Venus flytraps cheap yesterday. Unfortunately the public don't appear to think they're as irresistible as I did. Give them some of the bread next to the box. Just watch they don't close on your hand, though. Some of those big ones could take your finger off.'

He winked at Alice.

'You certainly don't look like you hate your job,' Alice said bluntly.

The showman's smile disappeared from Kerry's face. 'No. But isn't that what we all do? Pretend we're happy when we're not?'

'I guess so,' Alice answered slowly. 'But you being around something nice like plants must help, surely?'

'I hate plants,' Kerry replied flatly. 'Give me a nice paved back-yard any day, and if you really want flowers, a few fake ones. Hell of a lot easier than growing the things.'

'You're serious, aren't you?' Alice looked at him closely.

'Sure am. I didn't like them when I started doing this and after four years I like them even less. Bloody dirty, high-main-tenance things. But don't tell my fans.' The mask slipped back into place and Kerry smiled playfully. 'A plant seller who thinks plastic turf is a fabulous option is not going to have much of a business.'

Alice didn't smile. 'So how did you get into this?'

Kerry puffed up his cheeks and blew out the air.

'Just one of those things, I guess. My folks have always run a little nursery on the south side. It's never done more than really provide a living, but then a while ago business got really crappy. One of those huge nurseries opened nearby and Mum and Dad just couldn't compete. At the same time, these farmers' markets were becoming bigger than Ben Hur.'

He pulled off his cap and ran his hand through the flattened curls.

'I was sick of fixing people's cars and I had an idea to help Mum and Dad out. It actually works pretty well. They grow the plants, drill into me what they are; I forget, they tell me again, and then we load them up to bring here for the weekend markets.'

He paused and then added, 'And then they tell me again what the plants are — I've got the worst bloody memory for plant names. It's a bit of a joke really. Customers think the big name tags on them are for them.

'Anyway, Mum and Dad have a bit of an income ticking over at the nursery. But most of the sales come out of these things.' He waved a hand around. 'I've also picked up some deals to supply apartment blocks and small offices around here. Flogging plants for my folks doesn't really set my world on fire. But neither does changing oil in fifteen cars a day. And I haven't had anyone knocking down my door to have me restore their cars — or to offer me a hundred grand for my car that I restored. Guess I've gotta be realistic, huh?'

He took a breath. 'So — glad you asked?'

Alice looked at him squarely. 'Actually I am,' she answered.

Their eyes locked.

His assistant's head poked around the side of the van.

'Kerry, I've got chaos out here. You revved everyone up for those bonsais and then buggered off. Come on!'

He disappeared and Kerry stood up, jamming the cap back onto his head.

'Duty calls. Better go . . .'

He smiled and ducked back around the corner.

Claire

I knew I should have said no before I put the phone down. Megan isn't even a friend. I have no idea why she wants me. Desperation, I guess. But I find it hard to see how it's going to help her when this so-called fashion consultancy is a total and utter disaster.

I called her straight back. She must have gone into class, though, and I just got her voicemail. When I eventually got hold of her hours later, she launched into all of the things she'd arranged that day. In my typical pathetic way, I didn't have enough courage to cancel on her.

Claire stood at the school gate, stomach clenching. The oval was a hive of activity. People strode around carrying ladders and hammers and unpacking styrofoam boxes of goodies onto trestle tables.

It was only eight in the morning but the sun burned out of the cloudless sky with an intensity that seemed to drill straight through her skin.

Cargo shorts, old T-shirts and Birkenstocks were clearly the order of the day. Claire felt like the party guest who hadn't been told the fancy dress theme was cancelled. Her white dress gathered under the bust and floated to just below knee level and she had grave doubts of being able to navigate the potholed ground in her high brown wedges.

She felt like a fraud. Not because of what she was wearing, or even what she was about to do. This was not her world. The world of school fetes was one for parents.

Being a family was normal. Nothing special, just normal. And yet it was something that some type of supernatural being seemed to have whimsically decided to deny Claire.

She bit her lip and pressed her bag tightly against her side. Her Prada bag, which no parent supporting three children could ever dream of owning, bought in the good old days before money had become tight.

'Claire!'

She followed the direction of the voice and saw Megan waving wildly at her from beside a canvas tent which looked like something Claire's parents had holidayed in years ago.

Claire picked her way across the grass, trying to ignore the interested glances.

'See, you're already making an impression,' Megan commented as Claire reached her side. 'First time anyone's worn heels that high to a school bonanza!'

'Is it too much?' Claire asked uncertainly. 'I figured if anyone was going to take me even slightly seriously I would have to look the part.'

'Don't worry,' Megan commented dryly. 'This mob get whiplash if someone wears anything not featured in the local paper's fashion pages. You should have seen the reaction when I tried to leave my nose ring in.' She stopped herself. 'Sorry, that's another story. You look really fancy and I think it's perfect. Let's knock the socks off everyone. Right – now this is your tent.'

She gestured at the tent and Claire read the large letters printed on a banner across the doorway: *Free Fashion Consultancy Services*.

At least it was free, she thought; it was hard for people to complain when they weren't paying anything.

'And these,' Claire followed Megan as she walked inside the tent, 'are your clothes.'

She gestured with a flourish to a metal rack crowded with garments.

Claire walked over to the rack and flicked through the hangers. After a moment she looked up at Megan.

'Are there any others?' she asked hopefully.

'Ah, no,' Megan pursed her lips. 'These are it. They've been supplied by a local boutique. Trust me, I had no role in choosing them.'

'I believe that,' said Claire, looking at Megan's short tunic dress worn over black leggings. They're just very . . .' She paused.

'Mumsy? Suburban?' Megan supplied helpfully.

'Yeeesss,' Claire agreed. 'Fashion is about beautiful things that make you feel good. These are just kind of ordinary.'

'Well, you can't work miracles,' Megan assured her. 'Don't forget you're at a primary school fete. You just need to adjust your thinking a bit. Don't forget, we're supposed to flog these things. They wanted to have a fashion parade but I convinced the principal to try this instead. People can leave orders with you and the shop staff will follow up with them next week. But I'm told no sales will make the shop owner very grumpy and will mean they don't help us out next year . . .' She trailed off. 'Well anyway, I'll leave you to it – let you familiarise yourself with the stuff.'

Megan headed for the tent opening, but turned back. 'And Claire? Thanks. This isn't exactly glamorous, but you're saving my life. I really appreciate it.'

Claire looked at her for a moment and then smiled.

'The only other thing I'd be doing now is sitting not talking to my husband over the weekend papers. Don't worry.'

Megan looked at her silently for a moment.

'Okay. Well my class is in charge of the sweet stall. Can you believe it? Talk about leaving the fox to guard the geese. Anyway, I'd better go and make sure some of the fudge actually goes on the table. If you want me, just yell.'

With that she was gone.

Claire looked over at the rack again. It would be hard to change anyone's life with those items. There was nothing actively wrong with them. They were just unremarkable and unexciting.

Copies of designer clothes that had somewhere along the line lost the edge that made them special.

Panic clutched at her stomach. What in God's name was she going to do with the people who came in to see her? Could she really tell them they should buy these things?

As she stared at the rack, a quiet voice came from the doorway.

'Hello?'

Claire turned and saw a small woman dressed in jeans and an old T-shirt.

'Sorry, you're probably not open yet. It's just . . . Well, I thought I might beat the rush. But why don't I come back later?'

The woman turned to go.

'No,' Claire yelled, surprising both of them.

Her voice echoed around the canvas room.

'Sorry,' she tried a smile. 'What I meant was, why don't you come in? I'm just setting up, but we're expecting a lot of people so it's a good idea to have a look while it's quiet.'

Why had she said that?

The woman took a step or two forward and stood awkwardly, looking at Claire for guidance.

'Why don't you have a look at the clothes and see if there's anything that takes your fancy,' Claire gestured toward them.

The woman stood with her back to Claire, the metronomic shriek of the clothes hangers against the metal rack the only sound.

Claire chewed her thumbnail nervously. What the hell did she do now? She detested hovering sales assistants, but she was supposed to be a consultant, which surely meant she should do something more than stand there like a store dummy.

She walked around to the opposite side of the rack and plastered a smile on her face.

'Anything you like?' she asked.

The woman turned her head a little, not meeting Claire's eyes.

'Ah, yes, they're lovely . . . but I've got to get back. Thanks very much.'

She was gone in a moment and Claire was left staring at the empty doorway.

Well at least now she knew what not to do.

She walked back to the rack and pulled the clothes out one by one. They weren't actually so bad if you looked as them as basics. Teemed with something interesting, they could be okay. Claire put together some combinations and then walked around the tent, hooking the hangers into the rope slung around the walls at ceiling height.

Next she pulled a foolscap block and some pens out of her bag. Not for any real purpose other than the fact that she figured stationery looked official. She put them on the folding card table which was set up in the corner.

She tried sitting at the rickety chair beside the table, but had a sudden vision of herself perched there in her white dress just like Little Miss Muffet.

There wasn't much more she could do with the clothes so she walked to the doorway and looked out.

The umbrellas were up over the tables. Across the other side of the oval Claire could see the mechanical rides juddering into use. Over to her right, an already tired-looking donkey had his first small rider of the day.

The unmistakable smell of sausages being barbecued floated in the air and Claire turned her head, spotting the source.

She ate very little meat and never sausages, but all of a sudden she was ravenously hungry. Breakfast had been a cup of tea drunk alone. Peter had left on an early morning bike ride, which had at least meant she'd had no need to explain where she was going. On an impulse, she walked toward the food tent.

'Hello,' Claire greeted the woman behind the barbecue. The woman was wearing a loose white singlet and khaki cargo pants, her brownish hair pulled back from a face which was starting to show the first serious lines of age.

'Hello,' the woman smiled in reply, looking Claire up and down. 'You know, I'm not sure I can recommend one of our sausage rolls – the tomato sauce is just destined to end up on the front of that dress.'

'You're probably right,' Claire agreed. 'Not likely to inspire confidence in potential clients.'

The woman looked at Claire quizzically for a moment and then her eyes cleared. 'Ah, you're the fashion lady. That makes sense, I didn't think you'd be doing the trash and treasure stall in that outfit.'

'Yes, well, I'm not really sure what I'm supposed to be doing, to tell the truth. I'm doing this as a favour, but I have no idea how to go about it. I think it's actually going to be a complete disaster.'

Claire had no idea why she was saying this to a complete stranger.

The woman looked at her levelly. 'Well, you look fantastic, so my guess is that you know what you're talking about. I don't think it'll be too hard to impress this crowd,' she gestured around her.

'You know . . .' she broke off and then started again. 'I've got my twenty year school reunion coming up next weekend. There were some absolute cows at that school who always made me feel bad about what I wore. I'd love to go along knowing that for once I look good, but whenever I try something a bit different on in the shops I look totally ridiculous. I don't suppose you'd be able to give me some ideas?'

Claire looked at her for a moment. She knew without looking that there was nothing in the tent that would work. But she had a stack of magazines in the car which might help show the woman what she should be looking for.

'I'll give you a free sausage?' The woman held one up in a pair of tongs.

Claire laughed. 'That I can't resist. You're on.'

Rebecca

I yell at someone every morning.

Sometimes Sam, when he poos in his underpants just before it's time for me to leave. One of the many unspoken rules in the nanny–employer relationship is that one does not hand over a child with steaming pants. So I take off my jacket and sort it out, trying not to flick brown globs onto my shirt as I do so.

Sometimes it's Jeremy when he asks me once again if I've seen his wallet and BlackBerry. 'I need to glue them to your goddamn forehead!' I scream silently, usually managing a vaguely civil, 'Have you checked on top of the microwave?' He has no idea that if I applied the same degree of organisation to the household that he does, we would all be lying starving on the floor with rats nibbling at our fetid clothing.

More than sometimes it's Bianca. Mornings are a battle of wills. The more I show stress and try to move things along, the slower she goes. School shoes are lost, finding white socks an impossible quest. Black eyeliner goes on – and has to come off again. Each day I watch her slouch in the school gates with relief. At least it's six hours before I have to worry about her again. We haven't repeated our morning off together. It has become just another disastrous glitch in our relationship which we're both ignoring. Well at least I am. I don't know whether Bianca gives any thought to me at all.

So this was why people wrote diaries. It felt good – the problems were still there afterwards, but somehow bashing the words onto her keyboard made her feel slightly better. Rebecca had to push out of her mind the idea that all the others were reading what she wrote. But hell, she read theirs. What did it matter?

The house had a glistening lounge area, designed around an amazing leather sofa chosen by the architect. But for some reason it wasn't where Rebecca ever felt like being. She'd stand beside the sofa, cup of coffee in hand, and then walk over to the kitchen bench. It was at the bench where she was sitting now, laptop perched on the stainless-steel counter, a tall glass of wine beside it.

She reopened last night's email from Alice.

You may well be an avid gardener. But somehow I don't think so. On your way home tomorrow stop in at City Gardener. It's on the corner of William and Mary Streets and they're open until six-thirty – I checked. Buy yourself a rosebush in your favourite colour – take it home and plant it in a very sunny spot. Preferably somewhere where you'll see it a lot. Oh, and make sure you can smell the roses. My grandmother believed that scentless roses were modern travesties that should be outlawed.

Rebecca smiled. Despite herself, she was enjoying this. Alice was a bit out there, but at least she wasn't predictable. She looked over at the sink. The bush had deep green leaves and only one bud. The shop assistant had looked at her questioningly when she'd ignored the other bushes crowded with blooms and picked up this one. There was something about picking the runt of the litter she liked, but mainly it was the colour of the bud. A pink, which started at the lightest blush and finished at the shade which wove with yellow in a glorious sunset.

As instructed she'd checked the smell on the plants with open blooms. Rebecca had walked out of the shop, wallet decidedly lighter but with a smile on her face. Now all she had to do was plant it.

Sam's cry echoed down the stairs. Rebecca hesitated, waiting to see if he'd settle himself. The crying settled into a continuous wail and she pushed back the stool.

By the time she reached Sam's room he'd found his bear and settled back into sleep. Rebecca walked over to the cot and ran her hand over the curve of his cheek.

'Sleep well, darling,' she whispered.

Rebecca paused outside Bianca's closed door. No light showed from inside and she knocked softly then opened the door a crack. Bianca's bedroom had become a guarded fortress and Rebecca never went inside uninvited. And invitations were few and far between.

Two green lights pulsed from the desk near the window. As Rebecca's eyes became accustomed to the dark she saw the computer and mobile phone. She'd bought Bianca her own computer two years ago when everything was good. Now Rebecca bitterly regretted it, the internet having become Bianca's own private world from which her family was totally excluded.

Bianca was asleep, one arm thrown up above her head, sheet tangled at her feet. She wore a faded black T-shirt that had bunched up over her small breasts. A bar of light from a street lamp was angled across her body, catching the side of her face.

Asleep and without her perpetual scowl, Bianca's face had softened and she looked again like a vulnerable little girl, long eyelashes brushing her face.

Rebecca had always checked on her daughter before she herself went to bed, smoothing her hair, or tucking a sheet up over a bare shoulder. That had stopped abruptly about a year ago, when Bianca began shutting her door and making it clear that it was to stay that way.

Denied her late-night moments with her daughter, Rebecca had felt as though she'd lost something precious. One night when she was sure Bianca was asleep she'd cracked the door open and peered in. She'd stood in the doorway, drinking in the sight of her daughter as she had always been. Since then she'd done it every night. She never went inside the room, just looked at her daughter for a few minutes, closed the door softly and went away.

Each night she vowed it would be better the next day. And each day it wasn't.

Bianca stirred and Rebecca jumped, worried she'd wake and see her standing there. But Bianca turned onto her side and settled back into a deep sleep. Her body rested in the strip of light and Rebecca's eyes caught on some lines across her stomach.

Her first thought were that they were pen marks, but then she noticed the flecks of red along the lines. Some kind of injury then?

Her mind registered the precision of the cuts at the same time as she rejected the idea that they could be scratches from a cat. Rebecca crossed the barrier of the doorway without thinking, striding toward the bed. She looked at Bianca's soft white stomach, unable to believe what she was seeing. The lines she had seen were cuts, clearly made with a sharp object of some kind.

Rebecca stepped back, mind whirling with shock. Her beautiful daughter had cut herself, her stomach − with a knife − many times.

For a moment the scene morphed into a memory of Bianca as a seven year old lying back on the pillow smiling up at her, gaps showing through her front teeth. 'Mummy, do you know the words to "I'm forever blowing bubbles"?' she'd asked.

The memory was snatched away abruptly and Rebecca was left staring down at the slices through Bianca's white skin.

She backed out of the room, not bothering to close the door. Blindly, she lurched to the toilet. She flicked the toilet seat up and leaned over the bowl, hair hanging down around her face, wracked with dry heaves.

Slowly she straightened. She walked back to Bianca's room and pulled the door shut silently. Robotically she went down the stairs and into the kitchen. Her wineglass still sat on the bench, condensation pooling at the base of its fine stem. Ignoring it, she leaned on the sink, staring out into the blackness of the night.

She heard Jeremy's car pull up into the drive. He was still doing his best to avoid spending time with her.

Suddenly she couldn't face his coldness and silent disdain. She picked up her car keys and met him at the door.

'Oh hi,' he said in surprise.

'I'm going out,' Rebecca announced. She pushed past Jeremy and strode toward her car.

'Hang on.' Jeremy was beside her.

Rebecca dropped the keys and scrabbled for them on the driveway. She found them and stood up, hand reaching for the door handle.

'Rebecca, slow down.'

She paused, head turned away. She needed to be alone somewhere so she could think about this.

'I'm just going out for a while. You'd rather be alone anyway. Don't worry, I'll be back soon.'

It was his touch, the first nonessential contact in weeks, that stopped her.

Rebecca looked down at Jeremy's hand over hers. She threw her head back and stared up at the sky, gulping in air, trying to figure out when everything had gone so wrong.

'What's wrong, Bec? You look terrible.'

Jeremy's words were soft and had a kind tone she'd almost forgotten.

Suddenly all her energy drained from her and she slid down the side of the car and sat on the concrete, legs drawn up to her chest.

Jeremy sat beside her and put his arms around her, pulling her against his chest.

Rebecca took a deep breath. 'Bianca has been cutting herself. With something sharp. I just saw the marks. On her stomach . . .'

She started crying, softly at first and then in huge racking gulps.

'Shhh Bec,' Jeremy said, pulling her closer. 'Shhh, it'll be all right.'

The words hit her like a slap and she wrenched herself out of his arms and scrambled to her feet.

'No. Don't you get it? No. It won't be all right. My baby is hurting herself on purpose. Nothing will ever be all right again.'

Rebecca

Jeremy and I decided that confronting Bianca about what she'd done before we knew how to deal with it would only end badly. So we decided to find someone to talk to — an expert. Someone who deals with these things all the time. Then we would make a plan so that we could fix it in a way that it would never, ever happen again. Which all made a lot of sense at the time. But now I am sitting here at three in the morning wondering how, in four hours' time, I am going to pretend to my daughter that I haven't seen what she's done to herself.

I keep trying to figure out why.

Is there something I don't know about — bullying at school maybe, or some kind of abuse?

Or is it because of me? Because Bianca was my whole life until Jeremy, then Sam arrived on the scene. Maybe, though, it's simpler than that. Even before the others arrived I'd never been like other mothers. Can not being there to take your daughter home from school to feast on oven-warm chocolate-chip cookies make her hate you and herself enough to do this?

Rebecca's BlackBerry beeped. She pulled her eyes back from the window where she'd been staring without seeing the magnificent view down the river.

3 pm Coffee w Claire, the built-in diary warned her.

Rebecca had fully expected Claire to call her daily about the whole group thing, agonising with her over the tasks set for her or what Claire should put in her diary entries. She hadn't, though.

One morning last week, Rebecca had pulled up the website. She'd read a few lines of her entry about the breakfast with Bianca and then, cringing, been unable to read more. The next entry down had been one from Claire. Sadness had permeated Claire's words and Rebecca had impulsively picked up the phone and called her. She'd reached her voicemail and had left a message suggesting a coffee. Two answering machine messages later, they had arranged to meet today.

That was before Rebecca had discovered Bianca had been cutting herself. In the early hours of the morning she'd given up all attempts to sleep and turned on her computer. She'd written about what had happened, posting the entry on the site before she could change her mind.

Rebecca rubbed her eyes. Elbow propped on the desk, she rested her head on her closed fist. Perhaps Claire hadn't looked at the website this morning and hadn't read Rebecca's entry. What the hell was she doing anyway? What kind of desperate loony wrote private details in an online diary she knew a friend would be reading? It was different for all the others, they didn't know anyone else in the group, and no one outside the group could access the website.

In the dark hours of the early morning, writing in the diary had seemed soothing and constructive. In the burning heat of early afternoon it looked like madness.

The reminder only gave her fifteen minutes. Claire would be in the city by now; Rebecca could cancel but it would be incredibly rude. Not that that would necessarily stop her. She'd spent years cancelling social occasions or just being extraordinarily late. Suddenly, though, she didn't have the energy to make up an excuse.

Slinging her handbag over her shoulder, she walked out of the glass-fronted office.

'I'm heading out for an appointment, Angela. Back in an hour or so.'

Her assistant smiled back. 'Okay – see you later.'

Hartman Consultants were on the tenth floor of one of the glass towers fringing the Brisbane River. They'd undergone a facelift by a team of interior designers two years previously. Chrome, caramel and dark brown had replaced a medley of blues. A sheet of sparkling glass was all that separated the corridor from the offices on both sides. Rebecca cast a look at the tiny internal offices in which she'd spent years. Each was now filled with a twenty-something year old intent on being the best and brightest in recruitment. Just watching their enthusiasm made her feel tired.

Eyes averted from her boss's corner office, she reached the bank of lifts and pressed the down button. The lift was blissfully empty and Rebecca stared at herself in the mirrored walls. Her hair was pulled back into a high ponytail; only now did she realise how drawn it made her face look. She pulled mascara from her bag and brushed another coat onto her lashes. A quick swipe of her favourite lipstick and she looked passable. Or like a drag queen ... sometimes it was hard to tell the difference.

Rebecca's sunglasses misted as she stepped out of the airconditioned building. The air was still and soup-like, the sun ferocious. She slowed her pace deliberately, but still felt the sweat spreading across her skin.

She stepped gratefully into the airconditioned cafe. Claire was there, sitting at a small table in the corner. As always, she looked as though she'd just stepped out of a fashion magazine. Her dress looked fresh and summery, the navy offset by a long string of red beads and matching shoes. Rebecca felt crumpled, tired and outdated, her suit one she'd been wearing for years. A dart of resentment that Claire had time to pull together outfits like that shot through her.

'Hey,' she stood next to the table.

Claire looked up and smiled. 'Rebecca – hello.'

'How are you?' Rebecca asked as she sat down.

'Fine, fine,' Claire answered.

As Rebecca looked closely at her, she saw the dark circles under Claire's eyes, the fine lines pinching the corners of her mouth. She felt a pang of shame that she of all people could have felt envious of Claire's spare time.

'Are you okay?' Claire asked.

Rebecca didn't meet Claire's eyes. 'Me? Sure.'

'Sorry, I didn't mean to be rude. Peter's mother always does that to me – asking if I feel all right, implying that I look awful.' Claire hesitated. 'You don't – look awful, I mean . . .' She smiled nervously. 'It's just that I read your diary entry this morning.'

Rebecca nodded slowly, fiddling with a small red cardboard box which held tubes of sugar.

A young man with a black apron and a harried air arrived at their table. They placed their orders, silence settling again as he left.

'Look,' Claire said finally. 'We don't have to talk about it if you don't want to. I just wanted you to know that I read what you wrote.'

Rebecca looked up at Claire. For a second the last seventeen years disappeared and they were friends who told each other everything.

'Not saying anything to Bianca this morning was one of the hardest things I've ever had to do.'

Rebecca paused and Claire stayed silent.

'Jeremy and I decided we had to pretend everything was fine. From the second that Bianca walked into the kitchen I started acting like some demented housewife. I asked everyone about their plans for the day, even poked my head out the window to assess the weather at one stage.' She laughed bitterly.

'Jeremy kept looking at me like he expected me to lose it at any second. But I didn't. I didn't stop chatting until I dropped Bianca at school. Then I managed to drive around the corner and park before I fell apart. By the time I got to work Jeremy had lined up an appointment with a counsellor. About the only efficient thing I did all morning was to reschedule my 11 am appointment so that we could see him.'

Rebecca became aware that her fists were clenched, fingernails digging into her palm. She forced herself to relax.

Their coffees arrived, but they both ignored them.

'It's called self-harm and apparently is frighteningly prevalent in teenage girls. The counsellor didn't have any answers. He just said that what Bianca is doing is both a way of saying something is wrong and that she doesn't want or need help. Try and make some sense of that if you can.'

Claire kept her eyes locked on Rebecca's, not saying a word. Rebecca cupped her hands around her water glass, feeling the condensation cooling her palms.

'He thinks that the very thing Bianca keeps pushing away – us and the whole family thing – is what she needs. He thinks we need to try and pull her back. That even though she'll kick and scream, deep down she really wants to be part of the family and be loved.'

'Does he think she'll do it again?' Claire spoke quietly.

Rebecca took a shuddering breath. 'He thinks she almost certainly will. And he said it is up to us whether we confront her and tell her we know.'

'Really? Surely you have to talk to her about it?'

Rebecca shook her head. 'He gave us a whole bunch of articles to read – apparently forcing her to stop could make it worse. He called it "removing the coping mechanism". The fact that she is cutting her stomach indicates that she doesn't want anyone to know – if it had been her arms, that could be a cry for help, but this . . .

'So,' she laughed shakily, 'I get to keep doing my Stepford Wives act for the foreseeable future while trying to get her hooked up with someone she can talk to. The counsellor suggested talking to her school and seeing if there is a teacher there who could help. In the meantime we have to force her to eat with us and plan some fun family outings.'

'Is Jeremy helping?' Claire asked, sympathy written all over her face.

'Actually, that's the only good thing that's come out of this whole thing. My husband is talking to me again.' Rebecca paused. 'You know about what I did, I suppose?'

Claire nodded briefly.

'So on a positive note, at least I'm not feeling guilty about that for the moment.'

Rebecca pulled her coffee toward her and dropped a large spoonful of sugar onto the top, watching it sink slowly into the foam.

'Do you think maybe that not knowing her father has anything to do with it?' Claire asked tentatively. 'She seemed pretty upset about it the night you came around to our place.'

With Claire's words, the reality of the situation slammed back down on top of Rebecca. What on earth had she been thinking, unburdening herself to Claire of all people?

Rebecca picked up her handbag and stood up. 'I'm sorry Claire, but I have to go.'

The look of hurt which crossed Claire's face sent a stab of guilt through Rebecca.

'I'll call you,' she lied, and unsteadily wound her way between the tables and out of the cafe door.

Megan

I know this diary is supposed to be about me but I just had to correct something in Claire's last entry.

She said the clothes consultant stall at the school fete went 'quite well'.

Bollocks. It went brilliantly.

She failed to mention that not only did she sell almost half of the clothes (if you'd seen the clothes you would appreciate what a miracle that was in itself). She also gave everyone who came in a personal style guide to take home with them. Colour suggestions, styles – the works. She cut pictures out of magazines to give them an idea of what they were looking for.

This woman has talent.

As for me, I actually did your last task. I baked a cake. Not just any old cake either. A beetroot and chocolate cake, thank you very much.

One of the teachers at school has started a veggie garden. Apparently the only thing he can grow is beetroot. So that's what he's growing. Half a backyard of it the way he tells it. Consequently no one is allowed to leave the staffroom unless they have taken their quota of beetroot.

When I saw the cake recipe in The Courier Mail I knew it was meant to be. Doesn't taste too bad really – considering it is a cake with a vegetable in it. Half a tonne of icing probably helps.

*And baking is as good a way to kill another long, hideous
Sunday as any other.*

As soon as she hit enter, Megan realised she'd probably given
away the fact that she hadn't really done any reading at the
old folks' home. She'd also admitted how much she had come to
hate the weekends – clearly designated family days. She couldn't
even concentrate on the computer game she'd been developing
over the last few months.

Megan took another bite of the cake.

There was no way she was the only one faking it. Ignoring
a slight twinge of guilt, she'd emailed Greg the password to the
site several days ago. His theory was no one was actually doing
anything – they were all just pretending. Megan had warned him
about the entry in which she said it was one of Alice's tasks that
had stopped Megan breaking up with him. He'd found it amus-
ing, though, and Megan had wondered, not for the first time, how
serious he was about her.

She'd bet Rebecca had skipped a few tasks. She hadn't struck
Megan as a joiner – in fact, she'd seemed completely the opposite. And she was busy. Surely she hadn't done everything she
claimed to have?

Oh well, what were they going to do? Smack her?

She eyed the enormous cake in front of her.

It was all right for Alice to tell her to 'bake a cake from
scratch', but she'd be willing to bet Alice's kitchen was rather better equipped than Megan's. Instead of the spring-form cake tin
the recipe required, Megan had only been able to come up with
a small banged-up heart-shaped tin.

The tin had only taken a small part of the enormous amount
of chocolate and beetroot cake batter. Megan had tipped the
remainder into a largish saucepan whose handle had come off.
Much to her surprise, both cakes had risen beautifully.

She now had a lifetime supply of beetroot and chocolate
cake.

Megan's mobile rang.

'Hello.'

'Megan. It's Claire. I'm returning your call.'

Claire didn't sound especially friendly. Megan wondered if she had already read the diary entry she'd posted. Perhaps she was annoyed at Megan for butting in on her diary entries. She decided to ignore Claire's marked lack of enthusiasm.

'Hi,' Megan answered. 'Sorry to bother you. I just wanted to check something.'

There was no response.

'I . . . the principal is sending out a newsletter – a sort of post-mortem of the fete. She wanted to check that it's okay if she puts your mobile number in it. Apparently people have been calling up the school asking for your website and the receptionist is getting dirty about it.'

'I don't have a website.'

Megan rolled her eyes. 'I know you don't yet. But that won't take long. You could tell people it is under construction and you'll call them back with the details. These are great leads for a start-up business like yours.'

'I don't have a business. I was just helping you out.'

'But the mothers loved it. And trust me, they are a tough audience. You can't pass this up.' It's not exactly like you've got anything else to do, Megan added silently.

There was another pause. 'It was a school fete – and it was free. It's not much of a business if no one gives you any money. Besides, I don't know anything about running a business.'

'Me either. But I know this is how a lot of successful businesses start.'

Claire seemed determined to prove she couldn't do it. 'I have no idea how to set up a website.'

Megan suddenly lost her patience. 'Oh for God's sake, Claire. Who the hell made you Captain Negative?' The silence stretched. 'Okay then, well let's not worry about it. I'll see you around.'

Megan went to hang up.

'You really think this is something that could work?' Claire's voice was soft.

'Yeah, I do. And I can set up a website for you. Easy.' As the words came out of Megan's mouth she wondered what the hell she was doing. She was a bystander in this group thing. Helping Claire out was absolutely stupid.

'Don't worry. You've got better things to do. Maybe if I just talk to the people.'

Megan sighed silently. 'No way. That's not how it works these days. Look, it's no big deal. You need to register a domain which costs less than a hundred bucks. I can put up a template website to get you started. It won't be fancy and you'll need to get someone else to put some stuff on it later, but at least people will know how to contact you. Consider it payback for digging me out of a hole at the fete.'

There was yet another silence on the other end of the line. Then a faint, 'Okay.'

Megan was tempted to hang up the phone. What was wrong with this woman? She was obviously standing behind the door when personality was handed out.

'Okay what?' she asked, feeling as though she was speaking to one of her students.

'Okay, I'm in.'

This was like pulling teeth. 'Okaaay. Any ideas on a name?'

'What do you think of "The Real You"?'

Megan didn't even hesitate. 'Nope – sounds like a Dolly Parton song.' She thought for a moment. 'What about "Va Va Voom"?'

'No.' It was Claire's turn to be definite. 'Too trashy. Sounds even more like Dolly Parton. What about "Style File"?'

'Not bad,' Megan said. 'Hang on a second and let me check if the domain name is taken.' She typed for a few seconds.

'No go, someone already has it,' she said. 'It's pretty hard to find a good domain that hasn't been registered these days. Unless you're happy to just get an Australian domain name, that'll be a lot easier.'

Claire laughed. The sound was a marked contrast to her flat tones of earlier.

'Is that a real question? I want dot com of course. For when we open our offices in the States.'

They threw around a few alternatives, all of which were taken.

'How about Fix Your Wardrobe.com?' Claire suggested. 'It's not exactly beautiful, but it's what it's about.'

Megan typed it into the domain search engine.

'Yes! It's free. Right, let's grab it.'

'How do you know all this stuff?' Claire asked while Megan logged into the purchasing page for the domain name website.

'I went out with a computer nerd called Ben for most of uni,' Megan answered. 'Last time I spoke to him he was moving to the States. I haven't heard from him in years, but my guess is he's either a wonder boy at Microsoft or some kind of super computer hacker wanted by the FBI.' She smiled, remembering Ben's total incomprehension that other people could understand so little about computers. It was he who had given Megan her love for computers, but what she knew was just a fraction of the information rattling around in Ben's brilliant mind. All that information hadn't left much room for her, though.

Megan changed the subject. 'So how's this business going to work? Do you have to go shopping with everyone? That'll get old pretty quickly.'

Claire sounded thoughtful. 'Maybe not. People seem to think looking good is done with smoke and mirrors but I don't think it is. It's not even having lots of money – although that does help. If someone sent me honest photos of themselves and answered a few questions, I could give them a pretty good idea of what to look for when they're shopping. Maybe even tell them the best places to go. Do you think anyone would pay money for that?'

'If your popularity at my school is anything to go by I'd say definitely. By the way, what is your full name?'

'Claire Menzies. Why?'

Megan didn't answer, but typed for a few moments.

'All right, I need your credit card number for the domain name and the template website.'

Claire hesitated. 'Okay,' she said finally. 'Give me a second.'

Claire read out the number, hoping there was still enough credit on it, and Megan entered the details.

'Right,' Megan said after a moment. 'You are the new owner of the domain name www.fixyourwardrobe.com. Give me a couple of hours with the template and you will be open for business.'

Alice

The nights were hers.

It was the one time when Alice didn't clean benches or pick up errant shoes. And the hallway was mercifully free of whining calls of 'Muuum . . .' The downside of hours spent awake while everyone else slept was obvious. She'd regret it in the morning when her eyes felt as if they'd been dragged through the sandpit. But while she was awake she felt as though she were in a dream-like bubble.

There was a ritual to it. Once she'd accepted that sleep had slipped from her grasp, she'd slide out of bed and pull the bedroom door shut behind her.

This was the only time she didn't wear shoes and her bare feet would sink into the carpet pile on the steps as she made her way downstairs. She'd flick on a light, not the fluorescent light but a soft lamp, and pull a milk carton from the fridge.

She'd pour the milk into a saucepan and set it on the back of the stove. It took longer than the microwave, but she loved this time. These few minutes while she looked out the kitchen window into the black silkiness of the night and up to the cool glow of the moon.

Milk warm, she'd tip it into a thick mug and curl up on the sofa. No newspapers or school notices to read now. This was when she read a novel – something enthralling that took her away to other worlds and lives. This was how reading used to be – hours which disappeared like minutes lost in a story that was more real than her own. Not even close to the five minutes she'd manage each evening before giving up, too tired to even hold up the book.

The last sip of milk was always cold by the time she'd stretch her legs back to the floor and close her book, folding over a corner of the page. No bookmarks – she'd given up on them years ago, tired of having successive toddlers delight at throwing them to the floor. She'd flick off the light and make her way back through the warm darkness, eyes accustomed to the faint light by the time she reached the bottom of the steps.

She'd stop at the boys' room, breathing in their energy that had been set aside for the night, to be taken up again with their first awake breath of the morning. Then at Ellen's room. In sleep the years seem to slip off. Alice would stand there, drinking in the sight of her daughter looking as she had when boys had still been evil beings who brandished sticks in her direction.

Finally she'd walk back to their bedroom, gently turning the handle to avoid its click waking Andrew. She'd slide beside him, touch her fingers to her lips and run them over the back of his hand. Each time it occurred to her to wonder why she'd never think to do that if he was awake.

Then she'd close her eyes and try to reclaim the sleep which lay heavily over her family.

Tonight, though, the ritual didn't work. As she touched Andrew's hand, her stomach twisted, milk sour in the back of her throat. She slid out of bed again and walked downstairs. Tonight the darkness was threatening, not benevolent, and she turned on the overhead lights to banish the shadows. Finally she sat down at the computer and logged on.

Megan had uploaded some software and changed the format of the website. Alice was now the proud owner of a 'blogger page' to which everyone who had the password could add their diaries. She had to admit it did work much better this way.

Kerry, though, continued to communicate with Alice via email and his latest message was sandwiched between one from the school P&C and a confirmation of an order for a new dishwasher.

He had been frank about his sex life in the initial questionnaire.

The only women I felt comfortable sleeping with after Sandra and I broke up were cougars — at least there are no possible issues with commitment. But I got tired of that pretty quickly.

Alice had asked him what a cougar was in an email yesterday.

She opened his email now and re-read his response.

Cougars are the women you meet in dark bars. The women who look as though they've come down from the mountains to take a mate for the night. The kind that don't want you to stay until morning. The exact opposite of you . . .

Alice knew that letting Kerry continue to think she was single was unfair. She also knew that she was betraying Andrew. Exchanging this type of email was just as wrong as if she were having real conversations with Kerry.

She clicked on the reply button and typed a quick email telling Kerry she was married – apologising for not having told him before. But with her finger poised over the send button, Alice pictured the next day, and the day after that. Long hours in her suburban house, providing for a husband and children who seemed only to care about what she did for them. There had to be more to life than this.

Alice read Kerry's words again, feeling that long-forgotten thrill creep up her spine. Slowly her finger moved to the delete button and she watched her words disappear from the screen. She typed new words: *Perhaps if you did see me in the morning you'd wish you'd left in the night!! Sleep well . . .*

Lillian

The maître d' looked up as Lillian opened the restaurant's front door. His steel-grey hair had been cut in a precise line against his head and his black suit was definitely not off the rack.

'*Bonjour madame . . . mademoiselle*,' he greeted each of them with a polished smile.

Lillian had told Kyla she wanted to go somewhere special to commemorate her mother Nessie's birthday. Now that they were here, though, Lillian wished they'd chosen somewhere less intimidating.

The restaurant was in a huge white building, perched like a squat wedding cake on a sweeping gravel drive. Only a ten minute drive from the Eiffel Tower, it was in the middle of a forest and seemed a world away from the tourist bustle they'd come from.

And if it was one world away from the Champs Élysées, it was at least five worlds away from the Spring Moon, the Chinese restaurant which had been Lillian's sole dining experience until she was about forty.

'*Bonjour monsieur*,' Kyla answered breezily.

Lillian felt relief that Kyla had dealt with the initial greeting, and then shame that she was relying on her daughter. She pulled herself up. This was a once-in-a-lifetime experience. She was going to take it as a compliment to herself that she'd brought up a daughter who could take this in her stride.

'*J'ai une réservation pour Grant.*'

The maître d' smiled welcomingly. '*Oui, mademoiselle.* This way please.'

He hadn't even looked at the reservation book and, despite herself, Lillian felt important. From the sidelong smile Kyla threw at her, she felt the same.

They followed him through the cavernous reception area, moulded plaster cherubs encircling the ceiling. The dining room and the small one beyond it were totally empty. Twelve o'clock was clearly the time for lunch. No one other than a naive suburban Australian mother and daughter would arrive fifteen minutes before that. They'd had trouble getting taxis over the last few days and Lillian had insisted they leave with plenty of time. That of course had meant that they'd picked up a taxi immediately and arrived here too early.

The maître d' offered them a choice of tables – none near the window though, Lillian noticed. Clearly they were reserved for those with enough class to know what time lunch started.

Lillian sat in the chair pulled out for her and, with clammy fingers, flattened the glowing white linen serviette which had been laid solicitously on her lap.

The ceilings soared above them. Heavy butter-yellow drapes framed the huge glass doors which led onto a terrace but today were closed against the unseasonably cool autumn weather. Thick cream carpet extended across the room and she had a sudden vision of what it would look like with a glass of red wine spilt on it.

Kyla leaned across toward her. 'Mum – relax. You look like you're expecting the guillotine.'

Lillian managed a smile before a waiter returned with their menus. Kyla opened hers briefly and reached across to her mother's.

'Excuse me. Yep, I thought so. You and I need to swap menus.'

She exchanged the heavy books.

'Yours had the prices, mine didn't,' she answered her mother's inquisitive look. 'I figured it was better the other way around.

'Phew . . .' she exhaled. 'I was right.'

'Really, is it horrendous?' Lillian asked worriedly.

'Not at all, it's very reasonable,' Kyla lied blithely. 'Order what you want. Actually,' she corrected herself, 'let me order. I have an idea.'

The waiter returned so silently Lillian wondered if he'd been hiding behind the metres of curtains. 'Would you prefer that we speak in English?' he asked.

'*Non, merci*,' Kyla answered. '*Je ne parle pas bien français, mais j'essaye.*'

She smiled at Lillian. 'That means that my French is lousy but I try. It also means I can order anything I like for my unsuspecting mother and she won't be able to complain.'

The waiter's practised smile softened into something more genuine. '*Très bien mademoiselle. Est-ce que vous avez choisi?*'

'*Oui . . . le menu dégustation, s'il vous plaît.*'

He nodded, without writing anything down. '*Merci mademoiselle.*'

'You know, I'd pay anything in a place where everyone calls me mademoiselle,' Kyla whispered as the waiter disappeared as quietly as he'd arrived. 'In Australia I'm thirty and not married, which equals sad and desperate. Here I'm a mademoiselle. Is it any wonder the French consider themselves more civilised than everyone else?'

Many times over the past week, Lillian had been awed at how well Kyla fitted into this alien world. When she'd first come through immigration at Charles de Gaulle Airport she'd scanned the crowd unsuccessfully for her daughter. It wasn't until Kyla had waved wildly and hurried toward her that she saw her. In her long cream trench coat, and with a hair cut that could not have been done anywhere but Paris, she blended in perfectly with the locals.

Lillian looked at her now. Her blonde curls were cropped to jaw level and her hazel eyes were large and clear. Kyla had grown into her looks in the last ten years. She was still not beautiful,

Lillian's nose guaranteed that. But with the French chic she'd acquired, she was definitely very attractive. Kyla maintained that her French was awful, but to Lillian's ears it was extraordinary. She had taken several days of holidays since Lillian had arrived and had shown Lillian around the city like a local.

Looking at her daughter, Lillian felt a surge of pride. Kyla's job was based at the Sorbonne, Paris's largest university, recruiting foreign students for Australian universities. She'd come for a year and had been so successful that she was still there three years later. Being with her again, slipping almost instantly back into their loving relationship, Lillian realised how much she had missed having Kyla near her.

'Now,' Kyla continued, 'I ordered the full degustation menu – about seven courses, I think. It'll take most of the afternoon, but there's nowhere we need to be and I have a feeling Nana would approve.'

Lillian felt sick at how much this would cost, but another waiter appeared at their table before she could say anything.

'*Voulez vous un apéritif?*'

The only word that Lillian recognised was 'aperitif' and immediately her mind flashed to the McWilliams dry sherry she'd drunk for years as a before-dinner tipple. She couldn't remember exactly when people had stopped drinking that – long enough ago to make it very uncool now. A smile curved at the corners of her mouth at the thought of it.

'I thought this occasion called for champagne,' Kyla said as Lillian returned from her 1970s reverie.

The waiter returned, pushing a silver trolley bearing four ice buckets.

'You're kidding,' Kyla muttered under her breath. 'It's a bloody champagne trolley – we get to choose which champagne we want!'

Sure enough the sommelier lifted each bottle of champagne, the accompanying descriptions lost on both of them.

Lillian had noticed that one of the champagnes was pink and caught the word 'rosé'. It seemed like a good enough differentiating factor.

'Ah, the rosé, *s'il vous plaît*,' she managed haltingly.

Kyla chose the same and they lifted their glasses in a toast.

'To Nana,' Kyla said.

'To Mum,' Lillian replied.

She thought of Nessie and various scenes flashed through her mind. Easter-egg hunts where her mother had led balls of wool from each child's nest back to their bedroom. The birthday cards she used to sketch for each of them. Her mother straightening from digging in the garden and leaning on the pitchfork to survey the flowerbed.

Kyla was looking closely at her. 'This is supposed to be a celebration, Mum. Don't be unhappy.'

'I'm not, darling,' Lillian said truthfully. 'I am so glad that Mum died before she got too sick and before she couldn't live with me any more. It was the right time. If she can see us, I know she'd be delighted.'

'I hate to think how many bottles of instant coffee this bill would cover,' Kyla mused.

Lillian laughed. Nessie had never shaken the habit of economising, which she'd learned painfully during the Depression. She'd pore over the supermarket catalogues when washing powder and coffee were on special and wheel her trolley to Coles and stock up. It didn't matter that she was the only one who drank instant coffee, or that Lillian and Nessie's washing was minimal. A bargain was still a bargain as far as Nessie was concerned.

Any time Lillian objected to the pile of jars at the bottom of the pantry, Nessie would shake her head. 'They won't go off, Lillian. You'll use them, trust me. At that price, it's a crime not to buy them.' It had been eighteen months since she had died and Lillian still had a cupboard full.

Kyla interrupted Lillian's thoughts. 'Well, I've done a bit of wining and dining since I've been here, but this is definitely the fanciest place I've been to.

'I was chatting to the head of my department at a function last week . . .' She stopped suddenly. 'Actually, that was a lie,' she corrected herself. 'I was haltingly speaking to him in French the other day and told him I wanted a nice restaurant to take you to lunch. He immediately said this was where we had to come and wouldn't even suggest anywhere else.'

She looked around. 'He's done well.'

Lillian took another large sip of her champagne. She sat the crystal glass back on the table, watching the delicate baby pink bubbles shimmer in fine lines to the surface. She could feel the alcohol whispering through her limbs, simultaneously relaxing and enlivening her. It occurred to her that the last time she had drunk champagne was at Alice's evening. An urge to tell Kyla about that and about her illness struck her, but she pushed it away. This was a time to celebrate that she was here today – drinking pink champagne in a ridiculously fancy restaurant with her daughter.

She smiled at Kyla. 'I am very glad to be here,' she said simply.

'Me too, Mum,' Kyla replied.

They looked at each other for a moment and Lillian thanked the divine hand that had given her this daughter.

'Now admit it,' she smiled. 'You're very glad that you didn't get that tattoo.'

Kyla laughed suddenly. A man at the closest table turned his head and Lillian realised that almost a third of the restaurant was now occupied. Lillian met the man's eyes, feeling guilty that they'd broken the decorous murmur which was the only noise she could hear. But instead of a disapproving frown, the man was smiling slightly. He was seated at one of the tables next to the windows and had paused in the act of handing his menu to a waiter. Lillian smiled in reply and turned back to Kyla.

Their champagne disappeared quickly and was replaced by a bottle of white wine Kyla ordered.

The sommelier filled two glasses, draped the neck of the bottle with a linen serviette and placed it reverently in a silver ice bucket.

'That's the thing about places like this,' Kyla whispered as he left. 'They treat our wine, which happens to be the cheapest on the menu, the same way they would something that cost ten times the price.'

A pair of waiters arrived simultaneously, distracting Lillian from any reply.

They placed a silver chalice in front of each of them and disappeared as quickly and quietly as they had arrived.

The food in front of Lillian looked like some type of sculpture, rather than something to be eaten. A bright green puree had a wafer balanced in it at an amazing angle and was surrounded by a tangerine froth.

'Don't ask me what it is, because I have absolutely no idea,' Kyla pre-empted. 'One of my reasons for choosing the degustation menu was that I didn't have to try and make sense of all the choices.'

Lillian dipped her spoon into the dish and put a small amount of the food into her mouth. The flavours spread across her palate.

'I don't think it really matters what it is,' she said. 'It's absolutely amazing.'

'It's so good to have you here, Mum,' Kyla said. 'I've been worried about you since Dad died.'

'It's been a big change,' Lillian acknowledged. 'He was such a good man and a wonderful husband and father.'

'Mum . . .' Kyla started tentatively.

Lillian looked at her.

'Dad was a great man – we all loved him. But you know, he wasn't perfect. He was great when he was around, but when he was in la-la medical land it was like we didn't count. None of us.

'Do you remember that time when I ran in the Queensland Athletics carnival?'

Lillian nodded. 'Your dad didn't make it.'

'No,' Kyla said. 'I pretended it was okay, but really it wasn't. That was a huge thing for me and he was stuck giving some damn paper somewhere.'

'It was a big conference, he was supposed to have spoken earlier but everything was pushed back . . .' Lillian trailed off, looking at Kyla. Her expression said that she'd heard this all before.

'I know, Mum. It's all right, it didn't make me turn to drugs or prostitution. But he should have been there.'

Lillian was silent, not knowing what to say.

'Mum, I didn't tell you that to make you sad. I just hate that you have this ridiculously idealised picture of Dad in your head. He was a good man, but he wasn't perfect. You lived in his shadow your whole life, working around what he wanted. I loved him too, but your life hasn't gone with his.'

Lillian began to speak.

'Nope,' Kyla interrupted. 'We're not going to debate this here. This is a celebration. For Nana, but also for you. I know how big a thing it was for you to come to France by yourself. So just make it the beginning. Life's out there, Mum – you've just got to grab it.'

Lillian smiled slowly. 'How'd you get so smart?' she asked fondly. 'Okay, sweetheart. I guess on that note we'd better order another bottle of wine.'

Each dish was presented by silent but attentive waiters and proved to be extraordinary.

Lillian felt more relaxed than she could remember. She looked around. They were clearly the only foreigners in the room.

As they ate, they speculated on their fellow diners. From a pair of politicians, to businessmen, to a very well-heeled couple who looked as though they did this regularly. The couple both wore wedding rings, but whether they were married to each other, Lillian and Kyla couldn't decide.

The man Lillian had smiled at earlier was the only person dining by himself. He looked in his seventies, was incredibly suave and incredibly French. Kyla's theory was that he was a hero from the Resistance.

'Oh no,' Kyla exclaimed. 'Look behind you.' She gestured at a trolley being wheeled to their table, loaded with handcrafted sweets and chocolates.

'You have to have some,' she ordered. 'It's obligatory.'

They both managed some chocolates as they sipped their coffees.

Kyla drained the last of her espresso from the tiny cup and placed it carefully back on the saucer.

'Well, I do believe that's it. I think it's time for the bill.'

Lillian nodded reluctantly, sorry to leave this glorious bubble of an afternoon. She looked around and noticed that there was only one other table of people still in the restaurant.

Kyla signalled to the waiter. '*Ah, l'addition s'il vous plaît,*' she smiled.

'*Oui mademoiselle,*' he replied, disappearing again.

He was back within moments and spoke to Kyla, gesturing toward the table next to the window.

She shook her head and spoke to him in French.

The waiter handed Kyla a piece of heavy cream paper.

'*Merci,*' she replied, a bemused look on her face.

Kyla looked at the paper and handed it to her mother. 'You're not going to believe this, Mum. But apparently the man who was sitting at that table has already paid our bill.'

Lillian glanced at the now empty table of the resistance hero and then down at the paper which bore the restaurant's name. There were no contact details, not even a name. Just a message in red ink.

What a pleasure to watch such happiness.

Kerry

So I took out an extra line of credit to fill up the tank and took the Aston Martin out for a spin this morning.

I haven't done it in more than a year so I figure it qualifies for my last task.

Went up to Mt Glorious. It was a great day and, except for the hordes of motorbike riders intent on killing themselves on the next bend, fairly peaceful.

Still it didn't work for me. I just kept thinking of all the crap I was pumping into the air. I didn't even stop for a coffee. Just turned around and came home.

Maybe next time I'll take Annie . . .

He was going to cause a car accident. Or be the victim of road rage. Already he'd had two irate drivers honk at him as he was slowing down to take a corner.

'What are yaw, mate? A little old lady?'

He wondered if it would make any difference if he'd made up a sign and stuck it to the back window of his ute. *Fairy on board.*

Then again, as he was the only one travelling in the car, that wouldn't be such a great look. It would probably only increase his chances of getting beaten up.

He used his hand to signal that he was slowing down and

pulled up outside Sandra's shopfront. The parking situation was even more diabolical than usual and there wasn't a spare spot within sight. He hesitated, then pushed the gear lever into park and pulled on the handbrake. A hundred metre walk in thirty degree heat could just about destroy his creation. He was prepared to take whatever the parking inspectors could throw at him.

Pink and white balloons were tied to the door off to one side of the shop. He could hear laughter and excited screams coming from inside and glanced nervously at the cake.

Sandra had begged him to buy the cake. She knew someone, she said, who could design just about any cake you could imagine. They could even pass it off as his if he really wanted them to.

When he'd refused, she'd rolled her eyes just like she had when they were together. Strangely, though, it no longer bugged him.

It wasn't some crazy test of love, she'd said. Annie knew he loved her. Baking a birthday cake from scratch wouldn't prove anything. Besides, remember the last time he'd made Annie a cake?

He'd laughed with her at the time, savouring the intimacy of a shared memory. The night before Annie's first birthday, he and Sandra had decided to make her a teddy-bear cake. In the process they'd opened a bottle of wine, then another, and by the time they were finished, they had moved on to Drambuie shots – the only thing left in the cupboard. Consequently, both they and the cake had looked rather the worse for wear the next morning.

But something in one of Alice's tasks had struck a chord. Traditions. Family traditions.

Annie's birthday cakes could be his thing each year. It had seemed like a sensational idea at the time.

So with Sandra still rolling her eyes, he'd told Annie that he'd make it for her and asked what she'd like. A balloon? The number four? Maybe another teddy?

It was then Annie had hit him with the fairy thing. Long after he could gracefully back out.

She wanted a fairy cake. Not to be confused with fairy cakes.

She wanted a cake made into a fairy. A beautiful one. Like the ones in *Flower Fairies of the Garden*, a book Kerry had given her shortly after he and Sandra had broken up. According to Sandra, Annie had slept with it under her pillow for months.

And the dress had to be red. With tiny pink and yellow flowers.

'Just so you know, I'm holding this for someone.'

Kerry turned toward the voice.

Sandra was standing beside the front door, guiltily holding a burning cigarette.

As long as he'd known her, Sandra had smoked when she was stressed. Never more than one and never at any other time.

She was one of the few people he knew who could go for months, sometimes years, between cigarettes. No matter where they had lived, though, there was always a half-packet stashed somewhere 'just in case'.

He smiled at her. 'Smoking over a four year old's birthday. C'mon now. Surely not?'

She exhaled and gestured him closer. She really did look wound up, he noticed.

'It's not the four year olds,' she hissed. 'It's the parents. I thought they'd just drop the kids and run, but they all stayed.' Her voice rose at the end of the sentence and she took another long pull on the cigarette.

'Thank God for your parents. Your dad went out and bought some champagne and they've been loading the parents up with it for the last hour.'

Kerry tried not to smile. This was clearly no laughing matter.

'And you're late. Tell me the cake is all right. Annie's been asking about it all morning.'

'Sorry. I had to do some . . . running repairs.' He ignored her question and pretended not to notice her worried look.

A bit more than running repairs, he thought as he followed Sandra into the house, holding the cake container gingerly.

He'd been determined to prove to Sandra he didn't need to cheat. He'd visited a cake-decorating supply shop and thrown himself on the mercy of the woman behind the counter.

She'd sent him home, armed with almost a hundred dollars' worth of professional-grade icing supplies that she swore would help him create his masterpiece.

And he'd totally ballsed it up.

The monstrosity he had created looked more like roadkill than a fairy (red being the only colour he'd managed to get right).

Just then there was an earsplitting shriek and Annie, dressed in a pink tutu, came flying down the hallway like some kind of mad banshee. Out of habit, he stepped in front of Sandra as she hid the cigarette butt in the palm of her hand.

Kerry had only just managed to pass the cake to Sandra before Annie jumped into his arms.

'Daddy, I'm foooouuuuuuuurrrrrrrrrr.'

He couldn't help but laugh.

'Annie, I kkkkkknnnnnnnnooooooowwwwwww.'

He swung her around and set her back on her feet.

'Did you bring my fairy cake?'

Kerry nodded.

'Can I see it?'

Laughing, he shook his head. 'Why don't you and your mum go out the back with everyone else? I'll follow you in a minute. With the cake,' he added as Annie's face started to crumple.

He turned to Sandra, taking the cake back off her. 'I just need to add a few finishing touches.'

Once they had gone, Kerry walked into the kitchen and prised the lid off the plastic cake container.

He'd gone to bed at midnight. It would look better in the morning, he'd assured himself. It was just that he was too close to it all and too tired. Thankfully he'd arranged for his assistant to handle the stall at the market by himself the next morning.

Unfortunately, the cake had looked just as bad at six the next morning. Worse possibly.

He'd run through the options in his mind. His mother? Her cooking was a family joke and not a small contributing factor in his leaving home at nineteen. She'd have bought a sponge cake from the supermarket. And asking Sandra for help was clearly not an option.

Which really only left calling in the experts. He'd pulled the Yellow Pages toward him, wondering at what time cake shops opened. Surely if he offered enough money someone could produce a fairy cake for him. He'd tried, that was all he could do. Maybe next year he'd be able to make Annie's cake himself.

Fifteen minutes later, he'd put down the phone, defeated. He'd called every cake maker in Brisbane. All he'd got was answer phones telling him to call back later. Later would be way too late.

That was it, the end of the line. He had no one else to call for help.

And then a thought had struck him.

He'd turned on the computer, filling the kettle and finding coffee while he waited for it to start up. A mug of steaming coffee in hand, he'd settled himself in front of it and logged onto Alice's website.

This is an appeal of gravest importance, he'd begun.

Without much hope he'd sat down at the table nursing his coffee.

He forced himself to drink half of it before he leaned over to press the refresh button to update the website.

Miraculously there was an entry from Rebecca.

Okay, you have now entered my zone of expertise. Homemade birthday cakes made under extreme time pressure and duress. You will need – a cake tin shaped like a doll's skirt with a hole in the middle, packet cake mix and a Barbie. My guess is that you have none of these so I will drop them around this morning. You then cook the cake, stick the Barbie in the hole in the middle, ice the skirt with whatever you want, and Bob's your uncle. Email me your address – I'll be there by eight. Rgds Rebecca.

Rebecca had arrived at seven fifty-eight and parked outside, motor still running.

With her hair pulled in a ponytail and a white T-shirt over denim shorts, she'd looked tired but as attractive as he'd remembered. Thrusting a plastic bag into his hand, she'd brushed away his offers of thanks.

'Good luck. And by the way, if any of the mothers ask, of course you made the cake from scratch.' She'd smiled slightly and then clattered down the steps.

Even the enormous cake container had come from Rebecca – a Post-it note on top which said, *Figured you'd need this too.*

He looked at the cake now and felt a swell of pride.

Gingerly he slid his hands inside the cake container and grasped the edges of the plate. Inch by inch he raised it slowly until it was free. Balancing it on his palm he rotated it, examining it from all sides.

Red skirt, covered with pink and yellow flowers. Admittedly, a harsh judge could suggest that the flowers looked more like splodges. But anyone who knew anything about fairies would realise that Fairy Tatania's skirt had been made for her by elves who had in fact given painters like Degas the idea for Impressionist painting . . .

Fairy Tatania was also rather well endowed, Kerry thought with satisfaction. It looked like Disco Barbie was the first one Rebecca had been able to lay her hands on, but beggars couldn't be choosers.

Depositing the cake on the bench, Kerry pulled a pack of candles out of his back pocket.

'Shit!' he exclaimed looking at what was now a crushed packet housing a collection of small wax pieces hanging off string.

Sandra must have some birthday candles here somewhere. His eyes went instantly to the drawer to the right of the cutlery. Opening it up, he found the junk drawer which he'd expected. Rubber bands tangled with pens, and a bus timetable had wedged itself in the top of the drawer. Kerry wrenched it free, pulling the drawer out as far as it would go. A stack of letters rested on top and he put them on the bench while he picked amongst the loose change and hair bands. A handful of gritty candles were in the back corner and he pulled four out triumphantly. As he piled the letters back in, the envelope on top slipped to one side.

The letter underneath had a solicitor's letterhead and the

words *Final Demand* printed in bold type. Kerry read the words quickly. After a pause he replaced the envelope on top and pushed the drawer closed.

He stuck the candles into the cake, lit them and carried Fairy Tatania toward the gaggle of small fairies in the backyard.

Claire

I think I'm getting better at this lousy dinner stuff. Two nights ago I made scrambled eggs. Despite my intentions to make it easy and fast, I found myself thinking it wouldn't be that much harder to make a frittata. But then I could almost feel Alice looking over my shoulder saying, 'It doesn't have to be fabulous. In fact it doesn't have to even be good.' I'm considering adopting that as my new mantra.

Claire pulled up outside a nondescript warehouse and checked the address. She was in the right place. At least parking wasn't a problem at this ridiculous hour of the morning. Surely Alice had got something wrong. Nothing at all was happening here.

A white four-wheel drive pulled up behind Claire's car. Claire watched in her rear-vision mirror as the driver looked straight ahead – directly at Claire it seemed. The driver's door opened and a woman stepped out and walked toward Claire's car.

She stopped beside the door and Claire wound down the window.

'Hello Alice,' she said.

Alice smiled apologetically. 'Sorry I didn't tell you I'd be here. Thought it might be a bit much for you. After all, telling you to do volunteer work is a bit clichéd. It's just that, well, this is a good place and I thought you might like to give us a hand.'

Claire looked at her for a moment before nodding. 'Okay.' She opened the door and stepped out, following Alice back to her car.

'I collect yesterday's bread from a bakery nearby and drop it down a few mornings a week,' Alice explained as she opened the door at the back of the car and pulled out several large shopping bags. 'I started years ago when the kids were tiny and I was up early anyway. The kids don't come any more but I do.'

Alice smiled. 'All right, follow me.'

There was already a handful of other people at work in the large kitchen. Alice introduced Claire, but greetings were perfunctory. It was early, they were all there with a purpose, not to chat. Alice's bread was taken out of the bags for sandwiches. An older woman set Claire to work chopping pineapple. Alice left soon afterwards with a small wave across to Claire.

As they got underway, people relaxed and conversations started. Claire was mostly silent though, concentrating on her job. An hour later they began loading the sandwiches and fruit into big steel bins, then carting them outside to the van which had arrived earlier. Large urns were filled with hot water and two of the volunteers climbed into the back of the van.

'Right, that's it.' The older woman who seemed to be in charge rubbed her hands down the side of her jeans and headed back inside.

She turned back when she realised Claire hadn't moved.

'You can go with them if you want.'

Claire smiled slightly. 'I'd just get in the way. I didn't think it would all be so easy, that's all.'

The older woman smiled. 'It is when we've lots of helping hands – you should see the carry-on when there's only a couple of us.'

She hesitated. 'Will you be coming back?'

'Yes, I think so,' Claire replied.

'Great,' the other woman answered brusquely. 'You're a champion fruit chopper. It normally takes two people to do what you did this morning.'

Claire smiled slightly and headed for her car.

She pushed the radio on and pulled away from the footpath. A recording of a Boyer Lecture was on her normal radio station. It was about the nuclear threat facing the world. Claire knew she should be interested. It was the kind of thing she tried to listen to, something to casually refer to at a dinner party so she didn't appear to be a vacuous housewife, but she couldn't face bad news at the moment. She stabbed at the dial and the radio settled on a commercial station, with a witty duo doing the drive-time show.

Claire was normally asleep at this time, or nursing a coffee trying to decide how to fill the day ahead. Although she was on her way home, rather than to work, she felt strangely useful.

A song came on. 'Uptown Girl' by Billy Joel.

As soon as the first chords came through the speakers, Claire felt unreasonably happy. She turned the volume up, the music filling the car.

She sang along as she caught the good edge of an amber light, gliding through the empty intersection. The music carried her through the city, where the earliest office goers were pulling into empty carparking stations. The song finished and Claire felt deflated, wishing she could rewind it. But then another song took its place. 'Wake Me Up Before You Go-Go.'

Claire laughed out loud. There was a lot to be said for commercial radio. Peter loved music and always knew what was new and popular. There was no room for eighties hits CDs in their collection. Turning the volume knob even higher she let the music take her away, memories of George Michael posters and fluoro-lettered T-shirts filling her mind.

The song was just finishing when she pulled up outside home.

Claire sat for a moment, engine running, singing along wildly. The last bars sounded and she reluctantly took the key out of the ignition and opened the door.

It was only then that she saw Peter standing several metres away. His car keys were in his hand, bag slung over his shoulder, courier style.

Claire stood up, her arm resting on the top of the door.

'Hi,' he said. 'How was it?'

'It was good.' She hesitated. 'I think I'll go again.'

Peter nodded.

'Off to work?' she asked rhetorically.

The silence stretched. Claire truly didn't know what to say to the man she'd lived with for seventeen years. She felt as though their final common thread had snapped after the fight about the house plans. Not because of Peter's concern about the costs, that wasn't new. It was the realisation that he believed her renovations were an indulgence, not something skilful and valuable to them. Everything had shifted slightly now she knew what he really thought.

Peter raised his hand and walked toward his car, parked a little further down the street.

Claire was still watching him when he turned back.

'You know – I haven't seen you look that happy in a lot of years.'

Claire said nothing, following him with her eyes as he drove off. She only moved once the car was out of sight.

Lillian

Lillian reached the top step and stopped. After the concrete and tiles of the Metro system, the beauty of the street was astounding.

She stood still, people flowing around her.

The street was lined with aristocratic buildings, the colour of the plaster ranging from clotted cream to café au lait. Wrought-iron balconies decorated the buildings in graceful swirls. Large, flat, charcoal-coloured stones covered the roadway, and huge plane trees sat in the middle of footpaths. The street was crowded, people swirling around the small tabacs selling papers and drinks.

Parisians didn't dress formally as Lillian had always imagined, but in a dress code that looked something like 'impeccable casual'. Jeans or soft trousers were matched with light jackets, evidence of a well-founded suspicion of the autumn weather. The only people wearing open-toed shoes were tourists. The locals' feet were shod in cut-away flats or boots.

There was a cafe on the corner, its awning stretched out toward the footpath, rain from a shower earlier that morning glistening on the canvas. Underneath were small round tables, just big enough for two drinks. Nestled next to each were chairs, green and cream plastic strips woven to create a wicker type look. The morning was cool and only a few of the outdoor tables were occupied.

Lillian sat down, moving her scarf to better cover her neck. There was no way she was going inside and missing this view.

A waiter paused imperiously in front of her, taking her order for a coffee with a nod.

Kyla was at work. They'd caught the Metro together, Kyla sending her mother off the train at Saint-Germain-des-Prés station and continuing on her journey.

Lillian and Kyla had been on this street the week before, but being here by herself was a totally different experience for Lillian.

She smelt cigarette smoke drifting over her and breathed it in. She followed the white tendrils back to their owner, a man with dark chin-length hair pushed behind his ears, leather-jacket clad arm draped over a chair beside him.

It was almost forty years since Lillian had smoked regularly, but the smell suddenly made her crave it. It was a habit she'd taken up when she was a teenager, as a lot of people had in those days. Even then she'd known it had to be bad for her, and she had given up soon after she was married. But she had sometimes managed the occasional cigarette sneaked around the back of the shed, so the children couldn't see.

Lillian pictured David in those days. He'd been lean and muscled, playing competition squash two nights a week. Their marriage had been good, very good. They'd complemented each other well. He was gregarious, making friends without thinking about it. But it was Lillian who built those friendships and kept them going in the times when David was buried in another research project.

David had loved the children fiercely. But he focused on things intensely, to the exclusion of everything else. When it was the children, he was fun and constantly entertaining and they were besotted with him. But when it was work that took his focus, both Lillian and the children suffered.

Lillian had always known that. She'd become accustomed to it and had thought the children had too. But after Kyla's remarks the other day, it seemed that perhaps they hadn't.

Lillian thought back on those years. She thought of the times

David had worked until dawn and was unreasonably grumpy at being unable to sleep in the small family house. She thought also of the times when she'd realised halfway through a conversation that he had no knowledge of, and in fact no interest in, what she was saying.

Those bad things had been overlaid in Lillian's memory by the many good times. Perhaps Kyla was right, more and more of the bad things kept dropping off Lillian's memory while the good ones glowed brighter.

The waiter deposited a cup of coffee in front of Lillian, tucking the bill under a clip on the edge of the table.

Lillian ignored both, staring out at the street. Somehow things seemed more possible here than at home. She hadn't even thought of having another relationship. But perhaps it wasn't as ridiculous as it sounded. Kyla was right. David had been wonderful, but he was not an irreplaceable demigod.

As she watched, a man turned away from the tabac stand on the footpath with a packet of cigarettes in his hands. He ripped open the cellophane packet, flipped a cigarette into his mouth and leaned over to light it, hands cupped against the breeze.

Lillian stood up and walked across to the stand.

Too late, she realised she had no idea of the French word for cigarette.

The man behind the counter looked at her, eyebrows raised.

'Uh, les Galloises, please,' Lillian managed with sudden inspiration. Of course, if she was to smoke in Paris it could be no other brand.

She strode back to her table, intoxicated by her bravery. She was in a strange city, free of her real life. Why not have a cigarette? After all, lung cancer was unlikely to get her before the multiple sclerosis did. Lillian pushed away the thoughts of her illness which threatened to crash down on top of her if she let them.

Then she realised she had nothing with which to light the cigarette. She could go back to the tabac, but somehow that wasn't the point.

Her euphoria disappeared as quickly as it had arrived. She pictured herself, someone with wrinkled skin and sunspots on the back of her hands, sneaking a cigarette like a teenager. And as for contemplating another relationship, who was she kidding?

Lilian sat there, cigarette packet in her hands.

'Madame?'

The voice came from beside her.

She turned. It was the man who had been smoking at the other table.

'Would you like a light?'

His English was excellent but soaked in an accent that could not be more French.

He held out a silver cigarette lighter and flipped back the top.

Lillian hesitated for a moment and then put a cigarette in her mouth, leaning forward toward the flame and breathing in deeply.

She opened her eyes and exhaled.

'*Merci monsieur,*' she said.

Rebecca

I pretend like everything is normal. I pretend (although weakly, I suspect) that I still care what Bianca wears, that her music is too aggressive, that her latest report card has her slipping to Cs and Ds.

Whereas actually all I want is for her to stop hurting.

We do outings now that seem like a macabre game of charades. Pick the happy family. All of us piling into the car to drive to Wellington Point for fish and chips on a Saturday afternoon. Hell, we even went ten-pin bowling. Bianca was so mortified that she wouldn't join in, just sat there, glaring at the pins.

And every night when I know Bianca is in her deepest sleep I sneak into her bedroom. I stand over her bed and look at her stomach, desperately hoping not to see fresh wounds that will show my little girl has hurt herself again.

Alice, you say you don't know what task to set me when these things are going on. That anything you think of seems too trivial. As you say, you're not a counsellor. But to be honest, I don't think the counsellor has any simple answers either. Find something you used to like doing together and do it again, you say . . . Easier said than done . . .

Rebecca turned back to the start of the company profile she was attempting to read. After a few minutes she realised she was still taking in nothing and pushed the file away. The chrome hands of the clock above the kitchen bench showed it to be just before 6 am.

The first rumbles of morning traffic had always woken her. Normally she'd be able to fall back asleep for another hour or so, but that was impossible these days. So she'd push herself out of bed, make a coffee and do an hour's work before anyone else stirred.

Bizarrely, while the rest of her life was falling apart, she seemed to be able to do no wrong at work. After the loss of the candidate she'd met with the day she'd snuck out early, she'd found someone even better and the client was ecstatic. And an industry publication had named her as the best financial executive recruiter in Brisbane. Her boss Simon was all smiles and dropped into her office several times a day to chat.

She should have been delighted. This was the pinnacle of a steep, boulder-strewn mountain which she'd stepped onto the day she'd discovered she was pregnant with Bianca.

For as long as she could remember, Rebecca had wanted to be a doctor. She wasn't a genius but had studied much more than her friends to try to make it happen. The day she received her university entrance score had been a vindication of all her hard work. She'd accepted a place to study medicine two days before she realised her period wasn't just very late.

Rebecca had always done everything right. She'd been one of the best swimmers in the state and had been dux of the school each year. And she was going to become a surgeon.

Getting pregnant at seventeen wasn't something that happened to girls like her.

Her normally unflappable parents were horrified. As Rebecca watched them try to come to grips with the new reality she'd created with two words, she felt all of her achievements crumbling. Her father looked up from the table and the disappointment in his eyes cut deeper than any angry words.

At one stage Rebecca's mother had gently raised the

possibility of an abortion. Rebecca had thought about it when she first found out she was having a baby. It would have fixed everything and put her back in the position she should have been in. But somehow she couldn't. She had created a new life and she would have to deal with the consequences, whatever they were.

They had eventually worked out a plan. Rebecca would take a year out from study. A gap year. Lots of people did it.

She worked as a receptionist in a doctor's surgery until Bianca was born. The next year she started at university, leaving Bianca at home with her mother. But it didn't work out. She was totally different from the other students, whose biggest dilemma was whether to go to the recreation club or a local pub after classes on Friday. Studying with a six month old baby who woke twice a night was extremely difficult and she didn't see the first semester out.

So she found a part-time job in the mail room at an advertising agency. It didn't pay a lot, but enough to make her feel like she wasn't a total burden on her parents. She'd lost contact with her school friends and, despite her mother's urging, rarely went out without Bianca. Those early years were a blur, the only thing Rebecca remembered was her surprise at the love she felt for her daughter.

By the time Bianca began school, Rebecca had started as a secretary at a recruitment company. Someone left suddenly and Rebecca was given some files to handle. She did the job well and was given some more. Finally she earned enough to enable her to move the two of them into a little flat in an inner-city suburb. Two years later she was promoted, which meant a nicer flat and a bit more confidence that money would actually come out when she put her key card into the automatic teller.

Then someone from Hartman Consultants had called and asked her if she'd be interested in moving. She was. Within two years, she had taken her boss's job. Now she was the head of a team and, if the magazine sitting on her desk was to be believed, the best in Brisbane at what she did.

When she'd met Jeremy and become pregnant with Sam, she'd believed that she could have it all. Career, family, happy marriage . . . But since she'd found out about Bianca hurting herself all that had seemed like a farce.

When she wasn't worrying about Bianca, all Rebecca could think about was how tired she was. Tired of trying to manage a desperately unhappy teenager and a three year old, a nanny, a house cleaner and an ironing lady. Tired of trying to be a good wife, to keep a house stocked with food, the family clothed and all utilities connected. Tired of trying to convince a boss and colleagues that she was as focused and committed as them.

Lately she'd not been able to stop herself thinking about what would happen if she stopped and just let the balls drop where they may. The idea was seductive and Rebecca felt like an ancient sailor lured onto rocks by a mermaid's song. Right now, though, she didn't care. If she could sleep on the rocks that would be enough. If someone would bring her a cup of coffee when she woke up, she would sell her eternal soul.

. Sam's sandy head appeared around the doorway. He was grasping his teddy bear and looked like he'd only just woken up.

'Hello sweetheart,' Rebecca smiled. The mornings always brought with them a sense of expectation that maybe today everything would be okay. Except that it never was.

Sam smiled and ran over to her, burying his face in her legs. She spread her fingers through his hair and held him close to her. Having him there made her remember suddenly why she needed to keep going, why it was all unquestioningly worthwhile.

'Did you have a good sleep?'

Sam nodded solemnly, although she doubted he had any idea what a bad sleep was. He fell asleep at seven each night and didn't stir for the next eleven hours.

'Come up here.'

Rebecca reached down and pulled him onto her lap. He curled into her shoulder and she held him close. After a nasty spate of two year old tantrums, Sam had returned to the even-tempered toddler he'd always been. Definitely Jeremy's chromosomal input Rebecca had decided long ago.

'Where's Anka?' Sam asked.

Bianca was unquestionably Sam's favourite. The attachment was mutual. Bianca had been besotted with him since the first time Rebecca had put him in her arms. She'd play with him for hours, building towers and mounting complex dinosaur battles to keep him entertained.

'She's asleep, sweetheart,' Rebecca replied.

Bianca had always been an early riser. The time before breakfast had been a lovely slice of time for the two of them. Like everything else, that had changed recently, and Rebecca often wondered whether Bianca was really asleep or just didn't want to be around her.

Maybe that needed to change. Rebecca turned Sam around and stood him up on her knees.

'Hey Sam, I've got an idea. Do you want to go and wake Bianca?'

The little boy's eyes lit up with delight. He wasn't normally allowed into Bianca's room uninvited and he wasn't going to wait to be asked twice.

Rebecca lowered him to the floor and he took off for the stairs, small arms pumping like a sprinter.

It had taken all of Rebecca's willpower not to cry when she'd met with the principal of Bianca's school and explained what she had seen.

Far from being shocked, the principal had just nodded and touched Rebecca on the arm. 'We've seen this before, in other students,' she had said quietly.

Rebecca hadn't known whether to be relieved that this wasn't an isolated occurrence, or terrified by that fact.

In the end she'd settled on gratitude and had sat with the principal for more than an hour working out a strategy. Bianca had always liked her music teacher and the principal called her in to talk with Rebecca. Eventually they had all agreed that the teacher would try to spend time with Bianca where the opportunities arose and keep an eye on her generally. It wasn't much, but it was all they could do for now.

Now, Rebecca pulled on a set of crumpled clothes from the washing basket which was threatening to take over the entire laundry.

She braced herself as she heard heavy footsteps on the staircase and plastered a wide smile on her face.

Kerry

Annie loved the cake — as well she should have. Thank you Rebecca, a thousand times, for your help. I will return your container filled with gold sovereigns (or perhaps Lindt chocolates?).

I have now achieved legendary status amongst the mothers present. One of them even asked whether I had considered making cakes to sell. I assured her that the only thing I would be worse at than plant selling was cake making.

The fact that I have set myself up to repeat this experience every year fills me with great apprehension. Alice, I suspect I will be cursing your 'traditions' for years to come. Still, people have worse problems . . .

'A beer?'
Kerry turned to his companion as they entered the bar.

His question was rhetorical. This wasn't the type of establishment where you ordered a mineral water — or a mojito.

Craig nodded and Kerry headed for the counter.

Kerry and Craig had seen a lot of each other before Sandra and Kerry's break-up. But Craig's wife Jenny was one of Sandra's good friends and, despite assurances that no one was taking sides, Kerry had slid off their dinner-party list pretty quickly.

Craig was an accountant and had helped Sandra to set up the salon, another thing which had strained his friendship with Kerry.

Kerry had been meaning to catch up with Craig for a while. But it was the letter he'd seen in the kitchen drawer at Sandra's house the previous weekend that had made him do it now.

'So Sandra's doing okay in the salon then?' Kerry asked casually as he put the two beers down on the table.

'Not too bad,' Craig answered vaguely.

'She managing to pay down that big loan at all?'

'Not yet, no.'

Kerry tried again. 'How's she managing with the interest rate rises?'

Craig licked the foam off his top lip and carefully put his beer down on the paper coaster. 'What's going on Kerry? You know I can't answer those questions. Client confidentiality and all that.'

'Yeah, yeah, I know,' Kerry looked across at the other side of the room. 'I was just wondering, that's all.'

Silence settled for a moment.

Kerry went to speak again.

'Kerry,' Craig said firmly. 'You are about as subtle as a sledgehammer. You invited me here to find out about Sandra's business, didn't you?'

Kerry looked over at Craig. 'Sorry mate,' he shrugged slightly. 'I . . . well I was at Sandra's last week and saw a letter from the landlord. I wasn't snooping or anything – I just came across it by accident. It was a final notice, telling her to pay the outstanding balance within thirty days or be evicted.'

Kerry let a silence fall, hoping that Craig would correct him and tell him everything was sorted out.

Craig looked over at him thoughtfully. 'All I can tell you are some general things, okay?'

Kerry nodded eagerly, not risking speaking.

'The rental market is very hot at the moment. Some commercial landlords are pushing rents up regardless of the fact that their tenants can't afford it. In the case of new businesses still getting on top of a cash flow, it can prove disastrous.'

Craig stopped.

'Right,' Kerry said. 'Shit.'

'Yes,' Craig replied. 'Shit indeed.'

'And before you move on to a different tack. No, she still doesn't have a boyfriend. Although why not, I have no idea. She's a gorgeous girl and it's time she was involved with someone else.'

He looked hard at Kerry.

'Okay then. Well yes, that does about cover it. Thanks,' Kerry said awkwardly.

'So now can we have a peaceful beer?'

'Yeah, no worries,' Kerry answered. His mind swirled with thoughts of what Sandra was facing.

'Ah, so how's Jenny?' he managed.

'She's good. Our youngest started school this year, so things have eased up a bit for her. She was sorry not to be able to catch up with you tonight. She always liked you. Asked me to find out how you were actually.'

'I'm okay,' Kerry answered slowly. 'Not a lot's changed, but I'm doing okay.'

God, what a sad effort. It was eighteen months since he'd seen Craig and he couldn't come up with anything more interesting than that to report.

'I've met a good woman though,' he blurted, regretting the words as soon as they were out of his mouth.

'Yeah?' Craig was interested.

Kerry berated himself silently. His email flirtation with Alice was not anything worth reporting – particularly to friends of Sandra's.

Ah well, in for a penny . . .

'She's a few years older than me, but nice looking still. She's an author actually.'

'Is that right?'

Craig raised his eyebrows, clearly interested.

Kerry rushed on, trying to stop Craig asking where they'd met. He'd think Kerry was certifiable if he knew about the Red Folder Project.

'It's early days, though.'

What an understatement, thought Kerry, given he had hardly even touched Alice.

Craig looked at him for a moment, but allowed the topic to be changed.

Kerry moved gratefully onto the subject of cricket scores. But his mind was only half with the conversation.

What had made him think of Alice? He found her attractive and she was fun, he enjoyed their emails. But something had stopped him taking it any further, despite the fact that the possibility of sleeping with her was one of the things which had motivated him to join the Red Folder Project. She felt something too – that was obvious from the other day at the market and from her emails. With a conscious effort, he turned his attention back to Craig.

Claire

What I should say is that I loved being at the soup kitchen because I was helping out people less fortunate than I. The truth, though, is that I loved it because of how I felt — like I was useful. And of course I can now add fruit chopping to my list of things I am good at . . .

'Peter?'

Peter was sitting on the balcony, legs propped on the wooden table, the sports section of the newspaper open in front of him.

He pulled his gaze away from the paper and looked up at Claire standing beside him.

'What's up?'

She'd been wondering all day how to tell Peter. Should she make a big deal about it, or just leave the cheque lying around perhaps? In the end, she'd decided she had to tell him.

'I, I just wanted to show you something.'

Claire handed Peter the cheque.

He looked at it.

'O-kay, a cheque to you for fifty dollars, from,' he read the drawer's name, 'Mrs Sarah Roberts. Do I know her?'

'No,' Claire smiled. 'She's my client.'

Peter smiled slightly, a quizzical expression on his face. 'Your client?'

'Yep – the first client of my new business, Fix Your Wardrobe.'

Claire touched the cheque reverently. 'Fifty whole dollars,' she breathed.

Peter pushed his feet off the table and laid the paper down on the table. 'What's Fix Your Wardrobe?'

Claire sat down on the edge of a chair. 'A couple of weeks ago I helped a friend out at a school fete. She needed someone to help sell some clothes provided by a boutique. The clothes were dire, but I talked to a few women about what they could do to improve the way they looked. Apparently the school had some calls from people wanting to get hold of me. So I set up a website to help people contact me.'

Peter's expression was unreadable, but Claire continued anyway.

'They did, and I've done some things for a few women. And – well, one of them has paid me!' She pointed at the cheque.

Still he said nothing and Claire's confidence began to slip.

'It's not much I know, and it doesn't help with our money problems, but it's just the beginning. I've got ideas about how to put generalised advice on the website – things that people pay a subscription for.'

She could hear herself babbling nervously and forced herself to stop.

Peter picked the cheque up, turning it over in his hands.

'That's great Claire. Really great.'

Although his words were enthusiastic, he didn't smile. 'Why didn't you tell me, though? You've done all these things, set up a website . . . but you didn't tell me?'

Claire looked at the deck. Slowly she raised her face to Peter. 'I didn't think you'd be interested,' she answered honestly. 'Or that you'd just think this was another hobby of mine that would go nowhere.'

Peter ran a hand through his hair, leaning back in the

director's chair. 'Or you thought that I'd think it would just cost money, right?'

Claire nodded. Suddenly she couldn't keep it inside any more. 'Peter, it's awful. We don't talk, we don't do anything together. You act like I'm some person you don't even know who just spends your money.'

She paused. 'I think maybe we should think about separating.'

It was strange. They were the words Claire had always dreaded hearing from Peter. But now it was she who was saying them.

Fix Your Wardrobe was a long way from listing on the stock exchange. She would have to get a job doing something – anything. But for the first time, she felt like there was something for her outside this marriage.

Claire felt a stab of guilt. For a moment, she wished she could take the words back. This was a marriage. You don't just walk away from a marriage.

But the guilt was only momentary. Alice was right, life should be good. And hers wasn't – that was pretty clear.

'Tell me what you want, Peter,' she said in a voice she hardly recognised. 'This,' she swept out her arm 'is not working for either of us.'

'For God's sake, Claire, I don't know! We've been like this for ages now. It's just worse right now because my work is stressful.'

'Work has got nothing to do with us, Peter. If you'd let me close to you I could even help you, but you won't.'

'It's not that simple. It's been hard living with you. This baby thing . . .' Peter's voice trailed off briefly and then he started again. 'It's exhausting. Every time we have a conversation I have this dread that you're going to turn the topic to it. Each month I know you're going to be unhappy when you find out you're not pregnant again. It just goes on and on. When I saw you singing in the car the other day, I honestly couldn't remember the last time I'd seen you look so happy.'

Claire sat silently for a minute, head bowed. Finally she looked up. 'You're right. I know and I'm sorry. It's something I have to come to terms with – I don't know how. But I have to, otherwise

I'm going to go mad. For the last few years, though, it's like I've been on my own with it all. I'm really –'

She broke off, swallowing the tears that rose in her throat.

'I'm really lonely,' she said finally.

They looked at each other for a few moments.

Peter stood up. 'Come here,' he said, pulling Claire out of her chair.

Gently he wrapped his arms around her. Claire nestled her head on his chest, in the same place she always had, and then she let the tears come.

Megan

You told me to think of a part, however small, of teaching that I like.

There's a look that children get when they finally understand something. It's pretty nice. Anyway, I saw that look again today. Either I haven't been watching for it, or I've been doing a lousy job of teaching these children.

I still hate my job though.

Megan pulled up outside Greg's two-storey brick house in Toowong. Geographically it was only about five kilometres from her place, but emotionally it was another world altogether. The houses in this area were all very much family homes. Pools, basketball hoops hanging off poles. She would have bet a week's salary that there wasn't one sexy red bathroom like hers in the whole suburb.

She'd been amazed by the invitation. With Deborah and the children two thousand kilometres away in Cairns at a family celebration, Greg had sent her an email asking her to dinner at his place. Not a seedy restaurant. Not her place. His place. Because he wanted to cook for her and wanted her to stay the night.

She knocked softly and within seconds the door was pulled open.

'Hi.' Greg's smile was that of a naughty schoolboy.

'Hi yourself.'

In this neighbourhood, Megan was painfully aware of how they must look, the two of them framed by the light spilling out of the house. She could almost feel the curtains twitching as neighbours checked out the new arrival.

As if reading her mind, Greg kissed her demurely on the cheek as though he were greeting a younger sister.

'Come on in,' his voice was slightly too loud, slightly too like a scout leader.

The instant the door had closed, though, he covered her mouth with his and tangled his hands in her hair.

They hadn't even made it out of the entryway before they were both flinging their clothes off.

'We can't do this again,' Greg gasped in her ear. 'It's just having you here like this . . .' Megan bit his earlobe then and he lost his train of thought.

Some time later, when they'd finally made it past the entryway, she was shocked by how warm and domestic it all was.

Although she didn't look too closely, she could see dozens of photos carelessly pinned to the fridge with homemade magnets. Family happy snaps. Greg and his two daughters. Greg and a pretty blonde woman who could only have been his wife, Deborah.

There was a whiteboard over the kitchen counter with a picture of a glamorous-looking housewife from the fifties looking stern. Underneath it read, *Hand over the chocolate and no one gets hurt.*

In the message section was scrawled in a child's hand, *Don't forget to feed Jones!!! Love you Dad!* The dots in the exclamation marks were tiny hearts.

Coming here suddenly seemed like a really bad idea. And the sex that had only moments ago seemed impossibly exciting now just seemed dirty.

As Greg had so glibly pointed out, moral high ground wasn't exactly Megan's natural habitat, but surely this was a bit ordinary, even for her.

'I bought you a present,' he said.

Megan forced a smile, trying not to look as panicky as she felt.

As if it were the most natural thing in the world, Greg was pushing a beautifully wrapped present across the kitchen counter.

From the shape and weight, she figured it was a book.

The thick, purple ribbon felt almost like velvet as she gripped it between thumb and finger and pulled the knot loose. *The Art and Architecture of 3D Animation.*

Megan looked at Greg, who smiled sheepishly. 'Thought it might give you some inspiration,' he shrugged.

'Thank you,' she managed.

Grateful for something to do, she flicked through the pages.

'You should do it, you know,' he said.

'What's that?'

'Programming – something you enjoy. Even if it means taking a step backwards.'

He tied an apron around his waist and moved around the kitchen pulling out ingredients. He stopped to pour them each some white wine, kissing Megan on the forehead as he handed the glass to her.

Megan couldn't concentrate on what he was saying. She tried to think what it was that made Greg want to have her in his house. Didn't using his wife's saucepans to make a red wine sauce give him the jitters? Or cooking the steak in a frying pan she'd stacked neatly under the bench? She felt on edge, as though someone could walk in the door at any moment and catch them.

Not that it was her problem, she reminded herself. It was Greg's. He was married, not her.

It wasn't that her feelings about being with a married man had changed. It was more that this was all just too much in her face. An old pair of pink Havianas sat next to the front door; the pair of sunglasses pushed to the back of the bench were unmistakably female.

Greg placed the meal on the table with a flourish and lit the candle between them. Megan tried to relax and enjoy herself.

After a few minutes, Greg put his cutlery down. 'What's wrong?' he asked quietly.

'Everything. All of this.' She gestured around the house. 'This was a mistake. I shouldn't be here.'

Pushing back the chair, Megan stood up. She grabbed her car keys from the kitchen bench, then turned to look at Greg, still sitting at the table, two untouched meals in front of him.

'I'm sorry,' she said. 'I'll – I'll call you.'

Alice

A lice always baked when she felt guilty.
    As if by filling the house with the smell of homemade
cake she could find redemption for yelling when she should have
comforted. Or for rejecting Andrew's advances when she should
have been accommodating. Or for still being in the queue at the
supermarket when the hurdles final was running at the school
sports day.

A casual visitor, glancing at her collection of cookbooks,
would have thought she loved cooking. Two full rows of gor-
geously bound books. Nigella, Jamie, Bill, Delia – she had them
all.

The reality was a rotation of eight healthy and easy meals,
two dinner-party menus and about four slices and cakes that she
could make without even thinking.

Guilt, though, had the power to break through her food system and it was then that the cookbooks came out.

Today the guilt was substantial.

As she cracked eggs into a bowl, Alice wondered how on
earth she had let the situation get to this point.

The nature of the group was that she had known intimate
things about Kerry before she'd even really spoken to him. But
she knew intimate things about the others too.

Alice beat the eggs furiously, then tipped them into the cake mixture. She should have called a halt when she received the email about cougars. She should have emailed him back. Told him he'd got it wrong. That she was happily married. That emails like that had to stop.

But she hadn't.

She didn't need a degree in psychology to know why. Kerry made her feel good.

Alice spooned the mixture into a tin.

The email that had arrived in her inbox this morning was the end of the line. It had shattered the exciting little world she'd constructed out of nothing. She was a bored, attention-deprived housewife who should have found something better to do with her time.

She'd set Kerry a new task the day before. It was to go camping, the idea being that it would force him to slow down and think about what he really wanted. Kerry clearly had another take on it.

Come away with me. I know a great place. They even have cabins . . . log fires . . . That's kind of camping, right?

The strange thing was that the idea horrified her. Her exciting email flirtation had transformed into something dirty and illicit. Her marriage was far from good, but she had no desire to have an affair with Kerry or anyone else.

Alice slid the tin into the oven and closed the door gently.

She lifted the apron over her head and placed it on the counter. As she did, she noticed the drooping skin on the back of her arm. What had she been thinking? She was an overweight middle-aged woman who needed to find herself some kind of life.

Slowly Alice walked into the study and sat down at the computer.

Megan

Megan pushed her hair out of her eyes, trying to ignore the
fact that she should have washed it this morning.

The cafe's airconditioning couldn't contend with the wall of
humid air which oozed in through the doorways. It was too hot
for jeans and Megan stretched her legs irritably, denim sticking to
her thighs. Even her orange T-shirt, which usually made her feel
good, had a stain on the front she hadn't noticed at home.

She was here too late, Megan knew that. An early Sunday
breakfast could be a thing of joy. The cafe would be only half full,
with a couple of bikes parked outside and their owners celebrat-
ing the end of an exercise session with a dose of caffeine and
saturated fat. Maybe there'd be a father, unfamiliarly juggling an
infant, while its mother slept late. Possibly even someone sitting
at an outside table, weary dog lolling at their feet. Then there'd be
people by themselves. No apologies were needed for eating by
yourself early on a weekend morning. A crisp copy of the Sunday
paper was the only companion required.

But by about nine, the couples drifted in. Some were well
established, women handing over the sports section without
comment. Then there were the relationships which were as new
as the day and might not last it out. Those men eyed others' newspapers covetously, while the women tried to make small talk over
freshly squeezed orange juice.

The dress code changed too, from exercise wear or clothes which had clearly spent the night on the floor, to crisp leisure wear and elegant shoes. While unbrushed hair was perfectly acceptable at 8 am, it screamed 'single and not making an effort' after 9 am.

Megan took another sip of her coffee and closed the main part of the newspaper.

She knew she should read the news section, but the only sections she ever really paid any attention to were the colour magazine and the entertainment section. The rest of it just made her feel bad, reminding her that the world was in a shambles and she was doing nothing to fix it.

At least she didn't buy her own newspaper, she thought. Think of the trees she was saving. She pulled the glossy magazine toward her.

DICE MAN IN THE SUBURBS, screamed the cover.

Megan opened the magazine, thumbing through the early pages to the lead story.

A photo of Alice stared up at her.

She read the first paragraph feeling sick to the stomach. Slowly, not missing anything, she read to the end. It was all there – all of their stories. Even hers. There were no last names and no photos except Alice's, but the journalist had clearly done her research.

The 'Megan' in the article was a teacher at a northside school who lived in Paddington. She hated teaching and wanted to be a programmer.

'Duh,' as the kids in her class would have said. Even a passing acquaintance would be able to tell it was her.

And there in black and white was the fact that she was having an affair with a married man. While the man remained anony-mous, there were even details about the horrible dinner at Greg's place.

Megan had surprised herself by writing a diary entry when she'd arrived home after that evening. She'd woken ridiculously early the next morning in a panic, remembering that Greg had the password and could access the site. She'd quickly changed it, forwarding the new password to everyone in the group – under the guise of a regular security update. Fortunately no one had thought to question why she'd done it at four o'clock in the morning.

Images of different members of the group ricocheted around Megan's mind. Claire, Rebecca, Lillian, Kerry. Their lives laid bare.

How had this happened?

Megan paid her bill and walked outside. She paused on the footpath, disoriented, then remembered her bike. Unchaining it from the lamppost, she slung her backpack over her shoulder and climbed on. Although it was ridiculous, she felt as though everyone was looking at her, laughing.

All she wanted to do was get back inside her house, close the blinds and never come out again.

As she pedalled her bike up the steep hill to home, the anger rose up in her. Alice must have given the story to the paper. That was the only explanation that made any sense. Of course she had. She was a faded star and this was a good way to get back in the limelight. Bugger what it did to anyone else.

Megan finally reached her house and threw her bike down, not even bothering to chain it up as she usually did.

Still sweating and breathing hard, she logged onto the familiar website address. With a couple of key strokes, she crashed the whole site. Not just the diary pages but the whole thing.

Sure it was way too little, way too late, but it made her feel slightly better.

Rebecca

Jeremy was halfway through the sports section when Bianca's phone beeped.

Rebecca tensed, looking up from Sam whose face was covered with a gelatinous mixture of Weet-Bix and toast.

They were all supposed to turn their phones off during meals. It was a rule she'd set about six months ago in an effort to regain some family life. But she'd quickly run out of the energy required to enforce the rule. Bianca didn't even pretend to adhere to it these days.

Bianca picked up her phone, ignoring her mother's silent look of disapproval. She looked up from the phone's display and across at the pile of newsprint.

'Have you got the colour magazine, Jeremy?'

Jeremy didn't even look up, just pushed the pile toward Bianca and nudged his glasses back up his nose. 'In there somewhere,' he muttered.

Bianca spread the paper with a careless hand and pulled out the glossy magazine.

Intrigued, Rebecca watched her.

The cover was a picture of a large dice taking up a whole supermarket trolley. The shout line read, *DICE MAN IN THE SUBURBS.*

Rebecca remembered *The Dice Man*, the seventies cult book

in which the main character allowed his choices in life to be ruled by the fall of the dice. Good title for an article, she thought vaguely, turning her attention back to Sam.

Bianca stood up suddenly, knocking the chair backwards. It hit the terrazzo floor with a crack and Sam burst out crying.

'Bianca!' Jeremy exclaimed. 'What the hell is wrong with you?'

'Look at this!' She thrust the magazine into his chest. 'I'll bet she didn't tell you either.'

Rebecca lifted Sam out of the highchair and tried to settle him. She cuddled him into her chest and watched Jeremy silently.

'What is it, Jer?'

Bianca stood glaring at her and Rebecca only just resisted the urge to send her to her room. God, what she'd give for just one day of peace.

Jeremy didn't answer her, his eyes scanning the page. He read for what seemed like a year, turning the page slowly. Finally he looked up, pulling off his glasses and dropping them on the table.

'What is going on, Rebecca?'

'What do you mean, what's going on? I have no idea.'

'Maybe you should have a look at this, then.'

Jeremy turned the magazine around and handed it to her.

A photo of Alice stared back at her. A younger and slimmer Alice, but Alice nonetheless.

A terrible suspicion ran through Rebecca's body, tightening her throat and jolting to a stop at her fingertips.

Her eyes darted to the text on the opposite page:

Four women and one man have put their lives in the hands of Alice Day, a once successful author who hasn't been published in over ten years. Their aim – to fix screwed-up and unhappy lives. Their agreement – to do whatever Alice tells them to and then post their diaries on the internet.

> These are mature, seemingly balanced individuals. There is Lillian, the respectable sixty year old widow, Rebecca the successful recruitment specialist with Bianca the self-mutilating love child and Jeremy the stockbroker hubby . . .

Rebecca didn't need to read any more.

She looked up at Bianca and Jeremy. Bianca's eyes were furious and flashing. Jeremy's were flat and emotionless. Sam struggled to be put down and strutted off to the other side of the room.

The things she'd written in her diary entries tumbled through her mind. Her dissatisfaction at work, her fight with Jeremy – Bianca cutting herself. Suddenly what she'd done seemed totally and ridiculously stupid. Posting intimate details on a website. She should have known that the fact the site was only accessible by the group members wasn't good enough. Alice had said that the names would be changed in any book that she wrote about the group, but the article used their real names. No surnames were mentioned, but there was no need, they were clearly identifiable.

Rebecca stood up, nightdress sticking to her thighs.

She stepped around the table toward her daughter, who had picked the magazine up again and was reading.

'Bianca . . .' She touched her daughter's sleeve.

Bianca flinched as though she'd been struck. 'Do not touch me! What have you done? You think that you can tell everyone in the world about your terrible daughter and the disaster she has turned your life into.'

'Sweetheart, that's not it at all. It's something I got into without wanting to and I've been so upset about what you've been doing to yourself that I . . . well I kept writing about what I was feeling.'

'About me?' Bianca asked.

'Yes, but other things too.'

Bianca thrust her hands into the pockets of her jacket and glared up at Rebecca. 'So . . . you see that I've done something to myself . . . You don't bother to talk to me, you just write to a bunch of strangers on a website which every person that I know in this world will read? What kind of mother are you?' Bianca's voice reached a pitch which was not far off a scream.

She whirled around to Jeremy. 'Did you know about this?'

'This is about those drinks you went to that night, isn't it? You said it was a ridiculous thing you wouldn't consider being a part of.'

Jeremy looked at Rebecca with the flat stare she'd lived with for weeks after their last fight.

Rebecca broke his gaze. Jeremy would have to wait.

Bianca turned back to Rebecca.

'You don't want me in this family,' she ground out.

'Bianca, that is ridiculous. You're my daughter. I love you. Don't you remember how it used to be with us? Don't you remember when we were friends?'

Bianca looked at her mother, her irises matching the black lines around her eyes.

'No I don't,' she answered, and turned and ran out of the room.

Rebecca put a hand on the table, only just resisting the urge to sink down onto the floor.

She turned to Jeremy. 'Jeremy, I'm sorry. I didn't mean this to be anything big. I just kind of got pulled along. God, if I'd thought for a minute that anyone else would read it . . .'

Jeremy looked at her. 'What is going on with you, Rebecca? This is not your kind of thing. You'd normally laugh yourself stupid at anyone involved in something like this.'

Rebecca let out a shaky breath. 'God, I have no idea.' She combed her hair back roughly with spread fingers. 'Things have been so bad lately, I haven't known which way to turn.'

'Maybe talking to me would have been a good start.' Jeremy's voice was frosty.

'I know. I'm sorry.'

The front door slammed and Rebecca and Jeremy looked at each other in alarm.

As Rebecca reached the doorstep, the door to her Saab

clunked shut. Bianca looked through the windscreen, wild eyes set in a white face smeared with black eyeliner. For a moment their eyes met and then Bianca turned the key in the ignition.

The car whined as she threw it into reverse without releasing the parking brake. Suddenly it jolted backwards and careened down the sloping drive much too fast. It hit the gutter at the bottom and the undercarriage screeched along the bottom of the driveway.

A black shape caught at the corner of Rebecca's vision. She saw a four-wheel drive bearing down toward where Bianca had stopped, the back of the Saab stretching onto the wrong side of the road.

'Oh God,' Rebecca whispered.

At the last moment the driver swept the nose of the large vehicle up onto the left-hand gutter, skirting the Saab. Horn blaring it surged past and continued on.

'That'll scare her,' Jeremy urged, pushing Rebecca to one side and running down the driveway. 'Come on.'

He reached the car and spread his hand across the closed window on the driver's side.

'Bianca!' he yelled. 'Put the window down. Now!'

With a screech of tyres the Saab took off down the middle of the road. Rebecca reached Jeremy's side and stood there helplessly. The road curved to the left fifty metres away and Bianca took the turn fast. The car clung to the road, but its tyres lost the battle with the speed and drifted over the gutter, slamming into a power pole.

Claire

It wasn't exactly the Sydney Cricket Ground, but the Demons' home ground was humming.

This was a big match. The opposition had been the champions last season. The Demons were clear underdogs, but they'd played some good matches and were in with a chance.

A couple of dozen fourteen year old boys in white shirts and trousers milled around. Their parents were there too, fathers talking about the weather conditions, mothers setting up drinks and food.

The umpire walked out onto the pitch, signalling for the two team captains to follow him. The match was starting early in an effort to avoid some of the burning heat. It had been hot and dry all week and the tossed coin fell on a pitch which already had cracks in it.

Peter's team won the toss and elected to bat.

The Demons' opening batsmen had their backs slapped and received last-minute advice from their fathers. The rest of them sat down on the bench, both dreading and anticipating their turn to bat.

The woman beside Claire leaned over and said quietly, 'My God, you'd think it was India playing Australia, wouldn't you?'

Claire had been trying hard not to look as out of place as she felt. She'd been amazed when Peter had asked her to come and watch the match this morning, something he'd never even suggested before. The match was at a local high school and, having learned her lesson at the school fete, Claire had dressed casually in a long flowing skirt and tank top.

She looked gratefully at the woman beside her. 'I know,' she whispered back. 'I had no idea it was all so serious.'

She watched Peter talking to the batsmen. All eyes were glued to him as if he alone held the secret to victory.

Standing in the middle of the pitch, he looked as though he'd never had a moment's doubt about anything in his life. But Claire knew that Peter was as aware as she that they'd reached a crossroads. She'd been awake a lot during the night and, if Peter's tossing and turning was anything to go by, so had he.

On Thursday night they'd been closer than in a long time. Their discussion had broken down the barriers and when they'd gone to bed they'd made love. Without regard to timing or temperatures, just because they'd wanted to. But Friday morning had brought them back to reality. They were still the same people in the same lives with the same issues. Did they have enough to keep them together, or was it time to go their separate ways? Claire didn't know and she didn't think Peter did either.

The woman beside her offered her coffee from a thermos. Clearly used to cricket matches that could go for hours without much happening, she started to make conversation.

Eventually they got around to the question Claire always loathed. 'So what do you do?'

About to make her standard excuses as to why she didn't work, she suddenly changed her mind.

'I run my own small business, actually,' she said.

After all, this woman didn't need to know her small business so far had an annual turnover of fifty dollars.

'Really?'

Claire had never had anyone respond so enthusiastically when she'd told them she was a housewife.

'Yes, it's an online fashion consultancy.' God, but it felt good to be able to say that.

'Really?'

A woman standing in front of them turned around. Claire hadn't even known she was listening. 'What kind of stuff do you do?'

'Well, my original idea was that a lot of women want to look better but don't know where to start. I thought I could be a personal shopper – you know, helping people choose what suited them. But my first clients weren't that enthusiastic.'

Claire paused, half expecting someone would snigger at her use of the word 'client'.

They didn't.

'I'm not sure why – maybe it's because they thought they'd be pressured to spend money.'

'Or maybe because they didn't like the idea of someone seeing them in their underwear,' a woman on Claire's other side suggested.

Claire laughed. 'So what I'm doing now is getting clients,' this time she didn't hesitate over the word, 'to send me a photo and tell me about themselves – whether they have a job, stay home with kids, that kind of stuff. Then I email them some ideas on what kind of things they should be looking for, what they should be avoiding, and some shops they should look in.'

Claire hesitated. She'd said enough, they'd think she was big-noting herself.

But the women were still looking at her with interest, so slowly she continued.

'I've got other plans too. There aren't that many body types. If I could come up with some general stuff for maybe five different body shapes, I could put together a site people subscribe to. I'd have other things in there too – like fashion trends to ignore, or those that will last for a few seasons.'

'Maybe ideas about accessories?' one of the women suggested. 'I still can't figure out if your shoes are supposed to match your belt these days.'

Claire smiled. 'That's a good idea.'

There was a roar from the crowd. One of the Demons' players was out, caught on the boundary by a boy who was lying stretched out on the grass.

Claire looked for Peter. He'd be devastated – he'd been hoping the opening batsmen would make a big total.

She saw him twenty metres away. Strangely, though, he was looking not at the field but at her. Looking, she realised, at the small group of women who'd been listening to her.

Claire grimaced, pointing to the batsman, who was trundling back to the sideline, bat under his arm.

Peter shrugged lightly, smiled and turned back to his team.

'Claire?'

A dark-haired woman stood beside her.

Sharon and her husband were one of the couples Peter had invited to dinner at their house all those weeks ago – the dinner that Claire hadn't made it to. Sharon seemed fine about it, but Claire still felt a squirm of embarrassment whenever she saw her.

'Hi Sharon. How are you?'

'I'm okay, thanks.' Sharon hesitated. 'Ah, have you read the paper today?'

Claire shook her head. 'We've been here since the crack of dawn.'

'I think maybe you should have a look at this then,' Sharon said.

Claire looked down at the Sunday paper's colour magazine which Sharon was holding open. She jolted at the sight of the photo of Alice.

She looked at Sharon and saw sympathy in the other woman's eyes.

Claire took the magazine and began to read.

Lillian

Lillian should have known something was wrong when Ross braked gently, pulling up almost silently beside her.

She'd arrived home two days earlier, but had been heavily jetlagged, sleeping fifteen hours the night before last and missing yesterday's morning walk. So she hadn't seen Ross since her return.

'Morning, Ross,' she said cheerily.

'Hi Lillian,' he replied quietly.

She waited for him to ask her about her trip, but he stayed silent.

'I can't believe the colours in Australia. The blue of the sky, the green trees . . . It's all so vivid – so different from in France.' It was what had struck her on her return. She paused, giving him a chance to speak.

Instead, he pulled on the handbrake and stepped out of the car. 'Lillian,' he said without preamble, 'have you seen today's paper?'

'No,' she smiled, slightly confused. Ross knew that she always took her copy of the newspaper from him.

'There's an article there that . . .' He broke off. 'Look, let me show you.'

He dived in the window of the van and pulled out the colour magazine. Thumbing through a few pages, he folded it over and handed it to her.

Lillian took it, bemused.

She saw the photo of Alice, then read on. Skimming down the pages she saw her own name. Everything was there – her illness, everything. She flicked back to the start of the article. *Written by Caitlan Murphy.*

The name meant nothing to her, but the next paragraph did. *This paper has obtained exclusive access to the website used by Alice Day's group to record their part in this social experiment.*

Lillian hadn't used the website. But she'd known that Alice was putting her letters on there.

Ross interrupted her thoughts. 'So it is you?'

Lillian looked at him, nodding slightly.

'I thought so. Bit of bad luck that sickness thing.' Ross's words were light, but his eyes were dark and serious.

'Yes,' Lillian answered. 'It is a bit of bad luck, isn't it.'

She pushed her hand into the pocket of her tracksuit pants, feeling the tickets. They were to a friendly football match between Australia and Uraguay the following week. The match had sold out in minutes several weeks ago, but Max, one of her son's friends, was high up in the Queensland soccer world.

Years ago, Lillian had pulled Max together after a very drunken night, feeding him and washing his clothes before sending him home. Much to Max's amusement Lillian had called in the favour on her return from Paris and two tickets had been hand delivered the same day.

Lillian crumpled the tickets in her fingers. What on earth had she been thinking?

'I've got to go, Ross.'

Lillian turned, retracing her steps toward home.

Kerry

Kerry shifted the empty packet of chips from under his face and propped himself up on one elbow. As a bizarre kind of consequence of his marriage break-up, he now spent more nights on the couch. After an evening at the pub, his planned five minute flick through the television channels would inevitably finish at dawn, with the bad-tempered squawk of crows and an ache in his back.

This morning, the phone beat the crows.

He squinted at the window as he fumbled with the handset. It couldn't be later than seven, which meant it was his father calling.

'Dad.' Kerry's voice sounded husky and he tried to quietly clear his throat. He couldn't remember what time he'd got home but it didn't feel as though it was too long ago.

'Son – how are you this morning?'

'Great thanks,' Kerry replied.

'You're a liar,' his father replied gruffly. 'And you're also fired.'

Kerry pushed himself into a sitting position and tipped his head to one side, stretching the muscles in his neck.

'Sorry?' he replied vaguely.

'You – are – fired,' his father repeated.

Kerry ran a hand through his hair.

'Dad,' he said, 'I have a hangover that would kill a bull and I got about ten minutes sleep last night. I'm really not in the mood for jokes.'

There'd been a method to his drinking last night. It was only after about five large ones that he could forget his guilt about Alice. She didn't wear a wedding ring and he'd assumed she was divorced. But obviously not – he'd been flirting with a very nice married lady. A lady who was obviously not as sorted as she appeared, given that it took her over a month to tell him to get lost.

His father didn't hesitate. 'That's good because I'm not joking. You can sell things, but you haven't so much as a green thumbnail. I've never known anyone to be worse with plants than you. They wilt if you even look at them.'

'Dad, you're going to have to start again. I don't know what you're talking about.'

The old man's voice was softer now. 'Kerry, your mother and I had no idea you didn't like working at the markets.'

Kerry was suddenly wide awake. He scanned his memory for a drunken confession from last night which could have reached his father's ears. There was nothing.

'I don't hate it, Dad. You know that.'

'I thought I did, son. Until I picked up this morning's paper.'

Kerry wondered if his father was deliberately trying to confuse him. 'What the hell has the paper got to do with anything?'

For the first time, his father hesitated. 'You haven't read the paper?'

Kerry squinted at his watch. 'Dad, it's only just past six-thirty. Only bloody bakers and plant people are awake at this hour on a Sunday morning.'

His father sighed. 'Okay, have a shower and go buy the paper. Read the colour magazine and then call me. But you're still fired.'

Rebecca

Rebecca sat next to the bed, watching her daughter sleep. God they'd been lucky.

When they had reached the shattered Saab, Bianca had been unconscious, a thin trickle of dark red blood running down her face.

Jeremy had called an ambulance and arranged for one of the neighbours to take Sam inside. Rebecca had felt totally useless, her mind locked up like some kind of malfunctioning computer.

Bianca had regained consciousness within minutes but she'd looked frighteningly pale. The police had kept onlookers away as the paramedics lifted her out of the car and onto a stretcher and then into the ambulance.

Rebecca had held Bianca's hand for the short journey, Jeremy following behind in his car.

Bianca had concussion, a broken arm and lots of bruises. She had to stay in overnight for observation, but should be released tomorrow.

Every time Rebecca had turned her mobile on during the day, it had shuddered with the torrent of texts and phone messages that had poured in. It seemed that it wasn't too hard to identify her from the newspaper article even without surnames. Rebecca had ignored all of the messages, only calling Claire to see if she knew how this had happened. Claire had known as little as Rebecca.

Bianca had been on painkillers all day, speaking to no one, and had finally drifted off to sleep about six o'clock.

Jeremy had left to call his parents, who had arrived midmorning to take Sam from the neighbours. They'd managed to shield him from the worst of the crash, but he knew something terrible had happened to his beloved 'Anka'.

With Jeremy gone, the atmosphere had settled oppressively, lying over the room like a heavy blanket.

Rebecca ached to hold Bianca's hand but she didn't move, fearing that her touch might wake her. She didn't think she could take any more silent contempt today.

There was a tap on the open door.

'Come in,' she murmured, assuming it was another nurse.

But no nurse appeared and Rebecca looked over her shoulder.

Peter was standing in the doorway.

His jeans were worn to a soft blue and the collar of his polo shirt was folded underneath as if he'd thrown it on quickly.

Rebecca looked at him for a moment.

'Is Claire here?' she asked, knowing the answer.

Peter shook his head.

'I didn't think they would let anyone in here,' Rebecca commented, marvelling at how level her voice sounded.

'I told them I was Bianca's father,' Peter replied evenly. 'I am, aren't I?'

Rebecca had imagined this scenario many times. Even had different replies ready. But suddenly they all deserted her. Panicking, she glanced back at Bianca, relieved to see that she was still sleeping.

'Be quiet,' she hissed.

Peter ignored her. 'Aren't I?' he demanded.

Rebecca moved her hand closer to Bianca's.

'Yes,' she said in a voice little more than a whisper.

Peter's retort came back like a slingshot. 'My God, Rebecca! Why didn't you tell me?'

Bianca stirred. Instantly, Rebecca stood and moved past Peter in the doorway, forcing him to follow her or be left alone with the sleeping girl.

Mind spinning, she walked past several rooms until she came to a small alcove. She turned to him. 'Peter, I'm sorry. I really am, but we can't do this now.'

'Tell me when would be convenient for you, Rebecca? When were you planning on telling me that I am the father of your sixteen year old daughter?'

A nurse walked by and paused. 'Is everything all right, Mrs Jackson?'

Rebecca mustered a faint smile. 'Yes, thank you. It's fine.'

The nurse walked on with a glance back over her shoulder.

Peter slumped against the wall. 'Is she going to be all right?'

Rebecca rubbed her eyes wearily and nodded. 'Broken arm, lots of bruises. She'll be pretty sore for a while . . .' Her voice trailed off.

'Why, Rebecca?'

Peter's words were so soft she could hardly hear them.

She looked over at him. His face hadn't changed that much. His hair was still a sandy type of blond, his eyes somewhere between green and brown. His features had hardened and fine lines radiated from the corner of his eyes. Certainly older, but still good-looking.

It didn't take much effort to picture the boy she'd admired from a distance for years. The attraction had been mutual, she'd known that. But somehow one of them would always be seeing someone else while the other was not. Their paths were always parallel, but never converging. Until the after-formal party. Rebecca had gone with her Swedish boyfriend but that had always been a half-hearted affair, both of them knowing it was just a bit of fun before he went home.

Rebecca didn't normally drink much and after several beers was feeling very light-headed. The party was being hosted by one of their class mates who had liberal parents and a house on ten acres of land. She'd wandered past the spill of the lights, thinking some fresh air might sober her up. Peter had seen her go and followed her. Their first kiss had left her with sensations she'd never felt before and they'd lain in the long grass together. Alcohol and long-suppressed emotions had been a potent mix and they'd gone much further than either of them had intended.

Now, so many years later, she had to try to find the words to explain what had happened next.

'Everything is so different now,' she began. 'We have jobs, we're married. You would like a child.'

Peter's face tightened but he said nothing.

'Peter, remember how things were for both of us seventeen years ago. You were starting uni. By the time I knew I was pregnant, you had started seeing Claire.'

Even after almost two decades, she could still feel the piercing hurt when she'd found that out.

Now that Rebecca had begun, the words fell out in a torrent.

'You got your degree. I didn't even get to study. There didn't seem to be any point in ruining your life as well.'

She looked him full in the face. 'The easy part was deciding not to tell you at the beginning. The hard part has been not telling you since then. I've thought about it every single day – wondered whether I was doing a terrible thing not letting you be part of Bianca's life. But it seemed to get harder every year to tell you the truth, and easier not to. I kept hoping I'd hear that you and Claire had children – I thought somehow that would make it better. But you didn't . . .'

Peter rubbed his forefinger hard across his lips and shook his head slightly.

'I'm sorry, Peter. I really am.'

'God, Rebecca . . . when I heard that you were pregnant, I wondered if I could have been the father. But when I spoke to you, you seemed so sure it was that Swedish guy.'

Rebecca nodded. 'I thought I was doing the right thing for everyone. When you called me, I had my story ready. I just changed the dates a bit, made it look like it couldn't have been you. The truth is, I never had sex with Sven.'

Rebecca hesitated and then asked, 'What made you suddenly so sure Bianca was your daughter?'

Peter sighed. 'I guess I always wondered. When Bianca was at our place the other day, I noticed that she was left-handed like me. There was just something about her that seemed familiar. Still, I told myself, there was no point in digging up old bones. But when Claire told me she'd been in a car accident . . .'

He took a deep breath and spoke slowly, enunciating each word. 'I might have been crap. I might have told you to get an abortion or denied that she was mine. But, you know what, I might not have been too. And you never gave me a chance.'

He looked hard at Rebecca. 'You can't know what it feels like to suddenly discover you have a child. Claire has been desperate for a child for years and I thought I'd stopped caring. But knowing I already have one changes everything. I have missed so many things. Seeing her learn to do things. Birthdays . . . teaching her to ride a bike. Who taught her that – was it Jeremy?' He tried unsuccessfully to keep the look of jealousy off his face.

'No,' Rebecca replied quietly. 'I did.'

Peter looked away. Rebecca could see the Adam's apple in his throat move as he swallowed.

He waved his hand toward the room down the hallway where Bianca lay. 'She's almost an adult and she doesn't even know who I am.'

Peter dragged his hand across his face wearily and looked down at his feet.

'I'm sorry,' Rebecca said softly.

When Peter spoke again, it was almost a whisper. 'Why didn't you return my call after the formal party?' He turned his head toward her.

Rebecca looked at him in confusion. 'What call? You said you'd call and you didn't. And then you started seeing Claire a month after that.'

'But I spoke to your mother – you were still in bed. She said she'd get you to call when you woke up.'

'She never gave me the message,' Rebecca said. 'She must have forgotten.'

They looked at each other silently for several seconds.

Rebecca shook her head. This was ridiculous. A teenage fancy had nothing to do with where they were now.

Just then, Jeremy came striding down the corridor. He stopped short when he saw them.

'Peter,' he nodded, clearly wondering what was going on.

There was a pause, a couple of beats too long for comfort. Finally Peter broke the silence. 'I should get home.'

He looked at Rebecca. 'We need to talk about this again tomorrow.'

Slowly he turned and walked back the way Jeremy had come in.

'Rebecca?' Jeremy turned to her. 'What was that about?'

Rebecca looked at him desperately. 'Don't hate me,' she begged. 'Please don't hate me.'

The words she'd kept inside for so many years tumbled out. 'Bianca's father isn't Sven, the Swedish guy I went out with at school. Peter is her father. Nobody has known until today, not my parents, not Peter, not Bianca, no one. I always meant to tell Bianca one day – almost did a couple of years ago. But somehow I didn't. Then she started being difficult and it just seemed like one more problem to resolve.'

Jeremy was looking at her unblinkingly. Rebecca had a sudden sense that she was talking to a stranger, not the man she'd been married to for five years.

'When we met I told you the story about Sven, like everyone else. I didn't know I'd marry you then. Every day I didn't tell you the truth it just seemed harder to, and somehow it seemed wrong to tell you before I told Bianca.'

Jeremy's face was stony.

'I'm sorry.'

Jeremy shook his head slowly. 'Too many secrets, Rebecca.'

He turned, heading toward Bianca's room. Presumably to get his car keys and leave.

He stopped suddenly in front of Bianca's door.

Rebecca stopped beside him.

Bianca was standing next to the bed.

'Bee?' Rebecca walked toward her.

She expected Bianca to push her away, hit her even.

But Bianca let Rebecca fold her into her arms.

Her world was crashing down upon her, but still Rebecca felt an overwhelming sense of happiness to be able to hold her daughter again.

She pulled Bianca down beside her on the bed.

Her face pale against the white hospital gown, Bianca looked much younger than her sixteen years.

'Why didn't you tell me?'

Rebecca took a breath. Why hadn't she told Bianca, told Peter, told Jeremy? She could have avoided the years of guilt, the nagging feeling that pulled her from sleep and never left her.

Rebecca had truly felt she was doing the right thing at the beginning. But the lie had grown and become worse over the years. Telling Bianca and not Peter had never really been an option. Whenever she thought about coming clean, the repercussions seemed too great and so instead she took the line of least resistance – which was to do nothing.

'Bee . . . I'm so sorry. I always planned to tell you. I just could never figure out when the right time was. I didn't mean it all to be a lie . . . it just happened . . . and I didn't know how to back out. I was trying to protect Peter, we were just kids – almost the same age as you are now . . .'

The excuses sounded lame even to her own ears.

'Do you love him?'

'What? No – God.'

Rebecca remembered she was talking to a sixteen year old. A girl who might pretend to be grown up but who two years ago had still subscribed to a pet magazine. Babies, love and marriage all existed together in the land of princesses and fairy stories that Bianca hadn't left that long ago.

'No sweetheart. I thought I did at the time, but that was so long ago. I love you and Sam – and Jeremy.'

As she said his name, Rebecca looked up. Jeremy had gone.

'That's not true.' Bianca's words were quiet. 'You don't love me. You don't have time.'

Her words wedged in Rebecca's chest. Bianca was right, though. Rebecca treated her like the other responsibilities in her life – to be dealt with at the appropriate, prearranged times. But a teenage girl who was so unhappy needed much more than that. Rebecca's whole body ached with the thought of all the things she'd done wrong.

She took Bianca's hand in both of hers.

'Bianca. I love you so much. You were my whole life for so long. Sam and Jeremy are part of that life now too, but that hasn't changed how I feel about you one little bit.'

The silence descended again. Then Bianca spoke tentatively. 'A couple of months ago I found an old diary you had written in when I was small.'

Rebecca hadn't thought of the book for years. Even then, it had been an ancient notebook covered in paisley silk. She'd wanted to remember some of the small pleasures of Bianca's early years with messages like, *Spent the morning playing Poohsticks at the creek. You are convinced that if you run across the bridge fastest, your stick will win. We need to do a bit of work on your physics skills I think.* Or *Terrible night – again – surely it wouldn't kill you to sleep more than four hours in a row!*

They'd been messages across time to a grown-up Bianca.

Bianca continued, 'The entries just stopped. In the same year you met Jeremy – I checked. What happened? Suddenly I didn't rate any more? You had better things to do?'

Bianca's voice was raw.

'No!' Rebecca almost yelled. 'God no! It was just that you were growing up and I started to realise how little I had to offer you. When you were younger I was all-powerful. I could solve all your problems. But then you got older and suddenly I couldn't fix things for you.' She struggled to explain. 'I got scared,' she finished weakly.

She looked at Bianca again. 'When I first saw that you'd cut yourself, all I wanted was to hold on to you and to never let you go. To make everything better for you. I'm so sorry I put it on that damn website. Jeremy and I were so worried, we'd been to see a counsellor who told us to try to pull you back to us and to give you a little time. You have no idea how hard it was to let you out of my sight, wondering if you might be feeling so bad that you'd cut yourself again.

'We're going to fix this, I promise. We can find you someone you can talk to if that's what you want. But we'll do whatever it takes – together. Okay?'

Bianca pulled her hand free. 'I'm tired. I just want to go to sleep.'

She lay down on the bed, her back to Rebecca and her legs curled up against her chest. Slowly Rebecca pulled a sheet up over her, then sat down in the chair beside the bed to watch her daughter sleep.

Claire

The rage that welled up inside Claire was unbearable and she felt like she was going to shatter.

'Go! Just go!' she screamed at Peter, unable to control herself.

She wasn't angry at Peter. Even amongst her pain she knew he'd done nothing wrong. It was anger at the bitter trick the universe had played on her. But she couldn't bear to look at Peter, knowing that he had the one thing she wanted more than anything else.

Peter turned on his heel and walked out.

Claire sank onto the couch, arms wrapped around her chest and tears running down her face.

She needed to tell someone. To have someone understand how unfair this was. After all these years praying for a child — to discover this. But the only friend she had in Brisbane was Rebecca. For a moment she pictured Rebecca, sitting on a chair in the hospital watching over her daughter. Their daughter — Rebecca and Peter's daughter.

Desperate for something to dim the pain, Claire walked into the kitchen and pulled out a bottle of wine. She poured a huge glass full and downed it, wondering what she had done to deserve this.

Just when she and Peter had been trying to find a way back

together, they'd been hit with the newspaper article and now this. It was as though someone was trying to tell her something.

At least Claire's lack of friends in Brisbane had lessened the embarrassment of having her life spread out in the Sunday papers. Peter hadn't quite seen it so calmly, his delight at the Demons' victory earlier that day swamped by his anger and confusion at the way their life was revealed in the article.

Claire poured another glass of wine, then put it down untouched, willing herself to stop crying.

She tried to see past the ache in her chest and think rationally. Was it possible that having Bianca around sometimes might heal the wounds that years of infertility had caused in her marriage to Peter? Claire truly didn't think so. Bianca was definitely not the type of girl who would welcome another woman in her life – she was trying everything to push Rebecca away as it was. Even if Bianca and Peter could establish some kind of relationship, Claire would only ever be an outsider.

Claire thought of Rebecca again. Of the secret she had carried all these years. Where had she found the strength? What would the truth have done to her and Peter all those years ago? Broken them up for sure.

Claire knew Peter thought Rebecca had betrayed him by keeping it a secret. Claire thought it was the opposite. It had been an act of kindness, at least initially. The secret had taken on its own life, though, and it was inevitable that it end in pain and hurt. It was easy to say, as Peter had, that Rebecca should have told the truth, but when? There were always going to be people devastated by this revelation.

Claire walked out onto the deck. She leaned on the railing and looked out into the dark.

Her last sobs stopped and she wiped her eyes with the back of her hand.

Things had been different with Peter in the last few days. They didn't know where they were going, but it felt as though he was thinking about her for the first time in a long time. It was as if her business had made him look at her differently, like a real person. That thought had thrilled her initially. But if she was honest with herself, it also filled her with unease. It was as if Peter needed to admire what Claire was doing in order to be interested in her. What would happen if this business wasn't successful, or if his enthusiasm for what she was doing ran out?

Claire wondered how Jeremy had reacted to the news about Bianca. If he'd been half as angry as Peter, Rebecca must be feeling awful. Claire pushed off from the railing and looked down at herself. Her yoga pants were a washed-out grey, stretched in all the wrong places and covered in little balls of fluff. She would never normally dream of setting foot outside the house in them.

Sod it, she thought as she walked back inside the house and picked up her handbag. She was sure the hospital staff had seen worse outfits than this one.

Rebecca

Rebecca turned off the engine, but didn't move to open the door. A band of cloud along the horizon shimmered pink, the morning sky a ridiculously vivid shade of blue.

During the long night in the hospital, Rebecca had realised that things were suddenly very different. For the first time in seventeen years she had no secrets. Not from Bianca, Claire or Peter. Or from Jeremy.

Every now and then Rebecca felt for the guilt, like a familiar sore tooth. Amazingly though, the feeling that had followed her since the day she'd first lied about Bianca's father was gone.

There was a whole new set of problems to face now. But for a moment last night, she and Bianca had been closer than they had been in a long time. A surge of optimism swept over Rebecca. She would make it up to Jeremy. She'd find a solution to Bianca's unhappiness and everything would be okay again.

Rebecca leapt up the few steps in front of the door and let herself into the house quietly.

She smiled to herself. No doubt, Sam had slept with Jeremy last night. Jeremy loved having Sam in bed with him – would have let him every night if Rebecca hadn't put her foot down. She didn't even need to go upstairs to know how it would look. Sam would be spread diagonally across the bed, quite possibly upside down. Jeremy would be curled around him in whatever space was available.

Making as little noise as possible, Rebecca eased her keys onto a table by the door.

Deep in thought about a long hot shower, she was startled by a soft voice behind her.

'How is she?'

Jeremy was wearing the same clothes as the day before and looked as though he hadn't been to bed. His eyes were bloodshot, his hair rumpled.

Rebecca smiled at him, a wave of love curling inside her. 'You look terrible.'

Jeremy's quick laugh was harsh. 'You don't look so great yourself.'

Rebecca glanced down. She was still wearing the old shirt and trousers a nurse had found for her after Rebecca had arrived at the hospital still in her nightgown. Her shoes were a pair of heavy lace-up nursing shoes.

'I guess not.'

In a moment Rebecca's euphoria vanished and she was exhausted. All she wanted was to be held safe in Jeremy's arms. Something made her hesitate, though. She crossed her arms across her chest.

'No more news really,' she said, answering his question. 'Bianca woke a couple of times, but the nurses gave her more painkillers and she went back to sleep pretty quickly.

'She'd just woken when I left. She didn't want to talk to me but the doctors say she'll be okay to come home after their rounds. I thought I'd have a shower and then head back in. How's Sam?'

Jeremy ignored the question. 'Rebecca, we need to talk.'

Rebecca felt her stomach tighten. 'You know what they say,' she said lightly, trying to make a joke. 'Nothing good ever comes after those words.'

Jeremy didn't smile.

'I'm leaving,' he said.

'No!' Rebecca couldn't keep the shock out of her voice. 'Not now. You can't go now.' Not when I can finally make everything right, she thought to herself.

'You have too many secrets, Rebecca.'

Jeremy's face was so hard, Rebecca thought her heart might break. She thought she'd cried all her tears last night but more welled up behind her eyes.

Jeremy kept talking. 'From when I first met you, you always kept part of yourself locked away. I thought if I let you do it at your own pace, you'd let me in. Share yourself with me. But you never have. It's not just about Peter – or the group diary thing. It's that you've never trusted me enough to let me in. No more, Rebecca, I'm done.'

'But . . . where will you go?' Rebecca's words sounded ridiculously clichéd even to her. What the hell did it matter where he was planning on staying? But it was all she could manage.

'I've booked into a hotel in town for a few nights. After that . . . I'm not sure. Rent a house I guess.' He paused. 'I'm not disappearing, I'll be here for Sam – and Bianca if she still needs me. I just can't be here with you any more.'

'No. You can't do this, Jeremy. I love you, I am so sorry I didn't tell you about Bianca's father, but I couldn't. This shouldn't change anything between us. We're still the same.'

She paused.

'I need you, Jeremy,' she said urgently.

'See, that's not true,' Jeremy replied. 'You don't need anyone. You control your personal life like you do your work. It's all done according to your rules and your timetables.'

He picked up a suit carrier and sports bag from behind the sofa, pulling his keys out of his pocket. 'I'll give you a call tomorrow and figure out the best way to manage things with Sam.'

Rebecca watched as he walked out the door and toward his car. This pain was different from what she'd felt when Bianca was hurt, she evaluated clinically. With Bianca she'd been terrified, but kept together by the desperate hope that she would be all right. This pain, though, was flat and raw – an ache that she didn't think would ever go away.

Jeremy had been the love she'd never expected. Years of

fending for herself and Bianca had made her believe they were the team, that male company was a transitory pleasure, no more. Jeremy had changed that. He had loved Bianca and Rebecca together and then Sam had arrived.

Was Jeremy right? Had she always left him on the outside?

It was only as Jeremy reversed out of the driveway and onto the street that Rebecca moved.

Slowly she looked around the room on which they had spent a fortune. A black porcelain sculpture sat in the corner of the room. 'Gloriously sleek lines' was how the interior designer had described the piece. Rebecca had never liked it.

Deliberately she walked over to it and kicked it. Its middle section resisted the first kick from her shoe, but not the second. The noise was shocking in the still of the early morning, but Rebecca didn't flinch. She stood watching as the sculpture caved into itself and collapsed, the fall breaking the remaining pieces into shards on the polished cement floor. Only then did she turn around and walk upstairs.

Alice

'Seriously Mum. It's just a movie. You have no idea. It will be fun. Remember that? F-U-N.'

Alice looked at her daughter through eyes gritty with lack of sleep. She felt as though she was seeing Ellen for the first time in a very long while.

As a small child, Ellen's hair had been platinum blonde, almost white. Recently, though, it had darkened and was now almost brown. A small part of Alice wondered when that had happened. How had she not noticed? And when had her daughter started sneering at her? Just because she wouldn't let her go into town with her friends to see a movie.

Alice tried to explain herself again, trying not to sound as exhausted as she felt. 'Twelve is far too young to go into town by yourself. If you're that set on seeing the movie, I'll take you over the weekend. You could even bring a friend.'

'Yeah great.' Ellen rolled her eyes. 'Going to the movies with my mum is just what I want.' She started to turn away, mumbling 'Thanks for nothing,' under her breath.

For quite some time now Ellen had been convinced that Alice's mission in life was to ruin Ellen's. Alice told herself that it was okay. That all her friends' kids thought the same thing about their parents.

And then, like a boxer who knew she was beaten but wanted to inflict pain anyway, Ellen turned back.

'No wonder Dad's never home any more. Why would he want to be with someone as boring as you?'

And suddenly, just like that, a sneering daughter wasn't okay.

Without conscious thought, Alice slapped her. Hard. Across the face.

Just like that.

There was a moment of stunned silence. Ellen's face was pale except for a red mark where Alice's hand had connected. Ellen stared at Alice. Ellen who had never been smacked in her life. Not once.

Alice knew she should say sorry. She should step in, give Ellen a hug. Tell her she was just tired. Make it all right.

But she did none of those things.

Instead, she stood there, looking at Ellen. Watching Ellen watching her. Alice felt as though a well inside her had run dry and there was nothing left.

Alice knew Ellen expected an apology. And in fact, she probably deserved one. But the-Alice-with-nothing-left felt anything but sorry. In fact she felt great. She even wondered, briefly, about doing it again. God, but it had felt good.

After several more seconds of wordless staring, Ellen's face crumpled and she turned and fled up the stairs.

With shaking hands, Alice turned back to the kitchen counter, trying to focus on the task at hand. As usual they were running late.

She looked at the food she'd already laid out, ready for school lunches. Pumpkin and pecan cake – made without preservatives and with flaxseed oil. Multigrain bread and free-range roast chicken. With hummus for Ellen. With avocado for John. With mayo for Alex.

At least Andrew was still overseas. He didn't like roast chicken. She would have had to give him tuna, which he never really enjoyed . . .

What the hell was she doing? She was obsessing about a bunch of stupid lunch boxes, for Christsakes. Had she always been this pathetic?

Ellen's words swam in her mind. 'No wonder Dad's never

home any more. Why would he want to be with someone as boring as you?'

Alice had a sudden memory of a dawn in London many years ago. She and Andrew had been up all night. She'd taken an Ecstasy tablet. He'd taken who knew how many. She remembered the warmth of the chemical in her bloodstream. They were utterly in love with each other and with the world.

They'd sneaked away from the party and climbed out of the attic window. There was a small flat piece of roof. There, with the new day flooding across the rooftops, they'd made love. In full view, she'd realised later, of anyone who'd cared to look up. She'd felt as though her bones were liquid, that her whole body had fused with Andrew's.

Alice hadn't thought of that morning for years but now the memory of it was so strong she could almost feel the drug-induced euphoria.

She looked down at the kitchen bench again.

Had that been the real Alice that morning in London long ago? Or was the real Alice this woman worrying about tuna?

She knew the answer. Or at least she hoped she did.

This wasn't her.

She felt as though she'd woken up from a long dream and found herself in the wrong life.

Alice picked up the pumpkin cake and threw the whole thing into the bin. Not the compost. The bin. The one that contributed to landfill.

It felt good.

She followed it with the roast chicken. Then the multigrain bread. The avocado and then the hummus.

It felt really good.

Right. Lunches.

She turned back to the cupboard and pulled out a packet of Cocoa Pops. She'd bought it for Ellen's birthday treat the next week. Perfect. She filled three small Tupperware containers right to the top and broke her special packet of dark chocolate (high in antioxidants) into thirds. Each piece she put on top. That was morning tea covered.

Lunch. She stood in front of the cupboard for a moment and then was struck with inspiration. She pulled a loaf of white bread out of the freezer and smothered three slices in butter. She slathered jam on, then crunchy peanut paste, and covered each with another slice of bread. Her children would probably be expelled for bringing peanuts into the school yard, but that was their problem.

Ignoring the Tupperware containers lined up on the bench, Alice pulled an ancient roll of clingfilm out of the cupboard. Tearing off far more than she needed, she wrapped each sandwich in plastic. Excellent, that should ensure some chemicals leaking into their bread.

Alice's mind spun as she worked.

She had lain awake most of the night wondering how this had happened. It had to be someone in the group who'd given the information to the journalist. No one would have reason to know the website was there otherwise, even if they could some- how avoid the password protection. But all of the group were implicated in the article – not one of them came out of the arti- cle unscathed. It just didn't make sense.

The group had seemed like a nice idea. You can be happy now. Don't wait for a cataclysmic event that forces you to make changes. Make small changes in your life today. Be happy. Drink nice tea. Be kind to animals.

How could something so simple have gone so horribly wrong?

Claire had called Alice on Sunday to tell her what had hap- pened to Bianca. Alice hadn't heard from any of the others. She was sure they must blame her for the article and hadn't been able to bring herself to contact any of them.

The dark hours of last night had given Alice plenty of time to wonder what had happened to everyone else. It had also given her time to wonder what on earth to tell Andrew when he arrived home today.

She'd read the newspaper article so many times she could just about recite it.

It was so unfair, she had wanted to scream. She hadn't been

trying to control anyone. She had just thought her plan might work.

Now she was at war with her twelve year old daughter.

She pushed the lunchboxes into the appropriate school bags and carried them to the door.

'Time to go!' she yelled up the stairs, surprised by how normal she sounded.

Shoes were scattered all over the hall. Automatically Alice bent to stack them in the shelf next to the front door. Suddenly she stopped. Straightening, she aimed a kick at a large pile, scattering them even further. Calmly she picked up her car keys and walked out the front door.

Claire

Claire slid the last sock into the Ziploc bag and ran the white toggle along the top.

Quietly, she slid it into position at the top of the Samsonite suitcase and closed the lid. How many times had she packed like this for Peter over the years? Conferences, golfing weekends, she packed for them all. Shoes and jumpers on the bottom, shirts next and then underwear on top.

The zip whispered closed.

She started as she heard Peter's soft voice in the doorway. 'It's probably not quite normal for a wife to pack her husband's suitcase when he is leaving.'

Claire smiled sadly. 'We're both leaving,' she reminded him. 'It's just that you're going first. Hopefully we'll be able to sell the house soon.'

She still wasn't sure why she was so calm about her life crashing in around her. It was almost as if she'd spent years worrying about everything and now that the worst had happened there was nothing left to worry about.

In the end there hadn't really been a decision to make. The last sliver of Peter and Claire's love had disappeared some time ago, worn out by too much unhappiness and not enough good times. The thought that they could put it back together had been tempting but not real.

It had taken the news about Bianca to make Claire sure. She wasn't prepared to see that one through with him. It was time for her to be by herself.

When Claire had arrived at the hospital the night before, Rebecca had looked utterly beaten.

Claire had sat down beside her and they'd both sat in silence watching Bianca sleep.

Finally Rebecca had spoken. 'It happened before you and Peter got together.'

Claire nodded. 'I know.'

'I would never have cheated on you.'

Claire felt tears on her cheeks. 'I know.'

She stayed with Rebecca until just before dawn when the hospital started to wake up and Bianca stirred.

Then she called Peter on his mobile, not even asking where he was. It had been strangely clinical. Both of them had known it was over. All they'd had left to talk over had been the details.

Now, standing in their bedroom, Claire looked over at Peter. 'I still can't believe this house is worth so much less than we paid for it.'

The two real estate agents they'd had over that day had been pessimistic about the price it would raise.

Peter grimaced. 'We must be the only two people who have lost money on property during the boom.'

Actually, if she was truthful, Peter hadn't had much to do with it. She'd told him she'd loved the house, carried away by her vision of what it could look like. Instead of seeing a grungy, dingy verandah, she'd seen impromptu brunches as friends dropped in, long dinner parties and Sunday lunches.

So much for that.

It would have been very easy for him to blame her, to tell her it was all her fault, but he hadn't.

Once they'd sold and paid off the mortgage and credit cards, they would be barely in the black. It made Claire feel sick to think of it, so mostly she didn't.

Suddenly Peter strode forward and grabbed Claire by the

arms. 'Maybe we could make it work. Sell this place . . . move somewhere else . . .'

His voice trailed off as he saw Claire's face.

She was finished, there was nowhere for them to go.

Without another word Peter turned away.

Alice

Ellen had obviously told John and Alex what had happened. All three were unusually subdued during the ride to school.

In the rear-vision mirror Alice could see the children sneaking glances at each other, clearly unable to decide how to react.

Normally Alice would have felt forced to fill the silence. Start a conversation, turn on the radio. But not today. Today she felt strangely removed from the whole scene. As though she were just a passing stranger looking in the car window and wondering why everyone looked so unhappy.

All three kids were clearly relieved when she pulled up at the school gates and, with a quick chorus of 'bye Mum', they were gone. Despite the fact that she was in a two minute drop-off zone, Alice didn't pull away instantly. Instead she watched the three familiar backpacks linger briefly together, then separate and go their own ways.

She could almost imagine the conversation that had passed between them.

'She'll get over it,' Ellen would be saying in the smartarse tone Alice hated.

'She'll be feeling guilty as hell by this afternoon. I guarantee we'll all get extra PlayStation time tonight.'

Alice thought about that. Tonight. Tonight, it would start all over again. The fights over who wouldn't eat what. Who stole whose place at the dinner table.

Even after the backpacks disappeared from sight, she didn't pull away. She was aware of the glares shot by mothers out of car windows, but she just didn't care. On a normal day dallying in the two minute zone was a serious protocol crime. But today, it seemed, was not turning out to be an ordinary day.

She knew she should go home. Throw all the Red Folder Project stuff away. It was over, that much was clear. She might as well put it behind her. Failing that, the house was a tip again.

But when she finally put the car in gear, she didn't swing the car into its customary U-turn at a safe distance from the pedestrian crossing. Instead, she kept going. She almost turned left when she reached the Normanby five ways. She had her indicator on, intending to double back on her tracks, head home and pull herself together.

But she didn't.

Instead, she turned right and within minutes was on the freeway.

Alice flicked the radio to the country station she enjoyed, despite her children's embarrassment. She turned the volume up far too loud and let the music wash over her as the freeway took her away from the city. Away from home.

The song finished and another came on. More heartbreak and undying love. She twisted the volume knob even higher and drove faster. She knew she was breaking the speed limit. How long had it been since she'd done that?

She moved into the right hand lane, passing everyone.

One after another the songs rolled over her, blocking out the need to think as her car headed south. Alice passed freeway exits, shopping centres . . . All of them became a blur. The only thing that existed was the car and the music.

It wasn't until she reached a traffic jam that she slowed down.

As she did, she realised she'd hit the southern end of the Gold Coast. Surely she hadn't travelled so far?

On the side of the freeway was a sign advertising the Cur‐rumbin Wildlife Sanctuary.

Alice had a sudden memory of visiting the wildlife sanctuary with Andrew when she'd first arrived in Brisbane. She remem‐bered the heat radiating off the bitumen as they'd sat together on a low brick wall licking mango ice creams. It had been so hot it had been impossible to eat faster than the ice cream was melting and both of them had the sticky mixture dripping down their arms.

Abandoning his own ice cream, Andrew had run his tongue from her elbow to her fingertips and she remembered the feel of his mouth sucking her middle finger.

They'd laughed like little kids and in the end agreed the only solution was a dip in the ocean. They'd stayed the whole day, driving back to Brisbane as the sun went down. Sunburnt and ravenous.

Now, without any plans, she exited the freeway and pulled over next to the enormous Greyhound buses lined up beside the front door. The wildlife sanctuary was much fancier than she remembered. The unremarkable entrance she recalled had been replaced by turnstiles and a glass and stone booth.

Alice had no intention of going in. She'd been thrilled by koalas and kangaroos when she'd first moved out here. Fifteen years later, she was over them.

She looked down at her hands on the steering wheel and realised she had no intentions at all.

The clock on the dashboard read *09:57*.

She still had plenty of time to get home.

Except she wasn't going home.

Rebecca

Since Jeremy had left, Rebecca had operated on autopilot, doing everything that needed doing without allowing herself to think.

She had showered, woken Sam and headed back to the hospital to collect a sullen Bianca. Her attempts to talk to Bianca about Peter had been rudely rebuffed. Bianca had limped up the stairs to her bedroom as soon as they arrived home, closing the door tightly behind her.

Rebecca had called the office early, long before anyone would be in, and left a message on her assistant's voicemail. She'd then logged onto the system from home and put an out-of-office message on her incoming email saying she was on leave.

Although nobody from work had called, they must have seen the article and identified her. Rebecca could just imagine the furtive conversations that would be buzzing around the office. This would be gossip beyond their wildest dreams.

The thought of having Lorraine around all day was unbearable. So Rebecca had given her the day off, pretending not to hear the smirk in the nanny's voice. Sam's delight at having Rebecca home for the day was the only thing that had penetrated the shell around her, the guilt that it should be such a special event for him, cutting deep.

It wasn't until lunchtime, when Sam was asleep and Bianca

was doing God only knew what in her room, that Rebecca stopped and allowed herself to think.

Jeremy was gone. Gone.

With shaking hands, she called his mobile, but the call went straight through to his voicemail.

What message could she possibly leave?

'I'm sorry I got it so badly wrong. I never realised how much I needed you until you weren't here. I'm lonely. Come home.'

Silently, she hung up.

The phone rang immediately. Eagerly Rebecca hit the talk button.

'Hi Rebecca, it's Claire.'

'Hi.'

The word echoed down the phone line, followed by a silence.

Where did they begin? Rebecca had no idea.

It was Claire who spoke. 'How's Bianca?'

'She's okay. A bit battered and bruised and not too happy with the cast on her arm. But she'll be okay.' Rebecca paused. 'How are you — and Peter?'

'He left this morning. It's not about Bianca, it was the final straw, that's all. There was nothing left. It's time for both of us to start again.'

Rebecca said nothing, her thoughts swirling. Had she set them all on this path the day she first lied about Bianca's father? If she had told the truth, would Peter and Claire be in a different place to this one?

'It's okay, Rebecca,' Claire's words were strong and Rebecca believed her.

They were silent for a moment.

'Who do you think gave the journalist the information for that article?' Rebecca asked the question that had been in her head since the previous morning.

'I have no idea,' Claire answered.

'It had to be Alice didn't it? Think about all the publicity her new book will get from this debacle.'

'I don't know.' Claire paused for a moment. 'None of the rest of us would have done it, that's for sure. Who wants their personal life spread all over the weekend paper? But Alice? I don't know. She seems so – well, so nice.'

After Claire had hung up, Rebecca walked purposefully into the kitchen.

She hadn't eaten all day but she didn't feel hungry. Instead she made a coffee, adding an extra shot for good measure. She pulled her filofax toward her, trying to think which of the lawyers she knew would be able to help.

Rebecca knew what Jeremy would have said. 'It's done now, Bec. Let it be.'

But Jeremy wasn't here. That was the whole point.

Alice

Alice tried to ignore the waiter's curious look as he put the coffee cup on the table.

Surely she didn't look that out of place?

Only two other tables were occupied. One was taken by three soft-drink sipping boys, wetsuits stripped to below their hipbones. Alice wondered idly why they weren't in school. The other was occupied by a leather-skinned woman who looked as though she'd spent most of her life in exactly that spot.

Alice was in her standard school drop-off uniform of jeans and T-shirt – today's T-shirt happened to be black. She couldn't remember when she'd last washed her hair. It was forced into a ponytail which she knew didn't suit her.

Only a quiet road separated the cafe from the beach and Alice looked across at the stretch of glittering sand which looped to a point, a large flat rock at its end. The cafe had been a kiosk until coffee became a cultural essential. The owners had tried to enter the new era with stainless-steel tables and angular chairs. But the faded umbrellas and sandwich boards advertising ice creams betrayed its origins.

It was a place for holidays smelling of sunscreen and frying sausages. Not for a tired housewife who hadn't been in a bikini for a decade.

Andrew would have landed by now and arrived home to an

empty house. It had been almost a week since she'd seen him. Being at home to meet him wouldn't really have been too much to ask.

This was starting to get ridiculous. She had to get back.

It was just that she was so tired.

She shouldn't be. It wasn't as though her children were babies any more and waking for feeds every three hours.

They had all had been terrible sleepers as babies and she'd felt like a zombie for years. She remembered yearning for sleep, counting the hours before she could get back to bed, if only for a short while.

This wasn't like that now. It was a different kind of tired.

She was tired of being the grown-up that made things work as they should. And she was tired of feeling guilty.

Alice looked along the road. Currumbin was a lot fancier than when she and Andrew had been here. The one little guest-house on the corner had yielded to a multistorey hotel complex and there was a small but stylish looking hotel adjacent to the cafe. Maybe that was what she needed. To get a room and sleep. A little slice of oblivion might give her the energy to pull it all together again.

Almost unable to believe what she was doing, Alice paid for the coffee and walked into the hotel next door.

Fifteen minutes later she was sitting on the edge of a king-sized bed in a beachfront room.

She should call Andrew. He'd be wondering where she was. Why hadn't he called her mobile? Alice pulled her handbag onto her lap and pulled out her phone. Its screen was black and wouldn't turn on − battery totally out of charge.

Alice picked up the telephone beside the bed and called Andrew's mobile number, no idea of what she would say when he answered. She counted the rings, her stomach unclenching as they continued. Mercifully Andrew's voice message clicked on. As Alice listened, his voice sounded like that of a stranger.

'Andrew, it's me. I'm out all day, but will be back later this afternoon. Just in case it's after school pick-up time, could you get the kids today? I − I'll see you soon.'

She hung the phone up, kicked off her shoes and lay back fully clothed on top of the covers on one edge of the huge bed. Finally she allowed her eyes to drop closed.

Alice woke with a start. The light in the room had faded.

Although her mind felt as though it was stuffed with cloud, she knew instantly where she was and that she'd slept way too long.

She sat up in a panic.

The clock radio read *16:20*. God, she should have been home hours ago.

A terrible thought struck her. What if Andrew hadn't got her message? What if he wasn't even in the country yet — if his flight had been delayed?

Her stomach clenched in terror. What if no one had picked up the children?

Desperately, she fumbled on the floor for her shoes.

'Finally.'

At the soft voice, Alice spun around to see a shadowy figure sitting in a chair in the corner.

'Andrew! What are you . . .'

Before he could respond, she asked desperately, 'The kids. Did you pick up the kids?'

Andrew nodded without smiling. 'The kids are fine.'

Alice felt the tide of panic fade, replaced instantly by embarrassment. Even in the poor light she could see Andrew looking at her as though he'd never seen her before. She shook her head, praying she could keep back the tears she could feel behind her eyelids.

'How, how did you get in here?' She bunched the bedcover in her fists.

Andrew smiled and for a moment everything felt as though it would be all right.

'How do you think?' he asked.

'Oh no, I didn't, did I?'

Alice routinely left keys in doors. Andrew often walked

in at night, swinging the keys which had been hanging in the front door lock since Alice came home hours before. On one memorable occasion she'd even left the keys in the car door and then driven off with Andrew's set. They were ten minutes down the road before they figured out what the banging noise was.

Andrew smile disappeared and Alice knew that she needed to explain.

'Andrew, I'm sorry . . . I don't know what happened. I just wanted . . . I just couldn't go home and then . . .' Her voice trailed off. She had no idea what had happened herself, so how could she explain it to him?

'And then what?' Andrew pushed himself out of the chair and moved to snap on the switch, flooding the room with light.

'I land after an extremely crappy trip away to find about twenty messages about some goddamn article. Not one of them from my wife, I might add.'

He sounded as though he were struggling to keep his voice calm. Alice tried to interrupt, but he kept talking.

'And then I get home to an empty house. Car gone, wife gone. Just a voicemail message saying you were going to be late.'

He gestured around the room. 'This isn't late, Alice. This is gone.'

She tried again to speak but he clearly hadn't finished.

'What is going on, Alice? If you hadn't called my mobile from the landline here, I would have had no idea where you were. I'd have called the police by now.'

He was right. She knew he was. Nothing she had done today made any sense even to her. She'd been selfish and unfair.

And yet, now that she knew everyone was safe, she suddenly wasn't sorry.

She could see Andrew's lips moving as he kept talking but his words had stopped connecting with her brain. She stared at his face. Was this really the man she'd married? There had been a time when she'd loved him so much that she'd ached when they were apart.

The stupid little flirtation with Kerry, which she'd been

feeling so guilty about, didn't even rate on the scale of how she had once felt about Andrew.

That had been a long time ago though.

Maybe if Andrew had asked whether she was okay she would have felt differently. Or if he had sat down on the bed beside her and hugged her. Instead, it seemed the only thing he cared about was that she had abandoned her post. He hadn't even waited to hear what she had to say.

A moment ago she'd felt like bursting into tears. As he kept talking, she could feel anger coursing up her spine. His words echoed in her ears.

'This isn't late, Alice. This is gone.'

Gone? Was that what this was?

Finally his lips stopped moving and she assumed she was now permitted to speak.

Her voice sounded cold, even to her own ears. 'You know what? Maybe you're right. Maybe this is gone.'

Fuelled by adrenalin, she stood up, careful not to move any closer to Andrew than she had to. She briefly registered the surprise on his face.

'I can't do it any more, Andrew. Any of it. I surrender.' She raised her hands. 'I've failed. Failed at being a writer, failed at being a mother. Failed at being a wife. I think maybe it's time to wave the white flag and move on.'

Alice's grandmother had once told her that there were lines in every marriage that shouldn't be crossed. Some were obvious, while others were like tripwires hidden in the grass, obvious only when your chin cracked onto the rocky ground.

Alice knew that what she was saying now crossed all of them. But she couldn't stop.

'I can't keep the house clean. I can't keep the kids happy. Quite clearly I can't keep you happy. And I'm sure as hell not happy.'

Andrew opened his mouth but she raised her voice. 'It wasn't for lack of trying. I have read just about every book on home organisation and parenting that has ever been published. At last count I had three folders full of recipes from magazines that one day I was going to make. I have tried spending fifteen minutes every day spending quality time with each of my children. I have tried baking goddamn cookies one day a week.'

She slowed her voice down so there would be no confusion. 'I . . . can't . . . do . . . it.'

Her words echoed around the room for a moment, before disappearing and leaving behind a thick silence.

Andrew looked at Alice for a long moment. Slowly he walked toward her, lowering himself onto the bed beside her.

'So what happens now?' he asked quietly.

Alice turned toward him and was surprised to see a real look of fear in his eyes. 'You know, I have absolutely no idea.'

Andrew looked straight ahead for a moment. His voice was hoarse when he spoke. 'Do you know how many times I've walked in the door at night just wanting to sit down and talk to you?' He looked away for a moment. 'But all I'd get was a peck on the check as you stuck your rubber gloves back into the sink.'

He paused, as if deciding whether to go on.

'I'd get a time estimate on dinner and then have you banging around the kitchen exuding this self-righteous resignation at still having to be working at eight o'clock at night. I tried to suggest we get takeaway a few times, or maybe just have something simple. But you'd bite my head off as if I was complaining.'

There was silence, the tension reverberating around the small room.

Alice tried to reconcile the picture Andrew had just described with what she remembered. Achingly tired nights, when all she wanted was to walk away from the kitchen and fall into bed. Instead she'd think of something to make, clear the benches from the children's dinner and start again. Dinners made for a husband who didn't want them. The memory of an endless string of nights just like he'd described sped through her head and threatened to overwhelm her. How could they both have been looking at the same scene so differently?

'I thought that when you suggested takeaway it was because you figured I couldn't manage.' Alice's voice was almost a whisper.

Their eyes met. For a moment the two different worlds they'd inhabited for the last years aligned.

Alice tried to sift back through the indistinguishable stretch of evenings to the beginning. Was there a moment when she'd almost agreed to a curry from down the road? Or when Andrew had almost wrapped his arms around her at the sink instead of walking straight past her to the study? A moment that could have set them on a different road to the one they stood at the end of now.

It was the sense of ridiculous waste that consumed her – a waste of time and effort and a love that had been worth something once.

Andrew shook his head as if to clear it. 'I don't know, Alice. We used to be happy. The house, the business, the kids, they were all supposed to add to that, not destroy it.'

The angle of Andrew's head flipped Alice back through time to an afternoon in a pub in London's Camden Town. The insipid afternoon sun had stretched pale fingers across the glass tabletop and illuminated the beer sitting warm and flat in their glasses, English style. She'd watched Andrew as, eyes sparkling with a mixture of excitement and lager, he'd talked about the life they could have in Australia. He'd achieved exactly what he'd set out to. But his eyes were a flat brown these days.

'I'm sorry.'

Alice looked up at Andrew, startled by his apology.

He looked back at her steadily.

'I'm sorry too,' she whispered.

In a romance novel they'd have fallen into each other's arms.

In real life they sat there quietly for a moment, neither knowing what to do.

Finally Alice stood and picked up her handbag from the floor.

'We should go,' she said.

Megan

Megan sat on the front step, arm around her dog Merlin's neck. The long flat hours of early afternoon surrounded her.

She'd called in sick for a second day today.

Wearily she rested her forehead on the dog's neck, her cheek pillowed against Merlin's wiry coat. She screwed her eyes up tight, trying to force the thoughts from her mind.

Megan hadn't contacted Greg since the night she'd run out of his place and he hadn't tried to get in touch with her.

He must have seen the article – everyone else in Brisbane had.

Megan's answer phone had been blinking madly when she'd returned home from the cafe on Sunday. Her sisters had each left several messages but, in true family form, they seemed to have forgotten she was a sinner and had left messages of support and outrage at the article. Megan smiled at the memory. Even her mother had called, asking if she'd like to come home and stay for a while. For once that didn't sound like such a bad idea.

But from Greg, there had been no word.

The day was burning hot, the sun edging across Megan's feet, her toes sweating in her sneakers.

Megan rubbed Merlin's head for a moment and stood up.

She walked inside and re-read the email she had drafted to Greg.

Who'd have thought you and I were interesting enough to be in the paper?

And here was I thinking it was just a harmless little affair.

It looks as though I might have to take up your suggestion of a career change after all. My principal called this morning. When I admitted that 'Megan' from the article was actually me (there didn't seem much point in denying it), she made it very clear that my behaviour does not set a good example. She suggested an 'unpaid sabbatical', which I think is public-service speak for 'don't come back'.

So maybe I'll check out programming after all.

As for the rest of the group — who knows? Alice has called one last meeting at the bar tonight — God knows why. Hope she's wearing a bullet-proof vest.

And you and I? Maybe my moral compass isn't totally defective. Maybe it just went a bit haywire for a while.

It's time to finish this.

I wish you well.

Megan

She hit the send button.

Trudging into her bedroom, she kicked her shoes off. Jeans and singlet top dropped onto the floor and she pulled a rancid running shirt and shorts from the washing basket. White socks smudged with dirt were stuffed in the toe of her running shoes and she pulled them on.

She felt a fool before she even reached the roundabout at the end of the street. The sun forced sweat onto her forehead and her arms jerked awkwardly, her normal running rhythm lost in the heat.

Megan turned up the hill. The pain ripped through her muscles, but she leaned into it, forcing her body faster. She reached the top of the hill and fell back into a shambling run, pulling air into her lungs in gasping coughs. But still she kept going, up and down several more hills until finally she reached the river.

There wasn't even a cool breeze off the water, which sat slack and brown in the beating sunshine. Megan turned down the pathway alongside the river. Suddenly she could bear it no longer and stopped, head bent to her knees, as she fought to regain her breath.

'And people call me senile . . .' An unmistakably old voice rasped out the words.

Megan turned, the motion tipping a river of sweat from her forehead into one eye. She rubbed at it, seeing the old man in a strangely familiar blur.

The sweat prickled her flushed face.

She attempted a smile. 'You're right. Bloody stupid idea.'

Megan caught sight of the low-slung blond-brick building on the rise behind the river and it triggered her memory. 'You sit here a bit, don't you? I've seen you before when I run past here.'

The old man nodded. 'Hell of a lot more interesting outside than in.' He gestured with one sharply pointed shoulder at the retirement home behind him.

'Guess so,' Megan answered.

'Never seen you down here in the middle of the day though,' the man said. 'Lost your job have you?' he pried shamelessly.

'Looks like it,' Megan answered flatly.

A silence fell.

'Pull up a pew if you like.' He gestured at the bench.

The bench sat in a pool of shade. Megan sat down on the far end.

'I'm Ray,' the man introduced himself.

'Nice to meet you. I'm Megan.'

'Not a good day?' Ray asked conversationally.

'Nope,' Megan replied.

Ray nodded slowly.

'Likely to get any better?'

'Nope.'

'If you think you'll get any pithy proverbs from me, forget it,' he said. 'I'm a grumpy old bastard.'

'Good,' Megan replied. 'Pithy proverbs would make me throw up right now.'

Ray nodded.

A blue and white city cat cruised past regally and their eyes followed it around the bend in the river.

'Do you sit here all day?' Megan asked.

'No,' Ray replied. 'Just most of it. This bench is the reason I wanted to come here. Drove my son mad. Wouldn't take up any of the fancy new places on the north side of town. I stayed in my place until someone croaked and I got a bed here.'

Megan looked over at Ray. He was still staring over the water, face expressionless.

'It's a nice spot,' she ventured.

'Yep,' he answered.

'Is the retirement place okay?'

'Pretty good. Food's terrible but there you go. I put up with that for sixty-five years, a few more won't hurt.'

'Sorry?' Megan asked, not understanding.

'Beryl – my wife – was an awful cook. Never told her though. Sixty-five years we were married and I reckon she died thinking she was a gourmet chef.'

Megan turned and looked at the side of Ray's face. 'You're telling me you were married to your wife for all that time and never told her she was a bad cook?'

Ray turned to her. 'No, of course not. I loved her.'

Megan thought of her relationship with Greg. She thought of the nights out in bars drinking too much and of the frantic sessions of sex, knowing he wouldn't be staying the night. It all suddenly seemed rather sad.

It wasn't love – nothing even like it. She'd known that rationally, been told it by others, but she'd never quite believed it until now.

'That was kind,' she said, looking at her dirty running shoes.

He snorted a laugh. 'Kind? Nah, she'd have set on me with a wooden spoon if I'd complained. A real firecracker was my Beryl.' His eyes lit up as he said his wife's name.

Megan smiled, not believing him. She put her hands on her thighs and pushed herself up.

'Don't suppose you like chocolate and beetroot cake, do you?' she asked impulsively.

'Never had it. Doesn't sound good though,' Ray replied.

Megan laughed. 'You're right. Sixty-five years is enough. Don't worry.'

She raised a hand goodbye. The old man nodded in reply and Megan took a couple of steps back toward the path.

On an impulse Megan stopped and turned around.

'Do you remember when you yelled out something at me one day? You were sitting further up the hill, I couldn't hear you. I've always wondered what you said.'

Perhaps there was an answer, something that a lifetime of a good love had given him, which might give her some direction.

The old man paused for a second, an expression she couldn't place catching at the corner of his mouth.

'Nice legs.'

Megan must have looked blank.

'I told you that you had nice legs,' Ray repeated.

Megan laughed for the first time since she'd read the article.

The Red Folder Group

Alice's hands were shaking as she accepted the glass of white wine from the bartender. She was deliberately late, figuring it was better to confront everyone at once.

They were all there, sitting at the same table they had been at two months earlier: Rebecca, Claire, Kerry, Megan. Even Lillian.

Alice's hair sat loose on her shoulders, uneven kinks replacing the controlled waves of the first meeting. She was wearing jeans that she knew were frayed at the hems and just a little too tight. But her shoes and her lips were the same as at previous meetings – both defiantly red.

She had woken early that morning after a restless sleep punctuated by dreams. One thing she was certain about was that it couldn't end like this. She had to face everybody.

So before anyone else woke, Alice had sat down at her computer. Unable to access the website, she had typed an email to everyone.

The article was terrible for all of us. I'm sorry. If you can, come along to the bar tonight – 8 pm.

Alice had gone through the motions of making breakfast and lunches. The children had eyed her warily as if wondering what she'd do next.

She'd driven past Lillian's house on the way home from the school, dropping a note in her mailbox. Lillian had left the group long ago, but she had been mentioned in the article, so Alice thought she had a right to be there.

As Alice walked to the table, she noticed a woman sitting at the bar. The woman was staring into her glass, gripping it tightly, and it was the tension in her that drew Alice's attention.

'Other people have problems too,' she reminded herself as she forced her eyes back to the table.

Straightening her shoulders she walked over to them. The chair at the head of the table was empty, and Alice sank into it. She put her glass carefully on the table in front of her and looked up.

'You all want to know how this happened,' she said without preamble. 'I'm so sorry about the article, but it wasn't me. I truly don't know how the journalist had access to the website.'

Rebecca shook her head, a disbelieving smile on her face. 'Come on, Alice. Do you really expect us to believe that? Only six of us had the password. One of us leaked the information. You haven't written a book for years and all of a sudden there's some sensational story about your new one. You're the only one who gets any benefit from the publicity. The rest of us just get the consequences.'

'Hang on a minute,' Kerry said. 'However it happened, it's done now. Is there any point in dwelling on why?'

Megan opened her mouth to reply, but Rebecca beat her to it.

'Dwelling on it? Tell me you're joking? My daughter has had a car accident and my husband has left me. My in-laws have it in ink that my life is a disaster and you want to chalk it up to experience? No way!'

Megan leaned forward and spoke. 'Apparently there is a petition circulating at school asking for my removal.' She paused and for a moment Alice thought she was going to cry.

Then Megan shook her head and when she spoke again it was with her normal aggression. 'Okay Alice, so if you say it wasn't you, then who did leak the story? I want to know who it was and I want to sue their asses off!'

Rebecca put down her glass with a clatter. 'I've already checked it out. We put our diaries online. Someone else wrote about what was in them. It's not defamation because it's all true.'

'Are you serious?' Megan was outraged. 'How about invasion of privacy? Or breach of trust? How about –'

Megan broke off abruptly and the colour drained from her face. She was looking over Alice's shoulder.

'How about encouraging marriage-wrecking behaviour?' came a voice Alice didn't know. 'How about recklessly ruining the lives of innocent people who don't even care about your bullshit "little things"?'

Alice turned. The woman she'd noticed on the way in was standing beside her. She was clearly a little drunk and very, very angry.

'You!' she pointed a red-nailed finger at Alice, 'told one of these women,' the finger moved over the rest of the table, 'to follow her own road. To find something that made her happy and to do it without thinking about the consequences.'

Alice was vaguely aware that the bar had fallen silent. Out of the corner of her eye she saw the bartender move toward the phone, clearly wondering if the police were going to be needed.

'So she shagged my husband. Again. Shit, she even shagged him in my house. How's that for not worrying about the consequences?'

Alice looked back at Megan who was staring at the woman, transfixed.

'Lucky for me, my husband has used the same password for his phone and emails for years. I know what he did. I even know about the night at my house.'

Alice's mind tumbled as she tried to make sense of everything.

'Even luckier for me your ridiculous website made a great story. The editor loved it – reckons it's the best article I've sold him this year. Just a shame I had to use a pseudonym.'

The woman put out a hand against the wall to steady herself.

The silence echoed as everyone registered what she had said. Greg's wife was a journalist – it was she who had broken the story.

'So now all I have to do is figure out which one is Megan.'

The woman's eyes swept over the group, settling on Rebecca. Megan's chair scraped as she stood up.

'Deborah.'

Her gaze shifted reluctantly from Rebecca to Megan. They stared at each other for several seconds.

Deborah's words were low. 'So this is what he wants.'

'I'm sorry, Deborah.'

Deborah laughed harshly. 'Yeah great, thanks. That helps a lot.'

'It's over,' Megan told her.

'Yes, I do know that,' Deborah said, a mock brightness in her voice. 'And I know that it wasn't even my wonderful husband who finished it. It was you. Why?'

Megan didn't take her eyes off the older woman. 'It just didn't seem right any more.'

'Damn right it wasn't right,' Deborah yelled, anger back in full force. 'Shame you didn't figure that out a bit earlier.'

She looked around wildly. 'I hate you! I hate all of you and your stupid little tasks that ruin people's lives.'

Lillian spoke then. Her voice was soft but filled with quiet confidence. 'We are very, very sorry for your loss.'

A tear tricked down Deborah's cheek. Then another.

'I wish he had died,' she whispered. 'It would have hurt less.'

Deborah turned back to Megan, rubbed her hand over her eyes and then shook her head. Slowly she turned and walked out of the bar.

There was a moment of shocked silence.

Alice looked over at Megan, who was still standing, hands gripping the edge of the table, eyes fixed on the glass in front of her.

Alice was filled with horror. She had caused this tragedy. Her pithy little suggestion had led to the destruction of a family.

'It's not your fault, Alice.' Lillian's voice was firm. 'Everyone is responsible for their own actions. Just because Megan chose to take something you said to justify being with that woman's husband does not make it your fault.'

Megan sat down slowly and stared around at the group. She looked stunned, as if she'd just hit her head and was trying to figure out where she was.

'I'm sorry,' she said softly.

More silence, as if no one could think of anything to say.

'What I don't understand,' Kerry said finally, 'is how Deborah got access to the website. She said she'd seen Greg's emails, which means the information must have been there.'

'That means,' he said, turning to Megan, 'you sent him the password.'

Megan said nothing and Kerry kept speaking.

'I can understand why you'd tell your boyfriend what you were doing. But why would you give him the website and the password? This group has been private, the deal has always been that we share personal stuff, all of us. It was only ever going to be read by other people if Alice wrote a book and changed all our names.'

Megan paled, but met Kerry's eye. 'You're right. I told him the details, because I wanted him to look at the website.'

'You were laughing at it, weren't you – at us?' It was Claire who spoke. Her hair was tucked behind her ears, her face clean of make-up.

'Yes.' Megan didn't attempt to lie.

'Does it occur to you that you're the same as us? You're not some superior being who can sit in judgement upon us poor mortals?'

Megan went to speak, but Claire put up her hand. 'You don't realise, do you? You tried not to be part of it, not to tell us what you were about. But you did.

'You're bitter about having a job that you hate. You can't make yourself open up enough for a proper relationship. So the best way to avoid anything too serious was to take up with a married guy. You don't get on with your family, you have no friends.'

'Easy on, Claire,' Kerry tried to intervene.

'It's okay, Kerry,' Megan held out a hand and Claire continued speaking.

'You needed this group as much as any of us. It's made you realise these things – maybe even find a new direction. But just to prove you were too cool, you ridiculed the group, us, everything.'

'I think that's too harsh, Claire,' Lillian said. 'Things have happened to us all that we didn't expect. I think most of us still can't believe we were ever part of this group. It just . . . somehow happened.'

'But you weren't part of the group,' Claire said. 'You left.'

Lillian was quiet for a moment. 'Actually, I didn't really.'

She smiled at the looks of confusion.

'I just took a leave of absence while I was in Paris.'

Alice looked stunned, then laughed suddenly. 'You went?'

Lillian nodded.

'And?'

'And did I meet a debonair French millionaire who fell hopelessly in love with me, besotted by my suburban charm? Well no . . . But I had a good time.' She smiled. 'I had a very good time. And I realised that I wasn't buried with David.'

Claire leaned forward. 'So there's someone else then?'

She looked like a schoolgirl, Alice thought. Despite the carnage that surrounded her, Claire was still able to be delighted at the prospect of a new romance.

'No,' Lillian answered slowly, shaking her head. 'I can't ask someone else to spend their days watching me for symptoms, trying to protect me from whatever this illness is. And I can't in all honesty be involved with someone who doesn't know. But that's okay. Sometimes it's better to be by yourself.'

'Well I hope you're right,' Claire said, 'because I'm about to find out for real. Peter has moved out.'

Her words hit Alice like blows. 'Oh Claire, I'm so sorry . . . I never meant . . .'

Claire shook her head. 'It wasn't the group. That just pushed us over the edge. We've done nothing but go through the motions for a long time now.'

Kerry spoke as he put his arm in the air, signalling for the waiter. 'I think we need another drink,' he said.

'Can I have a beer please?' he asked the waiter.

'Actually,' he corrected himself a second later, 'can you make it a water? I'm driving.'

No one else wanted a drink and there was a strained silence.

'I want to apologise,' Alice said quietly. 'What I wanted to do was to make everyone's lives a little better. Not to end relationships or cause tensions in families. I'm sorry.'

'Don't kid yourself, Alice.' Megan had recovered her composure and her words were characteristically brusque. 'You told us to bake cakes, do good deeds, buy pretty necklaces. We did the other stuff – not you.'

'I think what Megan is trying to say – a little tactlessly,' said Lillian, 'is that we don't blame you. We're all grown-ups and if we'd had perfect lives we'd never even have filled in your red folders.'

'God, Lillian, speak for yourself. I've had my life turned upside down. I'll take my not so perfect life, thanks very much.' Rebecca banged her glass down on the table.

Lillian looked back at her, not even slightly intimidated. 'Really? Would you really, Rebecca? You don't think that perhaps this group has shown you how badly you need to fix things?'

She pinned Rebecca with a gaze that Alice was sure would have been the equal of any Rebecca had seen in the business world.

Rebecca looked back at her defiantly. But after several seconds she looked away.

Lillian spoke again. 'You all have lives. They can be good or bad. It's up to you.'

Lillian stood up.

'Goodnight.'

She picked up her bag and left, her slight figure looking surprisingly strong as she walked out of the door.

Kerry spoke after several seconds. 'You know what? How about we call it a day? What do you think, Madame Chairperson?'

His eyes met Alice's and lingered.

'Definitely time to finish it, yes.'

Alice paused, knowing there was something to be said, but having no idea what it should be.

'Thank you all. This isn't how I envisaged it would end. I'm sorry and I hope you can get on with your lives.'

They stood up.

Rebecca slung her bag over her shoulder and stepped up to Alice. 'Alice . . .'

'It's okay, Rebecca.'

They looked at each other, then Rebecca nodded slightly and turned toward the door.

Claire held out her hand to Alice. 'Thank you,' she said simply.

Alice squeezed her hand softly.

Megan slung her rucksack onto her shoulder. 'You'll be sorry to have me out of your life.' She smiled slightly.

'Devastated,' Alice replied. 'Be happy Megan.'

And then it was just Kerry and Alice.

'Kerry, I'm sorry,' Alice blurted out. 'I should have told you I was married, I just . . . I'm really sorry.'

To her surprise, Kerry smiled. 'Me too.'

She looked at him. 'What?'

'I'm sorry too,' he said cheerfully. 'I like open fireplaces.'

For a moment, Alice didn't know what he was talking about. Then she remembered his last email inviting her away for the weekend. She felt the heat rush to her face.

'I . . .' She felt like a fish with her mouth flapping open. 'I haven't told my husband.'

Kerry didn't miss a beat. 'Told him what?' he asked. 'That you turned me down?'

Alice wouldn't be put off that easily. She shook her head. 'That I wasn't honest with you.'

Kerry touched her arm briefly and then moved his hand away. 'You were honest enough to help me when I needed it,' he said. 'It's okay.'

He hesitated before continuing.

'I'm changing some things too, Alice. It's time to stop complaining about what's wrong with my life and make it right.'

Alice looked at him. He'd shaved off his goatee and he looked younger. Less glib and more vulnerable.

'Do you think maybe you can fix things with Sandra?'

Kerry shrugged. 'I don't know – maybe. For now, though, I need to fix things with me.'

He put his arms on her shoulders and pulled her toward him, kissing her gently on the cheek. 'Your husband is a very fortunate man, Alice.'

Their eyes locked for what seemed a long time, before Kerry dropped his arms.

He grinned suddenly.

'You know, you're pretty good at this group stuff. What do you say we start a book club?'

Lillian

L illian locked the car door and walked toward the house.
     She started as a human-shaped shadow moved against the
wall.

The shadow stepped forward and became a man. His hands
were held out in a gesture of surrender.

'Lillian, it's me. Ross. I'm sorry, I thought you could see me.'

Lillian held her hand to her throat, heart thumping. 'Ross,
what are you trying to do, scare me to death?'

'You haven't been walking. I just wanted to talk to you. I came
around after dinner, didn't expect you to be out. I just sat down to
wait for ten minutes and then figured I'd wait another ten.'

Lillian looked at her watch. It was nine fifteen – he'd been
here for hours.

'Come inside.'

She walked up the stairs, unlocked the door and pushed it
open.

Ross followed her, sitting uncomfortably on the edge of an
armchair.

'Can I get you a cup of tea?' Lillian asked.

Ross shook his head. 'No thanks.'

Lillian sat opposite him. 'What's wrong, Ross?'

'You haven't been walking,' he said.

'No.'

'Are you okay? Is it because of the – the illness?'

'No, I'm fine.' That was true. Lillian felt as good as she had in years.

'You've been avoiding me then?'

There didn't seem much point in lying. 'Yes.'

To her surprise Ross smiled broadly. 'That's great.'

'It is?'

'If you're avoiding me, it must be because you like me, but are worried about doing anything about it in case you're really sick. Right?'

Lillian looked at him for a moment, various arguments running through her head. She opened her mouth to deny it, but suddenly couldn't summon the energy.

'Right,' she acknowledged.

'Okay then.' Ross stood up, brushing his hands down the uneven creases in his trousers. 'Well I don't care whether you're sick or not. We'll figure it out. So I guess I'll see you in the morning then?'

Lillian smiled.

'I guess you will.'

Claire

Claire stepped into the empty house, flicking on the lights.
So that was it. Eight weeks and one marriage later Claire was finished with the Red Folder Group.

Claire's life had changed suddenly when Peter left. It was no longer defined by looking after him or waiting for him to come home. She'd met with a client earlier that day, but apart from that she'd spent most of the time at home.

That morning she'd left her bed unmade and dirty dishes on the counter in some kind of rebellion. She'd deliberately ignored the newspaper spread all over the sofa and dropped her bath towel on the bathroom floor. Claire didn't know what she was trying to prove, but it felt good.

She had also bought a Billy Joel CD which she'd played over and over.

The computer now sat in the middle of the dining room table. A copy of *Design Your Own Website* was beside it, bristling with yellow Post-it notes. Money was very tight and there was definitely none to spare for website development. So Claire had decided she would do the work herself.

Despite Megan's insistence that building a website from a template was simple, it was proving a daunting task for Claire.

She considered doing some more work before bed, but decided against it.

Before shutting the computer down, though, she clicked to her inbox. There was one unopened email.

Dear Ms Menzies
I write to ask whether you would consider me for a job with your company.

How bizarre. Why would someone be asking her for a job?
She flicked back to the email.

I heard you interviewed on the radio yesterday and think Fix Your Wardrobe sounds great. I have always been interested in a career in fashion and would love to learn how to be an entrepreneur like you.
I am finishing off my senior year so would be available after school and on weekends.
I look forward to hearing from you.
Andrea Brown

Claire stared at the email. What the hell was an entrepreneur like her? Someone whose website resisted all of her attempts to bend it to her will? Someone whose marketing plan consisted of pulling in a favour for a five minute segment on local radio? Someone whose house, which doubled as an office, was on the market and was littered with half-finished business plans?
And then she smiled.
She hit the reply button and started typing.
Dear Andrea, she wrote, *I am so glad you like Fix Your Wardrobe.*
She paused for a moment.

While all our positions are currently filled, we are anticipating significant expansion in the next twelve months. We will keep your details on file and contact you as soon as a suitable vacancy arrives.
Regards
Claire Menzies
CEO Fix Your Wardrobe

Kerry

Kerry walked up behind the ute, shaking the load to test it.
There was an esky, an ancient swag and a half-empty duffle
bag stuffed with a few T-shirts and shorts. He wouldn't be need-
ing much in the way of clothing.

What he would need would be some proper camping gear.
But he'd pick that up on the way.

The plan, such as it was, had occurred to him on Sunday. His
parents had made it crystal clear they had only been selling at the
markets because they'd thought it was good for him.

Their excess plant supply had been taken care of with one
phone call to another nursery and by ten o'clock on Sunday
morning he was a free man.

Last time they'd spoken, his mate Brian had mentioned that
he was heading to a big motorcycle event up north. At the time,
Kerry hadn't even thought about going, but all of a sudden he
had an idea. A weekend of motorbikes and then a month or so
of travelling.

After that, who knew?

The only glitch had been Sandra's reaction.

In hindsight he hadn't picked his time perfectly.

In fact, his timing had probably been perfectly wrong. Sandra
was already furious about the article. She was convinced everyone would be talking about her as well as Kerry.

'Who gave you the right to make my life public?' she'd asked when he arrived to collect Annie on Sunday. 'Do what you like with your life but keep the hell out of mine.'

Like an idiot, he'd told her that, actually, he was doing what he wanted with his life.

He'd thought she'd be pleased that he was finally moving on and doing something positive. Instead she'd exploded and he'd been thankful that Annie was in her bedroom gathering her toys.

'So how do you expect me to explain all this to Annie? Tell her Dad's just gone bush for a while to find himself?'

Kerry had tried to tell her that she didn't have to, that he'd talk to Annie himself.

'What do I do with Annie? I'm not like you. I can't just throw it all in and piss off.'

Kerry had been tempted then to tell her he knew her business was slowly bleeding to death. For one crazy moment, he had even thought about telling her to stop fighting and give up. To come away with him and see if they could make it work. But sanity had prevailed.

'Mum has offered to help out. Now they've scaled down the business, she'll have more time to spend with Annie. It will be great for both of them.'

Sandra had been slightly mollified, but had still been frosty when he returned Annie that evening.

Now, Kerry sat behind the wheel of his ute and flicked on the dim cabin light. He picked up the block of foolscap and pen sitting on the seat beside him.

Dear Sandra,

When you took the lease on the salon, I thought you had chosen to go your way without any regard for us. I am starting to wonder if maybe it wasn't the other way around the whole time. Maybe 'us' wasn't going anywhere because of me.

I've realised that there are better uses for that 'hunk of metal' than sitting under the house. The guy who has been hassling me about selling the Aston Martin to him for years couldn't believe his

luck yesterday. I thought maybe you could use the money to give your
business a good go. No loan, no strings — it's yours.
   I'll call Annie in a couple of days.
   See you in a month.
   Love,
   Kerry

Kerry slipped the bank cheque in with the letter, sealed the envelope and threw it onto the dashboard. He started the engine and shifted into gear. One more stop, to slip this into Sandra's letterbox, and he was on his way.

Megan

Megan took the corner too fast, feeling a spurt of adrenalin as she lost control. But she stopped the car's drift, pulling it back into the lane, heart thumping.

She drove the rest of the way home slowly, frightened by her carelessness.

The house was still and empty as she swung the door open. Maybe she should get a flatmate, she thought, knowing that wasn't really the answer.

Impulsively she ignored the light switch, kicking off her shoes and wandering through the house in the dim light which filtered in the windows.

The glow of her computer was like a beacon and she walked toward it.

Megan slumped into the chair, trying desperately to shut out the look in Deborah's eyes. What the hell had she thought she was doing?

Megan moved the mouse, floating the pointer over the icon for the virtual world in which she'd met Greg.

Decisively she jerked the mouse, clicking instead on the blue internet icon and pulling up a job recruitment website.

Megan needed a new job.

She knew that the school couldn't actually fire her. That it was within her rights to force the issue. But she'd had several calls from her friends at the school. The article had clearly set the place buzzing. If she'd loved her job, maybe it would have been worth fighting for it. But the way things stood, it all seemed too hard.

The website came up.

Under key words Megan typed *computer programmer*. She hesitated for a moment over the drop-down menu which set the desired location, then left it set at 'All'.

Fifty options came up. She scrolled through them quickly, rejecting the ones insisting on years of on-job experience. One caught her eye.

Junior Software Engineer – Computer Games – Melbourne

**Our Client is an online games leader, seeking
junior programmers to start immediately.
Great package in a pioneering environment.
Learn & work at the same time!**

*No previous programming experience needed, just a
high level of C++ proficiency.*

**** PASSION FOR GAMING IS A MUST ****

No mention of salary. Probably because it was below the poverty line.

Megan looked at the entry again. C++ was a programming language she'd been using for years.

Melbourne. Two thousand kilometres away. From Greg. From her family.

She pictured how shocked her mother would be if she told her she was moving. Imagined her sisters' reaction.

Grinning, she went to work on her CV.

Rebecca

Rebecca turned the key and pushed the front door open, plastering on a smile for the babysitter.

She stopped short.

Jeremy was standing in the living room, picking up his keys and sliding his phone into his pocket.

'Hi.'

'Jeremy – what?'

'Bianca called me.'

He saw the look of panic flare on her face and spoke quickly. 'Nothing's wrong. She's fine. She said she just wanted to talk to someone and asked if I could come over. I figured I might as well stay until you got home, so I paid the babysitter and told her she could go. I hope that was okay.'

'Yes, yes. Of course it is – thank you.'

Rebecca struggled to ask the next question. 'Did she . . . ?'

'Talk about cutting herself?'

Rebecca nodded.

'No. We just talked about . . . stuff really, nothing that big. But it was nice. Like it used to be.'

'Good, that's really good.' Rebecca couldn't think of anything else to say.

Jeremy was still in his suit and had obviously come straight from work. His tie was bunched in his hand, his white business shirt open at the neck and a smear of what looked like dirt on the front.

'Bianca said it was another meeting of that group tonight.'

Rebecca nodded. 'The last one. Turns out it was the wife of the guy Megan was sleeping with who wrote the article.'

She shook her head, then looked around. The remains of the sculpture she'd destroyed lay crumbled in the corner; she hadn't bothered to clean it up.

'Looks like that had a bad accident,' Jeremy said. 'Sam's football?'

'Ah no,' Rebecca answered. 'Me actually.'

Jeremy's eyes widened, then he smiled. 'Never liked it, did you?'

'Bloody awful thing,' Rebecca agreed.

Jeremy moved toward the door. 'Well, I'd best be off.'

Rebecca stepped forward. 'Jeremy – please don't go yet. I've been doing a lot of thinking and . . .'

Jeremy looked at her silently and she forced herself to take a deep breath.

'I've made some bad decisions. I am so sorry I didn't tell you about Bianca. I carried that secret for so long, I felt like I could never let my guard down, could never let anyone get too close. Every time you told me you loved me, I felt this pain in my stomach that I hadn't told you the truth.'

Jeremy didn't move.

'I'm going to pull this family together. I don't know how yet, but I'm going to help Bianca. I'll find a way to sort this out. If that means leaving work, then I'll do it. I've started from nothing for Bianca once. I'll do it again if that's what it takes.'

She stopped for a second, looking down at her feet and gathering her courage.

'But I really want for us to do it together.'

Jeremy moved toward her and for a wild second Rebecca thought he'd take her in his arms.

But he didn't touch her.

'Bec, I've been thinking too. When Bianca called tonight, I almost didn't come. I figured Bianca was your problem now, not mine. The only flaw in that argument was that it wasn't true. Bianca started being my problem the first time I stayed the night with you and I don't want it any other way.'

Rebecca didn't move, willing him to say the words she wanted to hear.

'I love you. Have done since the first day I saw you. I have a terrible suspicion I will until the day I die. But everything has changed now and we've got to take this slowly. Peter is Bianca's father, he has a place in your family too. You've got to figure out how that's going to work. And some things have got to change – really change.'

Rebecca went to speak but he interrupted her.

'Let's just take it one step at a time, okay? If there's to be anything more between us, it's going to have to be different this time.'

He kissed her on the forehead and Rebecca screwed her eyes shut, bowing her head.

Jeremy stepped past her and out the door, closing it softly behind him.

Rebecca stood still for a few long moments. Then she walked toward the terrace, sliding the heavy glass door open.

Slowly she sank into a chair, kicking her shoes off and stretching her toes.

Taking a deep breath, she looked up at the sky. Looking back down, Rebecca noticed a dark trail of dirt across the grassed area with bordered the terrace. Under the glow of a street light, it stood out clearly against the manicured grass which was maintained by a gardening contractor Rebecca had never even seen.

Rebecca pursed her lips, remembering that her rosebush had been sitting in that spot for the last few weeks. The pot was gone now.

That was strange. Lorraine certainly wouldn't have moved it. She was lucky to feed the children, let alone water a plant.

Curious, Rebecca followed the trail of dirt to where it ended, in the garden bed outside the kitchen window.

There, planted in the centre of the garden, totally inappropriate amongst all the native grasses, was the rosebush.

Rebecca stood there for a moment, trying to figure out what was going on. Suddenly she remembered the dirt on Jeremy's shirt.

Smiling she walked across the garden, pushing aside the fronds from a large fern. She knelt down beside the rosebush, ignoring the dirt on her suit. The bush still only had one bud, but with a bit of luck there'd be more.

Alice

A lice stood at the bathroom sink.

It was over. The Red Folder Project was finished.

But now that the meeting was behind her, the reality of her own situation pressed down once more.

Since Alice had followed Andrew home from the beach two days earlier, they'd spoken only when absolutely necessary.

The children had been subdued when she arrived home. But then the pizzas Andrew ordered had arrived. The day's drama had been quickly forgotten amongst the cardboard boxes and the choice between pepperoni and hawaiian.

Alice hadn't told Andrew about the meeting in the bar tonight. She had arranged a babysitter knowing he'd be at work until late. The babysitter was gone and Andrew in bed by the time Alice came home.

Alice pushed the door to the bedroom open slightly. Andrew was asleep on his side, his back turned toward her.

The one thing Alice had been certain of on the drive back from the coast was that something had to change. And yet nothing had. She'd just picked up her life and put it back on and no one seemed to have even noticed that anything had happened.

It was as though she'd missed her moment, as though there was a decision she should have made or an action she should have taken which would have changed everything. Maybe there was an Alice in a parallel universe who had shaken off the ties of domesticity, found a way to care for her children while discovering her own life. But this Alice was still washing up and folding socks. Still sleeping next to the stranger who had once been the closest person to her in the world.

Both Alice and Andrew knew the situation was unsustainable, yet neither of them had done anything to change it.

Alice stretched out her right hand, reaching automatically to the side of the basin. Only when her hand touched the porcelain did she realise her toothbrush wasn't there. Not sitting there with half a centimetre of toothpaste carefully piped along the top, like every other night in her memory when Andrew had gone to bed before her.

She thought of the stretch of nights before this one. The nights when she'd grumpily take her brush, wishing that Andrew had seen fit to pick up the children's clothes from the floor instead. The nights when she'd pick up the toothbrush thoughtlessly. On not one of those nights had she thanked Andrew and yet he'd kept doing it, year after year.

She tried to think of the things she'd loved about Andrew when they first met. The fun drunken nights, Sundays exploring a part of London neither of them knew, afternoons reading together in front of a fire. With all those things gone, how could their love have been expected to survive?

Alice flicked off the light and walked across to the bed. She slid carefully under the sheet and pulled it up to her chin.

Lying there, she put her fingers to her lips and touched them to the back of Andrew's hand.

'Thank you for the toothpaste,' she whispered into the dark.

Andrew's hand lifted slowly and slipped gently over the top of hers. He rolled onto his back and pulled Alice toward him, so that her head rested on his shoulder.

'Where've you been?' he asked softly.

'I met everyone from the group – I had to say sorry. And to try and figure out what happened.'

'Did you?'

'Yep.'

For a moment Alice thought of Deborah and Greg and their children. Then she pictured Megan sitting alone in her house.

'I still can't believe that I did all of this – changed all of those people's lives,' Alice said, pain in her voice. 'Goddamn little things – I must have been mad!'

Andrew said nothing, just bent his elbow a little, pulling Alice closer. 'So what's our destiny then, Alice?'

The words were light, but Andrew's tone was serious.

Alice had a sudden memory of her grandmother's words on the tape.

'The only person who knew what to do was your grandfather.'

Love wasn't just something that happened sixty years ago. Surely, it could exist amongst school runs, business trips and a mortgage. She and Andrew had been in love. Alice didn't believe it had disappeared. It had just been buried by unimportant things.

Alice rolled toward Andrew and kissed him softly on the lips.

'Do you think we could we try for happily ever after?' she asked.

Andrew was fast asleep, one arm thrown over his head.

Alice rested her arm across his chest, relishing the closeness which had been missing for so long.

Sleep seemed a long way away.

Like so many times before, Alice slid out of the bed, making her way into the kitchen. Slowly she warmed a pan of milk, pouring it into a mug. But this time she sat down at the computer and pulled up a blank page.

The words came quickly and it was all she could do to keep up with them.

This story had nothing to do with her grandmother. Except for the thread running through it. Love. The love she'd heard in her grandmother's voice whenever she spoke of her husband. The unwavering emotion which had been the one constant through their lives. The thing Alice and Andrew had once had in abundance and which Alice had to believe was still alive.

At first Alice thought she was writing a predictable

paperback romance. One she could write in a week and then sell to a company like Mills & Boon. But somehow, as she wrote, it became more complicated than that. Her chiselled-jaw hero had been damaged by an abusive childhood. The heroine with the heart-shaped face had never achieved her dreams because of crippling self-doubt. Real life intervened and made things different from what they had hoped.

The hours passed. Alice looked at the clock a few times, vowing to finish and get to bed. Then it was so late, she figured she may as well stay up.

When Andrew walked into the kitchen, rubbing his eyes, Alice was standing on the deck nursing a cup of coffee.

'Hi,' she smiled at him.

'Hello,' Andrew smiled back. 'You're up early.'

He paused, registering her pyjamas. Alice always dressed as soon as she woke in the mornings. 'Hang on – have you been up all night?'

Alice nodded, feeling slightly daring.

She wasn't tired. Besides, she could sleep later.

Andrew poured a cup of coffee and joined Alice on the deck.

He pulled her to him, kissing the top of her head, and then leaned against the railing.

The unfamiliar contact thrilled Alice and she reached up and kissed him full on the mouth, something she hadn't done in years.

'Are you okay?' Andrew asked, a look of concern on his face.

Alice smiled. 'I'm fine.'

'Not working on another group, I hope.'

Alice shuddered, shaking her head.

'I've started a book,' she said.

Andrew looked at her. 'A novel?'

Alice nodded slowly.

'It might be awful, but you know what, I don't think it is.'

She thought about telling Andrew the plot, but decided against it, wanting to keep her characters and their story to herself for now.

'You don't want to write about the Red Folder Project?' Andrew asked. 'It's quite a story.'

Alice shook her head. 'No, this is what I've been waiting to write. The entries on the website weren't material for a novel.'

She paused.

'They were other people's diaries. You don't write about those.'

For more, visit *www.kathywebb.net*